Sexy Berkeley

Sexy Berkeley

Sexy Series Book One

Dani Lovell

Copyright 2013 Dani Lovell

CHAPTER ONE
FRIDAY 14TH SEPTEMBER

An unwelcome breeze and a car door slamming, disturbs me from my precious, deep sleep. I grumble, snuggling back into my duvet, trying to ignore the pain pulsating through my forehead. The comfort of the warm covers cocooning me isn't enough to soothe the nausea seizing my body. *Sleep... go back to sleep.* If I open my eyes, this nasty, sick feeling will become all too real. It's so strangely cold... and really, *really* bright.

"Bea," a voice whispers from behind me. Please, *please* let this be a dream, no one is allowed to pull me into reality, the reality where I run for the bathroom and vomit violently before spending a day nursing a sickly headache and over-sensitive stomach.

"Bea." Ugh. There it is again, calling my name.

"No," I groan, my voice hoarse, "shh."

"Bea, I've brought you a drink, you should come inside now, doll." *What?*

I reluctantly force my eyelids apart, why *is* it so bright? It takes a moment to focus as the pain thumps through my skull, but I quickly realise that I'm on the balcony, wrapped in my duvet, curled up in a deck chair. *How odd.*

I look to my left to find Clare smiling sweetly at me, with a big glass of water and a headache tablet. "Clare," I whimper, closing my eyes, hoping for some instant relief from the horrendous nausea.

"Take the tablet, doll, drink this and go inside to bed. I'll lock up here, I've got to go to home and get ready for work."

"Shit!" I sit bolt upright in my chair and my hand instantly cups my head as I slink back down, immediately regretting the over-zealous movement. "Shit, work..." I grumble, my eyelids falling again, "I just need five more minutes, okay?"

"No, Bea, you're not in today, just go to bed. Don't forget though, you need to be up and ready to leave by about noon." Clare's voice is so gentle and calming, I've no idea what she's talking about, but I'm in no fit state to care.

I scrunch up my face and attempt to open my eyes again to look at her. "Can't move. Feel sick."

Clare pops the headache tablet in my hand and holds the water in front of me. "It's really early, Bea, you'll feel fine in a couple of hours." She helps me up and I stumble through the lounge to my bedroom. Crawling onto my bed slowly, bringing my duvet with me, I curl up like a baby. Clare lies next to me and gives me a big hug, so comforting in the world of poorly I'm living in right now.

"I'm off now honeybun, have a fab time. I'll miss you, but don't worry about anything here; I've got it under control."

"Huh?" I grunt, half asleep.

"I'll call you in a bit."

~~~~~~~~

There's an annoying noise. So annoying. *What the hell is it?* It needs to shut the fuck up and let me sleep. Its persistence wakes me fully, and I quickly realise that it's my iPhone, vibrating on the bedside table.

"Mmm," I answer.

"Morning, sleepyhead, how are you feeling?" It's Clare, sounding too bright and cheery for this hour of the morning.

"Mmm," I respond, "okay, what time is it? Why are you calling so early?"

"Bea, it's ten forty-five, you need to get up."

"What? What's going on? What day is it?"

Clare sighs, long and loud. "Oh lordy, okay. Listen, don't panic, but its ten forty-five and you need to leave your apartment at twelve for the airport."

"Fuck!" I sit bolt upright. "Airport? Oh my god, we booked me on a flight to LA last night, didn't we?"

"We did, doll. Tilly has hopefully left your apartment by now; she's got a cab coming to our place at noon."

"Oh my god, it's all coming back to me now, did I pack everything? Can you remember? Where's my passport? Why aren't you hung over?"

"Bea, calm down, your passport is with everything else, in your broken handbag. I went to bed much earlier than you

5

two, and you know what I'm like, I rarely get a hangover I can't handle."

"Oh Clare, you're so lucky." I hold my head and pray to god that this is one of those hangovers that gets gradually better throughout the day, as opposed to those that do the exact opposite. "Thanks for waking me up Clare, I better call my parents and let them know I'm going away, hopefully they'll keep an eye on my place for me while I'm gone."

"Okay, love, well if you need me to come by and check on it, let me know."

"Thanks, doll, you're a star. And thank you for looking after everything at work; I can't quite believe I'm about to jet off to the States!"

"Have an amazing time and send me the odd text to let me know what the pair of you is getting up to. I'm so jealous, wish I was coming with you."

"I wish you were too, we'll miss you." Ending the call, I stumble to the kitchen to start making tea, and realise that I have no bloody cups or mugs because I smashed my entire crockery collection during my shit-hole of a day yesterday.

I think back to how it started; rather an exciting day really, the last day of moving and my first night in my very own apartment. Clare and Tilly - my two best friends - were coming over in the evening for their first visit since I bought the place, and I was *so* looking forward to it.

The morning was standard, the second half of the day, however, was total, utter cow-crap. I had an appointment with two of the most awkward in-laws - ever, arranging their son's wedding cake. They hated everything, liked nothing, and were outrageously rude for the entirety of the meeting. *Bastards*.

That kicked off my hideous afternoon; I dropped a whole batch of newly decorated cupcakes that I'd made for the window display, the handle of my handbag snapped, I left the keys to my new apartment at work so had to make another journey to work and back, someone scuffed my beautiful new car in the car park, and to top everything off, the box of brand new, posh crockery that my parents had bought me as a housewarming gift, tumbled dramatically out of my car to the ground, smashing everything inside to smithereens. *Joy*.

I decided that lying down on the tarmac in the foetal position, wailing, probably wouldn't be an ideal first impression for the new neighbours, so resorted to sitting on the cold, tiled floor of my new kitchen, savouring the flavour of a huge glass of Cabernet. I remained there until my girls arrived.

So, as I have no cups and need my mandatory morning cuppa, I search about the apartment and decide to make do with a brand new porcelain toothbrush pot. There's no way I could get ready to leave for the airport without tea. It works quite well, all things considered.

I call my parents whilst moving the contents of my handbag into a less broken one. My dad tells me to cancel the cab; he'd rather take us to the airport himself, which is perfect. He's also giving Uncle William a call, I'm not entirely sure what he does at the airport, but sometimes he pulls some strings to get my parents upgraded to premium economy. I'm not expecting anything, though, I'm sure the flight will be fully booked already.

About an hour later, we're almost at Heathrow airport and I can't quite believe that I'm about to jet off to LA! This is one of the most random things I've ever done. Luckily, with the help of a few litres of water, my hangover has almost vanished, too. *Almost*.

Last night - what I can remember of it - was fantastic fun, and just the release I needed after that complete pig of a day. When the girls finally arrived and pulled me from the kitchen floor, I flung my arms around the pair of them, so excited to welcome them into my new home for the first time. I hadn't wanted them to see it before it was all finished and I had officially moved in.

"Happy new apartment!" Tilly sang, handing me a bag full of Chinese take-away. She grabbed my newly refilled glass from my hand, before barging past me to start her self-guided tour. Clare and I walked into the kitchen and she waved two bottles of wine in the air.

"Vin rouge darling, où est le... bottle opener?" she asked in the most 'British' French accent possible.

"Oh, you do have a way with the French language Clare," I respond, my voice laced with amused sarcasm. "I've

7

already got one open, I couldn't wait. Or..." I paused to open the fridge, slowly pulling out a bottle with the tell-tale yellow label. "Veuve?" I asked, peering through my lashes, knowing how much the girls love their champagne.

"Did someone say Veuve?" Tilly appeared at the kitchen door, grinning from ear to ear. "Bea, the place is stunning, I love, love, love it! And yes to the Veuve, please." She looked at her watch and gasped. "Tell me you're recording it, because if you're not, we're missing precious moments of Don Draper's mean sex appeal."

I laughed, "Mad Men is on record and Don is waiting for us as we speak."

"Well done Bea, excellent work."

Clare picked up the bottle of Veuve Clicquot and the bag of food while I took three champagne flutes from the cupboard. Tilly grabbed the cutlery and we strolled into the ample living room to make ourselves comfortable on the floor around the large coffee table.

"Oh, it's gorgeous in here Bea, so spacious," Clare said, taking her time to soak in the whole room.

"Um, any chance of a plate?"

"Gah, don't even go there," I rolled my eyes, "we'll have to eat straight from the boxes like we did in the old days, you would not believe what happened after I got home." I continued to tell the girls about the stresses of my evening.

"God, Bea, you've had a shitter of a day, poor you. You've moved in here and haven't taken a day off for weeks, thanks to me. Please take some time off now that I'm back, enjoy your new apartment, go away somewhere. It's my turn to take over Bear's for a bit and let you relax."

Bear's Cakery is our beloved business, set up about three years ago and going from strength to strength. Clare and I decided to set up shop together and it's the best thing we've ever done.

"Thanks love, I'll have a few days off soon, my birthday is coming up so maybe then. You excited for your trip Tils? When are you off?" I turned my attention to Tilly whilst popping the champagne and pouring it into the tall champagne flutes.

"Tomorrow! Whoop whoop!" Tilly sang, waving her hands in the air, "I'm going to Hollywood baby, yeah!"

"You must be so excited!" Clare enthused. "To new apartments and trips to Hollywood! Cheers!"

We spent the next hour focusing on Don Draper, scoffing Chinese food and enjoying the cool, crisp bubbles. This is something that the girls and I have always enjoyed, ever since we met in college. We hit it off straight away and have remained the best of friends.

Once the drool fest had finished and the bottles of champagne and Cabernet Sauvignon were exhausted, we cracked open one of the bottles of Temperanillo that the girls brought over, and got cosy on my plush new sofas.

"*So*, Tilly! I must know what happened with that guy you had a couple of hot dates with, I haven't had a chance to chat with you about him and Clare wouldn't tell me anything! You need to tell me before you go away, don't leave me waiting for the juicy goss!"

Tilly took a long swig of wine before entertaining us with a blow by blow account of her rendezvous with the man with the amazing apartment and hideous sex. "Oh for the love of god," she closed her eyes and shook her head, "if a man is going to be smoking hot, have a super sexy bachelor pad and kiss like a god, you'd think he'd know a vagina from a fucking arm pit." She cupped her forehead with the palm of her hand and shook her head in mock despair. "It was, without a doubt, the worst sex of my entire life. I literally wanted to run for the hills within about three minutes."

Clare and I fell about, howling at Tilly's hilarious rendition of her night from hell with the smoking hot bachelor. "Oh Tilly, that poor man," I cried.

Tilly looked at me like I'd just grown two heads. "That poor man?" she cried. "What about me? I'm the one who had to lie there afterwards, with him draped over me like some sort of beached whale, telling me how beautiful our 'connection' was. Yuck. If something is going to put you off a guy, shitty sex labelled as 'a beautiful connection' is gonna be it."

The tears poured down my face, my laughter turning into silent bursts of air, shooting from my lungs involuntarily. I had to put my wine down on the table for fear of spilling it on my perfect new sofa. Snorting, muscles temporarily malfunctioning, I had to roll onto the floor and wait for the fit of hysteria to subside.

"I told you," Clare managed, between fits of giggles, "you had to hear that from her mouth."

"Well, I'm glad you two find my repulsive experiences so amusing," Tilly piped up, trying to keep a straight face.

"Oh come on Tils," I manage, "that was hilarious."

"Well maybe now, it most certainly wasn't at the time while I was trying to get out of there!"

By the time we opened the next bottle, we were well and truly plastered. My stomach muscles ached from the laughter and I was successfully ignoring the red wine spillage on my cream lounge carpet.

"Ladiezz, where are you?" I slurred loudly as I re-entered the lounge after one of many trips to the loo.

"On the bul... bel... bolcany!" Clare shouted, sticking her head around the curtain of the french door.

"Shh! I don't want to upset the... the neeeigh-bours," I replied, pulling off a remarkable horse impression, as I joined them around the table on the 'bolcany'.

"Tilly, aren't you going to be a bit..." I gesticulated with my giant wine glass, swirling it around in the air,

"...icky, for your flight tomorrow?"

"Hmm, Beatrice, I think you may have a good point there, whoops!" Her nose crinkled and she bent forward, laughter exploding into the wine glass she held to her lips.

"What time's your flight? I hope it's not early! Ha!" Clare added and we all burst out laughing, clearly the thought of Tilly having to get up in a few hours with a hideous hangover was incredibly amusing.

"My flight's not until about four in the afternoon, I'm sure I'll be fine, fff-ucking hope so!" she giggled.

"Oh you lucky thing, Tilly, I'd love to jet off somewhere fabulous," I sighed, holding my wine glass to my chest, staring up at the stars.

"Oh... sighs." Clare tilted her head with a pout.

"It's alright for you," I pointed to Clare, "you only got back from Spain a week ago."

"Oh, I know, but Hollywood..." she replied and we both looked admiringly at Tilly.

"I wish you could come with me, you'd love it there... ooh!" Tilly sat up in her chair, inspiration struck.

"Come with me!" She stared at me wide eyed.

"Ooh! Ooh!" Clare cried out. "Go with her! Go with her!"

I looked at the pair of them like they were both barking mad, bouncing up and down in their chairs, wine sloshing all over the place. "I can't just go to LA, *tomorrow*. Come on now, get real."

"Why?" Clare looked like she was about to explode with excitement, her pitch rising. "Why not? I'll look after everything at Bear's. I went over the diary today, I know what's going on over the next couple of weeks, it's nothing the girls and I can't handle. Go on! You need a break, and this would be a-maz-ing!"

"Oh, come, come!" Tilly begged, practically wetting herself at the thought, before flicking through her iPhone.

Clare ran inside, I assumed because the excitement (and alcohol) had gotten too much for her bladder.

"Til, for starters, you stay with your sister, I can't just turn up with you and expect Gemma and her family to welcome me into their home, there won't be room... what are you doing? Who are you calling at this hour?"

Tilly had her phone to her ear, holding her forefinger up at me, wiggling it around.

While I waited for her to answer, Clare burst out of the french doors with my laptop, open on the Virgin Atlantic website. "It's Virgin isn't it Til? About four you say? She asked and Tilly nodded.

"Oh for god's sake girls, stop! I cannot get on a plane and go to America tomorrow, I only moved into my new apartment today! I haven't made any arrangements, I also don't have a load of spare cash lying about, you know!"

"Oh come on, Bea," Clare said, glaring at me, "are you telling me that you have no money left in your 'new apartment fund'?"

"Well, I do... a little, but that's exactly what it's for, my new apartment!"

11

"Come on! Live a little, you never know, you might meet a super-rich, eligible bachelor who'll fall at your feet and whisk you away on some romantic, Californian journey." She sighed and gave me the dreamy- eyed, fairytale princess look.

I imagined, briefly, how great it would be to get away; I have wanted to see LA for a long time. To drop everything and hop on a plane to the glorious sunshine, sounded... heavenly. But seriously, *tomorrow*? No, I just couldn't do that. I have a business to think of. I know Clare is more than capable of looking after things at work - we are partners, after all - but to piss off on holiday with a few hours notice just wouldn't be fair.

Tilly's loud shriek interrupted my train of thought. "Gem! It's me!"

At that moment I realised that Tilly had gotten straight on the phone to her sister. I started frantically shaking my head at her, "No! I'm not going!" I mouthed, but she just held up her hand and faced away, towards the green in front of the apartment building.

"Yes, I'm a weeny bit tipsy zzarling, but that's by the by. I just wanted to ask a teeny weeny, dinky tinky favour... uh huh, well, it's Bea. She's thinking of booking the same flight as me tomorrow, she needs a fucking break."

I flailed my arms about trying to get her attention, shaking my head.

"Do you think it'd be okay if she stays in the pool-house with me?" she asks. *Ooh, pool-house...* I looked over at Clare, tapping away at the keyboard of my laptop, swigging wine, on a mission. I couldn't just 'drink-book' a holiday to the States, less than a day before take-off without having packed a thing... *Could I?*

I stood up and stepped into the lounge, taking a sip of my wine - which I realised I should probably stop drinking if there's any chance of me actually boarding an aircraft tomorrow afternoon - and quietly contemplated the possibility. *I do need a holiday, maybe I could go in a few days and meet Tilly there...but I hate flying on my own and if Tilly is going tomorrow anyway, it would make sense for me to go with her so we can keep each other company on the long flight.* I felt a small flutter of excitement in my stomach. *No,*

12

no, no! I cannot do it; it's tomorrow we're talking about, for god's sake.

No, I decided. I'm not going, I'll have a weekend away somewhere in a couple of weeks, that'll be fine. I will be present and correct at work tomorrow and the next day as planned. I walked back out onto the balcony, purposefully, to tell the girls, 'no'.

"It's sorted, you're coming!" Tilly squealed, "Gemma said it's asobu... aslobu...asbolubly fine for you to stay with me in the pool-house, she said she's looking forward to seeing you and that she'll have a martariga waiting for us by the pool on our arrival."

"I think you mean margarita, doll," Clare giggled, "and we've checked the flights," her face still buried in the laptop, she continued, "you can get a seat on Til's outbound *and* return flight so give me your card and I'll book it for you now." She peered up at me through her beautiful long lashes with a broad grin. "You know you want to... cheeky margaritas by the pool, Hollywood hotties..."

I took another long, deliberate gulp of my wine, frowning. "I... I just..."

"Beatrice Victoria Hart, you are going to book this flight, go to Hollywood, and have a fucking fantastic time. You'll return to your beautiful new home in ten days or so, refreshed and invigorated with a smoking hot tan, just in time for your birthday. Understood?"

"Are you always this strict when you're drunk Clare? I don't recall ever noticing before..."

"Understood Beatrice?" she scolded.

I paused, momentarily. "Yes."

"So... so you're coming?" Tilly looked like she was about to explode.

"Looks like I don't have a choice!"

She squealed loudly and jumped up to throw her arms around me, almost drenching me in wine.

"Card," Clare demanded, holding out an up-turned hand, and I headed to the kitchen to get my purse and my passport.

When I returned, I checked the price and nervously handed over my bank card and passport.

"Right," Tilly said, enthusiastically, "we need a top-up, a suitcase, and an appointment with the wardrobe! Let's get packing!"

CHAPTER TWO
FRIDAY 14TH SEPTEMBER (CONT.)

Before we know it, we are boarding the aeroplane and heading... left! Good old Uncle William pulled some strings and managed to get us into upper class! I've never flown in upper before, it is just... wow. Each seat is closed into a kidney shaped area, relatively private and very comfortable-looking. The cabin colours, reds and deep purples, are quite romantic really.

As we stroll through the cabin with the very lovely Madeline, who's showing us to our seats, we realise that we haven't been seated together. Neither of us minds, after all, we're in upper class! A small burst of nervousness unfurls in my stomach when I realise that I won't be able to squeeze Tilly's hand for take-off and landing. I wouldn't say that I'm a terribly nervous flyer, it's only during take-off, landing and turbulence, that I can experience a minor panic attack.

We arrive at Tilly's seat first, she is in the middle row, facing north-west of the aircraft and a few short strides later, Madeline, points me to my seat on the left, facing north-east. I thank the stewardess and put my bag down on the seat, opening it to grab my iPhone so that I can text Clare to tell her about our fabulous seats. I look over to Tilly who is still standing, gazing at the plush surroundings. She catches my eye and I throw her a cheeky wink, we just can't believe our luck!

As I look away from Tilly to glance at my phone, my eyes skim past a tall, well dressed figure strolling down our aisle and I automatically double take. I subconsciously drag my eyes slowly from his shiny, black, designer shoes to his perfectly styled, light brown, gorgeous, short hair. He must be at least 6'3" or so. I'm pretty sure my chin has hit the carpet.

Dressed in an expensive-looking charcoal, three-piece-suit and pastel blue shirt and tie, the man coolly strolling towards me is a god. *Wow*. My eyes meet his and I'm snapped back to the present. *Whoops, caught blatantly ogling, how embarrassing.* I stare down at my phone, not doing anything

15

in particular with it, needing to look somewhere other than directly at the smoking hot man walking towards me.

Suddenly, he's standing next to me and I think I might faint. I can smell him and *oh, dear lord*, it's like a scent from the heavens... *why is he just standing there?* I finally look up to see him placing his briefcase on the seat behind me. *Oh good god!* He's sitting right behind me, this god of a man, how the hell will I cope for the eleven and a half hour flight with his heavenly scent wafting into my space?

He lifts his beautiful head to look at me through the most sexy greeny-blue eyes, and grins a broad, perfect smile. The light covering of stubble on his chin and upper lip begging me to drag my fingers along it, and that mouth. *Christ.*

"Hi." *Oh for the love of god, he talks.* His voice is deep and alluring and he's talking to me!

Well don't just stand there, you dork, talk to the man! "Um, hello," I manage with a small smile, and although his gaze lingers, I look away immediately. If I hold my stare on this sexy beast, I would have to physically fight back the desire to clamber over the seat and stuff his head between my breasts.

After a moment, he turns his attention to his briefcase and I look over to Tilly who is mouthing, "Oh. My. Fucking. God." at me, pointing to the Adonis. My eyes widen in agreement, I subtly start mock-panting and fanning my face with my hand. We both have a giggle and continue to settle into our seats. *Wow, he really does smell divine.*

~~~~~~~

The plane is picking up speed, hurtling forwards along the runway, getting faster by the second. *Oh, it's so bumpy, and so loud!* I squeeze my eyes closed, wishing Tilly was near me so I could grab hold of her, my hands frantically trying to find something to cling onto. As the nose of the plane lifts off the runway, my left hand automatically shoots to the wall of the aircraft, my right hand clings onto the headrest behind me. My eyelids still tightly clenched.

"Oh god. Oh god. Oh god. Oh god. Fuckety fuck. Shitty McFuck. Oh god, please?" I try hard to keep my unique prayer as quiet as possible, but I have very little control over my vocal scale at this moment, the aircraft's back wheels dragging along the runway after - what seems like - forever. My headrest is, most likely, going to need re-stitching by the time I'm done with it. The tips of my fingers chafe from squeezing so tightly.

Just as the back wheels start to lift and my stomach slowly drops, a hand peels my aching right hand from the headrest and the fingers curl into mine, holding on tightly. It feels so good, my fingertips no longer agonisingly squashed into the leather, the warmth of a human-being holding onto me, making me feel less... alone.

Something vaguely crosses my mind, mid-panic, about a super hot man sitting directly behind me, but the panic is still too deeply set in my rigid body for my brain to function adequately. I squeeze the living daylights out of the hand, grateful for the comfort, while we shoot through the sky above the houses and roads just metres below.

Just a little while longer, hold on to me just a tiny bit longer, just until we're a bit higher, through the clouds, on a more even gradient. I silently beg, my eyes still forced closed and feet pressing into the floor underneath me.

Clouds finally pass the window beside me, and as the wobbles begin to subside, my muscles slowly ease. I slide my left hand from the wall to my lap and the fingers of my right hand loosen their grip on the kind hand behind me. It's at this moment that the realisation hits. *Oh crikey,* it's the incredibly hot specimen of a man.

I look up at our hands, perfectly entwined, lovely golden skin and neatly manicured, yet, masculine nails... *Oh.* I slowly, reluctantly, pull my hand from his gentle grip, my face glowing with embarrassment. Thank god he can't see me.

"Thank you," I mutter in his direction, not knowing what else to say.

"Don't mention it," he responds immediately in his deliciously sexy voice. *Ooh, he's American.*

As soon as the seatbelt signs have been switched off, Tilly strolls over and sits on the little guest seat in front of me. "Just checking you're okay, how was take-off for you?" she asks.

"Ugh, it was horrible but I'm fine now, thank you," my voice narrows to a whisper, "and 'Mr. Smokin' hot' behind me was holding my hand over the head rest!"

"What the fuck?" she spits, animatedly. "What do you mean he was holding your hand? How? Did you talk?"

"Shh!! No, we didn't talk," she looks confused as I continue quietly. "I was clinging onto the back of the seat, f-ing and blinding to myself, and he grabbed my hand and held it until I relaxed a bit. I was kind of, oblivious to whoever it was, just grateful that I had someone to cling onto."

"Oh, wow. Did he say anything after?"

"I just said 'thanks' and he said," I revert to an overly-exaggerated American accent, "don't mention it."

"Bea, love, you need to 'tap that ass'," she says in an American accent, completely straight faced, "get talking to him."

"Tilly, could you please lower your voice before I die of embarrassment, what if he can hear you? And anyway, he's most likely married, or gay, or off the market. I'm not looking for a hot American lover to have a long distance affair with."

"Oh shoosh, he can't hear me, we're on an aeroplane for god's sake. And who said anything about long distance? Just have some fun, you're on holiday, baby!"

She stands up and raises her arms into a stretch whilst looking around the cabin, she moves her gaze down at the sexy American and holds her stare. *Subtle, Tilly, very subtle.* She bends down and whispers, "No ring, baby, no wife!" And with a wink, she strolls back to her seat.

As interesting as that piece of information is, I am not going to start chatting up the most incredibly gorgeous man I've ever laid eyes on, knowing I'll never see him again. He's far too good-looking, he's most likely, a complete arse-hole or gay. And what's to say he'd be interested in me, even if he was straight? Okay, I'm not totally hideous looking, but that man is way out of my league. He's just a super-hot guy, sitting behind me, minding his own business, and I should be doing exactly the same. I stand up and head for the loo at the front of the aircraft so I can settle back down to start reading book one of the raunchy new trilogy that I have just purchased on iBooks.

On the way back to my seat, I look around at the plush cabin, it really is much more luxurious. I wonder, idly, how all of these people are able to afford to fly like this, it must cost a small fortune.

When I arrive back at my little area, the gorgeous hand-holder sitting in the next seat looks up from his paperwork and offers me another beautiful, pearly white smile. *Knees. Weak. Can't. Stand.* I reciprocate with a polite smile and sit straight down before my skin flushes beetroot. *So hot.* Before I manage to compose myself, his head pops over into my section. *What the...*

"Hey, would you care to join me for a drink at the bar? I figured you could use one after take-off."

Fuck me. His voice is *so* sexy.

"Oh, um..." What do I say? Yes? No? I'm not really sure what to do. If this was 'Average Joe' asking me for a drink, I'd be able to make up my mind quickly and coolly, based upon how attractive or interesting I found him. But this man? Hell no. I am more physically attracted to my 'hand holding god' here, than any other man I've ever set eyes on. I'd love to find out more about him, not to mention shag him senseless, but his incredible, masculine radiance is knocking me sideways.

"I, er..." *Shit, come on Beatrice, say something!*

Before I get a chance to finish whatever I'm trying to stutter out, he interrupts. "I'd really enjoy the company, these long flights can be quite tedious when you're travelling alone."

"Um, okay then, that'd be nice, thank you." *Finally!*

"Great!" He flashes another dazzling smile and stands straight to remove his suit jacket. I stand and stroll behind him towards the bar at the entrance of the cabin, soaking in the rear view. *Oh lordy,* the waistcoat of his suit fits his gloriously toned body like a glove; broad, sexy shoulders, a small but perfectly-in-proportion waist. His backside is deliciously peachy, I can't help but imagine what it must look like without those tailored, designer trousers covering it.

Approaching Tilly, I notice that she's engrossed in something on the TV screen in front of her. She peers up as Mr. Sex-on-Legs passes and her eyes widen as she sees me

19

following him. A smirk grows on her pretty face, she raises an eyebrow, watching me as I follow hot stuff to the bar.

We each take a seat upon one of the stools surrounding the rectangular bar, and the attentive steward welcomes us.

"Good afternoon, welcome. What can I get you?"

"Good afternoon, I'd like a glass of champagne please, and my friend would like..." he turns to me in question.

"Oh, um, I'd like champagne, too, please." It's probably not the wisest choice, considering my hangover has only just about subsided, but how often does one travel in upper class? I may as well enjoy it while I can.

The bar steward busies himself preparing our drinks, and the 'god' sitting next to me peers at me through his thick, long eyelashes. Stunning blue - maybe green - eyes.

"I'm Daniel, Daniel Berkeley. How do you do?"

"Beatrice Hart." I take his proffered hand and an electric current instantly sparks from my fingers, through my body to the tips of my toes. His smell is out of this world, I'd like to grab hold of his face and sniff him like a dog to a crotch.

"How are you feeling? A little better now that we're in the air?"

I suddenly feel terribly embarrassed by my performance during take-off. "Yes, thank you. Once we're smoothly in the air, I'm fine. I have a little issue with take-off, landing and turbulence. Thank you for, er, letting me squeeze your hand, I hope I didn't hurt you." I feel my cheeks blush as I glance down to my hands and he offers me a reassuring, beautiful smile.

"It's my pleasure, I saw your hand squeezing your headrest, and the other sprawled on the wall, I thought you could probably use a little support... what was it? 'Shitty McFuck'?" His cheeky smirk conveying his amusement.

"Oh god, you heard that? Oh dear, I do apologise." *Mortifying!*

"So, Miss Hart, what brings you on board this Airbus today?"

"Please, call me Bea, most people do. I'm on my way to LA, on holiday. What about you Mr...." *shit*, I've forgotten his name already.

"Berkeley," he offers with a warm smile. *Mmm, oh yes, sexy, sexy Berkeley.* "But please, call me Daniel. I'm actually returning from a business trip, I live in Los Angeles."

Damn it, why can't he live in London?

"How long were you in the UK for? London?"

"Yes, I was in London. Only for two days, unfortunately."

I nod, not really taking in what he said. I'm too caught up imagining what it would be like to remove his clothes... *oh my god, Beatrice, get a grip!*

~~~~~~~

The next couple of hours seemed to fly by, so to speak. We talked about our lives a little bit, Daniel Berkeley works at his father's company as a 'CBDO'... I'm not sure what one of those is but it's of no relevance to me. I was more interested in ogling the covetable muscular frame sitting next to me. He has a sister who also works in the family business, a best 'buddy' called Luke who he likes to play golf with, and he loves skiing in Aspen. You can learn a lot in just a couple of hours!

We continue ordering drinks and relax in each other's company. He's so easy to talk to, if we were in the UK and he lived there, I would definitely pursue something further with this spectacular man. If he was interested. And single. And straight. But as it is, he's a hot mother fucker that I get to flirt with for a few hours before landing in glorious Los Angeles for the trip of a lifetime.

Gradually, as our fellow passengers dispersed from the bar, I loosened up, and had a hard time trying to suppress the urge to do dirty things to him. The way he was sitting at the bar, his heels on the stool's foot rest, his legs open, facing me, one arm resting on the bar, the other on his thigh, holding his glass. I could have ripped this man's clothes off and sunk my teeth into his hot flesh right there and then. His body language told me he must be straight... it might be presumptuous, but I'm pretty certain he'd been throwing me the odd flirtatious glance.

"So, Mr. Berkeley, I'd like to know a little more about you."

"Fire away, Miss Hart," he responds, his voice deep and sexy.

21

"Is there a Mrs. Berkeley?" Straight in there Bea. Good girl.

"There certainly is; Mrs. Rose Berkeley." *Oh, fiddlesticks.* "She's the most beautiful, incredible woman in the world." My foot stopped swaying of its own accord upon hearing his revolting declaration of love for the woman. "I'm proud to call her my mom. But I'm not married, if that's what you mean." His grin broadened, sexily, and I couldn't help but grin with him.

"Yes, that's what I meant and I think you knew that."

"How about you? I assume that there's no Mr. Hart, as you're not wearing a wedding ring and I've been calling you *Miss* Hart for the last two hours. You haven't corrected me yet."

"You assume correctly, Mr. Berkeley."

"Boyfriend?"

"Not currently," I replied. "You?"

"Not at the moment, but my preference is for women, so I think it unlikely that I'll have one of those in the near future." *Bingo.*

I rolled my eyes at him, even though I was thoroughly enjoying our banter. "You do like to play with me Berkeley, don't you?"

His eyes sparkled. "Oh, I'd love to play with you, *Hart*, was that an invitation?" *Whoa! Down boy!*

"It most certainly was not. Well, not if you don't answer the question, anyway," I grinned salaciously. I could see he was getting a little hot under the collar, but the naughty woman inside me just couldn't stop encouraging the poor man. Not now I know he's available for fun.

"Beatrice, fortunately, I don't have a girlfriend right now."

"Fortunately?"

"Very fortunately."

"You're not keen on having a girlfriend?"

"Oh, I am, but when I meet a beautiful, intriguing young woman like you, I prefer not to have one."

"Um, do you know where I can find a bucket?" I giggled.

"Hey!" he chuckled as he played wounded with the cutest, sexiest pout I have ever seen. *Swoon.*

I stroked his knee in mock sympathy. I can only imagine what his knees look like, outside of his clothes, I bet they're hot too. *Oh come off it, Bea, seriously? Since when have you found knees sexy?* God, I think I'd find this man's grunion sexy. "You know, Mr. Berkeley, I don't think I'll have any more to drink, I don't want to get into trouble on an aeroplane."

"Very wise, Miss Hart, very wise indeed. Would you like to return to your seat? I'd love to join you, I am thoroughly enjoying your company."

"That would be very nice, thank you."

Sitting for a while and consuming a few of glasses of bubbly at thirty thousand feet, does something to a little human like me. As I stood, I wobbled, trying to get my balance, and before I knew it, he had grabbed me by the waist and pulled me into his hard body. *Jesus Christ*, I could have had an orgasm, right there and then. I could feel that I was having a similar effect on him, by the large, hard bulge pressing into my stomach. As we paused briefly, I capriciously placed my hands on his hips and moved my body against his, ever so slightly. The sensation running through me was incredible, I wanted him so badly.

"Miss Hart, do you think we could wait here for a moment longer?"

"Yes, is there a problem?" I asked, knowing exactly what the problem was.

"Other than the huge tent you've just pitched in my front yard? No."

What? I looked at him, slightly confused. When he leaned back and glanced down, I immediately realised what the term 'pitching a tent' meant, and grinned at the terminology. "Ah, I see. I do apologise, that was rather an *awkward* place for me to pitch up," I smirked, this was very entertaining. I decided to be forward, highly unlike me but hell, I'd had a few drinks and I'll never see the man again. "Berkeley, can I be frank?"

"Of course, Hart," he looked intrigued.

"You're, um, smoking hot. I have an uncontrollable urge to kiss you right now, however, I'm not sure that would do much to help the camping situation in your trousers."

He chuckled, contagiously. "That was definitely, frank, Beatrice. But you're right, if we were to act on that, I fear we'd be stuck here until landing. I'd like to get back to your seat so I can tell you what else I'd like to do to you."

My knees almost gave way, I *so* needed to hear what that was, torturous as it may be. This was so hot, this situation was just so, so *hot*. The idea of fucking this man in a public toilet was becoming increasingly acceptable. It's disgusting and I wouldn't but... oh, how I wanted to. Why don't they have some 'mile high bedroom' for this sort of situation? Fuck. *If only.*

"Here, hold my hands and stay close," I said, turning away from him and holding his hands at my sides so he was pressed up against my behind. It felt good.

"No one will notice it if we walk like this, besides, everyone will be engrossed in their TV or laptops by now."

We strolled up the aisle, hand in hand, giggling at our private joke. We passed Tilly's seat and I looked down to see if she was awake, but she was tucked up, fast asleep. The effects of the mega-late night last night must have been catching up on her.

We arrived back at my seat after an amusing and terribly arousing stroll.

"Thank you, Beatrice, I think that worked."

"I think it did too. And call me Bea."

He leaned in towards me, his scent, intoxicating. *Wow*, he's so handsome. "So, Miss Hart, you were saying?"

"Yes, *Mr. Berkeley*, what was I saying?"

"Well, if memory serves correctly, you were telling me that I was - and I quote - 'smokin' hot', and that you had an uncontrollable urge to kiss me. How's that working out for ya?"

Good god, can I strip him here and now? Is that really illegal? I suddenly became unexpectedly shy, my cheeks blushing scarlet. Very strange considering I'd been quite the hussy, thus far. "Um..."

"Suddenly so shy, Beatrice?" His fingers reached for my chin and he gently pulled my face towards him. *Oh my god, oh my god, oh my god!*

I glanced at his beautiful mouth, his lips full and ready. He closed the distance and our lips met. The tingle that ran from my fingers, through to my crotch and down to the tips of my toes combined with the wild fluttering in my belly, deliciously. Our tongues brushed against each other, sensually, and my hand found the soft hair on the back of his neck. I pulled his face into mine, deepening the pleasure, his stubble grazing the skin around my lips, it felt good, so... masculine.

His hand stroked the side of my face as our pace picked up, hot and heady. We were in our own world. *More. I need more.* I wanted him naked, between my legs. I needed to feel him touch me. I vaguely noticed the buttons at the front of my jeans pressing into me where I was squirming down into my chair, fruitlessly trying to ease the overwhelming pressure.

As a ping from the cabin interrupted us, we broke away from each other, breathlessly. I rested my forehead against his. "Fuck," I whispered, dazed.

"Fuck indeed. Bea, you are... wow."

"This is, um, not like me at all, must be the alcohol and altitude. I'm sorry." I giggled, nervously. *God, I hope he doesn't think I'm a complete slag-bag.*

"Please, don't be, this is turning out to be a very entertaining flight, my most entertaining yet, and I fly a lot..."

"So you don't do this often, then?"

"Make out with an especially hot stranger mid-flight? No."

His response made me smile, shyly. I was still hot, needing more, I didn't want to stop. "You haven't told me," I whispered.

He reached for my hand and started to play with my fingers, twisting them around his. It felt strange, good-strange, something you might do after a couple of dates though, not after brief tongue encounter with a stranger you just met on an aeroplane. "Haven't told you?" he asked.

I smiled coyly at him, and looked directly into his hot greeny-blue eyes. "Tell me what you'd like to do to me."

His eyes burned brightly, he wanted me and I'd made it perfectly clear that I wanted him too. The fact that neither of us was going to 'get' the other was totally irrelevant, this was just, oh-so-exciting. Outrageous flirting on the eleven and a half hour flight that, this time yesterday, I had no idea I would even be on, was wildly unexpected and very hot.

In a few hours, when we disembark at LAX, we'll both go our separate ways and never see each other again, which, although slightly depressing, makes this so much more electric. What I'm doing is so unlike me, so brazen, but I feel alive, sexy and carefree.

I wasn't sure if it was the unbelievably gorgeous specimen leaning into me, licking and nibbling my neck, the alcohol mixed with altitude or the effects of my earlier panic attack that turned me into this outrageously horny, sex pest - maybe a combination of all three - but whatever it was, I was loving it, and in a few short hours I'd be back to my normal, boring self. So I decided to damn well enjoy it while it could last. I'm starting my amazing holiday with a bang... *Oh if only*.

~~~~~~~

We're ten hours into the flight and it won't be long until we start the decent into LAX. It has been, without a doubt, the most thrilling, exciting flight experience of my life and I do not want it to end. Usually, if I'm travelling alone, I'm crammed into a tiny seat, elbows nudging the smelly randomer next to me, counting down the minutes until a hideous landing. Not this time.

Since the very first moment that I set eyes on the centre-fold, stud-muffin that is Daniel Berkeley, I have been in a permanent state of arousal. When he talks to me, he makes me feel like I'm the only other person on the aircraft, his full attention on me.

He is a pro, I have to give him that, no girl has a chance when he sets his sights on her. He probably manages this with a different girl, every night of the week. Normally, that would bother me, but it doesn't today. This is a one off, sexually charged encounter on an aeroplane that I will never have again, and I'm loving every minute.

As I relax into my seat while Daniel has a 'bathroom break', I recall the moment he whispered in my ear between kisses, telling me all of the naughty things he wanted to do with me, and my stomach ties itself in knots for the millionth time. The buzz between my legs is almost unbearable. *Holy fuck, I'm horny as hell.*

I've hardly spoken to Tilly this whole flight. On a couple of occasions, I popped over to say 'hi', but she kept shooing me back to my seat to carry on cavorting with the god. She travels to her sister's a couple of times a year, so she's used to travelling alone. I think she's just revelling in the fact that she's sitting in this luxury. She donned the super sexy airline pjs and has eaten/drank/used, everything and anything that you don't usually get in economy.

I must remember to send a 'thank you' note to wonderful Uncle William. Without him, we'd be stuck in economy and I'd never have had my enthralling make-out session with Sexy Berkeley here. I'll leave that bit out of the note.

Daniel Berkeley strolls down the aisle, staring at me, smiling the sexiest 'I-want-you' smile I've ever seen. *Whoa!* There's that tingle again, god damn it. He stands in front of me, gazing down into my eyes. "You really are a beautiful woman, Beatrice." *Swoon.*

My cheeks blush. "Why, thank you, Daniel. You're pretty beautiful yourself."

He sits, smiling, "So can we meet up while you're in Los Angeles? Go for dinner maybe?"

Oh, please don't tempt me, it's a path to destruction. I must be strong! "Daniel, as much as I'd love for you to do all of those naughty things to me, this is just a bit of fun to pass the time until we land in LA. Nothing more. It'd only get complicated if we meet up."

"Well, that's a real shame, Bea. It's going to be hard, literally..." he winks as he continues, "to think that I'll never get to peel those sexy jeans down your legs, see your hot naked body, taste you..." *Drooling...*

"Hey! I think that's about as much of that talk as I can take."

He leans forward, taking my hands in his and I get a waft of his delicious smell again. "Kiss me," he says, his voice low, mellifluous. And it's not like he has to ask twice, I'm in there like my life depends on it. His tongue slowly joining mine, they move together, stroking, massaging, our lips parting further, allowing deeper access.

Picking up pace, it turns urgent, we can't taste the other enough, our teeth clash, an erotic, raw indication of our unsatisfied desire. Our hands searching, mine stroking his broad, muscular shoulders, his on my face and neck, trying to find some release from the agony of wanting.

"Fuck me," he whispers.

The whirlpool of electricity behind my pelvic bone is excruciating. Tingles run up my spine and through the soles of my feet, the goose bumps on my skin, painful. Every sensation craves release, I've never felt so powerless. I reach forward to touch him, there. He's hard, ready and... *wow*! He's a big boy! The fabric of his suit between our skin, an unwelcome barrier, the zip, an immense temptation. Should I? Could I?

"Whoa," he says as he takes my hand and brings it to his mouth. He kisses the palm and presses it against his cheek, peering up at me. "If you continue to touch me, something will happen and I don't relish the thought of walking through LAX with a stain on my pants. I want to touch you though, baby, so badly. You couldn't have worn a skirt?" he shoots me a gorgeous, cheeky smile and I melt.

"If only I was!" I fan my face with my spare hand and look to the ceiling.

He holds my hands in front of him. "I'm going to have to sit back at my seat soon, ready for landing. Are you going to be okay while we land?"

"I'm sure I'll be fine, thank you. I'm surprised that there wasn't much turbulence during the flight, actually."

"Oh baby, there was, I just think you were a little pre-occupied to notice," he raises an eyebrow and smirks.

Is that what this was all about? Was he just pre-occupying me so that I wasn't afraid? I hope not, although, it did work, if that was his intention.

"If you need me, throw your hand back and I'll hold you."

"Thank you, I'll see how I go."

All too soon, hot-lips is back in his seat and we're approaching the runway. I'm surprised that I'm only a little tired, considering it's about three in the morning, GMT. I plan on getting to Gemma's house, unpacking and enjoying a cup of tea before heading straight to bed. It's about seven pm here so that should work out well.

The landing was smooth, and I managed to remain relatively calm. I raised my hand once as we were seconds from touching down, to search for Daniel's, which quickly swamped mine and held it firmly until the aircraft slowed. He's either really smooth, or actually quite compassionate. It's no odds to me either way, but, for the sake of the women of California, I hope it's the latter.

As everybody stands to retrieve their hand luggage, Daniel looks at me and smiles. "I suppose this is it."

"It was a pleasure to meet you, thank you so much for helping me with take-off and landing. And all the fun bits in the middle." I blush and smile, looking down at my toes.

"Beatrice, it was my pleasure, and I mean that sincerely. It seems such a shame that we have to say goodbye now. Shall we?" He holds out his hand to let me walk towards the exit ahead of him.

"Thank you."

When I get to the ramp, Tilly is waiting for me and we all stroll together towards passport control.

"Tilly, this is Daniel Berkeley, he was sitting behind me."

"Well hello there," she purrs with a cheeky wink. *Oh my god, Tilly, did you have to?*

"Daniel, this is one of my best friends, Tilly Burton."

"Miss Burton, a pleasure. Where are you two headed? I'd love to offer you a ride, if I can?"

"Thank you for the offer, but my brother-in-law is collecting us, so we're fine for a lift. You could always take my lovely friend, here, out for some dinner though?" *Oh dear lord!*

Before Daniel gets a chance to respond, I intersect, "Thank you Tilly, for your interference, but I'm sure Daniel is a very busy man, and I am quite tired, so would like to get settled at your sisters and go straight to bed."

"Suit yourself," she sniggers, and I glance at Daniel who is looking ahead with a smirk. *God, how embarrassing.*

As we approach passport control, Daniel stops. "Well, ladies, unfortunately we'll go through separate lines here. Miss Burton, it was a pleasure meeting you, I hope you enjoy your vacation. Miss Hart, could I have a quick word over here please, before I go?" He motions to an area at the side, away from the steady flow of passengers.

"Oh, of course. Tilly, could you wait here for a second?"

"No probs, enjoy!" she smirks.

Daniel takes my hand and ushers me to the side. "Bea, do you really have to go? I would love to take you for dinner."

"I'm afraid so, Daniel."

He rests his briefcase at his feet and leans back against the wall. Placing his hands gently on my hips, he tugs me slowly towards his taut body. Sparks fly, yet again, I swear my knees would buckle beneath me if he wasn't holding me against him. A hot flush engulfs my body. "At least let me have one last kiss before you disappear?"

"What about all of these people?"

"Fuck the people," he whispers with a grin, and reaches up to curl one hand around the back of my neck. He pulls my face towards his into a mind blowing, panty-dropping, hardcore snog. My arms wrap around his neck, wanting as much as I can get.

A small groan escapes his throat and it sends shivers down my spine. I feel the tingle all the way down there and the warmth starts to pool in my core. I want him so much. How can I feel this way about a man I only met a few hours ago? I want, more than anything, to agree to meet up with him in LA, but I know it will cause more harm than good. Unless, of course, he's shit in bed, and that would actually solve all of my problems, but I'm not letting it get that far, I'm on holiday. I need to tear myself away from this man and forever remember how exciting this flight to LA was, and leave it at that.

I've no idea how long we've been pressed up against the wall. I begin to realise where we are and slowly break away before airport staff have us removed.

He opens his stunning turquoise eyes and exhales loudly. "Whoa."

"Indeed. Thank you again, Daniel, for everything. I'm glad I met you."

"You too, Bea. Enjoy your vacation. I don't suppose you could arrange to be on all of my business flights? They will seem so terribly monotonous now."

"I'll do my best, although, sadly, I think it somewhat unlikely," I pout and step back, holding his hands.

"Beatrice, it is, unfortunately, time for us to go."

"Goodbye, Daniel."

He kisses my hand and I take one last look into those beautiful eyes before turning to walk back to Tilly. He strolls down towards passport control and looks back once before he's gone.

"Crikey, that was some game of tonsil tennis you had going on there, Bea, are you sure you don't want to see him again?"

I clasp my hands together over my heart and briefly close my eyes. "Oh Tils, you have no idea how much I want to see that man again, he was... unbelievable. But I can't do it to myself. This was fun, but if I see him again, I know I'll like him even more and I'll have to leave the states in nine days feeling miserable. Holiday romances always make me feel like crap when I return home. That is the last thing I want right now. I want a fun, fabulous holiday with my old chum knowing that I had the most exciting flight of my entire life on the way."

"Good for you, love. I totally understand." Tilly gives me a reassuring smile and we continue to passport control.

Walking through arrivals a while later, we find Gemma's husband, Jay, waiting for us. We head straight for the car and arrive at the house in no time. Gemma is hopping up and down on the doorstep as we arrive and Tilly practically falls out of the car to get to her. I help Jay get the suitcases out of the boot and make my way over to the reunited sisters.

Gemma releases Tilly and offers me a warm hug. I've always gotten on well with Tilly's older sister, they're so alike, if you love one, you'll find it hard not to love the other. They even look the same, only Gemma has blonde hair, where Tilly's is golden brown with a cute, heavy fringe. They both have identical hazel eyes and dainty, elfin features. Tilly is tiny at 5'3" with a very petite frame, and Gemma is much the same, maybe a touch taller. She moved to LA about eight years ago, but the pair have remained just as close as they always were.

"Where's Jack?" Tilly asks her sister.

"He's sleeping now, I tried to keep him up but he was too tired. He'll be up bright and early to pester you tomorrow though."

"Good! I can't wait!"

Hmm. I picture a three year old bursting into my bedroom at some god forsaken hour, jumping on my bed and screaming at the top of his lungs. Oh dear god, is that what I've signed up for? I seriously hope not. I try to push that thought to the back of my mind and hope for the best.

We walk through the huge, beautiful lounge towards the sliding double doors that lead out onto the deck. The outside lights glisten in the water of the pool in front of us and the warm breeze makes a wonderful change to what we're used to at home. To the right of the pool, a couple of wide steps lead up to another sun deck, belonging to the pretty pool-house.

"This is stunning, Gemma, I love it!"

"Thank you Bea, I'm glad you think so. We built the pool-house for friends and relatives coming over from the UK and wanted it to feel like a holiday haven, so I hope you like it inside, too."

"I'm sure I'll love it, thank you so much for having me at such short notice."

"Nonsense, Bea, we're happy to have you. It's about time you came to visit!" she replies, warmly.

"I'm actually starting to feel exhausted now, so I think I'll probably head in to unpack before hitting the hay, that okay with everyone?"

"Of course, love," Tilly replies, "you go and make a start and I'll be in in a bit."

Jay has left my suitcase in the pool-house for me so I head up the steps towards the french doors. I take a look at the pretty little house, it's a white, wooden house with a tiled roof. Very quaint. The front has double french doors with full length windows on either side.

I open the doors and walk into a stunning, nautical themed lounge room, the slatted wood walls and floor have been lightly white washed and a giant hessian rug covers most of the floor. The two plush sofas with washed-navy and white stripes, are crying out for me to kick back and take a seat. The curtains at the windows and doors match the fabric of the sofa and a pale blue chenille throw sits on the arm of each chair.

The stylish, white, antique furniture, housing a selection of navy and white vases, pots and candle holders, compliments the room perfectly. The table in front of the sofas has a pale blue vase filled with beautiful, short stemmed white roses. My favourites.

To the left of the french doors is a round white dining table and four chairs. The table is already set, with a vase of white roses in the centre. It's just like a mini show home. It's all very much my taste, I love it!

Beyond the table is a small kitchen which I'll explore later, and to the right of the living area is a small but ever-so-pretty bedroom. The walls are again white washed, and the double bed is the fluffiest, cosiest bed I've ever seen. A door leads to the small bathroom which has another door, giving access the lounge, too. This really is a haven, I feel so lucky to be here.

I put some of my clothes in the chest of drawers in the lounge, making sure I leave room for Tilly's clothes, and hang most of my other bits in the large wardrobe in the bedroom. It took much less time than I thought, so I wander out onto the deck to soak in the lovely LA evening, before bed.

Tilly strolls out of the main house with two cups of tea and a packet of chocolate chip cookies, and joins me on the deck. Handing me a cup she says, "Thought you might like this, I know I need one after that long, hellish journey." She winks.

"Ya sweetie, I don't think I'll ever be able to travel in upper class again! Yes, thanks Til, a cuppa is exactly what I need." We sit on the pool-house deck at the companion seat and look up at the clear, California night sky. My mind floats back to my magical flight with hot stuff.

"Thinking about him?" Tilly asks, a moment later.
"You can tell?"

33

"I just know you. I'd like some of the juicy goss now, if you don't mind. Gem's leaving us to it for the night, I've told her I'm having this and then going to bed, so... dish!"

Sitting out here, under the stars with a cup of tea, discussing my encounter with the 'hot slice', I feel warm and fuzzy, and although I do wish I could see him again, I'm happy to have had the chance to meet him. This is so relaxing, and I love my darling friends so much for making me come here.

We decide that Tilly can take the bedroom and I'll sleep on the sofa bed, which - by the looks of it - is just as comfortable as the bed. Tilly says that it has been made clear, by Gemma, that these are our quarters while we're here, we can come and go as we please and leave it as messy as we like. Neither Gemma, nor Jay will be coming in here, so we should treat it like home. Jack has been told that the pool-house is out of bounds and under no circumstance is he allowed to bring toys, musical instruments or 'loud behaviour' anywhere near our decking area before ten a.m. Music to my ears. *Hallelujah*!

When we've finished setting up the sofa-bed, I give Tilly a big, grateful hug. "Thank you so much, I just know I'm going to have an amazing time. You're so sweet to let me share your holiday. Love you."

"Love you, too. You're welcome and I'm so excited that you're here with me, I can't wait to take you to fabulous shops and out for yummy food!"

"Squee!" I cry, clapping my hands excitedly, like a child.

"Night Bea, see you in the morning."

"Night night, doll."

Tilly smiles before she closes the door to the bedroom and I get snug-as-a-bug-in-a-rug in the most comfortable sofa-bed I've ever slept it. I close my eyes and let my mind wander to Daniel Berkeley and his beautiful mouth.

⁄

CHAPTER THREE
SATURDAY 15TH SEPTEMBER

A sharp slap on my backside rudely awakens me from my heavenly dream about 'you-know-who'.

"Wakey wakey, sleepy head." Tilly is sitting on the side of the bed with a huge grin on her face. I realise that my night dress has risen up to my ribs, and where I've kicked the duvet off in my sleep, my bottom is hanging right out there for all to see. Thank god the curtains are still shut.

Covering myself, I smile over at Tilly. "Good morning, sunshine! Apologies for that, at such an early hour, too," I laugh, referring to my thong-clad behind.

"No worries, it's not like I've never seen it before. Sleep well?"

"Mmm, like a dream." A big, stupid grin spreads across my face.

"Yes, I bet you did dream, about Sexy McHottie, no doubt. What do you fancy doing today? The sun is shining and it's a glorious morning, we can either stay by the pool and catch some rays or head out for some retail therapy."

"I really need to buy some Hanky Panky knickers while I'm here, but I don't need to do that today. Shall we laze by the pool so you can catch up with your sister?"

"Sounds perfect, and then we can head out to The Grove tomorrow. I know Nordstrom sell Hanky Pankys, that's where I got them last time."

"Great. I'll go and get my bikini on then!"

I'm looking forward to getting out and about, exploring and soaking in all things 'California', but I know Tilly is desperate to spend time with her sister and nephew, and a day by the pool will be fabulous. A far cry from life at home! I'd like to catch some sun too, I'm feeling a bit pasty sat here in the glamour of Hollywood.

We make breakfast in the little kitchen - Gemma has stocked it with everything imaginable - and head out to eat on our deck. The weather is fantastic and there is a lovely smell in the air - fresh - different to home. Gemma comes out with

Jack, the cutest little boy with gorgeous blonde curly locks, and they sit on the steps chatting to us while we eat.

We spend the day sunbathing, laughing and playing in the water with Jack. When he went inside for some 'quiet time' during the afternoon, Tilly and I floated in the pool on huge armchair lilos and caught some more rays. Perfectly relaxing, just what I needed to take my mind off the teasing memories of Sexy Berkeley.

When the sun started to set, Jay and Gemma prepared a sumptuous barbecue feast for dinner on the main deck. We all sat around the table, talking about the UK, Tilly's job and the cakery, filling Gemma in on everything that's happening at home. When Gemma and Jay headed into the main house to retire for the evening, Tilly and I sat out on the pool-house deck, each with a throw from the sofas around us, drinking red wine and staring at the wonderful, clear night sky. We toasted California with one more glass of wine before heading in for a long, uninterrupted, very dreamy sleep.

CHAPTER FOUR
SUNDAY 16TH SEPTEMBER

I wake to the sounds of Tilly filling the kettle in the kitchen. Although the curtains are still closed, the french doors are open, sending a refreshing breeze through the room. My bottom is, thankfully, not making an appearance this morning. I stretch and revel in the glory of waking up in this heavenly place.

"Morning," I call into the kitchen from under my cosy duvet.

"Oh you're up! How did you sleep?" Tilly walks to the doorway and pokes her head out.

"*Amazingly*, thank you. How about you?"

"Oh me too, I always do here. It's times like this that I wish I lived here, dark circles would be a thing of the past."

"Oh wow, that would be amazing. I know Clare and I would miss you like mad, but you could easily come and live over here, Til."

"Yeah, I've thought about it, but I don't think I could. I'd miss everything at home too much and there's all the Visa stuff to think about."

"I suppose, but it would be fabulous."

~~~~~~

At eleven thirty, Gemma drops us by a fabulous looking apartment complex opposite The Grove, on her way to a 'Mummy/toddler' class, with Jack. The sun is shining and it's a beautifully hot day. I'm glad I wore my short, white, shirt dress, it's perfect. The tan ankle boots will probably be a little warm, in hindsight, but never mind, they look good.

We look around a couple of shops, before our bellies start to rumble. Tilly told me about a place she goes to with Gemma for noodles in the Farmer's Market, a few minutes away, so we decide to go there and head back to the shops afterwards. The market is very busy, but it's so vibrant and energetic, and the aromas are delectable. Tilly points to the noodle place and we approach the queue.

The line inches forward slowly and I contemplate the options on the menu plaque, it all looks mouthwatering. Just as I'm about to ask Tilly what dish she recommends, a familiar, velvety voice takes me by complete surprise. "Well, Miss Hart, what a wonderful surprise."

I turn so quickly, I'm surprised I don't do damage to my neck.

Jesus Christ, he's here, hot-pants himself. The very man who has dominated my dreams for the past two nights, stands before me looking... exquisite. I'm stunned into silence for a few moments while I gawk at this hot slice of heaven.

"Oh my god..." I just about manage, "Sexy Berkeley..."

His smile is magnificent as he raises his eyebrows. Tilly bursts out laughing and only then do I realise what I've called him. "Oh, um, I mean, Daniel!" I can't help but giggle, I'm not used to being so dumb-struck by a man's presence.

He puts his hand on the small of my back and kisses my cheek. The skin on skin contact is electric, I feel the tingle immediately and close my eyes to inhale his divine scent, melting into him. He draws away slowly and offers a cheek to Tilly. She presses her cheek against his and immediately pushes in front of me to order for the both of us. I wouldn't care if she ordered me a plate of dead rats right now, Daniel Berkeley is in front of me, looking hot to trot in navy Ralph Lauren shorts and a brilliant-white polo shirt. His face is even more beautiful than I remember. His collar is standing up against his neck in the sexiest way.

"Bea, how are you? It's so great to see you. How unexpected!"

"I'm very well, thank you. A little shocked to see you, as I'm sure you can tell! How are you?"

"I'm good, all the better for seeing you." He smiles a shy and utterly gorgeous smile as he slides his hands in his pockets and rocks back on his heels. Tilly arrives at our sides with two plates of... something - who cares - I'm far too interested in Sexy over here.

"Oh, please join us, we're sitting right here."

Us? We? Oh please god, don't be with a girl... *Please?* He wouldn't invite us to join him and another woman... would he?

He gestures towards a round table with another unbelievable hottie sitting at it. Christ, do you have to be ridiculously handsome around here or something?

"We don't want to intrude, Daniel." I mumble, still in a state of shock.

"No, please, it would be our pleasure to have you join us." He walks ahead of us to the table. I look at Tilly and she shrugs, smirking, before she turns to see Daniel's gorgeous friend rise from the table. Her tongue practically rolls out into her noodles. He is stunningly attractive, remarkably well built and dons the most handsome smile. Okay, maybe not as handsome as Daniel's, but I know Tilly is peeing her knickers with excitement, looking at him.

"Luke, I'd like you to meet Beatrice Hart, and her friend Tilly Burton, I met them both on the flight from London on Friday."

Luke gives Daniel a knowing nod before shaking my hand. "Well, what a coincidence. It's a pleasure to meet you Miss Hart." He turns to Tilly and I grab the plates so that she has a free hand.

"Miss Burton, enchanted." He lifts her hand to his mouth and holds her gaze as he kisses her knuckles, winking sexily. Ah, so he's a smooth talking mother fucker too. We have no chance!

We all sit around the table, Daniel sits opposite Luke and scoots his chair around a bit so Tilly and I can sit together. Daniel and Luke pick up their forks and continue eating while Tilly and I poke about with ours.

"So Beatrice, what brings you here today? Are you staying nearby?" Daniel asks.

"Tilly's sister's house is about fifteen or twenty minutes away, and we decided to do a spot of shopping here. Do you live around here?"

"I live over in Hollywood and Vine, but Luke lives across the street at The Palazzo, so we come here quite a lot."

"Oh okay, I think that's where we got dropped off, it looks lovely."

"Yeah, I used to live there with Luke, it's a great location."

"Tilly, that's an unusual name," Luke says to Tilly.

"Um, thank you, I think? Luke, that's... not a particularly unusual name." She shoots him her cheeky smile and a wink. I can feel the sexual chemistry between them already!

I look at Daniel and he's watching me, intently with a slight smile on his face. His eyes are sublime in the natural light of day, it's almost like a creamy turquoise, the palest greeny-blue. "Bea, I'm just so stunned to see you. I thought our 'goodbye' at the airport was the last I'd see of you, but here you are, sat at my table at the Farmer's Market. Well what d'ya know." He grins and shakes his head, raising another forkful of noodles to his mouth, reminding me that I have a plate of untouched food in front of me. I hook my fork into some noodles and pop it in my mouth. It tastes unbelievable.

"Mmm, this is amazing!" I mumble, covering my mouth with my fingertips.

"I know, right? Luke and I eat here all the time."

"So, where are you ladies headed after this?" Luke asks.

"Well, Bea wants to go to Nordstrom..." *Please Tilly, please don't tell them why I want to go to Nordstrom.* "...To buy some hot, kinky underwear." *You little witch!* She looks at me and giggles her 'I'm-gonna-get-in-trouble-for-that-later' laugh, nudging me with her elbow.

I notice Daniel look up from his plate with his mouth ajar, holding his fork mid-air. "Whoa, is that true or is she just trying to embarrass you?"

Heat rushes to my cheeks, I must be the colour of ketchup. "Um, probably a bit of both actually, although you can take out the kinky part. Thanks for that Til."

She looks thoroughly pleased with herself and continues. "And I want to get something for my little nephew. Then, I planned to take Bea for a drink somewhere. What are you two up to? Wanna come?" she directs the question to Luke and takes a long, obvious look from head to toe, checking him out. He mirrors her perfectly and they both grin salaciously at each other.

Daniel answers the question, "Well, I'm not sure about you two," gesturing towards Luke and Tilly, "I think you might need to get a room, but Luke and I *were* planning on heading over to the Apple Store. Why don't we all go shop together? There's something I need to pick up in Nordstrom, too."

The thought of spending leisurely time with Daniel is exciting. On the plane, our time was limited, and although I'm slightly embarrassed by how forward I was, it was thrilling. Out at the shops, strolling with Tilly and Luke too, maybe I won't feel the need to tear his clothes off and jump him every five minutes. *Who am I kidding?*

"That sounds great... does that sound good to you, Til?"

Still gazing at Luke, she waves her hand in my direction. "Yeah, yeah, whatever."

I know I should be saying no, I should be steering well clear of this man, I'm going home in just over a week and I really don't want to start liking him any more than I already do. But I can't tear myself away. Just today, I tell myself, that'll be all. I won't see him again.

When we have all finished our food, we make our way back towards the shopping precinct. Tilly walks ahead with Luke, they're still making eyes at each other but have actually stopped gawking and started talking. Daniel and I walk side by side, occasionally looking up at the other in disbelief.

"So, how's California treating you?" he asks.

Gosh, he's just so hot, even his voice does delicious things to my nether regions. "It's wonderful, thank you. We had a pool day at the house yesterday, so today is my first day out and about. I'm really enjoying myself."

"I'm glad to hear it. I must say, you look like you've caught a little sun, you look radiant."

I tuck my hair behind one of my ears and smile down at the ground feeling shy. "Thank you, Daniel. You look very handsome yourself." I turn to look up at him through my lashes. Oh how I want to touch him, we've known each other for no time at all, but I want to hold his hand, stroke his muscular shoulder blades. His back is so broad, and through his white polo shirt, I can see the definition of the muscles all over his back. *Christ, take it off, man, let me see you in your full glory.*

As we approach Nordstrom, Tilly wolf whistles over to the male models standing outside a neighbouring shop with nothing but their pants on. On any other occasion, I'd have had a good old perv myself, but right now, the only person I want to see with no clothes on is walking along beside me.

"Right, shall I go to the... um... *department* that I want, while you boys get what you need?" I ask as we enter, praying that they'll let me buy my knickers in peace.

Luke responds immediately, "It'll be easier to stick together, and much more fun that way. I, for one, *love* panty shopping." *Ugh*, great. Luke winks at Tilly and she giggles, his smile that of child let loose in a toy shop.

Daniel puts a gentle hand on my waist and leans in to whisper, reassuringly, in my ear, "They're only panties, don't be embarrassed. I'll buy some boxers and you can all help me choose, how about that?"

The sensation of his hand on my body is enough to make me stop breathing for a moment. All of my hard work trying to forget this man yesterday clearly hasn't paid off. His lips skimmed my ear as he whispered, and that unwelcome, yet, exquisite tingle ran right down to my very own underwear department.

We all enter the lift, and Daniel presses the button for the appropriate floor. Tilly and Luke silently flirt - there's no way these two aren't going to 'get down and dirty' by the end of the day. Daniel stares down at his brown deck shoes, hands clutched behind his back, trying to suppress a super cute smile. I wonder if I could bury my face in his neck and sniff him silly without him thinking I'm some sort of lunatic...

I manage to tear myself away from thoughts of Daniel's sexy skin, and mentally prepare myself for the task ahead. As the doors open, I shoot out of the lift in search of the Hanky Pankys. I thread between rails at the speed of lightening, ducking and diving to get where I need to be without giving the others a chance to catch up. James Bond, eat your heart out.

I finally come across my favourite knickers, and in a matter of minutes - seconds even - I have grabbed ten pairs of the lace hipster thongs in a variety of pretty colours. As I'm still alone, I choose three lace bras in my size so I have three matching sets. I have probably spent a small fortune, but I know I won't be here again for a long time, if at all, so I may as well make the most of it. They're not easy to find in the UK, and will set you back a pretty penny.

I stroll, basket in hand, towards the nightwear section. I can see Tilly a few rails away, seductively holding a super-sexy black corset with suspenders against her body, in front of Luke, who's grinning like a Cheshire cat. The two of them seem so similar, overly flirtatious, afraid of nothing and up for a laugh all the time.

I focus back on the night wear and look at the vast selection of nighties. I've always been a fan of silky, pretty night dresses, I've never really been one for wearing t-shirts or big baggy things to bed. I do have a few pairs of pyjamas, but they're silk bottoms with camisoles or vest tops. I like to feel pretty in bed, even if there's no one with me, as is the case, most of the time.

A beautiful cream and black, polka dot nightie with lace detail grabs my attention, and next to it, a black lace nightie with a matching short robe. I start to look for my size in the black lace as an arm slips around me from behind, resting on my tummy. I turn my head in surprise and my lips almost touch his cheek as he leans forward. His close proximity, electrifying.

"Excellent choice, Miss Hart. Although I like your first choice, too," he says, pointing with his free hand to the polka dot nightie. "What size are you? Four?" He steps back and slowly slides his hand from my belly. *Touch me, touch me, again.*

"Well, it's a little confusing, at home, I'm an eight, so yes, I think that makes me a four here. How did you know that?"

"Lucky guess, I suppose." He starts to look through the hangers, pulls out my size and drops it into my basket.

"Oh, I'm getting that, am I?" I smile at him.

"I think it would be a great shame if you didn't. And the lace one."

"I do like them, but I won't get both. I'm already purchasing about a hundred pairs of knickers." *Holy moly*, I'm talking knickers with a hot man I hardly know.

"You're doing things to me, Beatrice, I think you should stop talking about panties." I laugh as he continues. "If

43

you're only going to get one, I think you should get the lace one, it's a little cheaper, it's very different to the others and also... it's sheer," he smirks.

"Daniel, I believe you have a point, thank you for your helpful assistance." I smile, swapping the nighties over.

"Oh, anytime, Beatrice. Anytime." He rocks back onto his heels and smiles, his teeth are so perfectly aligned, simply dazzling.

"Right, I'm going to go and pay, shall I meet you over by the lift? I'm not sure what Tilly and Luke are up to..."

"They're probably trying on underwear together, those two seem to have hit it off. I'll meet you downstairs by the door in a few minutes, I need to get a couple of things too. Unless you really would like to help me select boxer shorts?"

I giggle, he's very endearing. "Oh Daniel, I think that as you gave me a moment to select my own 'panties' - as you call them - I will let you 'boxer-shop' in peace."

"I didn't have a choice, you practically sprinted out of the elevator, I don't think an athlete could have caught up," he grins, "see you in five or ten."

I head to the cash desk and unload my basket, smiling. I love to shop, but to flirt 'n' shop is a whole new, exciting experience. I want to wrap my arms and legs around that man and... oh, the rest.

I meet Tilly and Luke back at the lift, both looking naughty and extremely pleased with themselves. What they've been up to, I don't want to know... *okay, I do.* But I'll find out later. We head back down towards the main door leisurely, stopping to look at this and that on the way.

When Daniel returns to us, we stroll outside into the beautiful sun and decide to skip the rest of the shopping, and go straight for a beer. The boys take us to a place close by, where we sit and each order a beer, basking in the wonderful weather and great company.

Luke tears himself from his flirtatious conversation with Tilly briefly to raise his bottle. "To great days in LA and hot British chicks."

We raise our bottles, laughing, and Tilly adds, "And super-sexy American boys." I'll drink to that!

Three beers later, we're all thoroughly enjoying ourselves, conversation is flowing freely and we're finding out a lot about each other. I already know a little bit about Daniel, but it's nice to find out about Luke, the fitness trainer best friend. He and Tilly have calmed their outrageous flirting, somewhat, and seem to be enjoying normal conversation.

It has been almost impossible to resist temptation, sitting here, next to Daniel. My eyes have been drawn to his sexy, tanned thigh so close to mine, my hand struggling not to reach out and stroke it. I have visualised running my fingertips up and down his strong, muscular arms, pretty much every five minutes.

As we all get close to finishing our drinks, Luke puts his bottle down to address the rest of us. "Hey, I have a great idea, it's a nice day, why don't we all go over to my place for a swim?"

"That sounds like fun!" Tilly answers, immediately, and I nod in agreement. "Let's nip into one of the shops on the way back and grab a bikini each," she adds.

So we head towards Luke's place over the road, taking a detour to buy a bikini. Tilly and Luke, again, walk ahead of Daniel and I, so we get a chance to talk some more.

"So, did you grow up in the town that you live in now?" he asks.

"No, I grew up in a small town called Rickmansworth, and that's where my business is, but I live in a larger town called Watford. My parents still live in Rickmansworth and my apartment is only a short drive away."

"Okay, and your friends?"

"Til and Clare live just around the corner from my apartment, so I'm close to everything important. My complex was built right next to the Metropolitan Line train station, so it's really easy to get everywhere if you don't want to drive. Especially London, we're very close to the City."

"That's great, maybe I'll come visit next time I'm on business in London," he says with a smile.

"Hey, that would be great!"

"You're beautiful, Beatrice, do you know that?" *Whoa, change the subject - why don't you, Daniel.* "Oh, and before I

45

forget... I bought you a little something." He hands me a Nordstrom shopping bag.

I accept it, stunned. "Daniel, that's very kind of you but you shouldn't have, you hardly know me."

"Please, I wanted to. I like buying gifts for people, please accept it."

"Thank you Daniel, that's very sweet." I hold open the bag, and at the bottom, I see the pretty, polka dot nightie. My first thought, is that he's been painfully sweet and bought me something he knows I wanted, but I quickly begin to wonder if he's buying me sexy nightwear to get me into bed. He wouldn't, actually, need to buy me anything to get me into bed, I've never been so sexually attracted to another human being in my life, but the thought of him expecting sex because he's bought me this, is quite unsavoury.

As if he read my mind, he says, "Please, don't think I bought you this for any other reason than knowing you liked it. Of course, any red-blooded male would love to see a beautiful woman like you, dressed in something like this, and the thought is making blood rush to places that I'd rather it didn't - in public - but I certainly didn't buy this to get anything out of it, other than the joy of buying someone a gift."

He's either throwing me a line or being totally genuine and right now, I think I'll give him the benefit of the doubt. "Daniel, thank you very much, I love it, that's so sweet. Thank you." I slow to a halt and lean in to kiss his cheek. Sparks fly like fireworks between our skin, and before I can lean away to continue walking, his arms wrap gently around my waist.

He gently pulls me towards him and his lips skim mine, our eyes burning into each other's. Lips touching, but not moving, breathing heavily against me, he lifts his head slightly to brush his bottom lip against my top lip. My eyes close automatically. I'm no longer on the pavement, carrying shopping bags alongside a busy road; I'm in a whole other world of arousal and electricity and tingling and butterflies. He increases the pressure, and we kiss a slow, gentle, sensual kiss. No tongues, no mad animalistic frenching, just a simple, ambrosial kiss.

"Spit spot, lovers!" Tilly shrieks from the other side of the busy road and my eyes open, looking directly into Daniel's.

"Come on, plenty of time for that later!" she shouts.

Daniel smiles and I melt, I could stay in this embrace for the rest of the week, easily. We gradually separate and start to walk towards The Palazzo again.

We arrive at Luke's apartment and it's gorgeous, Tilly's mouth dropped to the floor the moment we walked through the door. It's an elegant, stylish, luxurious bachelor pad, decorated in rich browns and reds.

The boys lead us to the spare bedroom upstairs to change into our swimwear while they get their trunks on. Apparently, this is Daniel's room when he stays here. It's very simple, a low, king size bed with simplistic wooden head board, two matching bedside tables and a plasma TV against the far wall. Two doors lead to the en-suite and walk in wardrobe.

We close the door and Tilly immediately whispers a squeal. "Eee! This is so much fun! I cannot believe you didn't arrange to meet up with him!"

"I know, it's so weird that they were there! I'm really glad though." My face bursts into a huge grin and Tilly's mirrors it.

"Daniel is so hot, Bea, and as for Luke, Christ on a bike. I am hot for his bod. I am going to get some sex!"

I laugh out loud and return to a whisper, "But aren't you worried that you'll really like him and then we'll have to go home?"

"Not at all, I want some sex, he wants some sex, so we're both gonna get some sex. Yes, I fancy him like mad, but I'm not going to fall in love with him or anything, he's not exactly boyfriend material. Just fun, fun, fun in the sun, sun, sun! Whoop whoop, baby!"

I wish I was able to think like Tilly, I'm so worried that I'm going to really like Daniel, and then I won't want to go home. Holiday romances always make me feel like shit, so I try to avoid them at all costs. I just can't seem to tear myself away from Daniel today.

We throw our clothes back over our new bikinis and head downstairs where Luke leads the way to the fabulous pool. We place our belongings on sun loungers and are the only ones here, which seems odd for such a large complex.

Tilly quickly strips down to her bikini to wolf whistles galore from Luke, she sashays over to the edge of the pool and expertly dives straight into the water. Luke strips in record time and shows off his immaculate, muscular body. Tilly's eyes almost fall out of their sockets, I know she's in her element as Luke dives in and swims up to her.

I look over to my right at Daniel as he kicks off his shoes and smiles in amusement at Luke and Tilly. He grabs his polo shirt by the hem and leisurely lifts it up and over his head, the muscles on his torso ripple under the flawless tanned skin. *Fuck me*. His body is outstanding. He pulls his shorts down to reveal navy, Ralph Lauren swimming trunks, and, although I am aware that I'm ogling, I can't seem to stop. My mouth is watering at the sight of this Adonis, my tongue must be hanging right out there.

It takes a while, but I manage to drag my gaze away from the burning chunk of eye candy and focus on the glorious, tropical surroundings.

"Aren't you coming in?" Daniel asks.

"Yes, I'm just chilling out for a bit, I'll join you in a minute."

"Okay, don't be too long," he grins. I want to eat him.

He dives into the water from the end of the pool and it's a sight for sore eyes. Utterly gorgeous. I watch him swim for a moment before I start to undress. Once I've laid my dress on the lounger, I take a few steps over to the edge of the pool and sit, dangling my legs in the water. It's so refreshing, not too cold but not too warm.

Daniel swims over to me and stands up by my feet, it's just the right depth for him, but too deep for me to stand in. He runs his hands up the backs of my calves and the goose bumps spread over my skin at top speed. How does his touch do this to me?

"Come on in, it's great."

I wriggle forward so that my bottom is at the very edge of the pool. He rests his hands on the edge, either side of me, as I lower myself into the water, sliding my body down his. It's erotic, I want nothing more than to wrap myself around him. Once my body is submerged, I bend my arms up, either side of my head, to hold on to the edge of the pool. Daniel's face is mere centimetres away from mine and my legs are freely floating around his.

"Put your hands on my shoulders," he says, his voice rich and velvety.

I let go of the edge and gently hold onto his wet shoulders, savouring the feel of his hot, wet skin. He runs his hands down my sides to the backs of my thighs, and pulls my legs around his waist. The flutters in my stomach become full on thrashes, a wave of heat courses through my veins, my fingers and toes tingle, not to mention down there. I'm wrapped around him, it feels like every inch of my body is touching his. His erection presses against me, in between my legs. If this was a private pool, and Tilly and Luke weren't here, I'd be pulling my bikini to the side and in the throes of passion already.

"Bea, what are you doing to me?" he whispers, looking into my eyes. "Your body is perfect, your skin feels like silk. You're incredible." His eyes full of desire as he strokes my back gently. My heart races as he glides one of his hands up to the back of my neck, his eyes gazing down at my mouth. My tongue tentatively reaches out to run along my bottom lip, slowly, in anticipation.

His mouth wet from the pool water, a tantalising invitation that I gladly accept, eagerly embracing the deep passionate kiss, his tongue warm, he tastes delicious. Natural instincts urge me to flex my pelvis, grinding myself against his solid erection. *No, no! Stop this, Beatrice!*

My hands explore his broad, naked back, I impulsively run my nails gently up his spine. He lets out a quiet, deep, masculine groan, spurring me on even more. I can feel the quivering inside building, my internal muscles twitch in response to his hard cock moving against my lady bits through the fabric of our swimwear.

I drag my hands back to Daniel's delectable shoulders and gradually slow the kiss until it fades, reluctantly creating space between my groin and his manhood. "We need to stop, Daniel."

"I want you," he says, trailing kisses down my neck. A wanton moan escapes me, I need his naked body against me, preferably in a bedroom, though, and without the trunks and bikini shielding the important bits.

"I think you know that I want you too, Daniel, but ideally not in a communal swimming pool, we can continue later."

He lifts his head slowly from my neck and looks at me with those hypnotic turquoise eyes, full of desire. His mouth casually curls into a sexy smile as he grabs my behind and gently brings me against him again. This time he tips his pelvis and pushes his rock-hard erection against my bikini bottoms right about, there. My stomach flips. I gasp silently and close my eyes, it's heaven and hell, I want him so much, but not here.

He rocks against me slowly, again and again. I drop my face to his shoulder, I can't bear it, I'm going to... I so want to, but no I don't, not here! I can hear Tilly and Luke messing about in the pool, splashing each other or play fighting... or something.

"Daniel..." I moan, my voice a whisper, "no..."

"Yes," he whispers in my ear.

The quivering inside is now a shuddering, it's uncontrollable, inevitable, even if he stopped rubbing me, I'd probably still come. I clasp my hands around his neck and whisper a moan into his ear. "Please, uh..." I plead, trying to remain as normal to the outside world as possible.

"Let it happen." The tone of his whisper is so rough and dangerous. I have no chance.

"Daniel...Daniel, oh god...no," whispering so silently that only he could hear.

"Yes, baby. It's so hot when you say my name like that, I want you so fucking badly."

"Uh huh, yes..." I'm clinging onto his neck, my face pressed up against his ear, the waves are rolling thick and fast and as the release pierces through my core, I bite Daniel's ear to keep me from crying out. It goes on and on, ripples forcing their way through my body, the longest, strongest orgasm I've ever had, and we're not even having sex! The imposing tingle through the arch of my foot spreads to my toes and gradually, the sensation begins to fade. *Wow*.

"Daniel... Oh, Daniel."

"You have no idea how hot this is for me, baby."

"Oh my, that was just... so good." I pull my face away from his, I can't believe he just did that. I frown and swat his bicep. "But so bad! Daniel, that was so, so naughty."

The biggest 'cat-got-the-cream' grin spreads across his handsome face. "I couldn't help myself," he murmurs, quietly, "but it was so hot, now I want you so much more, if that's even possible. I need you."

"I think we should have a little swim now, don't you?"

"Oh," he pouts, "do I have to let go?"

Tilly and Luke are doing handstands and amusingly attempting synchronised swimming in the shallower end, and Daniel finally releases me to swim a length, do what one should typically do in a pool. I cannot believe I just had an orgasm in a communal fucking swimming pool. But oh my word, it was magnificent.

~~~~~~~~

An hour or so passes, and we're all lounging by the pool, chatting and laughing. We've had such a brilliant day with Daniel and Luke, I'm so pleased that we bumped into them. It has only been a few hours but I feel like the four of us have known each other for years. It seems Tilly and Luke are completely oblivious to anything other than their own carnal desires, so I'm not feeling so embarrassed by what Daniel and I were doing earlier.

We are sitting face to face on a sun lounger, his legs straddling it and mine crossed underneath me, in-between his. He has been playing with my fingers, which I find irresistible, and we've been flirting non-stop. Tilly and Luke are having another 'pash' on their lounger which gives Daniel and I some more space to chat.

"I want to ask you some questions, to know more about Beatrice Hart."

"Fire away, I have some too, so this will be fun," I respond, grinning.

"Okay, question one; who was your last boyfriend, how long were you together, why and when did it end?"

"I do believe that was four questions, but I'll answer them all anyway, seeing as it's you."

He smiles and I itch to kiss him again, he's so cute when he smiles, yet so masculine the rest of the time.

"My last boyfriend was Dylan, we were together for five years, things weren't going well, he cheated on me and we broke up four years ago."

"Wow, what an asshole. I bet he regrets that every day of his life." I smile shyly, what do you say to that?

"Four years is a long time, why no boyfriends since?" he asks.

"I haven't met anyone that I've liked enough to put myself back in that vulnerable situation with," I shrug, "simple as that. How about you? Who, how long, why and when?"

"Well, she's called Holly, we dated for two years, she wanted something more than I was prepared to give so we finished it two years ago," he says in a very matter-of-fact manner.

"So what did she want that you didn't want to give?"

"She wanted to settle down, she wanted to come off birth control and start a family and it came as quite a shock. I wasn't ready to do that, certainly not with her. I always felt that she was merely a stepping stone to a more serious relationship, and I certainly didn't think that she thought of me as the man to start a family with."

"So, you were using her? As a stepping stone?"

"Maybe. Not purposefully, I'd never intentionally lead somebody to believe something that wasn't true. I thought she felt the same way as me, which is why I was so shocked when she wanted marriage and babies with me. We didn't even live together."

"Do you want to have a family one day, Daniel, or is that not your 'thing'?"

"One day, with the right person, yes. Holly wasn't the right person and it wasn't the right time. And you? Do you want hundreds of babies running around?"

"Hundreds? No! But I'd like a family one day, two or three kids maybe. I'm still young, it's not something I'm thinking about right now."

"What *are* you looking for right now?"

"Well, right now, I'd like nothing more than to be locked in a bedroom with you." *Whoa*! Down girl! But the thought of being wrapped around his naked body does send a tingle down my spine. Judging by the grin on his face and the speed at which his eyebrows shoot up, I think he's quite taken aback by my forwardness, too.

"I'm sure something can be done about that, in fact, I'm certain of it. I can't think of anything that would give me greater pleasure.

I grin, mischievously, and continue, "My turn to ask now, um... do you sleep in pyjamas, underwear or in the buff?"

Daniel chuckles and his eyes twinkle. "In the 'buff?'" he imitates my British accent, "Why, how personal!" He grins. "Boxers, usually. Now I must ask you the same, although I think, after our recent shopping spree, I already know the answer to this."

"You'd be surprised, Daniel. But, yes, I do sleep in nighties...when I'm alone."

"And when you're not alone, Beatrice?"

"Oh, that'd be telling."

"Maybe I'll find out."

The sexual chemistry is building thick and fast. We're going to have to stop this sooner rather than later, we're not submerged in water now. "I expect you will, Mr. Berkeley."

"Is it getting hot out here or is it just me?" he asks as he runs his finger around his polo shirt collar.

"Oh you're definitely hot, Daniel, very, very hot."

"You make me hot, for sure... I won't tell you what I was forced to do when I got home from the airport on Friday." He looks down and grins, before looking back up into my eyes through his super long, super gorgeous thick brown lashes.

I grin, salaciously. "Oh really? Someone was feeling a little... frustrated?"

"Someone was," he says, matter-of-factly, "I met this hot little fox on an airplane who got me hot and horny and left me with no release. What's a guy to do?"

For some reason this really turns me on. I lean forward and curl my hands around the back of his neck, gently running my nails through the short, soft prickles of his hair line. I whisper in his ear, "Were you thinking of me?"

He gasps and his hands suddenly hold either side of my face. In a split second, my mouth is against his, his tongue searching mine. It's so hot. We can't kiss like this, not here, I need more as it is. We need to take this inside before we give the residents something to talk about. I gently pull away.

"Daniel, not here. You make me want more."

He sits back with a look of amused frustration, and runs his thumb and fore finger up and down the stubble on his jaw. "You're something else. Maybe we should think about heading out for dinner, cool off for a bit?"

"Sterling plan, let's do that."

"Great, oh, and Bea, in answer to your question, yes... I was." *OH lordy*. If I was a man, that tent would be firmly pitched and able to survive a gale force wind right now. I smile, suggestively and wink before standing to collect my things. I need to cool off!

We head back to The Grove for food, and a couple of hours, four full bellies and a few drinks later, we're strolling hand in hand back to Luke's apartment. Tilly and Luke ahead, holding hands and looking like the perfect couple. I don't know how she can be so blasé about all of this, I really, really like Daniel and already I'm petrified of just how much more I'm going to like him if I see him again.

When we get back, Luke pours us all a glass of wine and before we've even had a sip, he and Tilly shoot up the stairs, giggling like teenagers. We hear the bedroom door slam and I laugh.

"Guess it couldn't wait?" Daniel jokes as we stroll through to the living area.

"It certainly looks that way, patience is a virtue, you know."

"Is that right?" he says as he takes my wine glass from my hand and sets it down on the coffee table, along with his own. He hooks his fingers into my belt and pulls me against his hot, hard body. "It's a damn shame I'm not a patient man, then." He wraps his arms around my waist, resting his hands on my backside. I snake my arms up around his neck and move in to kiss him. One of his hands slides up my spine and rests in-between my shoulder blades, pressing my chest into his. My nipples pucker as his tongue caresses mine.

We groan as the kiss becomes more intense, and our hands wander, exploring each other. He firmly cups one of my breasts, eliciting my desperate moan; I'm so ready for this man, I need him, I won't cope much longer without feeling his naked body moving against mine.

I bend my right leg, dragging my thigh up the outside of his body. He grabs it and pulls it higher, pushing it into his side as he firmly runs his hand underneath my dress to my bottom. He kneads and squeezes and it's unbearable, our kissing becoming faster, erratic. I moan again, loudly into Daniel's mouth and he automatically responds. His hand slides down from my buttock, over my thong to my wet centre, pressing his fingers against the gusset of my knickers. I buckle.

"Daniel," I whimper as I pull away from the kiss.

"I need to be inside you," he says with an arousing dominance, "upstairs." *Oh, I like horny, bossy Daniel.*

Before I can turn to make my way to the stairs, he wraps an arm tightly around my waist, and lifts me, my legs automatically wrapping around his body. *Christ, he's so strong.*

Walking towards the stairs with me hooked onto him like a Kuala, kissing manically, Daniel doesn't waste a minute. He practically runs up the stairs and bursts through his bedroom door, slamming it behind him.

Still immersed in an almighty, carnal kiss, he presses the light-switch by the door and unexpectedly walks away from the bed, pushing me up against the wall with a thud. His brute force, raw, and his kiss so deep, so animalistic. He groans loudly as I undo the button on his waistband, sliding the zip down before pushing my hand inside his boxers and grasping hold of his hot, hard cock. Powdery soft skin covers the huge, steel hard rod, I can hardly wait to feel every inch of him inside me.

"Ah, Bea..." he moans against my mouth as he closes his eyes. We're getting louder and I don't care.

I squeeze him tightly and move my hand, smoothly, up and down his thick shaft. His mouth pulls away from mine and he runs small kisses down my neck to my collar bone.

Still pinned against the wall, he starts to undo the buttons at my chest, kissing and nibbling my neck.

"Ever since I watched you undressing by the pool, I've been thinking about this moment. You looked so hot," he whispers. He pulls away to gaze down at my body through my open dress, my hand still squeezing him as he pulls one of my lace bra cups down. Growling, he takes my hard nipple in his mouth, and sucks.

"Oh, Daniel," I whimper.

"Mmm..." he moans back, licking and flicking my nipple with his tongue. Without stopping, he reaches to his back pocket and pulls out a condom. Although what's about to happen was inevitable, this increases my excitement, tenfold.

Confirmation that this gorgeous man will be inside me in a matter of minutes, and he wants it just as much as I do.

Keeping me pressed against the wall with my legs tightly squeezed around his waist, he pulls his polo shirt over his head before grabbing my waist and returning his lips to my nipple. I release his cock and push his shorts and boxers below his bottom, freeing him completely. I take the packet from his fingertips and tear it with my teeth, taking the condom and dropping the packaging to the floor. I roll it onto him between my legs, and he takes his mouth from my breast to claim my lips again.

He slides his hand inside my knickers and gently strokes my clitoris, sending excruciating spasms through my body. As he slowly moves down, he bites my bottom lip and simultaneously pushes two fingers inside me.

"Ah!" I moan, loudly, Daniel's teeth still clamped to my lip. It's erotic and *oh, so good.*

He releases my lip to kiss my neck under my ear. "You're so wet, baby, I want to be inside you," he whispers.

"Uh huh... now, Daniel," I beg.

He gently takes his fingers from me and pulls my knickers aside, guiding his cock to my entrance. Holding his tip there, he teases, pushing gently.

"Daniel!" I shout, my voice a high pitched cry, "Now!" I throw my head back, eyes clenched shut.

"Look at me," he grunts. I open my eyes and lower my face to meet his, and our eyes lock together.

"Don't look away, I want to see you."

I nod as he eases himself into me, inch by inch, stretching me exquisitely. Holding my hips, he sinks further inside me, filling me deeply. His eyes burn hot with desire into mine, the pure arousal from watching each other during this hugely intimate moment is extreme. He pulls back and pushes into me again, faster and harder this time.

"Oh, god, yes!" I cry, still looking into his hypnotic eyes. The feeling of him driving inside me, his hot soft skin, hard muscles rising and falling in unison with my body, the skin of my inner thighs rubbing against him. His hardness is hitting the spot over and over with excruciating accuracy.

The quivering inside turns to the inevitable shuddering, the buzz spreads from my spine as a rush of heat engulfs me and I moan loudly, still holding his gaze. "Oh god! Daniel, yes!"

"Come, don't close your eyes, look at me and come, I want to see it."

The rhythm picks up again, faster and harder, thrusting over and over. "Yes, yes..." I cry, clenching my eyes shut, the pressure building up, about to explode.

"Look at me!" he shouts, his voice deep and dark.

"Daniel!" The ripples dart through me, it's a mighty energy, exploding deep inside my body.

He slams into me hard, and groans loudly, his eyebrows furrowing in pleasure."Oh, baby!"

The glorious tingle runs again from the arch of my foot to the end of my toes and the delicious sensation begins to subside. I close my eyes, dropping my head to his shoulder, and I lay soft, wet kisses under his ear. He smells divine. Our bodies still against each other, twitching in the aftershock.

I raise my head and look into his eyes again, my eyelids heavy, my smile, shy. "Daniel, mmm."

"You're amazing, that was... amazing," he whispers, breathlessly, laying a soft kiss on my lips. He holds me around my waist, carries me to the bed and slowly lowers me down onto the mattress, before laying next to me. He removes the condom, dropping it into a bin by the bed and moves onto his side, leaning on his elbow to face me. His finger trails from the dip in my throat down my chest to my exposed breast, and he replaces my bra cup. I kick off my boots and turn to face him.

"Bea, today was unbelievable. I'm so glad that we bumped into each other, I don't think I've ever enjoyed a girl's company as much as I have enjoyed yours, today."

"Well, I should think not! We haven't even been on a proper date and you still got your wicked way with me... tut, tut." I grin and shake my head in mock disgust. Truthfully, I am surprised that I felt comfortable enough to go so far with Daniel, so quickly. I would never normally sleep with someone, having only met them a couple of times, and without even a date, but it felt right with him.

He leans over me and kisses my neck, under my ear, down to my throat, it's incredible. He nibbles my ear lobe gently and whispers, "You smell exquisite. You are exquisite." His fingers trail up my thigh slowly, finally reaching the hem of my dress. He starts to unbutton the bottom of the dress with one hand, still laying kisses on my neck. "But one more thing I need, is to see you. All of you. Your beautiful body, silky, smooth skin," he murmurs between kisses. I tangle my hands around his neck as he brings his face to mine and our lips meet, gently, tantalisingly.

He finishes with the buttons and pulls away, sweeping the fabric from my body. His big, strong hand lightly skims my stomach, slowly over my hips and down to my knickers. His fingers slide under the lace at the side and moves them down as I slowly wriggle my hips to help him. He slips them off my feet and sits up. "Take the dress off."

I rise to pull the dress from my shoulders, dropping it to the floor and I ease back down onto the bed, slowly removing my bra. I hear Daniel's sharp intake of breath as he instantly caresses me with his hand, leaning down to take a nipple in his mouth.

"Mmm," he groans, his voice deep and gravelly. I arch back, grabbing handfuls of duvet, and moan as he takes his hand from my breast and inches slowly down my belly to rest between my legs.

"Uh," I moan, deep in my throat, it's ecstasy as he hovers over my clitoris. He's so close that I can feel the heat from his skin, but so far that I ache for him to press down. His lips release my nipple and immediately take my mouth, forcefully. I writhe beneath him and moan loudly, begging for his touch.

He moves his hand to my face, and breaking the kiss, he buries his fingers in my mouth. I suck, instinctively, rolling my tongue around the end of them. He withdraws them slowly and slides them down to my impatient folds, where he, indulgently, circles my clitoris, agonisingly slowly. This beautiful man is laying next to me, his full attention on my body, my needs, my pleasure. My hands find his neck again and pull his face to mine, our tongues entwining, needing each other, devouring each other.

I pull away from the kiss and bury my face in his soft neck. "Yes..." I cry, the flutters ripening to wild shudders, it's approaching thick and fast. "Oh yes, Daniel, yes!"

"Uh huh, I want you to come so hard for me." And as he says it, he slides his fingers into me and pushes deep and hard, circling slowly. I explode.

"Ah!! Fuck!" I shout, clamped to his neck, my body pulsating around his fingers.

"You're so fucking hot, baby," he mumbles into my ear, "I want to do that again and again."

"Oh, Daniel... I've never... that was... oh." I give up with whatever I'm trying to spit out and open my eyes to look at his face. He's smiling beautifully at me. I lie still, unable to move for a moment, waiting for my breathing to slow. My heart thumps through my chest and Daniel places a hand over it.

"Can I see you again?" he asks quietly.

I pause, momentarily. "I'd like that, but please, don't make me like you too much, I am going home in a week."

He smiles and puts an arm around me, pulling my back into his front. "I can't make any promises, but I can try. I like you too much to not see you again, though."

Oh god, I like him so much. Why can't he live in bloody England? Or be a complete arse-hole so I hate him? I'll agree to see him once or twice, that's it. I can't deal with the heartache that will inevitably follow if I start wanting more.

"Me too, let's just have a little fun, and leave it at that."

He kisses my neck and squeezes me tightly. "If we must, Beatrice. How about dinner, tomorrow night?"

"So soon? You really are an impatient man."

"Bea, If I didn't have meetings all day tomorrow, I'd have whisked you off somewhere first thing. But as it's Monday, and I do, I'll have to settle for dinner. Will you stay with me tonight?" he asks, running his fingers up and down my arm.

"Well, I'm not sure what Tilly is doing, but if she's staying, then, yes, I'd like to stay with you."

"Good. I'm pretty sure Tilly's staying. I can take you both home early in the morning before work, or Luke will take you back. "

"Thank you, Daniel."

He switches off the light and we lay together, talking comfortably before I drift off into a wonderful, deep, cozy sleep, enveloped by his spectacular body.

The sun gleams through the open curtains as the alarm on Daniel's iPhone wakes me from a luscious, deep sleep. Wrapped in his strong, muscular arms, I stretch, letting out a slight sigh, and wriggle back into his warm body. He tightens his hold around me and kisses my neck softly, over and over.

"Mmm," I mumble sleepily, closing my eyes again to enjoy the feel of this deliciously hot, naked man pressed against me.

I wake again, a short while later, to Daniel, smoothing my hair away from my face. He is crouched in front of me, at the side of the bed, fully dressed. "Good morning, sleepyhead," he whispers.

"Mmm, good morning," I smile, "are you going?"

"I've got to get back to my place to get ready for work, so I have to leave, but I'd like to give you a lift home, if I can?"

"Yes, thanks, that would be great. I'll just get dressed."

I sit up, covering myself with the duvet and yawn quietly. He looks at me and reaches his hand to my neck, pulling me towards him. I take a slight detour and kiss his cheek.

"Thank you for yesterday, and last night, Daniel. I had a wonderful time. I'd kiss you on the mouth but I haven't cleaned my teeth yet... I don't 'do' morning breath'."

He chuckles and flashes his spectacular smile. "You're welcome, I should be thanking you, I haven't had so much fun in a long time. I'll leave you to get ready." He smiles at me before heading into the bathroom. I would love nothing more than for him to join me in bed and have mad, passionate sex again, but I know he has to go. *Sigh.*

As he returns from the bathroom, I'm dressed in yesterday's clothes, making the bed, getting ready to leave.

"You don't have to make the bed, Bea," he says as if I'm doing something alien.

"It's okay, I always have to make the bed." I smile at him and shrug, knowing that a maid will most likely be stripping it later anyway.

"Shall we?" he asks, motioning to the door and I nod.

As he opens it, I whisper, "Oh... do you know if they're up?" I point to Luke's bedroom door, "I need to tell Tilly that you're taking me home."

"I don't know, I don't hear anything downstairs, why don't we knock?" he suggests.

"Okay, good idea."

Daniel knocks on the door and we wait for a response. Nothing, so he knocks again. We both lean in to the door, trying to listen for signs of life.

"Why don't you open the door and poke your head around?" I ask, not willing to do it myself.

"And what if Tilly is running around Luke's bed, naked? You do it."

"No way! What if Luke is running around the bed, naked?" I respond with a giggle.

He laughs out loud. "Well I'm not doing it."

We both pause for a moment, leaning into the door to see if we can hear anything. Just as I lean into the door further, Daniel's hand darts to the handle, and he opens it so quickly, that I stumble into the room and fall to the floor. I hear his laughs as I find myself on the carpet of Luke's bedroom, on my hands and knees, peering straight at Luke's naked backside, in between Tilly's legs. *Oh for the love of god!*

"Oh my god!!! I'm so sorry!" I cry as I shuffle back towards the door with my hand covering my eyes. "Um, as you were..." I giggle as I stand and rush out of the door, slamming it behind me.

"You bastard!" I shout, swatting his arm and laughing with him as I run down the stairs behind him.

Daniel laughs cheekily and wraps an arm around my waist. "Shall we go? I wish I had time to take you for breakfast, but I need to go to my place and get ready before work. I'm sorry," he says as we reach the lounge.

"Oh, don't worry about breakfast, I'll eat back at Gemma's. Do you think Luke will bring Tilly home? I can't believe I just saw them having sex, I'll get you back for that."

As I say it, the bedroom door opens upstairs and Tilly shouts down, "Bea, are you going back now?"

"Yes, do you want to come or will Luke take you home?" I call up the stairs.

"Luke has work so I'll come with you. I'll just be a sec."

"Okay, don't be long," I add.

In a couple of minutes, she's downstairs with her t-shirt back to front and her hair all over the place. They obviously enjoyed their time together!

"Looking good, Til," I joke with a wink, and she swats my arm, running her fingers through her hair, giggling.

We head down to the underground car park and walk towards Daniel's car.

"Wow! Nice car!" Tilly says as she climbs into the backseat. I'd have to agree. "What is it?"

"It's a Bentley Continental, GTC V8. Thank you, I like it, too."

"It's lovely, wouldn't mind one of these myself!" I add, sliding into the front passenger seat next to Daniel.

"What exactly is it that you do, Daniel?" Tilly asks, "These cars don't cost peanuts..."

"Tilly!" I scold, she may as well have asked him his annual wage.

He laughs, "It's okay. I work for the family company, my sister, Alexia, and I both work for the business with my dad who's the CEO. I'm the CBDO."

"Right... and that means?" Tilly responds.

I'm listening, intently. I know we discussed this briefly on the plane but at the time, I was a little distracted. Now, I want to know everything. He starts the engine and makes his way up the ramp and out onto the street.

"Chief Business Development Officer. Simply put, I look for new sales perspectives and design processes to support growth. I work closely with my sister who is the Chief Marketing Officer, we develop marketing strategies and generally run the business with our dad." He shrugs as if the information would be boring for us, but I'm riveted, hoping he continues. He's so sexy when he talks shop, too. *Mmm*.

"And what does your company do?" I ask, intrigued.

Daniel looks genuinely surprised by my interest. "I don't know if you'll have heard of us, considering you're from the UK, it is a global business but it's heavily based in the US. The UK division is growing rapidly though and that's why I was in London. It's called 'Henry Berkeley.'"

I shake my head. "No, I don't think I've heard of it."

"I didn't think so. Anyway, my dad founded the company, back in the seventies. It started as an automotive business in the States, but it was very successful and expanded quickly to become an integrated commercial and services organisation. We now have five divisions; automotive, insurance, services, real estate and retail." *Oh Daniel, keep talking...*

"Wow, so you must be really proud of your dad?" I ask.

"I am, very proud, and I'm proud of the business," he smiles. He clearly likes to talk about the business, and I'm more than okay about that, I find this man fascinating.

"Tilly, can you give me directions? I just realised that I don't know where I'm headed," he asks.

"Oh sorry, if you head to Santa Monica Boulevard and then do a left onto North Cahuenga Boulevard, I can direct you from there."

"Great, thanks."

The short journey is over before we know it, and Daniel is dropping us outside Gemma's. He gets out to open my door and helps Tilly climb out of the back, before handing us our shopping bags from yesterday. Tilly kisses his cheek and thanks him before heading to the side gate and disappearing around the side of the house.

Daniel leans against his car and tugs on my dress to bring me against him. "Thank you again for yesterday, I had a really great time. I hope you'll still let me take you out for dinner tonight?"

I smile shyly and place my hand on his chest. "I had a great time too, so thank you. Yes, dinner would be lovely, but please, like I said, let's not get heavy or anything, just have a little fun enjoying each other's company before I head home."

"Sure, I understand. Can I take your number?" He fishes his iPhone from his pocket and enters the number I give him. "Thanks, I'll look forward to seeing you, all day."

I smile and touch his beautifully defined biceps. "I look forward to it, too. I'd better let you get to work, we couldn't have the CBDO late for his Monday morning meeting, could we?"

"You're right, Miss Hart. How will I ever get through the day with last night on my mind?"

"You'll have to try your best, Mr. Berkeley. Now, go and get ready for work, I have a sun lounger waiting." I lean in to kiss his cheek and he puts his arms around me, pulling me into an embrace. Oh, how I love the smell of this man. He lowers his mouth to my neck and lays light kisses under my ear. *My god, I really like this guy.*

"Mmm, I could stay here all day," he mumbles against my neck.

"Mmm," I respond and let out a barely audible sigh, "me too."

"But I've got damned work." He pulls back, seemingly reluctantly, and smiles that irresistible smile. "But I'll pick you up later and we can continue."

"Looking forward to it," I say as I take a step back, "text me to let me know when I should be ready."

"Sure, see you later, Bea." He climbs back into the sexy car without taking his eyes off me. I'd like to get down and dirty in that thing.

"See you later, handsome," I say with a wink and turn to walk towards the side of the house. I close the side gate behind me and skip around to the pool before hopping up the steps and collapsing on one of our sun loungers, my hands clenched on my chest. "Oh, good morning Los Angeles!" I say with a smile.

Tilly strolls out and hands me a cup of tea, she's grinning from ear to ear, her eyes as wide and excited as mine. "Oh. My. God! How amazing was that?" she squeals.

"*So* amazing!" I wiggle, excitedly, careful not to spill boiling tea all over myself.

"I want to know everything!"

"Are you kidding, Tilly? I want to know everything! I can't believe I saw you two having sex!!! O.M.G. you two were going for it!"

"Why don't we get breakfast sorted and then come out for a sunbathe and a good old gossip? Then you can tell me how you came to stumble into the bedroom while Luke and I were 'taking the log to the beaver'... so to speak."

I howl with laughter. "Tilly, you're so bad! Oh, by the way, Daniel wants to take me out for dinner tonight, is that okay with you?"

"Of course, that's fine, I might ask Gemma if she wants to go out somewhere and have a catch up."

"Great, it's a plan Stan."

~~~~~~~

A couple of hours later, I'm sitting on the side of the pool, my feet dangling into the cool water with the sun burning down on my shoulders. It's heavenly. I feel like I haven't had a proper holiday for years, and this is what it's all about. Gemma and Tilly are floating around on the lilo chairs and we're having a boisterous chat about yesterday, filling Gemma in on Daniel and Luke.

Jay has taken Jack over to his mum's house today, giving us some girly time alone. Tilly has arranged for them to go out for dinner tonight too, and although it would have been fun to join them, I'm really looking forward to seeing Daniel again. I'm trying not to get too excited, I can't get attached to this lovely man, but I do really like him. Really, really like him. *Oh dear god.*

At about eleven thirty, my iPhone chimes from under the sun lounger so I stroll over to retrieve it. It's a number I don't know.

~

17 Sep 11:33
Pick you up at 8pm, looking forward to seeing you. Been thinking about you all morning. Daniel xx

~

Eee! I'm so excited!

"Who's that?" Tilly asks, "is it Clare? I was supposed to text her yesterday, whoops."

"No, it's like, three in the morning at home. It's Daniel," I reply, a giant smile spreading across my face.

"Ooh!" she teases, "What does he say?"

"Just that he's picking me up at eight."

"Is that it?"

"And that he's been thinking about me all morning." I blush and cannot wipe the smile of my face.

"He's got it bad. You're gonna get married and have like, fifteen babies. And he's stinking rich," she says casually as she tilts her head back, towards the sun, relaxing into her lilo.

"Oh Tilly, stop it. He's got a nice car and good job, that's all we know, and that's not what I like about him. Besides, it's just a bit of holiday fun, nothing serious."

"Yeah, yeah, holiday fun." She raises an eyebrow and chuckles while I try to hide my smile, and turn towards the pool-house so I can reply in peace.

~

17 Sep 11:36
Hi, 8 is good for me, I will be ready and waiting. Been thinking about you too... and last night. Might doze by the pool and dream about it for a bit ;-) Bea xx

~

~

17 Sep 11:37
You've got me hot and bothered. Can't stop thinking about last night. You're amazing. Can I join you for a doze? Daniel xx

~

Oh my god, yes please, how I'd love a little 'afternoon delight'. I reply,

~

17 Sep 11:39
I'm sorry for getting you hot and bothered, I'll try to hold off until later... There's nothing I'd like more than for you to join me on

a sun bed for a nap. Or no nap...
;-) When can you be here? xx

~

~

17 Sept 11:40
That's not what I call 'holding off'. You're
doing things to me and I'm at work! If I
could, I'd be there in 5 and there would be no
napping whatsoever. But I have a meeting
and I'm afraid I'm going to have to explain
to my dad, sister and the entire proposal
team, why I have a pole in my pants. :-(xxxx

~

~

17 Sep 11.42
Mmm, don't talk to me about
the pole in your 'pants', you
might find me wandering
around your office after your
meeting, wearing nothing but
that gift you bought me... Xxxx

~

~

17 Sep 11:43
feeling faint I don't think I can take
anymore. I would love that. My day will be
excruciatingly boring now, no hot girl in a hot
silk slip to have hot office sex with. Sad. :-(
Wear it to dinner? Xxxx

~

~

17 Sep 11:45
I think the other diners might
object to my wearing lingerie at
the table. Boo. I'm going to have
a margarita, float in the pool
and dream of 'Daniel's office
sex'. Mmm :-) xxxx

~

~

17 Sep 11:46
I'm going to my meeting. Enjoy your
margarita, I'll kiss the salt from your
lips later. Down boy! Xxxx

~

Oh, oh, oh. I so *love* flirting with him. And text flirting with him is super-dooper exciting! He's so... wonderful. I can't wait until tonight. I'm letting my guard down and I mustn't, I'm going home in less than a week, I need to enjoy tonight and then not see him again. *Stop getting carried away, Beatrice.*

"Bea," Tilly's voice calls from outside. I've been on another planet, I stand and walk to the french doors.

"Sorry! Everything okay?"

"Margarita's ready!"

I spend the rest of the afternoon exactly how I told Daniel I would, floating in the pool, day dreaming of surprising him at work for wild, office, desk sex.

Before I know it, it's six thirty and I need to start getting ready. I decide to wear a silk, fitted, button down, leopard print dress with 3/4 sleeves. It's very elegant, and short enough to show a little leg, but long enough not to be tarty. I'll team it with a black, patent leather belt and matching heels.

After I shower, I dry my hair and slightly curl the ends so that it's voluminous and flicky. I do some super sexy, smoky eyes and slightly rouged cheeks. I thought about adding a touch of colour to my lips, but decided that I'd like to kiss Daniel this evening, without having bright smudges all over my face. So pearly gloss will have to do.

I take my dress from the hanger, and just before I slip into it, I have a brainwave. I rummage around my shopping bags and pull out the sexy nightie that Daniel bought me. It's silk, and fitted with bra cups, so I could wear it under my dress. Just because no one can see it, doesn't mean I'm not wearing it to dinner, as he requested. I smile, excited with the idea.

I leave the pool-house with about ten minutes to spare. Tilly and Gemma are enjoying a glass of wine by the pool before they head out.

"You look lovely ladies," I say, walking towards them. I take Tilly's glass from her hand and have a sip, trying to calm the butterflies, fluttering in my stomach.

"Thank you, doll, so do you. Do you want one?" She asks, pointing to the glass.

"Oh no thank you, Daniel will be here in a minute. I'll just have another sip of yours." I smile, gratefully, before giving it back.

"Bea," Gemma says, "obviously we don't want random men hanging about the house at all hours, but you know, if you want Daniel to stay in the pool-house with you at any point, that's fine by me. I trust your judgement."

"Thank you, Gemma. I'm not sure if that'll happen or not, but it's nice to know that you don't mind."

A car horn sounds from the front of the house. "That'll probably be him." I grab my clutch bag and give the girls a kiss on the cheek. "Have a wonderful evening, see you in the morning. Don't wait up!" I add with a cheeky wink.

"You too!" they say in unison as I walk towards the gate.

"Don't do anything I wouldn't do!" Tilly shouts.

"Oh god, I wouldn't!" I shout back, laughing as I open the gate, and bump straight into Daniel.

"Oh, hello!" I shout, surprised.

He steps back and looks me up and down slowly, silently.

"...Hello?" I repeat, expectantly.

"Bea, you look... breathtaking, wow."

"Thank you." I lean forward, put my hand on his shoulder and reach up to kiss his cheek. Oh, that smell. He puts a hand on the small of my back, and holds me against him briefly. He kisses my neck and gently releases me. When he steps back, I manage to take a good look at him, and good god, he looks fine.

"Bea, please excuse what I'm wearing, I had to work late so I came straight from the office. I didn't want to go home to change and be late."

"I think you look lovely! Don't apologise." He's wearing a three-piece grey suit, similar to the one he wore on the plane. His shirt is a crisp white and his navy tie finishes it off perfectly. Gosh, he looks so important and powerful. So masculine.

"Shall we?" he asks, holding out his arm.

"How very gentlemanly of you, Mr. Berkeley." I hook my arm in his and walk with him to the car.

He opens my door and waits for me to climb in, before closing it and walking around to his side. The top is down and the car looks gorgeous, very elegant.

He starts the engine and turns to look at me. "You really are beautiful."

I smile and look down at my hands. "Thank you. I think you are too." I look up at him, and by golly, he really is sex on legs. I can't believe he's taking me out on a date. *Me*! Shame nothing can come of it, but still. He leans towards me, staring into my eyes, and places a gentle, soft, lingering kiss on my lips. *Uh*, if I die now, I would die a happy, happy woman. I close my eyes and savour every second. Goose bumps spread over my skin, and I raise my hand to run my fingers down his cheek. Again, no tongues, no mad pashing, just soft, luscious kissing.

He slowly pulls away with a smile. "I have wanted to kiss you all day. I've wanted to do more to you all day, but there's a time and place for everything. There's something about you that's so different to anyone I've ever met."

"In a good way?" I ask. I doubt he's going to come out and say 'no, a bad one', but I had to ask.

"Oh, Beatrice, way, way more than good."

"Glad to hear it, Daniel, but I think I know what the 'something' is, and it's not that great."

"Okay, what's your theory?"

"It's because I'm from the UK. I'm going home soon and you'll probably never see me again. It's exciting and fun because there's no great threat of me getting clingy or annoying later down the line, I'll be gone. You see?"

He nods and then shakes his head. "I understand what you're saying, but no. That's not it, I can assure you. It's just you."

"Hmm. Okay, well I'm sure you'll figure it out."

He grins and starts to drive us to wherever we're going. I hope I've dressed appropriately.

It takes a short while to get to Santa Monica Boulevard, the roads here are so complicated and busy, I don't think I could ever get the hang of driving over here.

Daniel opens my door for me and I get out, hooking my arm through his. I feel like I've known him forever.

We enter a restaurant called 'The Palm', which apparently is one if his favourite places. He explained on the way here, that his dad used to take the family here when the kids were younger, and they still come here regularly now. It has been here since the seventies apparently.

We're quickly guided to our table and as we make our way there, I notice that the walls are covered with cartoons, caricatures and signatures. I could spend all night walking around, just looking at the walls. We sit at a cozy table for two, opposite from one another.

"What would you like to drink, Bea? Wine?"

"Yes, please. I like red, do you?"

"I love red, I like the Argentina Malbec in here, how does that sound to you?" he asks.

"Perfect."

Daniel orders the wine and rests back in his chair, watching me as I peruse the menu. I feel his eyes burning into me so I look up at him. "Hello?" I ask, questioningly.

"Hey. Just looking."

I smile, nervously, feeling quite the centre of attention. "Okay, I'll leave you to it then. Do you know what you're going to order?"

"Yes, I think I'll start with the jumbo shrimp, and then the filet mignon with peppercorn sauce and fries." Considering he hasn't even glanced at the menu, I think it's safe to say he knows his stuff here.

"Oh wow, that sounds amazing!"

"You like steak?" Daniel asks, sounding very surprised. Am I not supposed to like steak? *I love steak...*

"I love it, why?" I ask, apprehensively.

"No, it's great! Most girls I know are all 'salad and rabbit food'. I love that you love steak!" He does seem genuinely happy about this, and it's just as well really because I'm not eating rabbit food for anyone.

"I do like a caesar or niçoise, but I like steak more."

He looks surprised again, so I look away before I become too self-conscious, and have another look through the menu. I decide on the Crispy calamari to start and the steak for my main course, except I go for asparagus fritti instead of chips. It all sounds mouthwatering.

We order and sit quietly, smiling at each other.

"I've really been looking forward to tonight, Bea. I think I've mentioned it once or twice." Daniel smiles and flashes those gloriously perfect teeth again.

"Me too. How was work?"

"It was good, thank you. I managed to get all of the London work wrapped up from my trip last week, and my meetings were, although a little boring, all very fruitful. How was your margarita in the sun?"

"Delicious, I had a wonderful float in the pool too."

"Sounds very relaxing."

"It was, I have been working non-stop recently and although I love what I do, I needed a break. So chilling out by the pool with a cocktail was blissful. Not to mention my day dreams..." I smirk and wink at Daniel whose ears seem to have pricked up.

"Day dreams, you say? What exactly did these 'day dreams' entail, Beatrice?"

"Now that would be telling, but I'm sure you can imagine, Daniel."

I've had a few sips of the smooth Malbec and I'm feeling flirty. I lift my foot and slide my ankle slowly up the side of Daniel's leg in front of me.

He smiles cheekily and leans forward. "That feels good, Beatrice. Feel free to keep it up."

"I could say the same to you, Daniel, but I think that talk should be kept in the bedroom."

His eyes shoot open and his tongue practically rolls out of his mouth. "Beatrice, I thought you were a nice girl," he teases.

"Oh, but I am Mr. Berkeley..." I reply in a soft voice and I pout. "Only a nice girl would wear exactly what her 'gentleman friend' asks her to wear on a date." I smile, sexily as Daniel frowns, looking confused. I pull the neckline of my dress down a little, just enough to show a little of the sexy fabric underneath.

Daniel audibly gasps and raises his eyebrows with - what I assume is - pleasant surprise.

"Oh, Miss Hart! We need our food and we need it now! I've got to get you home!"

I giggle. "Patience Mr. B., I like to take my time when I eat," I tease. Daniel laughs with me and almost immediately, our starters arrive. It looks scrumptious.

~~~~~~~

The food really is delicious, the wine is divine and the company is superlative. We talk freely throughout the meal and I feel so comfortable with Daniel. He seems so genuinely

75

interested in my life, asking questions about the cakery, about Clare, my parents and Oliver. I, in-turn, ask all about his business and his family. He really is such an interesting, genuine guy. God damn sexy as hell, but also really interesting.

"Would you like dessert or coffee?" Daniel asks.

"The desserts sound incredible, but I don't think I could fit another thing in my full belly right now. And no to coffee, thank you."

"We could pick a dessert and take it away with us?"

"Brains and beauty, Daniel, I like it," I grin, "why don't you take me back to Gemma's for dessert?"

"That sounds perfect. I'd like to see what's under that dress at some point too."

"I'm sure that can be arranged, Daniel."

"Right, it's too much, we're going..." Daniel announces, making me laugh.

I order a bag of warm doughnuts with cinnamon sugar and chocolate sauce, and Daniel gets key lime pie with whipped cream. The restaurant staff kindly package it up for us to take home. Daniel pays the bill, or the 'check' as he calls it, and we make our way out to the car.

"Daniel, thank you so much for dinner, it was delicious."

He puts his arm around my waist and pulls me into his side as we walk to the car. "Anytime, Bea. And I mean that. I only wish we could do it more. Maybe you'll let me take you out again this week?" *Oh, don't say that!*

"Daniel, I'm nervous about spending more time with you. I'm leaving in six days and I'll admit that I really do like you. A lot. If I see you more..." I trail off.

Daniel is quiet for a moment, and as we get to the car, he places the dessert on the soft roof and turns to me, gently resting his hands on my waist. "I completely understand what you're saying, but I also think, as you do live in England, that we should enjoy as much time as we can together. Really make the most of it?"

"Oh, Daniel, I don't know. But look, we know we're spending tonight together, I would hope that you picked up on that." I grin, salaciously. "So why don't we just enjoy it and decide what's best, tomorrow. Forget about it for now."

He steps closer to me and dips to kiss my neck. "Okay."

I lift my head and close my eyes, enjoying each tender kiss. I place my hands on his broad, hard shoulders and glide them up to his neck, feeling his lovely warm skin and hair line. "Oh, that's lovely," I mumble.

"Mmm," Daniel groans into my neck, his tone deep and sexy, "you smell... exquisite," he adds, between kisses.

"Mmm," I respond again, I'm too far away with the fairies to think of something else to say.

Daniel sighs and rests his forehead on my shoulder. "Shall we head back now? I think we'll be able to enjoy this more once we're back at your place."

"Yes, let's go." I'm itching to get him into my bed.

He gently kisses my mouth before collecting the dessert from the roof and opening my door.

The journey home is quick and easy, and as we stroll towards the side gate of Gemma's house, Daniel, unexpectedly, holds my hand. It surprises me, but I like it. I turn to offer a smile, and he reciprocates.

It's so confusing. If Daniel had turned out to be a complete arse hole or done something to put me off, then I could have had my fun and forgotten about him. Instead, he is proving himself to be the gorgeous, kind hearted, super-sexy man that I really, really like, and now everything is going to be so much more difficult.

Tilly and Gemma are out on the deck when we turn the corner, drinking more margaritas and chatting away.

"Oh hello, you two are back early, I thought you'd be out partying," I say, surprised to see them.

"Hi Bea, hello Daniel," Tilly responds. "No, we decided to come back after dinner and chill out. We'll all have a girly night out dancing another night."

"Gemma, this is Daniel. Daniel, this is Tilly's sister, Gemma."

"Hey Gemma, it's great to finally meet you." Daniel shakes her hand.

"Hi, Daniel, you too, I've heard lots about you, and your friend, Luke." She smiles and winks at Tilly.

"I'm going to make some more margaritas," Gemma says, standing up, collecting the two empties on the table, "would you two like one?"

"I'd love one of your famous margaritas, please," Daniel says with a grin.

"Yes, me too please, Gem."

"I'll put the desserts in our fridge," I say, holding my hand out for Daniel to pass me the bag. Instead, he holds my hand.

"I'll come too, you can show me where you're staying."

"You do that!" Tilly says with a gleam in her eye and a smirk on her face. I roll my eyes at her and make my way up the steps to the small deck before opening the french doors and leading Daniel inside.

"Wow, This is great!" he says, looking around the living area, "Did they build this just for guests?"

"Yes, it's lovely isn't it?"

"It's great."

"There's the kitchen," I point, "and the bedroom there. Tilly sleeps in the bedroom and I sleep on the sofa-bed here." I walk into the kitchen with Daniel following me. He hands me the bag and I remove the doughnuts, leaving them on the top before bending down to open the under-counter fridge. I put the key lime pie in, and just as I'm about to stand, Daniel trails a finger down my spine before putting both hands on my hips and pressing into me.

"You look incredible like this, Bea." I smile as I slowly stand, keeping my rear end pressed against him. He kisses under my ear, making me shiver.

"Wasn't there something that I was going to show you?" I turn against him and look up at his face.

"Was there?" he asks, curiously.

"Uh huh, I'm sure there was..." I slowly un-do the top two buttons of my dress and he realises exactly what I mean. He steps back to give me room to continue, his eyes, smouldering. I toy with the third button in between my breasts and pause. "...But we have margaritas on the way, you'll have

78

to wait a little longer." I beam, patting him gently on the cheek, winking at him.

He frowns, gorgeously, and pouts like a child. Irresistible. Just as I'm about to wrap my arms around him and take him down, Gemma calls from outside.

"Bea, Daniel, margaritas!"

"Well how's that for timing?" I give him a quick peck on the cheek and head back outside.

"Thank you, Gemma, yummy." I hand Daniel his and he takes a sip.

"This tastes great, thanks."

We sit at the companion seat on our deck, while Tilly and Gemma stay down on the main deck, chatting. I gaze at his beautiful face. "Do you drink cocktails a lot, Daniel? You don't strike me as a 'cocktail' sort of a chap."

He smirks. "No, I don't drink cocktails much. I'm more of a beer or wine kind of a guy. But I enjoy the odd one here and there, outside pool-houses in the company of beautiful ladies, such as yourselves."

I smile as he takes another sip from his glass, and a small patch of salt remains on his lower lip. I can't help but stare, his lovely, soft, delicious lip. I want to lick it. I beckon him with my forefinger and he leans into the small table between us. I move towards him until our faces are almost touching. I whisper, "You have salt on your lip," before running my tongue along his bottom lip and taking it in my mouth, sucking gently. I bite down momentarily, before releasing it.

"Hey, I thought *I* was going to kiss the salt from *your* lip?"

I smile, remembering his text from earlier.

"You know I can't stand up for quite some time now, right?" I laugh, Daniel and his erections!

"I want to see you out of that dress," he whispers, and I close my eyes briefly. I'm so turned on.

"As hot as you look in it, I want to see you out of that suit, I haven't seen you with no clothes on, not properly."

"Really? You didn't see me naked last night?" he asks. Last night seems like forever ago.

"Nope, not completely, it was all a bit, you know... against the wall and everything. And then on the bed, I wasn't really taking notice." I grin and look down at my glass.

"Well, if you'd like to see, I'd be happy to show you." *Yes, yes, yes!* "Bea," he says, loud enough for Tilly and Gemma to hear, "I'm hungry for key lime pie now, what do you say?"

"Good idea, let's go in."

We stand with our drinks and I look to Tilly who's grinning. She's not daft.

"Enjoy!" she shouts, "oh, and Bea, I'm going to stay in the main house with Gem tonight, Jay's in with Jack because he's not sleeping well. You've got the pool-house to yourself." *Result!*

"Okay. Enjoy your cocktails, girls."

"Will do, enjoy your...um... key lime pie!"

I giggle quietly and follow Daniel inside. He stands in the centre of the room while I close the doors and the curtains. "Would you really like key lime pie, Daniel?"

"Amongst other things, yes, why not."

"Okay, I'll go and get it, make yourself at home."

I put the pie on a plate and take a fork from the drawer, and just as I turn to leave, Daniel walks through the kitchen doorway. He halts, saying nothing, just looking me up and down, his determined eyes blazing. He steps towards me tentatively, stunning turquoise eyes burning into mine. Suddenly, he takes my face in his hands, our lips meet and we're immediately locked in a lustful, prurient kiss.

I hold the pie to the side of me as Daniel moves one hand up and under my hair to the back of my neck, and the other down to my bottom. His tongue slow and precise. I'm completely lost. No one will ever compare to this, Daniel's kiss, his ability to transport me to another universe, just him. He's... *Oh god. This is bad.*

I lower the plate to the counter at my side, needing to touch, to curl my hands around his gorgeous neck and try, if possible, to deepen the kiss further. We up the tempo, moaning and sighing with pleasure. He brings his hands to my front and slowly starts to undo the buttons of my dress. Unbuckling my belt, he lets it drop to the floor, continuing with the lower buttons, still immersed in this hot, lascivious kiss.

When my dress is open, he slides it off my shoulders, sending it floating to the floor. He pulls me into him tightly and starts to slow the kiss, our breathing rapid, lustful. He gazes into my eyes for a moment before stepping back. "I need to see you... Now, *that* was the best purchase I've made all year, and I've made a few. You look so desirable, beautiful," he says, still exploring me with his eyes, his mouth slightly ajar. "Although, now that I've seen you in it, I do have one small request."

"Oh really? What's that?" I ask, intrigued.

"Don't let anyone else see you in it. I want this view to be mine, just mine."

I mull it over for a moment, amused. "Okay, since you were lovely enough to buy it for me, I'll agree to that." I look Daniel in the eye and run my tongue along my top teeth. "So, tonight, in *your* nightie, I'm yours. What will you do with me?"

He comes close again, fire in his eyes, running his hand up my thigh, pushing his body against me. He brushes the side of my face with his and whispers in my ear. "I know exactly what I'll do with you, if you'll let me." *Game on.*

"Help yourself." I grin and then giggle loudly as he lifts me off my feet, squeezing me, and carries me, effortlessly, through to the living area, putting me down on my feet by the sofa.

"Let's get this bed made," he says, his eyes twinkling with excitement.

A few moments later, I have the bed made to perfection, and I look over at Daniel, leaning against the wall, watching me. "To your satisfaction?" I ask sweetly.

"Fuck," he says, shaking his head as he practically sprints towards me. His hands slide around me and his lips are on mine, again. I unbutton his waist jacket at top speed, and with that on the floor, I pull his shirt out of his trousers and start to remove his tie.

He pulls away. "Let me," he croaks, breathlessly.

I let go and crawl onto the bed, watching as he empties his pockets onto the coffee table and swiftly removes the rest

81

of his clothes. And there he is. This glorious sex god looking absolutely fucking *incredible* in the buff, standing right before me with a whopping, great boner. He walks to the light switch and turns it off, leaving just the dim light from the kitchen.

Crawling up my body, he straddles me, hovering over me on his elbows. "You look delicious, Beatrice." he says, looking quite edible, himself. He lowers his body to mine, careful not to squash me, and brushes his lips against mine. My eyes close in anticipation, and he runs his tongue along my top lip.

"Mmm," I moan, he's hardly touching me but it's so good, I can feel his hardness digging into my thigh, it's arousing to say the least.

He sucks my lip and I moan again. "You like that?"

"Uh huh," I respond in a whisper.

"Me too. I want you." He continues to suck my lip and soon turns it into a deep, erotic kiss.

My fingers trace the outline of his shoulder blades and run down the muscles at his sides. He's so strong and perfectly shaped, I love the feel of his firmness under his silky smooth skin.

With one hand in my hair, cupping my head, and the other at the small of my back underneath me, he rolls to the side, taking me with him so I end up on top. With his tongue still enticingly caressing mine, I raise my bottom and bring my knees up to his sides.

I pull away and sit up on him, against his erection, placing my hands on his gloriously toned abs. I gaze down at him, smiling. "You're hot, Berkeley."

"You're hotter, Hart," he responds, running his masculine fingers up and down my thighs.

I raise an eyebrow and smirk, edging slowly backwards, down his legs. His erection springs free from underneath me and I hold him in my hand, squeezing gently.

Daniel groans and whispers, "I want to be inside you, baby."

I move my hand slowly, up and down, twisting ever so slightly around the tip. "You want to fuck me, Daniel?" I ask, my voice low and sultry.

He smiles, surprised by my frankness. "Nicely put. Yes, I want to fuck you, so badly." He draws in a breath through pursed lips. I hold my hair to one side and lean down slowly, seductively looking up through my lashes into his eyes. I indulgently lick the tip of his cock.

"Oh, god," he moans. I lick his tip again and then kiss it before taking it into my mouth and slowly sucking on him. He raises his hips as he drops his head back into the pillow. With my hand at the base, I take in his tip again and continue down further, taking in as much of him as I can.

I pick up the pace and suck hard whilst swirling my tongue around his tip, my hand following the rhythm, up and down on his hardness. "Mmm," I moan as I taste him and enjoy the feel of his silky skin on my tongue. It's so good. I try to take all of him but he's too big, and gagging in the middle of such a moment probably wouldn't be a huge turn on, so I stop trying.

I pick up the pace even further so my hand and mouth are simultaneously pumping Daniel's hard cock, while he pants and groans in pleasure.

"Stop," he moans.

I slowly take him from my mouth to respond, "No." I drag my tongue from his base to the tip, slowly, thoroughly enjoying myself.

"I don't want to..." he reaches down and cups my head in his hands, "come here."

I crawl up to him until our noses are touching and he curls his hand around the side of my face. "You're really... amazing at that," he says, smiling cutely.

"I really enjoyed it, I'd like to carry on," I reply, feeling quite surprised by how much I enjoyed it. I'm not really much of a 'bj' person, normally.

"No, I don't want to come yet and you're making me real close. I want to come inside you... somewhere else. You look so hot in this," he tugs the fabric of the nightie, "I want you so bad." He brings my head down so my lips meet his, and we are immediately caught in a wild, fervent kiss again, his need apparent.

He rolls over again, taking me with him. My fingers are in his hair, playing, pulling. My legs wrap around him, inviting him, and he lowers his lips to my neck. He trails his hand slowly down my body to the hem of my nightie, and pushes it up to my waist, hooking his fingers into my lace knickers. I untangle my legs from around him and wiggle my hips to help him free me of the underwear.

He slides down to the end of the bed and runs his hand down one leg, pulling the knickers with him, before slipping my shoes off. He drops my knickers to the floor, making his way back up my body, slowly, stopping to gaze down at my lady garden on the way. *Oh god, how embarrassing...* must he stare at it like that?

"Bea, you're so beautiful. You look after your body, I like that."

I suppose I do, I'm not one to have a great, overgrown bush, so yes, it's neat and tidy.

He leans down and kisses just below my small landing strip. I'm still very shy with him gazing at my bits and bobs like that, but luckily he doesn't linger and moves up to my face. I wrap my legs around his waist again, open and so ready for him.

He looks into my eyes before planting soft kisses all over my face. My heart thumps in my chest and I want, desperately, to close the distance between our wanting bodies. My hands travel up his strong, muscular arms and rest on his shoulders. God I love this part of his body. Mind you, all of him is pretty spectacular.

"You're incredible," he whispers in my ear, between kisses. He lowers his body to mine and reaches down to stroke my clitoris, gently. I gasp as he moves his fingers lower and pushes two inside me, gently.

"Oh!" I cry as I arch my back and my chest collides with his. Desperate for more, my insides are melting, tingles rushing all over my body.

"You want me," he whispers.

"Yes, Daniel, so much." I need him. Now.

"I want you too, all the time, ever since the first moment I saw you," he murmurs in my ear.

He gently slips his fingers out of me and guides himself to my entrance. Just the feel of his tip, pushing against me is enough to make me cry out loud in pleasure. He slowly and sweetly eases into me, pushing himself deep, stretching me, filling me completely.

"Oh god! Daniel!" I cry. It's exquisite, nothing else matters right now, nothing but Daniel and the ecstasy of feeling him move inside me.

"Oh, baby," he growls, "I need you." He flexes his hips and grinds into me again, the heat darts through my veins, the shuddering inside coming all too soon. He continues to grind into me, again and again, harder, stronger. I moan over and over, this feeling is... I've never felt this... oh god, I can't think straight.

"Daniel, oh, Daniel!"

"I love you saying my name like that, baby."

My feet are tensing, my toes curling tightly, the waves imminent and it's coming, strong and hard, and far too quickly! I tighten my legs around his waist, squeezing him firmly. "Daniel! Uh huh, Daniel, Daniel, Daniel! Oh god!" I shout, panting between each word, burying my head in his shoulder, my arms wrapped tightly around his neck, and the waves erupt into an almighty, over powering, explosion inside me. I sink my teeth into the flesh on his shoulder, my nails digging into his back.

"Baby, yes... Bea... fuck!" he growls as he thrusts into me rigorously. Deliciously.

Our bodies lay tangled together, hot and sweaty, our breathing rapid, and I can feel his heart thumping through his chest into mine. I soon realise that my nails are still wedged into the skin of his shoulders.

"Oh god, I'm sorry," I say, breathlessly, "did I hurt you?"

"No, you didn't hurt me, don't worry about that, Bea. That was phenomenal." He raises his head and smiles at me, his eyes sparkling.

"Oh, it was... " I'm in a daze, that has left me speechless, dumb-struck. I've never had orgasms so intense in all my life. How does he do that? I look up at his gorgeous face, his handsome features, and smile at him. I like him so much, I'm in my element laying here, underneath him after such an incredible sex session. I'm forgetting that I can't like him, that I can't fall for him. Right now, all I want to do is savour the feeling and enjoy every second of it while I can.

"Daniel," I say, huskily.

"Yes, baby?"

"Daniel, Daniel, Daniel, Daniel... You like me saying your name?" I smile broadly.

He beams. "Yes, I like it a lot, you make it sound so... sexy."

"Well, fancy that, Daniel, Daniel, Daniel."

"Again, again!" he laughs. He plants kisses from my neck up to my mouth. Having the full attention of this sensational man is something to treasure. He's so caring and kind but also wildly sexy and powerful, and a whole new experience in bed. He seems to be able to press buttons that have previously been completely ignored.

Daniel suddenly stills, he raises his head and stares at me like he's seen a ghost.

"Daniel? What's the matter? Are you okay?"

"Fuck, Bea, we, um... we didn't use anything." Oh Shit. *Whoops*.

"Oh god, how did we forget that?"

He looks really concerned. I feel such a fool, what if he has some god-awful disease or something? I'm sure he hasn't but what if? You can never be sure.

"Daniel, you don't need to worry about babies or anything, I'm on the pill, I have been for years. Also, I don't have anything... you know. I have recently been to the... you know. For a... you know. I feel such a fool though. Shit, how careless."

The colour appears back in his cheeks, he visibly relaxes. "Oh no, Bea, I've been tested recently, Luke goes all the time so I go with him occasionally, so we're all okay there." *Phew*! "Babies were my main concern, although that does sound very naive, you never know do you?" he says, relieved.

"No, you don't, so just as well for us that we're both in the clear. And no, no babies on the horizon. As beautiful as your babies would be, I don't really fancy trying out the whole pregnancy/motherhood thing just yet."

"So I can get back to nibbling your neck then?"

86

"Nibble away, Daniel, nibble away."

He grins. "As much as I love this nightgown, I think I've seen enough, I want you out of it."

"Oh," I pout, "but I'm not allowed to wear it again."

"I didn't say you couldn't wear it again, just not for another guy. I don't like the thought of anyone else seeing you in it."

"Okay, I'll have to wear it when I'm all alone, thinking of you."

"I'd rather be there with you, but if I can't be, yes. And take a picture and send it to me... please?" *He's so adorable!*

"I think I can manage that... *Daniel,*" I say, emphasising his name. "If you'll excuse me for a moment, nature calls." I wriggle underneath him to free myself.

"Of course," he says, rolling onto his side, "don't be too long, baby."

I stroll to the bathroom and close the door. I love that he calls me 'baby'.

I do what I need to do and wash my hands. Looking in the mirror, I notice how healthy I look, flushed and glowing. 'Daniel sex' and California must be agreeing with me. I decide to take off the nightie and surprise Daniel with naked Bea. I'm not usually comfortable with my naked body but what the hell, I'm doing lots of things I'm not usually comfortable with at the moment, and it's not exactly brightly lit out there.

When I step out of the bathroom, Daniel is sitting up under the duvet, looking gorgeous. I'd prefer if he wasn't covered so that I could have a good look at his naked body, but never mind, I'll look forward to joining him under there shortly. He turns to look in my direction and his mouth drops open when he sees me. His eyes slowly travel from my head, to my feet and back again as I slowly walk towards the bed.

"Would you like a drink, Daniel?" I ask casually, as if I walk around with no clothes on all the time.

"I... um... yes please."

"Wine? Water? Fizzy pop or *'soda'* as you'd call it?"

"Water please," he replies, his eyes still fixed on my naked body.

I collect his empty margarita glass and waltz into the kitchen to put it in the sink before taking two bottles of water from the fridge. A huge grin spreads across my face. I try my hardest to regain the sexy, impassive look that I managed in the living room, but I'm having difficulty, I'm just not that cool in real life. I put the water on a tray with the key lime pie and doughnuts and make my way back into the lounge.

"I thought you might like some dessert now, we became somewhat 'preoccupied' earlier."

"Great idea, won't you join me?" He pats his hand on the bed.

"I'd love to." I put the tray down on the coffee table and pick up a bottle of water for Daniel. I walk around to his side of the bed and bend to offer it to him. "Your water, sir."

"Why, thank you, Miss. Actually, there is just one more thing, while you're there."

"Oh?" I ask, standing upright. He puts his bottle down and rests his hands on my hips. He leans forward and lays soft, wet kisses all over my bare tummy. Butterflies flutter yet again and my knees start to feel weak. I run my fingers through his hair and close my eyes. He slows and puts his ear to my stomach. I look down at him, confused. *What the hell is he doing?* "Hello?" He knocks on my hip bone with his knuckles. "Hello? Anyone there?" He puts his ear to my belly again as I laugh.

"No, sounds pretty good to me. That's definitely a 'bun free' oven, right there," he says as he lays one more kiss just under my belly button and releases me. "I think we're safe to do that again," he adds with a cheeky smile.

As I slide under the covers, next to him, he leans across and kisses me. "You really are beautiful," he whispers.

"Thank you," I say, shyly, tucking my hair behind my ear.

"Would you like a bite of doughnut, *beautiful*?"

I smile. "Yes, please."

He takes a doughnut, dunks it in the chocolate sauce and lifts it to my mouth, holding his other hand underneath it to catch any drips.

I open up and take a bite. "Mmm," I moan, covering my mouth with my fingertips, "that's amazing!"

"I know, right? I've had these before. Want to try the pie?"

I wait to finish my mouthful before responding. "Okay, just a little taste please."

He uses the fork to slice a piece off and brings it to my mouth.

"Mmm, that too, wow."

Daniel has a forkful and frowns as he nods in agreement. "They do great desserts. They do great everything, there."

"Yes, they do, Daniel, dinner was fabulous. Thank you again, I had a lovely time."

"You're welcome, Bea. I'm still having a lovely time."

"Well, yes, me too."

I watch as Daniel dunks his forefinger into the pot of chocolate, looks messy. He lifts his hand and again, holds his other beneath it to protect the bed from drips. He surprises me by bringing it over to my lips. "Open," he says, and I do as I'm told. He puts his finger in my mouth and I close down on it, sucking gently. I grab hold of his hand to keep it in place while I swirl my tongue around, the way I did with his cock. I look up at his face and he smiles, sexily at me.

"Mmm..." I pull his finger from my mouth and lick it slowly.

"Well, Bea, I think it's safe to say that you enjoyed that. Lay down, baby."

I slink down in the bed and he pulls the duvet down, exposing my torso. He leans down to place the tray on the floor, emerging with the pot of chocolate sauce, and straddles me, swiftly.

"I want you to put your finger in the chocolate and then put it on your body."

"Where?"

"Wherever you want me to lick it off." His mouth curls into a sexy, ardent smile.

I slowly dunk my middle finger into the chocolate, Daniel watching eagerly as I trail it down the middle of my chest, between my breasts. I dab the remainder on my lips, finding it torturous not to lick it off.

He puts the tub down on my side table and bends to lick my lips. He gently takes each in his mouth, one at a time, and sucks softly. It's so intimate, his delicious scent and the feel of his warm mouth caressing my lips, is tantalising. The sucking soon progresses into a luscious, full on kiss and I can't get enough. My hands run through his soft, short hair and I moan, lustfully.

He breaks away and moves further down my body, gazing at my chest. He lowers his face to slowly run his tongue along the trail of chocolate. It's burning hot, this slow, sensual movement sparks desire deep inside. He laps up the chocolate and quickly travels to one nipple. Taking it in his mouth, flicking with his tongue and gently nibbling, he moves his hand to the other and gently caresses it between his fingers.

"Mmm, Bea," he mumbles against my breast before moving over to the other.

Goose bumps spread over my skin, I bend my knees either side of his body, resting my feet flat on the mattress. My groin circling beneath him, of its own accord. He releases my nipple and moves to take my mouth again. My pelvis still rotating below him, grinding into his hard cock. He pulls back slowly and kneels between my legs, reaching for the pot of chocolate sauce.

"Don't get carried away too fast, baby." He looks so sexy, his short hair tousled, his tanned skin glowing in the dim light. "I want you to dip your finger in the sauce again."

I do as he asks and as I swirl it around in the pot, he continues, "Get a lot on there, it tastes so good from your skin. Now, put it on your body, again."

I take my finger from the pot and hover over my chest, deciding whether to put it on my nipples or belly button.

"Not there," Daniel says, clearly. My eyes dart to his and he's staring at me, intently. "Lower," he adds, dominantly.

I slowly move my dripping finger, mid-air, to my belly. I look at him for guidance, *my belly button?*

"Lower," he says again.

Oh gosh, this really *is* exciting. But I'm nervous, I know what he wants and I want it too, but it's so personal down there, so intimate. I don't want him to look at me from that angle. I only want him to see the pretty bits.

I pause, briefly, before lowering my finger slightly, so the chocolate drips just above my pubic bone.

"Lower."

I look at his face, the apprehension clear on mine. *Oh god, should I? Shouldn't I?* I bite my bottom lip, considering my next move.

"Don't be shy baby, I want to taste you." He gently takes hold of my wrist and moves my hand infinitesimally lower, and let's go. "Touch yourself, baby."

I look into his eyes as I rest my finger, lightly on my outer skin, slowly moving in and over my clitoris. He's gazing at me, into my eyes, this is so carnal, surprisingly good.

"You look so hot right now," Daniel whispers, looking down at my fingers between my legs. He reaches down and takes my hand, lifting it to his mouth and sucking the chocolate off.

"Mmm," he moans, looking at my face. *Christ on a bike.*

He gradually removes my finger from his mouth and lowers himself to my belly. He licks and kisses each drop of chocolate from my skin, indulgently, nearing the main attraction. I clench my eyes shut, tightly as he pauses, gazing down at me. *Please! Stop studying it, just get on with the task at hand, I can't bear it.*

Eventually, I feel his hot breath hovering immediately above my delicate skin, his tongue gently sweeps over my outer lips before moving centrally to my clitoris. He swirls his tongue over and around, licking, flicking, sucking and oh god, it's divine. I arch my back and moan loudly.

"Uh huh," Daniel mumbles against me, still caressing me skilfully with his masterful tongue. His slowly glides his hands up to my waist, pressing firmly into my flesh with his fingers. My body is weak, I feel like jelly, his tongue working over time, stroking and brushing against my love button.

My hands grip the sheets below me, my pelvis raises off the bed, involuntarily, my muscles inside clenching tightly, preparing for the almighty burst fast approaching. Daniel's hands move to my lower belly and push me down into the bed, he wraps them around the front of my thighs, pulling me towards him.

"Daniel, yes, oh, Daniel," I cry. The quivering inside takes over, it's coming thick and fast, the huge waves join together, and just at that moment, Daniel takes my clitoris to his lips and sucks, hard.

"Oh, GOD! Yes!" I cry, my thighs tightening around his head, my hands gripping and tugging at his hair, the sparks burst inside me, my insides pulsating uncontrollably. I throw my head back onto my pillow, my heart beating through my chest and my stomach rising and falling rapidly with my panting.

"Oh, god," I whisper.

Daniel gently strokes me with his tongue and kisses me, lightly as I release his head from my thighs and the grip of my hands. I'm shaking.

He crawls up my body, a huge, gorgeous smile on his face and kisses my mouth. My eyes close, I'm spent.

"You are so beautiful, I don't know why you're shy, your body is incredible."

I can't speak, I'm exhausted, that was breathtaking.

"You're shaking, come here," he says as he pulls me into a close embrace.

I'm in his arms, on my side, facing him. One of my legs is curled in between his and we are truly wrapped up in each other. He pulls the duvet up and over us and showers my face with sweet, soft kisses. "Was that good, baby?"

"Mmm, hmm," I respond, I'm so sleepy, it's all I can offer.

He chuckles, quietly. "Is that a yes?"

I smile and nod, nuzzling my face into his neck.

"Good, because that was pretty amazing for me too. You really are the most beautiful creature. Everywhere. I want to do that all day, every day."

"Mmm, me too."

He kisses my head and we lay there, curled up together and drift off.

CHAPTER EIGHT
TUESDAY 18TH SEPTEMBER

I am so cosy, so snug and comfortable as I stir in my bed this morning, I don't want to wake up. I move slightly and realise I'm tightly wrapped in Sexy Berkeley's arms, my head buried in his neck. It's lovely. I open my eyes and pull my head back to look at Daniel's beautiful sleeping face. He looks adorable, so peaceful and handsome.

His iPhone alarm starts to beep over on the coffee table and I remember that he has to go to work. *Oh.* I run my fingertips along his cheek and call his name softly. "Daniel," I whisper, "Daniel," a little louder.

His eyes slowly open and lock with mine. He smiles a beautiful, genuine smile and pulls me into him tightly.

"Daniel, your alarm is going off," I whisper again.

"Uh huh. Mmm," he murmurs, still holding me tightly.

"Should I turn it off?"

He sighs and loosens his grip around me. "No, it's okay, I should get up."

He sits up slowly and stretches to the ceiling. *Oh heavens above,* his delicious body, the muscles beneath his skin, he's so big! He climbs out of bed and strolls, sexily to the coffee table, stark bollock naked, looking fine. He switches the alarm off and looks at the time. "Uh, it's so early," he grumbles, "I want to stay in bed with you." He pouts and comes back to the bed.

Climbing over to me, he pulls the duvet down, revealing my naked torso. His eyes run over my body before he rests his lovely head on my chest, he's so warm and delicious. I run my fingers through his hair, my nails lightly running across his scalp.

"Oh, don't stop, that feels so good," he mumbles.

"What time do you have to go, Daniel?" I can't help but sound disappointed. I am. I know I shouldn't be seeing him anymore, I told myself that last night should be the last time we see each other, but I can't help but want him to stay here, with me. Prolong it just a little.

"Really soon, unfortunately. I have to get back to shower and change clothes."

"Oh, do you want to have a shower here?"

"On my own?"

"Yes, Daniel, I think if we showered together, you'd be quite a lot late for work, don't you?"

"No then, I'll just do it at home. I can't shower knowing that you're just metres away, naked and willing."

"I won't be naked for long, and who says I'm willing?"

"You're willing."

"I am?"

"You're not?" He grins and I pause momentarily.

"Okay, I am," I giggle. "I'm just going to brush my teeth. Do you have time for tea?"

"Yes, thank you," he replies with that beautiful smile of his.

I climb out of bed and quickly dash to the bathroom, it's daytime and I'm naked. I find my nightie from last night hanging on the back of the door, so I slip into it and start to brush my teeth at the sink. It feels great to rid myself of morning breath, I never understand why, on TV, everyone wakes up and has a full on pash first thing, I mean, eur, seriously!

I check out my eye make-up from last night in the mirror, very well slept, Beatrice, not a single smudge. I bend down to rinse my mouth and as I stand up, Daniel is standing behind me, looking at me in the mirror.

"Oh god!" I shout, jumping.

He wraps his arms around my middle and kisses my shoulder, he's dressed already. "Sorry, baby, I didn't mean to make you jump. You look beautiful in this."

"Thank you, I think you mentioned something along those lines last night," I say with a smile.

"Can I borrow your toothbrush? I want to kiss you before I go."

"Yes, help yourself. I'll go and put the kettle on."

Flicking the kettle on and grabbing two cups from the cupboard, I reminisce about last night. Daniel is so... *Oh.* I want more. His phone interrupts my reverie, this time it's ringing.

"Daniel..." I call out from the kitchen, "Daniel, your phone is ringing."

He dashes out, toothbrush still hanging from his mouth and grabs it. "Hey, Alexia," he answers. He winks at me before making his way out of the french doors onto the deck, still brushing his teeth. He told me more about Alexia last night over dinner. She's two years older than him, so I think that would make her thirty four. They sound very close, a bit like Oliver and I, I imagine.

Soon after, Daniel walks through the living area again, toothbrush in mouth. "Uh huh, yeah. Eleven thirty... hang on," he says with a mouth full of toothpaste and disappears into the bathroom, emerging a few moments later, toothbrush free and speaking clearly. "That's great, thanks Lex. Okay, catch ya later."

"How do you like your tea, Daniel?" I ask as he hangs up and joins me in the kitchen.

"Black, no sugar please. So, what are your plans today, Bea?"

"I'm not sure, I haven't spoken to Til about today yet. I'd like to go to a beach or something. I'll see what she wants to do." I hand Daniel his tea and throw the teaspoon in the sink.

"I'd like to take you to the beach. In fact there's a restaurant I'd love to take you to on the beach, you'd love it."

"I would love that, but you have to work. Also, Daniel, we really need to cool off a bit, I mean, I really, really don't want to, but you're not doing anything to make me dislike you! Everything you do makes even more fond of you, which is really unhelpful considering I'll be leaving on Sunday."

Daniel laughs and puts his tea down on the counter. He approaches me and wraps his arms around my waist. "Bea, I really don't want to say goodbye yet, we're having such a great time together. Besides, I just took today off." A mischievous grin crosses his face and his eyes twinkle.

"What do you mean?"

"Exactly what I say, I took today off, I want to spend it with you. Will you let me take you out?"

I'm so excited, he took the day off! He's a big, important CBDO and he's just taken the day off to be with me! "Really?"

"Yes, really!" he says, rolling his eyes. "Why?"

"Well, just because, you should be working, and I'm just... "

"You're not 'just' anything. Bea, I really like you a lot. I know that you're going home and I know that it can't last, but while you're here, please let me spend time with you, make the most of whatever we have got? Please say you'll spend the day with me?" He pouts again, he's too damned gorgeous for his own good. Or mine!

"I'd love to, Daniel," I say with a shy smile.

God I could ravish this man, right here on the kitchen floor.

"Good. That's settled, and as it's so early, let's go back to bed."

"Well, I was thinking of having a shower..." I beam, I can't resist.

His eyes widen and a grin spreads across his face. "To the shower!" he yells and I laugh out loud as he sweeps me off my feet and heads to the bathroom.

I sit up on the sink vanity to watch him undress. His body is taut and shapely, his muscles are so hot, the way they tense and ripple with every movement. I smile as I watch the show. Daniel looks over at me and pauses.

"Are you watching me?"

"Yes, I am," I say, matter-of-factly, crossing my arms and grinning from ear to ear.

Daniel smiles, salaciously and continues to pull his shirt off his shoulders, slowly, giving me a sensational view. His shirt drops to the floor and as he unbuckles his belt, he turns his back to me. He rears up to me, gyrating his hips so his bottom is grinding against me, making me laugh out loud.

"Come on, give it to me, Magic Mike!" I run my hands across his shoulders, my hands seem so small against his big body.

He slowly pulls his trousers below his bottom so they drop to the floor and I glide my hands down to give both cheeks a squeeze. He ripples his body against mine and I trail my fingers around his waist to rest on his hard abs. He turns and opens my legs before resting himself between them. I see his amused expression before he moves in and kisses my neck, grinding his hips into me again. His erection rubs against me through his boxers.

"Mmm," I murmur, he feels so good against me, his lips on my neck.

I feel his smile against my skin. "You like the show?"

"Definitely, yes."

"Let's shower," he says, pulling away.

"Oh," I pout," I was enjoying that."

"You like that, huh? So you like the movie? Magic Mike?"

"I *love* that film. But I prefer it when you strip for me," I add, fluttering my eyelashes at him.

"Good, I'd rather you watched me," he says with a grin. "Now, let's get you out of that nightgown and into the shower, then I can show you some of the real moves."

Daniel's naked body, wet, is even more delicious than I remember. In the pool, with trunks on was different though, this is so much more intimate.

Kissing in the shower has always been something I've found a huge turn on, but as with most things, it was even hotter than usual, with Daniel. It was so erotic, and inevitably lead to shower-fondling and mind-blowing shower-sex. I'm worried about the next time I have to have sex with someone, I'm afraid it's going to seem terribly standard and frankly, very boring. I can't imagine finding anyone else who has the same effect on me. *Oh god, how depressing.*

After all the sex, Daniel and I stood against the wall of the shower together, slowly kissing and exploring each other's bodies. It was romantic and intimate, something lovers might do, but it felt so... right. I can't get enough of him, I want him near me all the time, touching me, kissing me. I know it's a lust thing, and I'm certain it's magnified because of the very limited time that we have together, but I can't ignore the realisation that it's so much more than I've felt with anyone else. It must have taken me months to feel so strongly for Dylan, he never made me feel as amazing as Daniel has, let alone in a few short days.

"Shall we get out now, baby?" Daniel asks.

"Okay... *baby,*" I tease.

He grabs a towel and stands, waiting for me, outside the shower. As I step out, he wraps me up and puts another towel around his waist before we both go through to the lounge. I take a quick look in the mirror on my way out and am relieved that I somehow managed to avoid panda eyes. I'll wash and re-apply when I'm alone in here in a minute, I can't let him see me au-natural, don't want to scare the man away.

I fasten the towel under my arms, before removing all of the pillows and duvet from the bed. I'm very surprised to see that we didn't get a single drop of chocolate on the bed sheet. Thank god, I wouldn't have wanted to explain that one to Gemma.

Daniel is playing with his iPhone, texting work I presume, while I put bed linen in the chest and walk back to the sofa-bed to close it up.

"No, no, baby, wait," Daniel calls as he jumps up, tossing his phone on the coffee table. "Let me do it."

"Daniel, it's fine, it's not that heavy."

"Even so, I can't sit and watch you do that when I'm right here."

"If it makes you feel better, it's fine by me," I smile and stand back.

"Good, thank you." He folds the bed and places the cushions back on the top, perfectly. "Now, go get dressed before I rip that towel off you and we spend the rest of the day naked on the sofa."

"Don't tempt me, Berkeley," I say with a wink as I enter the bedroom to get some clothes from the wardrobe.

I realise that Daniel has nothing but the suit he was wearing yesterday, and wonder if we'll go back to his place for him to change.

I choose a pair of straight-leg, white jeans and a mint-green, over-sized, silk blouse, teamed with nude ballet flats. When I emerge from the bedroom with my make-up bag, Daniel is still in his towel looking stunning.

"You look lovely," he says.

"Thank you, although I haven't done my hair or face yet, so hold your horses."

"Horses held, baby, but you look beautiful anyway...
Listen, I've got Luke coming over with some clothes for me, is
that okay? I thought it would be easier than going back to
mine, and he wanted to see Tilly."

"That's fine by me, I should probably warn Til though,
what time?"

"In, like, fifteen minutes."

Twenty minutes later, Tilly fore warned and my make-
up removed and re-done, I hear a beep out the front. I put my
head between my legs and tie my hair in a messy top knot
before making my way around to the side gate. Luke is
standing against his big, black 4x4 with an over-night bag. He
looks very rugged in his low-slung shorts and fitted grey t-
shirt. Tilly *will* be excited when she sees him.

"Hey, Bea! Looking beautiful today." He strides
towards me and kisses my cheek.

"Hi, Luke, thank you, how are you?"

"I'm good thanks, where's Danny boy? I've got his
stuff." He holds out the bag in his hand.

"He's out the back, come through."

He follows me around to the back where Daniel is
waiting on the pool-house deck, in his towel. "Dan!" Luke
calls as he approaches him, and they smack each other on the
back, affectionately.

"Thanks for that Luke," Daniel says, taking the bag
from him.

"It's cool, I wanted to see hot stuff, where is she?" Luke
asks, looking around the garden.

"Tilly's in the pool-house," I say with a smile on my
face, "come in."

The boys follow me inside and I head to the bedroom.
She's tying her hair up as I walk in, she looks stunning with a
peach, floaty summer skirt hanging from her hips and a short
white top, flashing her tanned, flat belly.

"Wow, you look gorge, Til."

"What, this old thing?" she says, trying to hold back a
smile.

"Lover-boy's waiting for you out there, he called you
hot stuff," I say, grinning and wiggling my eyebrows.

"I hope he's going to give me another seeing to."

I gasp. "Tilly! You're awful! I wonder how long he'll stay for."

"Long enough, hopefully!"

"You like him, admit it Tilly."

"Oh, I'll admit to that, I do. He's hot, funny and fucks like a pro, what's not to like? But I'm not up for some long distance relationship, if that's what you mean. For starters; I know that he's not a 'relationship' kind of a bloke, he has a new bird every few days, I expect. Secondly; long distance doesn't work, and last but not least; I don't want a relationship either. I'm having fun, Bea."

"Okay! Sorry I asked!"

Her words are a little depressing to hear, I'm glad Tilly can be so casual about her fling with Luke, but it just brings home, the fact that Daniel and I aren't going anywhere. The more I like him, the harder it's going to be to leave. I can't just 'fuck' him, like Tilly and Luke, I'm getting emotionally involved and it's bad. Really bad.

"Right," she says as she checks her face in the mirror, "will I do?"

"You look fab, he won't last five minutes without getting you back in here."

"That's the look I'm going for," she sings.

I open the door and head out to the lounge with Tilly behind me. Luke is sitting on the sofa alone, looking very comfortable. He turns around when he hears us emerge and immediately wolf whistles at Tilly, before standing up.

"Hey, foxy! You look hot!" He steps towards her, and before she even has a chance to respond, he wraps his arms around her, tipping her back into a dramatic pose and kisses her fervently. I can't help but stare, grinning, it's so... affectionate.

Daniel comes out of the bathroom and stops when he sees Luke and Tilly. He rolls his eyes and laughs before looking at me and shaking his head. He looks edible in stone coloured chinos, hanging low on his hips, with white plimsolls and a navy, fitted polo shirt. "Are you two going to come up for air at some point?" he asks, putting the over-night bag on the sofa and strolling over towards me. He puts an arm around my waist and kisses me.

"You look so hot today, baby," he whispers. *Swoon, I love this man*. Oh god, not like, love-love... you know what I mean.

"Thank you, I was just thinking the same about you, Daniel. Hot with a capital 'huh'."

"Thank you," he says, leaning in to give me a lingering, delectable kiss.

I turn into him and press myself again his chest, it's just too good not to enjoy for a bit longer, so I wrap a hand around the back of his neck and introduce my tongue, tentatively. He readily accepts it and we're heading into a full on, delicious pash. I hear Luke and Tilly's voices in the background, so I know that they've come up for air, and I gently, reluctantly end our kiss.

Daniel keeps hold of me and looks over to Tilly who's still wrapped up in Luke's muscular arms. "Tilly, you look lovely today."

"Thank you, Daniel. What are you two up to then?"

"I was going to take Bea to the beach for some lunch, what about you two? Luke are you working?"

"Um," Luke responds, "I had a couple of sessions today, but I think I'll cancel them." Looking down at Tilly, he smiles and winks.

"Would you like to join us or do you have other... '*plans*'?" Daniel asks with a grin.

"Thanks, Daniel, but I think we've got other '*plans*'." Tilly replies with a gleam in her eye as she looks up at Luke.

"Let's go to mine," Luke says to Tilly and I turn to Daniel, having heard enough of their '*plans*'.

"Daniel, what do I need today?"

"Well, we'll go to the beach and a restaurant for lunch, so bring a bikini and a towel, and whatever else you need."

I grab my over sized beach bag, a towel and bikini from the drawers, and put my handbag inside the beach bag. "I'm done!"

"Okay, catch ya later," Daniel says to Luke and Tilly, and steps out of the pool-house, putting his Ray-bans on. They *really* suit him. Does anything *not* suit Daniel?

"Bye you two!" I shout, leaving them gazing at each other.

101

"Come on, baby." Daniel reaches for my hand and we walk together to his car.

The sun is shining, the roof is down and I'm spending the whole day with Sexy Berkeley. Today is a good day. Driving towards Santa Monica, I look through my aviators at Daniel, and smile. He's so sexy in his casual clothes.

"Thank you for this, Daniel. I'm really looking forward to today."

"Don't thank me, Bea, I want to take you out. I enjoy spending time with you, so much, I only wish we had more of it."

I sigh, "Me, too. Let's just have a great day."

He places his large, masculine hand on my knee and smiles that beautiful smile. "Let's do that."

He parks up and walks me back out to the street, and down to the Beach. As we walk along the promenade, I put my hand in his and hold it tightly, looking out towards the sea. I would normally be nervous, making this move, but somehow, with Daniel, it just feels so comfortable and right. I pause and turn to face the beach, it's gorgeous.

"Would you like to sit out on the beach for a while, or eat first?" he asks.

"It's quite early, so why don't we have a stroll along the beach and then eat. Then, if we want to, we can lay out in the sun after lunch?"

"That sounds like a perfect plan, Beatrice. We're eating right here." He clenches my hand and points to 'Shutters on the Beach' with the other. It's a beautiful white hotel building, very posh looking.

"It looks beautiful, Daniel."

We stop to take our shoes off and stroll on the sand, towards the water. We're not particularly loquacious, just holding hands, enjoying each other's company. I wonder what's going through his mind. He suddenly stops walking, prompting me to turn and look at him, questioningly.

"You okay?" I ask, and he tugs on my hand, gently pulling me towards him, against his chest. The feelings I have for this man, after such a short time, are immense. I look up at his handsome face and smile, I could stay pressed against him, like this, in these beautiful surroundings, forever.

He leans down to kiss me, his arms snaking around me and holding me close, and I kiss him back slowly, romantically. It's not about sex, right now, it's something meaningful and I'm pretty sure he's feeling it too.

~~~~~~~

Lunch was perfect. Daniel had specifically asked for a table by a huge, open window and he sat with his back to it, giving me a view of the beach. Something about that small, thoughtful gesture tugged at my heart strings.

I opted for a Caesar salad with prawns which was delicious, while Daniel had grilled salmon with asparagus and lemon. We drank champagne and enjoyed every moment of our '*date*'. After Daniel asked for the bill, he leant forward and held both of my hands across the table.

"The sun has been catching in your eyes all this time, they are the most beautiful green, and the golden streaks are extraordinary. I've never seen such exquisite eyes before."

Wow, he's really been looking, very few people notice the gold streaks. "You obviously don't look in the mirror much, Daniel."

"My eyes aren't that interesting, I could gaze into yours for a lifetime." *Stop, please? Stop making me want you.*

"Your eyes are beautiful, Daniel. But please, could you stop being so..."

"Cheesy? Full-on?"

"Nice."

He frowns and smiles a little before responding. "Nice? You want me to stop being... nice?"

"I love you being nice, but when you are, I want you more. Then I think about Sunday, and I get a horrible feeling in my stomach. This is what I was trying to avoid, I already know that Sunday is going to be a great, hairy ball of shit."

Daniel chuckles and leans in a little further. "Please don't think about Sunday, think about today, and how many more hours we have, and tonight, and how many days we can see each other before... '*then*'."

"Daniel, I don't think we can see each other again... after today, I mean. I really want to see you, all day every day until '*then*', but I can't do it. I need to go home feeling refreshed, not depressed, and I fear it'll be the latter, if I don't

103

stop seeing and wanting you so much." I feel unexpectedly emotional. I'm not going to cry, because that would be ridiculous, but I don't want to stop seeing him. I want to curl up in bed with him and stay there for the next four days, but if I want to be sane when I return to the UK, this is how it has to be.

"Please don't say that, I don't think I can go to Sunday - knowing you're here - and not see you. I'll regret not spending that time with you. Once you're gone, that'll be it, I won't be *able* to see you, but while you're here..."

"Please don't, you know that's what I want too, but it won't be conducive to a healthy, happy state of mind for me later. Let's not ruin what may be our last day together, worrying about what will or won't happen over the next few days."

Daniel's shoulders drop a little, his expression, apprehensive. I want to wrap my arms around him.

"Daniel, doesn't it strike you as a little odd that we're having such a discussion after having met, only four days ago?"

"It really does, Bea, I've never felt so strongly about anyone is such a short space of time before. It's new to me and I don't quite know how to handle it." *Holy moly*, he's being very honest. 'Felt so strongly'? What does that mean?

"I've never had someone say anything like that to me before. This is all rather new to me, too."

"Now, *that*, I don't understand. The fact that you don't already have a boyfriend is crazy enough."

"You're sweet, Daniel," I say, lifting our hands together and kissing his. And he really is, he's so thoughtful and kind. *Where are all the men like this at home?*

The bill/check arrives and Daniel puts his card on top.

"Daniel, I'd like to buy lunch, please."

He looks horrified. "Oh no, that's not happening."

"Please? I'd really like to buy you lunch, it has been so wonderful and I'd like to thank you for bringing me here."

"I'm sorry, Bea, I can't do that," he says, gently shaking his head, "I'll take a kiss or two later, but no, I won't let you buy lunch."

I pout and flutter my eyelashes, "Pweeeease?"

He shakes his head firmly, but let's go of one of my hands to run the backs of his fingers up and down my cheek. "No, baby."

I lean my face into his fingers and he opens his hand to caress it, gently. "Thank you," I whisper.

"You're so welcome." We pause for a moment in silence, Daniel still grazing my cheek, looking into each other's eyes. It would seem quite awkward with anyone else, but with him, it's just so right. I'm not sure how much time passes, but eventually, the waiter collects Daniel's card and takes payment on the hand held terminal, bringing us back to reality.

"So would you like to sit on the beach for a while?" Daniel asks.

"Yes, that would be lovely, I need to get my bikini on though."

"Why don't you go to the bathroom and put it on here?"

"Good idea, Sexy, I'll do it now."

"I wish I could come help." He pouts again, god love him.

I stand up and collect my bag, and Daniel immediately stands like a true gent. "Don't be long, I'll be right here waiting for you."

We leave the restaurant, hand in hand, having both changed into our swimwear. It feels so normal to hold his hand, even though we're not boyfriend and girlfriend. I still get those sparks flying through me every time we touch, but when we're holding hands, it's like a continuous warm buzz.

Daniel's phone rings, so he tells me to find somewhere to settle while he speaks to work. I stroll down the beach, towards the sea, enjoying the fine, warm sand between my toes. I settle on a spot with very few people, and sit, gazing out to the water. It's picturesque. I want to stay forever.

I take off my blouse and rest back on to my elbows, listening to the soft waves lapping against the shore. I close my eyes and breathe it all in, thinking of Daniel and the time that we have spent together. Today is perfect and I so want to enjoy it as much as I can, but it's tainted by the horrible reality of what's to come. If I'm feeling like this already, what will it be like if I spend more time with him? How can I go back to 'real life', without being able to see him, talk to him, touch him? *What have I gotten myself into?*

"You look deep in thought, baby." I turn to see Daniel crouching behind me, smiling. He sits behind me, facing sideways and stretches his legs out. "Here, lean back," he offers, patting his washboard belly. I rest my head back onto his stomach and turn to look at his face. He's smiling at me and looks so handsome. He gently runs his fingers through my hair, I close my eyes again and enjoy the feel of his warm stomach beneath my face, gently rising and falling in time with his breathing, his fingers playing with my hair, it's so relaxing.

"Are you okay, Bea? You seem a little quiet."

"Yes, I'm fine," I say, reaching for one of his hands and holding it to my mouth. I don't want to have to let go of him.

"I'm just thinking about the time we have spent together and how I'll be so sad to say good bye to you."

His mouth curls into a small smile. "I know, baby. Me too."

I smile back, "I like that you call me 'baby', even though I'm not your girlfriend. Makes me feel... nice."

"Oh, Bea," Daniel sighs, looking out towards the sea, "Come here..." He sits up and opens his legs, prompting me to sit between them, facing him with my legs curled around his hips. He takes his sunglasses off and hooks his hands together around my waist, gazing at me. "I wish you lived here."

"Me too, or that you lived near me," I sigh.

"I don't like to hear you say '*even though I'm not your girlfriend*'. It means that you can be someone else's, and I don't like that, not at all. I want you to be mine... my girlfriend." *Oh, Daniel!* Butterflies suddenly break free in my stomach.

I smile, sadly and look down at the sand between us. I love that he wants that, but at the same time, I want to cry. "Me, too. Do you see why this is so hard? Why we need to stop?" I look up into his lovely face and he leans forward and kisses me gently. I rest my head on his shoulder, facing his neck and lay small kisses on his skin.

"I understand why you want to, but you know I don't agree. I want to see you as much as I can, fuck how I feel after. I'll feel a hell of a lot worse if I don't make the most of the time I can have with you."

"I can't do that, Daniel. I have to leave this lovely relaxing holiday to go home and try to function properly. I have a lovely new apartment, a business I love and my family at home, I want to enjoy that, not be too sad to appreciate it. I'll be as much use at work as a chocolate teapot, missing you."

"I understand. But I need you to know that I want to see you, every day, until you leave. And if you let me, I'll be there. I can take Friday off and spend a long weekend with you, I can see you after work tomorrow and Thursday, please think about it."

"You can't keep taking time off, Daniel."

"I can, and I will. I rarely take time off work, the business can cope without me for a day. I have to work tomorrow and Thursday, but they don't need me Friday. Please think about it."

"I will, Daniel, but..."

"I know, baby," he cuts me off, saving me from going through it all again.

I wrap my arms around him, I already know we won't be spending any more time together after tonight, and it's such a horrible thought, but I'll be heartbroken when I get home if this continues.

"It's hot, huh?" I'm pleased that he's changed the subject, I so want to try and enjoy every moment. I'm wasting it feeling sad, prematurely.

"Yes, I think I'll take my jeans off and sunbathe for a bit. I don't want to swim though."

"That's fine, I don't usually swim here, the water is quite cold."

"That, and you might try to bring me to orgasm in the water again." I wink at him.

"You didn't like that? I did." He pouts, I love it when he pouts!

"You know I did, it was incredible, but we were in a communal pool!"

"Hmm... I don't think you minded that much," he grins. He stands up and removes his t-shirt and trousers and I smile,

107

thinking back to this morning's 'Magic Mike' show in the bathroom. He looks at me with a raised eyebrow and I can tell he knows what I'm thinking. He turns and wiggles his bottom as he pulls his trousers down.

"Daniel! Don't get me started! Don't you remember how that ended this morning?"

"Yes, I do and if I recall correctly, it was extremely pleasurable for both parties."

"Unfortunately, though, now we're not in the confines of the bathroom, so we have to control ourselves."

"Yes, Ma'am. Now take off your pants and show me that hot booty."

~~~~~~~

The next couple of hours are thoroughly enjoyable, we don't mention the '*Sunday thing*', just talk about everything and anything else. Daniel plays some music on his iPhone quietly in the background, along with the sound of the sea.

"I love this music, Daniel."

"Me, too. It's the Pure Moods album."

"Oh, I thought I recognised it. It's so relaxing."

We sit listening for a while, with me in between his legs facing away from him, leaning against his toned chest. He kisses me constantly, he's always touching me one way or another and I love that he's so tactile. It does feel like he's my boyfriend, and that we're a lot further into a relationship than a matter of days but, reluctantly, I like it.

An Enigma song follows a little later, the French lyrics hypnotising me, drawing me into a pacifying, sensuous lull. I lean sideways in Daniel's arms and look up at him. "I'd love to know what these words mean, do you?"

"Uh huh, the background lyrics are in Latin, I think it's a prayer, I'm not great at Latin."

"The main lyrics are French," he continues, repeating the lyrics in French, and translating for me.

Fuck me sideways. Daniel speaks French. It's fascinating and so *HOT!* I gawk at him for a moment, slightly tempted to sink down on him, right here, right now. "You speak French?"

Daniel laughs and shrugs his shoulders, "No."

I raise an eyebrow at him, pursing my lips.

"Yes, I do, baby. You sound surprised?"

"I suppose I am, although I'm not sure why, I probably know very little about you."

"I want you to know everything."

I smile. I want to know everything, too. "You know the words off by heart?"

"I listen to this album in the car a lot, I've always liked this song in particular."

"It would be a great sex song."

His eyes dart to mine, his mouth slightly ajar. "Let's do this!" he says, a grin spreading on his gorgeous face.

"Here?!"

He nuzzles my neck and kisses it, squeezing me tightly in his arms. "Mmm, will anyone notice?"

"I think they might, Daniel."

"Okay," he grumbles and lifts his head, "anyway, don't you mean *'great music to make love to'* as opposed to *'a great sex song'?*"

"Well, yes, but I'm a bit funny about saying 'make love'. I think you can only 'make love' when you're 'in love'. So for two people in love, yes, it's *'great music to make love to'*, but for us, it'd be great music for us to have sex to."

Daniel doesn't say anything for a moment, as if thinking about what I've said. "It's starting to get late," he kisses my shoulder, "what would you like to do later? Go out? Stay in at yours or come back to mine? You haven't even been to my place yet."

"I know, but I think I'd quite like to stay at the pool-house tonight. I could make you dinner there, that way you don't have to bring me back before work tomorrow." Truthfully, I just don't think I want to see where Daniel lives. I don't want to see his belongings, sleep in his bed, and see how he lives day to day, it would make me feel even closer to him and I'm reluctant to take another step into his life, I'll get in too deep.

"Okay, that makes sense, baby, although I would love to have you all to myself, in my home. Maybe another day?"

"Daniel, please don't."

He wisely drops it. "Let's go back." He stands and dusts the sand off before putting his clothes back on, and I follow suit.

"I love the way you wiggle when you put those pants on," Daniel says with a chuckle.

"Every time you say '*pants*' I think of great big, ugly, granny knickers. I don't *do* granny pants, Daniel."

"I am fully aware of that, Beatrice. You wear smokin' hot panties and I'd like to see them around your ankles right about now."

"Shame I'm wearing my bikini then," I respond with a wink.

"You look smokin' hot in that too."

I put my blouse on and shake out the towel before rolling it up and putting it in my beach bag. "Right, I'm ready to go, are you?" I ask.

"Ready," Daniel says, putting his sunglasses back on and holding his arm out to me. He wraps it around my waist and I snuggle into his side to walk back to the car. "So what are we going to make for dinner?" he asks.

"Are you going to help, Daniel?"

"I'd like to."

"Okay, how about... pasta? Can we go to the supermarket?"

"Sure, sounds good, we'll stop on the way."

When we get back in the car, I dig in my bag for my phone to text Tilly to see if they'll join us for pasta. When I find it, there's a text from Clare.

~

Clare 18 Sep 16:24
Hey, doll-face! What have you been up to? Can't wait to hear all about lover-boy! Call me! Everything is good at Bear's, don't even think about home. Just have fun!! Miss you loads :'(Love you xxxxxxxx

~

It's so good to hear from her, I miss her too, so much. So Tilly's told her about Daniel, I wonder what she's said.

~

18 Sep 17:49

110

I'm sorry I haven't called yet... bad friend :-(I miss you too, wish you were here, you'd LOVE it! Daniel is dreamy. You'd like him. I want to bring him home :-(. Did Til tell you about her bit of fluff? Luke? Yet another hot piece of eye candy! Will call, promise. Love you loads xxxxxxxx

~

I giggle and smile down at my phone.

"All okay, baby?"

"Yes, I had a text from Clare. I wish she was here too, you'd like her. But if she was, you'd need to find another hot, single friend for her." I grin.

"So all three of you are single? I don't understand it."

I laugh. "Well, you and Luke are single, aren't you?"

"Of course. But Luke is single because... well because he loves it, I expect he'll always be single. I'm single, just because."

"Same here. Tilly likes to have fun, like Luke... well, probably not as much as Luke! But she's not interested in settling down. Clare's much like me."

"You'd settle down?"

"Yes, if I found the right man."

"And what's the right man?"

My mouth half smiles and I roll my eyes, embarrassed. "Um... you." I whisper.

He takes a deep breath in and exhales loudly through pursed lips. He looks at me and shakes his head. "You can't say things like that, Bea."

"Why? You would be, if you were local and wanted the same thing."

"But that's just it, I do." Wow. So, we've established, openly, that we would embark on a relationship, if we lived in the same country. *Oh god, where does this leave me? How do I feel about this?*

"Well, since what we want can't happen, let's not talk about it, it's depressing. I better text Tilly to see if they'll join us for dinner." I decide that changing the subject is the best course of action.

Daniel looks at me, his expression, impassive. He turns to focus on the road and exhales loudly, but says nothing. *Is he pissed off?*

I have another text from Clare which drags my attention away from Daniel's apparent mood swing.

~

Clare 18 Sep 17:55
What?! No!!! She didn't tell me anything about a Luke! So both of you are getting it on! This is not fair! I'm coming next time! Daniel and BB sitting in a tree, K.I.S.S.I.N.G! Try to bring him back with you! Gotta go, time to decorate the 'Dawson' cake. Love you, have fun. Say hi to Daniel! ;-) xxxxxx

~

Daniel and I arrive back at the pool-house about an hour after my last text from Clare. No one seems to be home in either house. I still haven't heard back from Tilly, so I assume they're busy. I put my beach bag down on the sofa while Daniel puts the shopping bags in the kitchen. He has been uncharacteristically quiet since we left the beach.

I wander in to join him as he unloads the shopping, deep in thought. I stroke his shoulder, affectionately. "Are you okay, Daniel?"

He pauses for a moment, looking down and not answering. I move to stand in front of him, and I have to push him away from the counter a little, as if he doesn't want to let me in. I rest my hands on his chest. "Daniel? What's wrong?"

He looks into my eyes, a strange, blank expression. Not the happy, lovely Daniel I've seen, thus far. Why isn't he talking?

"Daniel?" I prompt, but still no response, "Daniel!" I shout again, my voice urgent.

Eventually, he answers. "I think you're right," he whispers.

"What? What about?"

"I think we should stop this. Sooner rather than later."

Oh. I know I should be pleased that he's agreeing to what I asked, but hearing him say it, seeing him so cold... it's horrible. What happened to wanting me to be his girlfriend? Now he doesn't even want to look at me.

"Oh. Okay, so after tonight, we stop seeing each other?"

He pauses again, "I think... I think I should go now."

"What? Why? What's happened, Daniel?"

"Nothing. I have just realised that you're right, Bea. This will only get harder, the longer it goes on."

He steps back, away from me and grabs his keys from the side before walking out of the kitchen.

"You don't want dinner?" I ask, chasing after him like a puppy.

"No."

"Daniel, please."

He runs his hand along the back of his neck and closes his eyes for a brief moment. "I'm going to go, Bea. I... "

"Please don't go, Daniel. I was *so* looking forward to spending tonight with you." I rest my hand lightly on his arm and he quickly pulls away.

"Fuck, Bea! You're the one that wanted this," he spits, his voice harsh, "you don't stop going on about how this can't amount to anything, how you don't want to see me again in case it's 'too hard' later. You wanted this, Bea, not me. You."

What the fuck? "Not like this, Daniel, and you know that! Why are you being like this?" I can feel my eyes burning as the tears well, I don't want to cry but I can't seem to control it.

"Look, like I said, I just realised that you're right. We can't do this anymore. Enjoy the rest of your vacation, I hope you've enjoyed the past few days. I... I've got to go."

"But, Daniel, don't..." Tears begin to tumble over my lashes as he takes one long, last look at me, flexing his hands and clenching his jaw. He closes his eyes briefly and turns to leave the pool-house, practically sprinting off. I stand, staring at the door, not really understanding what just happened. How could he be so cold? Today was so wonderful, and then... *that.* What happened to him wanting to see me every day until I go? I know I said 'no', but he asked me to think about it.

I walk, dazed, into the kitchen and look at the shopping on the counter. I was going to cook for us, for our lovely evening together, we were supposed to talk and kiss and be intimate. He was supposed to stay and wrap me up in his big, strong arms.

I well up again, thinking about what tonight was *supposed* to be and how, now, it's a big, deflated nothing. I slide down the wall and slump to the kitchen floor, my heart beating so hard and fast it feels like it'll explode in my chest. I rest my head on my knees and hug my legs, tightly. I feel physically sick. I sounded like a desperate, clingy teenager getting dumped. Is that why he went? Was I too clingy? I'm just so confused.

~~~~~~~

114

Twenty minutes must have passed, still curled on the kitchen floor, running through everything we did today. I try to recall what happened, what I said. He kept saying that I wanted this, but I don't, not *this*. I just feel so much for him, and am too aware of the inevitable hurt that's ahead, why can't he understand that I'm trying to shield myself from deeper pain? I wipe my wet cheek with the back of my hand and rest my head back against the wall. Determined to stop crying. He's gone. It's done. Finished. Deal with it.

The french doors slamming makes me jump out of my skin, my head shoots up as he bursts though the door frame and drops to his knees in front of me, wrapping his arms around me. "Oh god, I'm so sorry, baby, I'm such an asshole, I'm sorry." He plants small kisses all over my face. *What the fuck?!* I'm happy to see him, but I'm so confused, what just happened?

He pulls away and holds my face in his hands, staring at me, intently. He wipes away my tears with his thumbs. "Please don't cry, I'm sorry."

"Daniel, I... what happened?"

"I... I just panicked, the thought of you leaving suddenly overwhelmed me. And all that talk of how we don't 'make love', it kind of got to me. I mean, what we do is incredible and I love it, *a lot*, but I think too much of you to just be 'fucking' you, Bea.

"Having to deal with the fact that this can't go any further in such a blunt way, I don't know, I feel so... helpless, like I'm trying to convince you to want as much as I do, to no avail. I shouldn't have ran out like that, though, or got pissed at you... it was completely selfish of me and a shitty thing to do."

"Daniel, for god's sake! Convincing me to want as much as you do? How many times have I made it fucking *obvious* how much I like you? How can you not know? I'm trying to protect myself, and every minute I'm with you that gets harder and harder because I'm feeling so much more. What you just did was so fucking horrible! Yes, I'm blunt about how we move forward, I don't know how else to be, I haven't been in this situation before, Daniel, but one thing I do know, is that if we carry on, this is going to go from being god damned sad, to being completely and utterly fucking broken, when I leave. Okay? Can you understand that?"

He puts his head in his hands and winces. "Fuck. I've fucked up. I'm so sorry, baby," he whispers. "Yes, I can understand it. I just don't want it to be that way, like if I don't think about what's ahead, it'll somehow change, and every time you remind me that you're leaving, something inside drops. And I flipped.

"I appreciate that our fucked up situation is not your fault, and fully accept what a total douche I've been. God baby, Bea, I'm so, so sorry. Please let me stay? Make it up to you, continue as we had originally planned before I made a royal fuck up of everything? I really don't want to miss out on this short time I have with you." His darling face looks so worried. I start to stand up and Daniel does the same, his eyes on my face the whole time.

"Please can I stay? Have dinner and stay the night? From tomorrow, we can cool off if you like, I really do understand where you're coming from. It will be hard, knowing you're right here, but with every day that I'm with you, it gets harder to think of you leaving. So I'm okay doing it your way, if that's really what you want." He grabs my hands and holds them between us, kissing them. "My feelings for you are growing, fast. I think what I felt today, was the feeling you've been describing about Sunday."

I nod, I believe him. "It's okay, Daniel. Stop apologising."

"I feel so shitty that you're upset, because of me."

I tug one of my hands from his and place it gently on the side of his face. "Please stop it. It's okay, you're back now. We've talked. Yes, I'd love for you to stay for dinner."

"Thank you." He leans forward and kisses me lightly. "I won't stay the night if you don't want me to."

"Daniel, stop it. I want you to, of course I do. Let's just forget it."

He gazes at me and smiles. "You're amazing." He steps forward and lifts me so I'm sitting on the counter, butterflies float in my belly and tingles run from my navel to my chest. I wrap my arms around his shoulders, running my fingers over his muscles, his arms tightly wrapped around my waist.

"I'm sorry," he whispers, softly, his face serious and his eyes intense, the beautiful turquoise that enraptures me so thoroughly.

I look down for a beat before meeting his eyes again, slowly lowering my gaze to his invitingly pouty lips and back again. "Daniel, it's okay, really." I stroke his neck. "Now, pucker up buttercup."

He chuckles, turquoise twinkling as he lowers his face to meet mine. He gently runs his nose up and down mine, our lips brushing against each other. It's so sensual, so intimate. A small moan escapes me as he pushes his mouth against mine, forcefully, locking us together.

Our tongues find each other, gently caressing, the heat runs under my skin from the excitement of having him against me, wanting me. I finally realise that this situation is equally hard for both of us, it gives me a bizarre thrill, knowing he wants me as strongly as I do him. The sound of Daniel's passionate groan sends desire rushing through my veins. My hands run through his hair, pulling his face into mine, I need him, now.

I glide one hand down his front, to his waistband. I yank it towards me, making my intentions very clear and Daniel smiles against my mouth. I unbutton his trousers and slowly glide the zip down before slipping my hand inside the waistband of his swimming trunks, and down to his rock hard, ready cock.

"Uh," Daniel groans as he tilts his head backwards, away from me. I grab his hair with my free hand and force his face back to mine again.

"Kiss me," I growl against his lips. I tighten my hold around him and glide my hand up and down his thick shaft slowly as I kick the door with my foot, slamming it shut.

Daniel slides his hands underneath my blouse, gliding over my breasts and around to my back where he unties by bikini, dropping it to my thighs. He immediately gropes my breasts, firmly and I moan in ecstasy. His fingers flick over my nipples before his hands move lower to my waistband. He unfastens the button and grabs my backside, pulling me off the counter so my feet drop to the floor. He steps with me to the back of the kitchen door and presses me up against it, unzipping my jeans.

Pulling away from me, forcing me to let go, he sinks to his knees in front of me. He tugs at both sides of my jeans, pulling them down to my ankles. He gazes at my bikini briefs for a moment, before slowly pulling the bows at either side so they drop between my legs. String swimwear is super convenient for this type of thing.

Daniel moans, licking his lips whilst gazing at me... at my bits. He leans forward and runs his tongue right up the middle, stroking my clitoris as he goes, making me shudder with pleasure.

"Ah," I flinch, it's so sensitive. He gently licks again before kissing me and standing up slowly to pull his swimming trunks down.

We simultaneously step out of our trouser legs and kick them to the side. Daniel pulls his polo shirt up and over his head, standing in front of me, totally naked and absolutely gorgeous.

He steps towards me so we're almost touching, he lifts my blouse over my head and we stand, gazing at each other, soaking in the view. Daniel's breathing, rapid, he grabs me, kissing me fast and furiously. His hands glide over my body, touching me, feeling me, exploring me.

I run my fingernails gently up and down his back, he groans loudly and grabs my bottom, pressing me against him, his erection pushing eagerly into my belly. I writhe up and down against him, wrapping my hands around his neck, pulling him closer. He lifts me, effortlessly, my legs curling around his torso, leaving me open, and ready.

Pressing me against the door, he positions himself below me and I gasp as I feel his tip, pressing against me, right there. "Baby," he growls.

"Daniel," I whisper, desperate for more, willing him to push further.

"Look at me."

"I am, I will, please, Daniel..."

"Keep looking into my eyes, please?" he whispers, almost pleading.

"Daniel!"

118

"Say it!"

"I promise, I will, Daniel. I'll look into your eyes. Please, I want you, I need you."

He kisses me and gently bites my lip, before pulling back to lock eyes with me. He slowly, delectably pushes all the way into me, so far, so deep. I cry out, desperately resisting the temptation to throw my head back in ecstasy, instead, baring to him, every moment of intense pleasure.

He pulls back and slowly pushes into me again, pushing deeper and deeper, it's almost painful but so, *unbelievably* good.

"Oh, Daniel, again, deeper," I moan, loudly, and he thrusts harder still.

"Ah! Yes, that's it. Daniel, fuck me hard, please!" He pulls back and slams into me, deep and hard, it's incredible.

Still staring deep into his eyes, showing him my every reaction to each thrust. Seeing his need, the pleasure in his eyes so carnal and heavy, and I need more.

"Yes, baby, keep looking," he breathes, his voice raspy.

Watching him, watching me, sends electrifying butterflies flitting, excitedly through my belly. "Oh god, Daniel!"

"Say my name again."

"Daniel, harder, please I need you, fuck me harder, Daniel!" It's fast approaching, the waves rising quickly, every thrust building the pressure higher, and I'm about to explode around him.

"Bea, I don't want to fuck you," he says, thrusting again. *WHAT?*

I frown. "Wh-what?"

"It's more, Bea," he says with another hard thrust, his eyes burning into my soul.

"Mmm, yes, like that, it's so good, Daniel... I, I don't know what you want me to say... oh, yes..."

"I want you... baby."

"I want you too."

He kisses me and there's a look of fear, fear and pleasure at the same time. *What is it?* "No, uh," he groans, frustration and pleasure combined, "no, Bea, I want you... I want..."

119

The waves build so fast, it's so good, I'm on the brink. "Daniel, Daniel, please...what do you want?" I cry out, desperately, as my toes start to curl under and the sparks begin to fly, he picks up the pace again and oh god, I'm ready. "Oh god, Daniel, tell me!"

"Oh, baby..."

"Uh huh, Daniel... I'm... it's..."

"I... I want to make love to you, baby..." he whispers, pained, closing his eyes and leaning in to rest his lips against my neck.

Suddenly filled with emotion, I whisper, breathlessly, "Daniel, make love to me, please." Tears spring to my eyes as I let go.

"Oh, baby, yes..." Daniel thrusts hard, as we both come together, it's so intense, so strong and it doesn't stop.

"Oh god, Daniel."

He tightens his hold on me, as if he knows my bones are turning to jelly. "Bea..."

As the waves diminish, the jitters take over, my insides convulsing in the aftershock of yet another remarkable orgasm. I drop my face onto his shoulder, trying to suppress the tears, and Daniel slowly slinks to the floor, taking me with him. He leans back, forcing me to lift my head and he grasps my chin with his fingers. "Baby? Are you okay?"

I smile and nod.

"Are you crying?"

I shake my head and look down, realising that I can't hide it, and reluctantly nod.

"I'm so sorry, I didn't mean to upset you before," he whispers, his voice laced with concern.

"No, Daniel, it's not that. It was just, you know, the whole... 'make love' thing..."

"I'm Sorry. I, well I..."

"No, it's okay, it just brings home what we're never going to have, you know?"

Daniel nods and pulls me close to him again. I rest my head on his shoulder and revel in his warmth.

After a minute or so, we're both disturbed by a knock on the kitchen door. I practically jump out of my skin.

"Hey!! Are you two still alive in there or have you fucked each other to death?"

My eyes widen in horror. It's Tilly. "Oh dear god!" I whisper, heat rises up my face.

Daniel bites his lip and grins.

I swat his leg. "It's not funny!" I whisper again.

"Uh, oh," Tilly shouts, "Luke, I think they're dead..."

Then Luke's voice! "Damn, that must have been some fantastic sex."

"Sounded like it!" *Mortified.* I put my head in my hands and wish I could shrivel up into a ball. Daniel is still silently laughing.

"What are you laughing at?" I scold, "I'm mortified!" I wriggle out of his hold and scramble to get my clothes together. Holding up my bikini I try to figure out how I put it all back together. "Oh fuck it!" I shout, "how the hell am I supposed to put this fucking thing back on?" I fiddle with the ties and Daniel stands.

"Baby, calm down. Stop worrying, you actually saw them at it the other day, they only heard us."

"Yes, but I walked in their room, they didn't exactly have a choice. I just had sex in the fucking kitchen in someone else's house, and let everyone know about it!"

He laughs again. "Come on, calm down, it's fine."

I hear Tilly speaking through the door for our benefit again. "Oh, it's okay, they're alive, I can hear Bea stressing about having loud sex in the kitchen."

"Oh fuck off, Tilly," I shout. I'm so mortified, and pissed off that she's making it worse.

It goes quiet and Daniel starts to put his clothes on. "Bea, don't worry about it, don't get pissed, she's only having a little fun with us." He rubs his hands up and down my arms and I frown and pout. I know he's right and I shouldn't have snapped.

I look up at him through my lashes. "Please can you help me get dressed?"

He grins, "Of course, baby."

Just as Daniel tries to fix the knot on the side of my bikini, the door opens ever so slightly and he jumps in front of me to cover me. My silk dressing gown slips through the gap, hanging from Tilly's finger. I take it, gratefully. "Thank you, love, I'm sorry," I say through the gap.

"Don't worry, sorry for taking the piss. Love you."

"Love you too, Til."

The door closes and I turn to Daniel who is smiling sweetly at me. He takes the gown and holds it out for me to slip into. "Thank you, Daniel. Sorry for being an idiot."

"You're perfect," he says, kissing my forehead and holding me tightly, "I'm the idiot."

Tilly and Luke kindly sit outside so that we can emerge from the kitchen without much more embarrassment. Daniel joins the two of them while I change into a pair of black silky pyjama bottoms and a black crop top before heading back to the kitchen to start dinner.

I put the water on to boil and start to prepare the puttanesca sauce whilst listening to Christina Aguilera singing 'Candyman' on my iPhone. Daniel walks in and stands behind me, wrapping his hands around my waist, grinding his hips into me in time to the music. The man's got rhythm!

"You look hot in this, baby. What can I do?" he asks, gesturing towards the chopping board in front of me.

"Nothing, there's very little to do, I'm just going to put the pasta in and finish the sauce."

"Can I chop the onion?"

"Nope, done that."

"I'll kick back and watch you then," he says, smiling as he sits on the adjacent counter top to talk to me while I cook.

An hour later, the four of us are sitting around the table, empty plates in front of us, drinking wine and chatting freely. I really like Luke, and in any other circumstance, I'd say he and Tilly were perfectly suited for a relationship. They look so good together, and they're constantly smiling and flirting with each other, how can she not be falling for him? She looks like she is, but when I talk to her, she's so blasé, stressing that they're 'fuck buddies' and nothing else. I don't understand it.

As relaxing and enjoyable as tonight is, I can't help but want to be alone with Daniel. Every time I look at him, I want to curl up on his lap or wrap my arms around him and kiss him... or strip him naked, throw him on the sofa and shag him rotten. He looks so handsome sitting back in his chair, talking and laughing, and for tonight only, he's all mine. So I want him to myself.

I stand to clear the plates, Daniel and Luke deep in conversation about some golfing matter. Tilly joins me, bringing some of the crockery into the kitchen. "Are you okay, Bea? You seem quiet?"

"Yes, I'm fine, Tilly, it has just been a funny old day, that's all."

"Are you pissed off with me? I'm sorry about earlier, I didn't mean to upset you."

"No, don't worry about that, I'm sorry, I was feeling a bit sensitive. I was embarrassed though!"

"Oh god, don't be! I'm sure I must have heard you having sex before when we lived together. I know I've heard Clare at home!"

"Yeah, I've heard Clare, too!"

"Is Daniel staying?"

"Yes, do you mind?"

"No, I don't mind at all, does it bother you being in the lounge? I doubt we'll need to come in, I'll take a drink to bed with me so we don't need the kitchen, and we have our own access to the bathroom."

"Great, just don't walk in without knocking." I laugh.

"I think me and Luke might go for a swim now," she grins.

"Oh, right, a *swim*. What about Gemma? Aren't they here?"

"No, Gemma and Jay are at a dinner party and Jack's at his grandma's. They won't be home for hours."

"Oh, okay. Well at least *they* didn't hear me having sex!" I say with a grin.

~~~~~~~

Daniel and I lay on the sofa together, talking, while Tilly and Luke have a 'swim'. He runs his fingers up and down my back as we talk about my new apartment.

"So... what floor is it on?" he asks.

"The first floor."

"How many floors are there?"

"I'm not sure, four, I think. Maybe five..."

"And... how many bedrooms are there?"

"Two."

"I'd love to see it, see your home."

"Well, it hasn't been my home for long, but I love it."

"So, you literally moved in the day before you came away?"

"Yep, I have owned it for a short while, but have spent the evenings, after work, decorating and putting furniture up. I didn't want to move in until it was completely finished, so I stayed at my parents until then. It was all finished on Thursday, so the girls came over for a house-warming. That's when we booked my flight."

He looks at me, surprised. "So you hadn't even booked your flight? It wasn't planned?"

"Nope. I was supposed to be at work on Friday but we all got a bit tipsy... a lot tipsy. We were talking about Tilly's trip away and I said how lucky she was, then the next thing I know, it was all arranged! I wasn't going to come but they practically forced me into it."

"Lucky for me that they did!"

"Yep and me, or it might be Tilly laying on top of you right now." I do not like that thought. I don't like the thought of any girl being close Daniel.

"Tilly's cute, in fact, she's very attractive, but nothing would have happened there. She's not my type."

I take this opportunity to ask something that has had me wondering, from the moment we met.

"Daniel, when you held my hand, on the plane, were you trying to get into my knickers, or were you genuinely comforting me?" I ask with a smile.

"Beatrice, you don't have a great opinion of me, do you?"

I giggle and kiss his nose. "I have a very high opinion of you, Sexy Berkeley, but at that time, you didn't know me."

"As much as I'd have loved to have gotten into your 'knickers', I was genuinely trying to comfort you. I had some naughty thoughts at the time, you have quite a tight grip," he winks, "but I wasn't doing it to get into your panties."

"I wanted you in my 'panties'." I offer him a salacious grin and he lays a gentle kiss on my lips.

"I'm looking forward to getting into them later."

124

"Me too," I say, softly. "Daniel..."

"Yes, baby?"

"I'm glad you came back." I rest my head on his chest and snake my arms around him to squeeze him.

"Me too. I'm sorry, baby, I was a total ass."

"Yes, you were. But it's okay, I forgive you."

"You're so sweet," he says, kissing my hair. I nuzzle into his chest and inhale his lovely scent.

"I've had a wonderful few days. I'm going to miss you."

"Me too, Bea. More than you know," he sighs.

We lay in silence for a few minutes. I'm savouring every moment of being so close to him, laying on his perfect, glorious body, smelling him, feeling his heart beating. He leans over to the coffee table, taking me with him, to pick up his wine glass. I lean up on his chest and grab mine too.

"Here, I'll sit up, baby." He sits up in the corner of the sofa and opens his legs for me to sit in between them. "I've got a question for you," he says, breaking the brief somber mood of a moment ago.

"What do you wear to work? Do you have uniforms?"

I smile at the random question. "Actually yes." I like that he's taking an interest in Bear's. "Clare and I decided that we wanted uniforms. We have logo'd, fitted t-shirts and aprons in different pastel colours, to match the interior of the shop. We tend to wear a different colour apron, to t-shirt, every day, so for example, on a Monday, I might wear my pink t-shirt with a yellow apron and Clare might wear her yellow t-shirt with a blue apron. You see?"

"I do, sounds great. I bet you all look very smart and coordinated."

"As smart as you can look baking cakes and getting covered in chocolate and icing all day."

"I'd like you to bake me a cake... and to get you covered in chocolate again."

"Well, one day, when you come to London on business, you'll have to pop in to the shop and I'll give you an extra special cake, on the house."

"I wish I needed to be in London every week! Unfortunately, I don't need to go too frequently, especially after what was achieved on my last visit."

125

"To be honest, Daniel, it's better that way. We need to make a clean break and not keep in contact. If we can't have a relationship, we shouldn't dangle carrots."

"You're right. I'm going to make the most of you tonight. I hope it doesn't go too fast."

I sigh and decide to change the subject. "Right, you asked about my work, my turn to ask you something."

"Fire away."

"Okay, let's see, what do I want to know? Um... ooh! Have you ever had 'relations' with any of your colleagues or employees?"

"Never. Next?"

"Really?" I bet they all want him.

"Of course not, that would be grossly unprofessional. There's no one of any interest there anyway."

"So, what if I applied for a job at your company? Would you give me it?"

"I'd give you something..."

"Seriously, what would you do? Employ me and keep your hands to yourself, or not employ me so you could shag me senseless?"

"I'd employ you and break all the rules so I could have you on my desk, every day."

"Mmm, sounds good, but you'd never get any work done."

"Hmm," he says, rubbing his chin, "that's true. Well, if you were applying for a job at my office, you'd be living in the States, so I think I'd have to employ you, keep my hands off at work, and then I'd get to take you home every night and have you all to myself. Which is still breaking the rules, but at least I'd get some work done."

"That's a well thought out plan, Daniel." *Oh, how I wish we could do that.*

"It's a little depressing, I want that to happen now. Will you come and work for me?" he asks and I pout.

"Oh, Daniel, I'd love to. But Bear's and the UK need me." I kiss his cheek and take a sip of wine. "Will you speak to me in French?" I ask, tactfully changing the subject again.

"Will you understand what I'm saying?"

"No, but I want to hear it anyway, I think it's hot."

"Sure, what do you want me to say?"

"Anything you like, whatever you're thinking."

"Okay, um... De tous les avions dans le monde entier, il fallait marcher dans la mienne. Vous ne saurez jamais combien j'ai besoin de toi. Je veux que tu restes ici, avec moi, pour toujours. Je pense que je suis tombé en amour avec toi, bébé." *Swoon.*

"Oh wow, that sounded so romantic, what did you say? Tell me it wasn't something terribly boring. I know you said 'baby' though."

"I just told you that I've had a wonderful time with you... yada yada, and yes, I said 'baby' at the end."

"You're so sexy, French. You're so sexy all the time, but especially sexy when you're being French!"

"I'll french you in a minute if you don't stop telling me how sexy I am."

"Be my guest, Monsieur!"

Daniel takes a sip of his wine and gently wraps his hand around the back of my neck, bringing me close for a deep, righteous kiss. It's slow and rich and thoroughly indulgent. I can taste the wine on his tongue and it's even more delicious this way. As my muscles loosen, the goose-bumps run over my skin and I let out a quiet sigh. I remain pressed against his lips as I turn onto my knees in-between his legs.

"Have some more wine, please, and then kiss me again." I ask in a whisper.

Daniel does exactly as I ask and as his tongue searches mine, I taste the delicious wine on his lips and moan loudly. It's sensual... erotic, even.

"Mmm."

"You like that, baby?"

"A lot. The taste of you with the wine is... mmm. Oh, and before I forget..." I lean forward and kiss him, again, gently. "Thank you for a lovely lunch, as you wouldn't let me pay, you said you'd accept a kiss, later, so, there you go."

"You're welcome, Beatrice. Always."

We sit, quietly chatting for a short while before Tilly and Luke stumble back into the pool-house, wrapped in towels and giggling. "Hello, you two. Good swim?" I ask, amused by their boisterousness.

127

"Very, thank you. We're um... just going to shower and hit the hay..." Tilly says with a giggle, Luke holding on to her around her waist, threatening to remove her towel. These two can't keep their hands off each other! It's a good job that they're both happy with a quick fling or there would be some serious heartache in the next few days. Makes me feel very alone, I know I will be really sad and no one will be able to fully understand to comfort me. *Snap out of it, Beatrice! Here and now!*

"Sleep well," Daniel says with a grin as they both head off towards the bedroom and close the door.

"I'll just lock up and then I'll make the bed up," I say as I rise off the sofa, "are you ready to go to bed, Daniel?"

"Of course, I can't wait to have you under the covers, all to myself. But I don't want to go to sleep yet."

"Me neither, I want tonight to last forever." Sounds a little dramatic, but it's so true.

I lock the french doors and close the curtains before strolling back to the sofa where Daniel is sitting. He stands up and comes close, looking down at my face. "What would it take for me to convince you to come and live here?" he asks in all seriousness as he holds my hands in front of me.

"Oh, Daniel. I wouldn't leave Bear's, or my family, and even if I did, we could go on another four dates and then decide we're not compatible!"

"I sincerely doubt that, I wouldn't let you go without a fight, baby. But in this instance, sadly, I have to. You can't leave everything you have, just as I can't leave everything I have, here."

"Especially not as we've known each other for no time at all. It's a great shame, if things were different, we could have had a wild time together."

"You certainly drive me wild, Bea," he says, sliding his hands around to my buttocks and leaning in for a kiss. When our bodies touch, as with always, an electric current runs beneath my skin and desire drives through my veins. I bend my knee, brushing my inner thigh against his side. He grabs it and pulls me against him, groaning as I press up against his erection. I'm ready to climb his body and ravage him.

"Oh," I moan loudly, my insides waiting, impatiently. I'm hot and wet, and I need him inside me, filling me. The buzz behind my pubic bone spreads to my knees, toes, fingers... everywhere!

"Oh, baby," he mumbles into my mouth, picking up the pace of the kiss and grinding against me. He quickly turns to sit on the sofa, taking me with him, straddling him. An expertly executed manoeuvre, because somehow, we're still kissing.

I rise to my knees, either side of him and edge further forwards, lowering right against his cock. He feels so good, I grind forwards and backwards making him groan loudly, we're so in need of each other. My hands make their way down, in between my legs, to his waistband, where I unbutton and un-zip his chinos.

Daniel gently pulls back from the kiss. "Stand up."

I do as he says and he quickly follows, pulling down his chinos and swimming trunks. He removes his polo shirt so he is standing, completely naked, in front of me. His burning eyes gaze at me with such intensity, I'm surprised my clothes don't drop off of their own accord. He slowly sinks back into the sofa without taking his eyes off me. "Take your clothes off, slowly," he growls.

He seems to have lost his manners, but it's very arousing and I want so much to turn him on as much as I am right now. I slowly lift my crop top over my head and drop it to the floor. Tugging on the hair band holding the top knot in place, I let my hair tumble down my back and over my shoulders, swaying my head sexily. I hook my thumbs into the top of my pyjama bottoms and very slowly glide them down so they float to the floor, leaving me nearly naked in my purple Hanky Pankys.

"Stop," he murmurs as he sits forward, taking my hips in his hands. He runs his fingers along the wide lace 'v' on my belly and leans in to kiss my stomach. He opens his mouth and gently licks with each kiss making his way to my belly button, which he swirls his tongue around. A wave of heat works its way around my body and I close my eyes, savouring every moment of his exquisite touch. Gosh, how I want to let myself fall in love with this man, he's everything that I could ever wish for.

I run my hands through his soft hair as he gently tugs on my knickers and pulls them down.

"You're so beautiful, Bea," he whispers, kissing from one hip bone, across to the other. He holds one hand on my hip and the other brushes up the inside of my leg, from my ankle to my thigh, and further. He strokes me, gently, still kissing my belly.

I moan, needing something more but not wanting him to stop.

He takes his hand away and raises it up to my face. "Suck my fingers, baby." I take them in my mouth and run my tongue around them, sucking gently. He withdraws them, slowly, before slipping them back in-between my legs. He lightly circles my clitoris, very gently and very slowly.

My legs begin to quiver. "Oh, Daniel!" I cry, the feeling is incredible but I need him, need to feel him. "I need you, inside me," I whisper.

Daniel groans and looks up at my face. "I want to be inside you, so much." As he says it, he inserts two fingers inside me, painfully slowly and pushes them deep.

"Oh, god..." I moan, my heart pounding in my chest.

"Look at me, baby." I look down to see him watching me, observing the pleasure on my face. "You're so beautiful, I need to see you."

He twists his fingers and circles them inside me, pushing deeply, brushing that all-important spot.

"Oh, god Daniel. Please, I want to..."

"What do you want?"

"I... I want to..."

"You want to sit on me? You want to fuck me?" he whispers, seductively.

"Uh huh... Oh..."

He pushes into me again, deliciously slowly. Indulgently. "No." *What? No? What do you mean, no?!*

"I don't want you to fuck me, baby. You know what I want." *Oh.*

"Uh huh." I need him so much, I need to feel him, now. "Yes, I want to."

130

"Say it, I need to hear it, I need you so much."

"We can...I want to..."

He kisses my belly again and I close my eyes, his fingers caressing me exquisitely.

"I want to make love to you, Daniel," I whisper and I feel his smile on my skin. He slowly withdraws his fingers and pulls my hips forward so I fall astride him on my knees. He grasps my face with both of his hands and pulls me towards him. His kiss is meaningful, romantic, he is kissing me like it's the last time. I'm pretty sure we'll be kissing before he leaves for work tomorrow, but it feels like the last time for me, too.

Full of emotion, every stroke of his tongue conveys a message, excitement, sorrow, fear, anticipation, lust... it's all there, and I feel and share each one. His hands smoothly glide from my buttocks to my neck, feeling every inch of me. My hands around Daniel's gorgeous neck, I wriggle forwards until I can feel him, twitching below me, he's so hot and hard. So ready.

"Mmm," he moans, "you feel so good, you're so soft," he says reaching down to touch me, "and so wet, baby. You want me." He kisses my neck.

"Of course I want you, I want you so much, Daniel."

"You can have me, baby, always."

A wave of sadness suddenly flows through me. No one has ever made me feel the way that he does. But tonight is the last time I will ever see him like this, touch his wonderful body, kiss his soft lips, look into his beautiful eyes.

His sweet lips kissing my neck sends shivers down my spine, the lump in my throat rises and tears begin to pool in my eyes. I close them - in the hope that I can hide the emotional outburst that's beginning to take over - causing the tears to spill onto my cheeks. I rest my head on his shoulder as I wrap my arms around him. I want to feel him, I want him to be closer, nearer.

I lift so that Daniel can position himself below me, and slowly lower myself onto him. It only adds to my emotion, it feels so good, so deep and intimate, I am closer to him, in this moment, than I'll ever be again.

"Bea," Daniel whispers, "you're so special."

I lift slightly and lower myself again, grinding forwards. "Oh..." I moan, he feels so good, so deep inside me, every inch of him. I wrap my hand around his neck and pull his face to meet mine, my eyes still firmly shut.

His tongue, gentle and sweet, he moves so slowly, one hand on my waist, the other wrapped around the back of my neck. I can only hope that his eyes are closed too, because the tears are still freely falling down my cheeks. I continue to move against him as he thrusts deeper, stretching me, it's deliciously painful. I feel the build up inside and know that it won't be long until I climax around this beautiful man.

I moan into the kiss, the emotion in my voice evident. I continue to drink in every intimate sensation, coming closer and closer. The energy swirls deep inside, preparing to explode. This is so slow, so moving, so beautiful. We're really making love.

"Baby," Daniel whispers against my mouth.

I drop my head onto his shoulder, eyes closed. *Please don't look at me.*

"Baby, what's wrong?" *Oh no.*

I shake my head against Daniel's shoulder and keep moving against him, I'm seconds away.

"Please, don't cry, Bea."

"Shh, please, don't," I whisper, gently.

Daniel holds my face and kisses me deeply, his concern, so sweet in my most fragile of moments.

"Daniel," I whisper quietly against his lips, resting my forehead against his, still clenching my eyes shut, "Oh, Daniel... oh..." It's here, the whirlwind of electricity, exploding around him. The tears pour down my face and I throw my head back, still holding Daniel's neck tightly and moan loudly. "Oh god, Daniel, make love to me."

"Oh, baby," he says with a smooth, velvety voice, soothing my throbbing head. "I want to, always."

A sob escapes my throat as I wind down from an incredibly, emotionally charged orgasm. Daniel's arms wrap tightly around me and I'm pressed against his chest. My hands around his back, under his arms, holding onto him for dear life.

"Baby, are you okay?" His voice is so soothing, I could drift off to sleep, listening to him.

I nod against his chest, "Mmm hmm."

"Okay, will you tell me why you're upset?"

I shake my head, I don't want to get into all the girly emotional shit.

"Okay. If you want to talk, I'm listening."

"Thank you, Daniel. You're wonderful, I will miss you."

"Shall we make the bed up? I want you in my arms, properly."

I wipe my face dry and nod, pulling away from him.

"Are you sure you're okay?"

"I'm fine Daniel, it's just a combination of emotions and wine."

He raises an eyebrow. "Whatever you say, sweetheart."

I smile a very small, shy smile and look to the floor.

"What?"

"Nothing, you called me sweetheart, it's nice."

Daniel appears to blush a little as he removes the cushions from the sofa.

CHAPTER TEN
WEDNESDAY 19TH SEPTEMBER

That damn beeping is waking me up again, I'm so cosy and sleepy, I need sleep. *Shh.* I attempt to move and feel myself familiarly wrapped in Daniel's gorgeous, naked body. I'm reminded of our amazing evening last night.

After the 'emotional sex', we spent the rest of the night, wrapped tightly in each other's arms, talking, kissing and making real, less emotionally-charged, love. It was the most delectable, romantic evening I think I have ever had. I'm sure it'll be etched in my memory, forever.

I don't want to wake Daniel, I don't want him to leave. I have to though, or he'll be late for work. I wonder how on earth he gets himself up when he's alone, his alarm clearly doesn't do much for him.

"Daniel, it's time to get up now," I whisper, gently, kissing the smooth chest that I'm pressed up against.

"No," he grumbles, sleepily, cuddling me, tighter.

"I don't want you to go, but you'll be late for work."

"I want to stay with you."

"Me too." I squeeze him tightly and snuggle into his warm, welcoming body.

"What time is it?" he groans.

"I don't know, Daniel."

"Let's stay here forever? Please?"

I grin, lazily. "As much as I'd love to, you have to work today, and I have to return to England in a few days." Back to reality.

"No," he says in a cute, stubborn voice.

I groan, laying soft kisses all over his chest.

"I'd better turn that fucking irritating alarm off," Daniel grumbles with a loud sigh. He slides away from me, and I feel empty already, watching as he walks over to switch the alarm off, before sitting on the side of the bed to pull his polo shirt over his head.

"Oh, I was enjoying the view, I want to remember it." I pout.

"Baby, I will remember last night for a very long time, you're one very special girl. It pains me to have to let you go."

"Daniel, you're sweet. I don't want this either."

"I know. I think it's best if I just get dressed and go. No lingering or tea, I'll only find some excuse not to leave and it'll make it harder."

"Like ripping off a plaster."

"Plaster?"

"Sorry, Band Aid."

"Oh," Daniel chuckles, "yes, like that. Would you like help to make the bed, sweetheart?" *He said it again!*

I smile. "No thank you, Sexy. I think I'll probably want to get back in it once you're gone."

"Don't say that!" Daniel says, putting his face in his hands.

"Daniel, I suggest you put your trousers on and clean your teeth so I can have a good, long kiss."

"Yes, ma'am!" he responds and gets right to it.

While he's in the bathroom, I get out of bed and find the lovely nightie that Daniel bought me and my long, silk dressing gown. I finish tying the bow just as Daniel walks out of the bathroom.

"I'll just get my bits together, okay?" he asks, looking me up and down, hungrily.

"Of course, I'll go and clean my teeth." I *need* to kiss him.

When I get back, Daniel is standing by the door, holding his over-night bag. "Baby, I've got to go." He frowns and pouts. I walk directly over to him and kiss him, hard. He drops his bag to wrap his arms around me, needy, strong and fervent. His hands pressing against my body, he makes me feel so cherished. I touch every part of him that I can reach, his shoulders, his gorgeous neck, his soft hair, buttocks, chest, big strong arms... I need to know that I made the most of this last contact with my lovely, California man.

Eventually, the kiss fades and we gaze at each other for a moment.

"If you ever decide to re-locate, please, please come here and be with me?"

I smile, gosh how this man has captured me. "I promise, and if you ever decide to re-locate, call me, I know a great place where you could crash for a really long time."

"I promise."

"Well, I can see how this is going to go, so let's just get it over and done with, I'll walk you out."

We stroll slowly around to the front of the house, and as we approach Daniel's car, I feel as though I've had a swift kick in the ribs. This is it.

He opens the passenger door and tosses his bag in before leaning up against the side of the car. "Come here, baby."

I rest against him and hold him tight. "I'm going to miss you, so much, Daniel. You mean an awful lot to me, even in such a short space of time."

"Bea, you have no idea... Un jour, je viendrai à vous et vous faire le mien. Cela ne peut pas être pour toujours. Un jour, vous et moi serons ensemble et vous m'aimez comme je pense que je suis en amour avec vous, ma beau dame."

"That sounded beautiful. What did you say?"

"You really should learn to speak French, Bea."

"Okay, I'll get right to it."

"I really don't want to go, but I have to." He slides his fingers around my waist, inadvertently pulling my gown open a little, revealing the nightie. "Oh, god, Bea! What are you wearing that for? Don't you know what this is going to do to me?"

I giggle, god bless this gorgeous man. "Sorry, Daniel, at least you can remember me in this." I grin.

"I'll remember you in it, out of it, in hot bikinis, in a white dress and boots, in tight jeans and a baggy sweater in upper class... I'll remember everything, baby."

He makes my smile broaden further. "You'd better get going, before I get in that car with you."

"You, in my car, with that on? I'll have an erection all day."

I laugh, leaning to kiss him slowly and gently on the lips, before brushing his pecks with my fingertips, and reluctantly stepping back.

136

"I'll miss you, baby. Whoever gets to be with you is the luckiest guy on the planet."

"Same goes for you, sexy."

He climbs into his car and puts the roof down. "And try not to call anyone 'sexy', that's my name."

"Are you going to stop calling girls 'baby'?"

"I don't want to call anyone else, 'baby'. Only you."

"Okay, then. 'Sexy' is yours."

"Bye bye, baby."

I don't want to say it. "Bye, Daniel. Take care."

He waves, and before I know it, he's gone. I stand on Gemma's front garden in my dressing gown, staring at the spot where, just a moment ago, Daniel's car was parked. The tears tumble down my cheeks as I turn to walk back to the pool-house. Miserable, lost and empty. I'll never see that beautiful man, again. How can I never see him again? He's everything I could ever want, and so much more.

Entering the pool-house, I completely ignore Tilly making tea in the kitchen, walk over to my bed and flop down, face first, weeping like a child.

A hand rests softly on my head. "Bea, what's the matter, love? Come here." Tilly's voice is gentle and soothing. I sit up and lean against her as she puts her arm around me. "What's happened?"

"He's gone."

"Daniel? Right, to work?"

"Yes, Til, he's gone to work, but I mean he's gone, for good. We said goodbye." I sniff loudly and wipe the tears from my cheeks.

"But we're not going home for another four days, did you fight?"

"No. We decided to end it, we can't have a relationship and are starting to have strong feelings for one another. So we thought we'd stop now, you know? Like ripping off a plaster... Band Aid..." and as I say those last words, I drop my face into my hands. "Oh... Tilly, I like him so much," I mutter through my hands.

"I know you do, darling. Anyone can see that you have feelings for each other."

"He's so kind, Tilly, and he's genuine, you know? He's not bull-shitting me all the time, or playing games like men usually do. He says he has strong feelings for me and I automatically believe him, instead of questioning his motives. How can I have found my perfect man over five thousand bloody miles away? It's not fair."

"No, it's not, Bea. Listen, you'll find it at home, you'll see. You'll find someone just like Daniel who lives just down the road."

"I don't want someone 'like' Daniel, I want Daniel. Oh god," I say, wiping my face and trying to compose myself, "where's Luke?"

"Oh, he's still asleep, don't worry."

"Phew. Are you seeing him again before we go?"

"I don't know, love, we haven't talked about it, might do. I'll defo see him next time I come though, phwoar!"

I laugh, but a pang of jealousy hits me in the gut. She can see Luke whenever she wants, without getting caught up, emotionally. She can come back to LA and experience this again. She'll probably see Daniel again, too... but I won't. She might see Daniel with another girl, they might double date. The thought is too depressing.

"Til, promise me something?"

"Anything, doll."

"Next time you come, when you see Luke, can you not go on a double date with Daniel and some other girl?"

She chuckles and gives me a big hug. "Of course I won't, darling. If I see Luke next time, we won't be going on 'dates' anyway, we're fuck buddies."

"How can you be so casual about it? Aren't you getting any feelings for him? You look like you're made for each other."

"Yes, I really like him, I think he's funny and sweet, not to mention wild in the bedroom, but I am keeping my emotional distance. I won't fall for someone like Luke. We all know he wouldn't do the same for me."

"He might, Tilly, you don't know how special you are."

"That's sweet, Bea, but he likes his ladies and I am not 'special' enough to change that. I'm aware of that, so that's how I can keep my distance, emotionally. It's different for you and

Daniel, you both want each other, you both want a relationship. Luke doesn't and neither do I."

I nod, although I'm not sure she's being entirely honest. If Luke vowed to become a one woman man and asked Tilly to be his girlfriend, I think she'd go for it (if they lived near each other, that is). I think he hides behind his womanising reputation to keep himself from getting hurt, and I think Tilly's reluctance to admit that she'd like a relationship, is her cushion against the blow of rejection.

But that's my humble opinion and I might be completely wrong. Maybe I think that because I cannot comprehend why two compatible people don't want to feel love for one another.

"Now, take some deep breaths, I'm making tea, would you like one?"

"Yes, please Til. What are you doing today?"

"Ooh, well, I thought we could do the theme park?"

"That sounds fun."

"Yes, and you need to do something fun to take your mind off it."

Tilly goes to make the tea and I decide that it's time to make my bed and get ready, try to enjoy my holiday, post Daniel. I don't really want to go to a theme park, I don't want to do anything, but I'm in glorious Los Angeles and I only have a few days left, I need to make the most of it.

~~~~~~~

About an hour later, I have showered, dressed and tidied the lounge. I make myself another cup of tea and sit on the sofa, reading the first part of the trilogy I was supposed to start reading on the aeroplane, before I got distracted.

I hear the click of Tilly's bedroom door, and turn to see Luke strolling towards me. "Hey, sweet lips!"

His greeting makes me smile.

He sits next to me on the sofa, making himself very comfortable, resting his ankle on top of one knee and spreading his arms along the back.

"Hi Luke, do you want tea or breakfast?"

"No, I'm good, thanks. Tilly made some earlier. So, she says Daniel's gone?"

"Yes, he left earlier."

"And you're not seeing each other again?"

I look down. This feels awkward, having this conversation with Tilly's fuck buddy, Daniel's best friend. "Um, no. We're not planning on seeing each other anymore."

"That's such a shame, Bea. You know, he really likes you. A lot."

My heart thumps violently, thinking about him feeling that way for me. "Thank you, Luke, I like him a lot, too."

"Bea, I've known Danny for over ten years, you know we're like brothers."

"Uh huh?" Where's he going with this?

"The thing is, I've never known him to like anyone, as much as he likes you, Bea. I know I'm breaking some brotherly 'code' or whatever, by telling you this, but honestly, I think he'd probably tell you himself, given the chance."

"Luke, please, I can't hear this right now. I want to see him, believe me, but it can't happen."

"Tilly told me why you're not seeing each other again, and I get it - I do - it makes sense, but I think you're both crazy. You two are so good together."

"Not when I'm in England and Daniel is here."

"Hey, it's not my place to get involved, but if you want him or need him, he'll be there in a shot. He's a good guy. Just saying." He holds his hands up in his defense.

"I know, Luke. And thank you. Look after him."

He winks at me and smiles a gorgeous, handsome smile. I can see why Tilly likes him, he's very good looking and really sweet, like she says.

Tilly strolls out of the bedroom holding their teacups, dressed in daisy dukes and a white vest, with wet hair hanging down her back. Luke wolf whistles and jumps off the sofa to follow her to the kitchen. "Dang, you're hot!"

"So are you, Lukey," she says with a smile as she exits the kitchen, passing him.

Luke stands against the kitchen door frame, arms crossed, eyeing her up. "So, what are you girls doing today?"

"We're going to go to the theme park, fancy giving us a lift?" Tilly answers, cheekily.

"Of course I'll give you a ride. Sounds fun, can I come? Pleeeease?"

"Um..." Tilly looks in my direction, nervously. I know she's worried that I won't want to be the third wheel but doesn't want to say 'no' to Luke.

"Of course you can, Luke," I reply, I know she wants him there, and he is great company. I'll just have to deal with him reminding me of Daniel all day. *Joy.* "But I have one rule, girls and boys," I add.

Luke's grin is contagious, he's really excited! He's like a little boy.

"Don't make me feel like a spare part."

"Of course not, Bea, I can't think of anything better than having two of the hottest, British girls in California, on my arm for the day."

~~~~~~~

By about six, we're in the car, driving home. It has been a fun day, Luke has been the most wonderful friend, not once did he and Tilly make me feel like a gooseberry. He treated us both like princesses and had us laughing all day. God bless that lovely man.

There were a few times, throughout the day, when I just wanted to curl up in a ball, but Luke somehow managed to pull me out of it and make me have fun. He really is a great guy, just like Daniel said, I just can't see how Tilly isn't falling for him.

"Do you girls want to grab a bite to eat? I'd love to take you out for dinner."

"That sounds fun, what do you think, Bea?" Tilly asks.

I don't want to go out, I want to go home, read a little and curl up in bed. I have managed to have fun today and it has been great, but right now, I just want to be on my own. "I don't really fancy going out, but you two go, I'm looking forward to reading my book in bed."

"I'll come with you, we can go out another night, can't we Luke?"

"No! Tilly, I want you two to go out and have fun, I'm fine on my own, you know I like my own space sometimes. Please, go and have fun."

"Are you sure, Bea?"

"One hundred percent, please. Have fun, you two, I'll be fine."

"Hey, Bea. Tilly and I can always stay at my place tonight, give you some time alone?" Luke says, and that's exactly what I was hoping for, the last thing I need is to hear them having sex.

"That sounds good. Thank you, Luke."

He drops me back at the house and they head straight out. As I walk into the pool-house, I take a deep breath and enjoy the silence, alone with my thoughts. I lock the doors, go to the bathroom to run myself a bath and then pour a glass of red wine. Sitting down on the sofa, I take a long sip and stretch my legs out to the coffee table.

I close my eyes and emotion fills me. It has been such a busy day, Luke and Tilly haven't given me a chance to get upset, but now that I'm alone, unwinding, the tears fill my eyes. Why is it so hard to stop thinking about him? I cling on to the hope that it'll get easier every day. I don't know what's wrong with me, it's not like we've been dating for months and just broke up.

My bath is so wonderfully relaxing, dunking my head under the water - it's like washing away some of the sadness, refreshing my soul.

I do feel better, strolling around the pool-house with no make-up on, clean, wet hair hanging down my back, nightie and dressing gown on, cosy and comfortable. I make up the bed, ready for me to curl up, with my iPhone, ready to read.

I lay tucked up, unable to concentrate on my book. It's everything I love in a book, raunchy, romantic, sexy, but I can't stop thinking about raunchy romantic, sexy stuff with Daniel. I'm holding my iPhone, wanting so much to call him, hear his deep voice, tell him how much I want him laying here with me. I almost wish I'd never met him, because at least then, I wouldn't know. I wouldn't crave him, need him, love... no, no. It's far too soon for all that, I'm upset and thinking irrationally, my emotions are on the extreme.

I stay strong, managing not to contact him. I curl up on 'Daniel's side' and drift off to sleep. Every time I stir, I can smell him on the pillow and it sends me back into another restless dream about him. I keep thinking I can hear his alarm, beeping, but as soon as I open my eyes, it's gone.

CHAPTER ELEVEN
THURSDAY 20TH SEPTEMBER

"Bea... Bea, wake up, love, it's okay."

I stir as a sob bursts out of my chest. A hand rubs my back, soothingly. I'm crying? Tilly leans down to hug me. "It's okay, Bea, what were you dreaming about?"

"Um," I sniff and wipe the tears from my face with both hands, "I didn't know I was crying. I was dreaming about him."

"Oh, doll, you've got it bad, haven't you? Are you okay now?"

"Yes, thanks. I'm fine. I didn't know you were home, what time is it?"

"About ten."

"Oh, I slept for ages, although I did wake up a lot, during the night."

"I should have stayed with you."

"No, Tilly, I wanted to be on my own, I was quite pleased that the two of you stayed at Luke's, no offence."

Tilly giggles, "None taken. What would you like to do today? I'd like to see Jack for a bit, I haven't spent much time with him, but we could do something else as well?"

"I think I'd like a day chilling out around here, if that's okay with you. Maybe a pool day? I can try to get into my book and get over hot stuff."

"Good idea."

"How was last night? Did you have fun?" I ask genuinely interested and wanting to hear all the goss.

"It was good, thank you."

"Hey! Don't hold back on the details just because I'm miserable. I want to know!"

Tilly grins and climbs into bed with me, and we talk about what she and Luke got up to last night. This is exactly what I need, chilling in bed with one of my best friends, chatting and giggling about her new, temporary lover-boy. We stay there for at least an hour before Tilly makes us both a cuppa and gets back into bed. She knows what I need.

I managed to pull myself out of bed and throw on a bikini, and of course, some mascara, before heading out to the pool for a relaxing day of floating, sunbathing and reading. Tilly had her play time with Jack, which she was so looking forward to. She's great with him, a fantastic Auntie and a natural with kids. I'm surprised she doesn't talk about wanting kids, she doesn't seem interested, but she's just so good with them.

I dozed a little on the lilo, attempted to read my iBook by the side of the pool and caught a few rays. I probably don't need to mention that I thought of Daniel every second of every minute of the day.

That evening, Gemma and Jay prepared another sumptuous barbecue meal, the table was covered in delicious meats and salads. It was wonderful, if only I could eat. I put a little salad and couscous on my plate and picked at it, but I couldn't stomach anything more than a few mouthfuls. I excused myself once everyone seemed to have finished and went to sit alone, in the quiet of the pool-house.

I close my eyes and put my head between my knees, I can't bear this feeling, my stomach hurts, my chest hurts and nothing will make it go away. I curl into a ball, close my eyes, and let the tears fall. *Good god, why am I being such a crybaby over all of this?*

CHAPTER TWELVE
FRIDAY 21ST SEPTEMBER

"Wakey, wakey, rise and shine, I can see your bot-bot!" Tilly chirps, cheerily.

I groan and throw the covers over my bottom, I must remember to wear my pj bottoms tonight. "Morning," I say, yawning and rubbing my eyes, they're sore and swollen from all the crying. And the kick in the gut strikes again. *Oh.*

"You slept quite late again today, sweet cheeks, it's quarter past ten."

"Ugh, I feel like I've had two hours."

"Hey, I had an idea." She sits next to me on my bed and hands me a cup of tea. "I spoke to Gemma earlier and we thought it'd be nice if we had a night out tonight, go for some drinks and dancing. They're getting a sitter so we can all have a fun night out."

"That sounds good, Tilly."

"Oh, a little more enthusiasm please, Beatrice! I thought we could go to Beverly Hills today, have a spot of lunch, treat ourselves to a fabulous outfit for tonight, and then come home, get dolled up and hit the tiles. Doesn't that sound fun?"

Initially, the idea of a night out was just 'okay', but now that I've heard the plan for the day, I want to kiss her. She really is trying to take my mind off everything and this sounds perfect. "That does sound wonderful, Til, thank you. How exciting!" Taking a sip of tea, I continue. "Aren't you seeing Luke tonight then?"

"Bea, he's not my boyfriend, you know. But no, we texted this morning, I said I wanted some girly time with you, and he's going to stay in with Daniel tonight, have some bromance time or whatever it is boys do, I'd rather not know," she says with a giggle.

The thud in the chest returns with a vengeance.

~~~~~~

It's twelve o'clock, and Tilly and I are strolling down Rodeo Drive, popping in and out of beautiful shops. I saw a pair of shoes that I loved, a beautiful dress in Dolce and

Gabbana, some super sexy, red sandals, a red jumpsuit and a black cocktails dress all from Valentino. I want everything, but it's all massively over budget. We decide - as we haven't found a dress that we like for less than a grand, on Rodeo Drive - to head to Neiman Marcus and see what we can find there.

It feels like I've tried on about four hundred dresses in Neiman Marcus, and I am in love with *everything*. As crappy as I feel about Daniel, shopping has really cheered me up somewhat, especially as I've told myself that I can have a treat on my credit card. When I get home to the UK, I'm going to have to eat cereal for breakfast, lunch and dinner to repay all the money I've spent. *Oh well.*

We both finally pick our dresses; Tilly chooses a grey, sequin dress. It's short with elbow length sleeves and is covered in large grey/black sequins. She looks stunning in it and in accentuates her gorgeous legs.

My dress is *amazing* and I adore it. It's a short, cream dress, covered with silvery beads and trimmed around the bottom with ostrich feathers. It is fitted and has a round, low back, and it fits me perfectly. I have never worn such a pretty dress, and too bloody right, it's costing me a small fortune! I found a matching, beaded clutch bag and Tilly has gone all out and bought a seriously expensive, beautiful, pewter clutch. I mean, we like to shop... a lot, and we have bought many a thing that was over budget before, but I'm not sure I planned to spend quite this much. But sod it, I'm having a fun night out in Hollywood tonight, and I've been feeling like total shit, so I'm going to treat myself and fucking enjoy it.

Tilly bought a pair of grey, high heeled pumps that match her dress perfectly, and I'm torn between some ridiculously expensive Manolo Blahnik silver glittery heels, and some nude, suede heels that I saw on Rodeo Drive.

"Manolo's!" Tilly shouts, enthusiastically.

"You would say that, they're the most expensive!"

"How much?"

"Six-fifty... quid, not dollars!"

"Do it, treat yourself, they'll last forever. Otherwise we have to walk all the way down to Rodeo Drive again. Buy them and let's eat, we haven't had anything since breakfast."

"Sod it, I love them. They're mine!"

"Yay! We're going to look hot, hot, hot!"

We find somewhere small and low-key to have lunch, and then the wonderful Gemma comes to collect us. It's amazing how fast time flies when you're shopping. As soon as we get home, we start to get ready. This constant distraction it's keeping me pre-occupied, Daniel is still on my mind all the time, but I don't have time to dwell.

~~~~~~~

Gemma knocks on the door as I'm applying my make-up. "Margaritas, ladies! Woohoo!"

"Oh, yum! Thank you. You look gorgeous, Gemma!" I say, taking the drink from her. She is wearing a short, purple, chiffon dress with heavy ruffles at the bottom and sheer cap sleeves, with matching purple heels.

"Thank you, Bea, you haven't seen me dolled up for quite a while."

"And you still look as lovely as you did the last time, if not, even more so."

"Thank you, sweetness. What are you wearing, not that I hope!" she says, pointing to my dressing gown.

"No, I'm wearing the fabulously expensive dress and Manolo's I bought today, can't wait!"

Tilly comes out of the bedroom looking incredible.

"Wow!" Gemma and I cry, in unison. "Tilly, you look stunning!" I add.

"Thank you. Bea, you'd better hurry up love."

"Oh I won't be long, just finishing my face and then all I need to do is get my dress on."

"Well spit spot," she says, as they both head out onto the deck, to wait for me to finish.

I take a deep breath and exhale through pursed lips, trying to push the sad thoughts of Daniel out of my mind. Beautifying myself isn't fun, knowing that he won't see me. I don't want to feel sexy unless he's there. But I need to snap out of this and feel good about myself. I can always pretend.

I apply the last coat of mascara and look in the mirror. My eyes are dark and sultry, my tanned cheeks slightly rouged and my lips blood-red. I'm not kissing anybody, so I will make the most of lipstick tonight. I slip into my dress and put on my

148

beautiful new shoes, before grabbing my clutch and margarita, and heading outside.

"Wow, Bea! You look fucking gorgeous!" Tilly shouts, almost choking on her drink.

"Thanks Til, I feel nice. Too bloody right, I can't believe I spent so much!"

"It's totally worth it, you look stunning, darling," Gemma says, sweetly as she kisses my cheek, "how are you feeling?"

"I'm okay thanks, Gem, don't be too nice to me, though, I might cry."

"Okay then, bitch, let's go."

I laugh, although I'm still crying inside, all I want is to cling onto Daniel's arm and stroll out with him right now.

"So where are we going, anyway?" I ask in the cab on the way.

"We thought we'd go to the 'W' Hotel in Hollywood. Jay knows someone having a 'do' in the club there tonight and we're on the guest list. I like the Living Room bar downstairs, so maybe we can go there first and see how it goes." Gemma replies.

"Sounds good to me."

We pull up outside the 'W' and clamber out of the car awkwardly in our short dresses, trying to remain elegant. Gemma and Jay walk ahead of us, towards the hotel, hand in hand. I watch them, looking at each other and laughing, wishing that Daniel and I could do that. How lucky they are, to have found each other, and be able to have each other.

"Hey! Snap out of it," Tilly scolds. "Here, hold my hand. I'll be your lover for this evening." She holds out her hand and gives me a sympathetic smile. I hold onto it, and she leans into me for a moment as we walk towards the entrance. "Love you," she says, quietly.

"Love you, too, Tilly. Don't be nice."

"Slag."

"Bitch," I respond, smiling.

"Whore."

"Thank you, love you."

We enter the Living Room bar and take the few steps down to the lower, main area. To the right of us is an amazing,

149

huge white spiral staircase with red carpet and a clear, sheet surround. It's fabulous. We sit in one of the clusters of leather sofas, and Jay goes to the bar to get the drinks. I wish Daniel was near. I want him to see me looking hot, I want him to see my madly expensive dress - I know he'd love it, and my sexy Manolo's. *Stop it, Beatrice. Stop torturing yourself.*

I get that jab-in-the-ribs sensation again and feel a little sick. Gemma and Tilly are talking about the last time they ate in the restaurant here, but I can only look through them, pretending to be listening, I can't concentrate at all.

"Ladies!" Jay snaps me out of my daze, arriving back at the table with an ice bucket and four champagne flutes.

"I couldn't remember all of those cocktails, so I just got champagne. Okay?" He puts the ice bucket down on the table, the yellow label glowing through the ice. Just what the doctor ordered.

"That's even better than cocktails, Jay. Thank you," Tilly says.

"I thought you'd say that, you and your sister are like peas in a pod," he says, pouring the weightless bubbles into tall flutes.

"Happy Hollywood Friday!" Tilly toasts, and we all take a sip.

I sink my glassful quickly, and before I know it, it's topped up. It's wonderfully refreshing, and my second glass is gone, just as fast. "I'll go and get another one," I say, pointing to the down-turned bottle.

"Bea, just get the cheaper stuff, this is like, over two hundred, and that's one of the less expensive ones here," Tilly says.

"Okay, as long as you're all happy with that?"

Everyone nods in agreement and I stroll to the bar to order the champagne. When I return, I place the bucket on the table and Jay begins to pour.

"I am going to stand, I think, I feel much more comfortable standing, and I get to show off my dress," I tell the girls.

"Good idea, I keep worrying that I'm bending my sequins!" Tilly says as she joins me.

There is a great atmosphere in here, it's quite busy, but not so much that people are pressed up against each other, and although I can't stop thinking about Daniel, I am enjoying myself a little.

My third glass goes down swiftly, and I head to the loo feeling the tiniest bit lightheaded. I don't need the loo, but I want a moment alone to check my make-up and gather my thoughts. I lean forwards onto the vanity, closing my eyes and taking a deep breath. I so want to cry but I will *not* ruin my make-up.

After a few moments, I stand straight, take my lipstick out and add another coat. I do look good, even if I say so myself. I pull all of my hair over one shoulder and puff it up a little before walking out, refreshed and confident. On the outside, anyway.

When I get back to Tilly, she has a small group of men surrounding her. No surprise there, she looks amazing, always does.

"Bea!" she calls as I walk towards her, "This is my friend, Beatrice." She hands me a glass of champagne. "These gentlemen kindly bought us another bottle of bubbly."

"Thank you very much," I say as I make eye contact with each of them, reluctantly.

Tilly introduces me to them, individually; how she remembered their names I've no idea. The last guy to shake my hand will not stop staring at me, he's really quite attractive, but he's not my type, at all. He's also, not Daniel. Tilly continues to talk to the other three while the remaining man continues to gawk. Marcus, I think his name is.

"You're very attractive, Beatrice." *Oh god, here we go. Fuck off.*

"Thank you, you look nice too."

"Thanks Hun. So, how long have you been in LA?" *Ugh... hun? I hate that with a passion.*

"Um, we've been here since Friday. A week."

"And you've enjoyed yourself?"

"Yes, it's been wonderful, thank you." All I can think is that I want Daniel. I want *him* here talking to me, not this prat. I want to feel Daniel's breath on my ear, not squirm every time I feel this man's warmth near my skin. There is nothing

151

that wrong with this Marcus guy, but he called me hun... and he stares... and I think he thinks he's getting somewhere. He's not.

"So, are you staying locally?"

"I'm not entirely sure where it is, it's about fifteen minutes drive away." I know that I'm giving very blunt answers, but I just don't want to talk to him! Could he get the hint and go chat up someone who might be interested?

"You really are stunning, Beatrice," he says as his puts his hand on the small of my back. I feel nauseous.

"Thank you, could you excuse me for one moment, please?" I walk away to the loo again, and lean against a wall. I can't do this. I want Daniel chatting me up, I want Daniel's hand on my back. I want Daniel! I'm tipsy, feeling lost and in serious need of a little boost. Getting chatted up would normally do it for me, but now it only repulses me. I want to hear from him, I want to make contact... *Can I?* What harm can it do? I won't be seeing him, just sending him a little text. Just a text. That's okay isn't it?

I pull my phone out of my clutch and start to type.

~

21 Sep 22:56
I'm out, dressed up in a beautiful new dress and gorgeous, expensive shoes, but all I can think about is you. I wish you were here with me. I miss you so much already. I'm also really tipsy, which is why I'm texting you. I've been so strong, up until now. Whoops :-/ I want to touch you and kiss you and hear you and... other stuff, you. I miss you, Sexy Berkeley. Xxxxxxxxxx

~

I hit send. Fuck it, why not? And I suddenly realise, what if he doesn't reply? I'm going to feel like complete and utter shit, that's what. *Oh dear, What have I done?*

I open the toilet door and stroll back towards Tilly, she's still with those bloody men. I consider going to sit with Gemma and Jay, but they're cosy on the sofa, engrossed in an obviously private conversation. *Great, Marcus it is.*

152

As I arrive back, he turns and offers me a great big smile. It's a very nice smile, but does nothing for me, so he might as well give it a rest.

"Hey, beautiful." Oh god, please do shut up.

"Hello." I take a sip of my champagne and look around the room, in the hope that he'll stop talking to me. I catch Tilly's eye and she holds a finger up, politely, at the man she's talking to and leans in towards me.

"Everything okay?" she asks into my ear, the music louder now.

"Yes thanks, he's just... not, you know..." I pull a face and she knows exactly what I mean.

"Oh, no. I agree, but they're buying and they're quite nice guys so I'm just chatting. Not... like 'that'."

"Good, unfortunately, I don't think this guy gets that."

"Okay, we'll break away in a bit once we've finished the champas."

I nod and smile as she returns to her conversation. I wonder if Daniel has replied, and just as I'm about to think of something to say to Marcus, my clutch vibrates.

As I take my phone from my bag, I get a swarm of butterflies in my belly and pray that it's a message from him. I see his name and smile automatically as I stroll over to the bar to read it. I put my champagne down and focus on my phone.

~

Daniel 21 Sep 23:04
Baby, I want to touch you too. I can't tell you how much I want to 'other stuff' you. I'm miserable. Don't get too drunk baby, please be careful. Do you need a ride home? I can't drive because I've been drinking but I will get you a car. Let me know. Thinking about you day and night. I miss you, too. So much. Xxxxxx

~

153

I clutch my phone to my chest and smile. I'm so happy that he replied, and that he feels the same. He's worried about me too, god bless him. I quickly reply.

~

21 Sep 23:06
Thank you, but I'm okay, we're out with Gem
and Jay, so we'll get a cab together,
later. Thank you for caring. I wonder what
these 'W' rooms are like. I'd like to book one
for you and I to be dirty in... or should I say...
'make love'? Wanna have text sex? ;-)
xxxxxxxxxx

~

Crikey, I must be drunk! But who cares, I can't meet up with him, why not have some text sex. I grab my glass and take a big gulp before returning to Tilly and 'the men'. I make small talk with dick-head, finding it hard to hide my joy at having been in contact with my California man. I hope Marcus doesn't think it's directed at him.

My phone vibrates again and I check it, a thrill running through me.

~

Daniel 21 Sep 23:12
Are you in Drai's????Fuck text
sex, I wanna have SEX SEX! I
miss your body. Xxxxxx

~

~

21 Sep 23:13
Drai's? I don't think so, we're in a hotel
lounge. I've had some dreary bloke chatting
me up and all I can think of is you. Sex sex?
Yes please. If you were here, I'd tear your
clothes off and straddle you on one of these
sofas. I want you so much. :-(I'm also very
drunk and will be annoyed, tomorrow, that I
gave in to a moment of temptation. This will
hinder my progress! I want to have you, here.
I want your arms around me. I want you to
kiss me. Xxxxxxx.

154

~

I put my iPhone back in my clutch and look back at the group, smiling at my own, private thoughts. Marcus tops up my glass and starts to talk again. *Ugh, fuck off!*

"So, who are you texting, hun? You seem to have perked up,"

None of your fucking business, you nosey little shit. And stop fucking calling me hun! "Oh, I'm sure you don't know them. I am perfectly fine, thank you, perky as ever."

Vibration!!! I pull my phone out again. "Excuse me, please," I say to the nosey shit and turn to read my text.

~

Daniel 21 Sep 23:18
Tell the poor man to leave you alone, if you're in need while you're in LA, you're mine. He's got good taste, though. How much do you want me? I need to know. Tell me what you're wearing. I bet you look so hot, as always. I want to kiss you too, EVERYWHERE. Baby, baby, baby, baby xxxxx

~

21 Sep 23:20
I wish I was yours. I want you so much. I am wet just thinking of you. I'm telling you this because I'm drunk. I'll be really embarrassed tomorrow, but I don't care. I'm wearing a short, cream dress with beads and feathers to tickle you with. I have glittery high heels on, which I'd like to see locked behind your back. You like? Sexy, sexy Daniel. Xxx I feel so naughty xxx

~

Oh gosh, I do feel naughty, but so good. Maybe I do need to keep in contact with him, by text. Maybe that'll make it easier, but it does make me want him. So much. I head back to slimy Marcus and he starts his annoying talking again, the volume in here has risen yet again, so he has to practically shove his mouth in my ear. *Bleugh.*

As he leans in, he puts his hand on the small of my back and pulls me close to him. I want to push him away but, politely, I wait to let him finish whatever it is he wants to say.

"So, you know what I think? I think you should stop texting whatever guy you're texting and let me take you home. The things I wanna do to you little lady."

What...The fuck? Did he really just say that? I want to punch his revolting little head in, how dare he be so fucking presumptuous. Just as I'm about to pull away from him and give him a piece of my mind, he shouts, "Berkeley! Great to see you!"

Berkeley? Not my Berkeley? No, it can't be... can it? I spin to see my Daniel stood right there in front of me. *Oh god, my gorgeous hero, I love... No, shh. You don't, Beatrice.* He looks... *Oh,* angry, really angry.

"Get the fuck off of her, Marcus," he yells, his face red, his eyes full of fury.

Yes, get the fuck off me Marcus! Hang on, they know each other? I pull away from him and Daniel swiftly pulls me into his side, clinging on to my waist for dear life.

"Berkeley, calm down, do you know this beautiful lady? We were just getting well acquainted, weren't we hun?" he says, winking at me.

"Don't fucking go near her again, do you hear me you fucking son of a bitch?"

Oh my god, what the hell is going on? I look over to Tilly who is gawking at Daniel. We both exchange confused looks and then her expression completely changes as Luke appears.

"Gentlemen, I'm afraid you'll have to find other company. I'd like my lady back now, if you don't mind," he says with a smile to the other three chaps.

Marcus and Daniel still staring at each other, Daniel's free hand, in a fist at his side.

"Hey, Daniel, no need to get shirty. So this is whose texts have been making your cheeks flush, huh? You're fucking Daniel Berkeley, well I never," he directs at me. I'm going to hit him!

"Who the fuck do you think you're talking to, you little prick? You don't talk about her like that, do you understand? Know what's good for you, you arrogant little shit, and fuck off. Now."

Marcus smiles, disgustingly at Daniel and fury boils in my blood, I'm not sure whether it's the alcohol I've consumed or the anger at the way this man is talking to Daniel, but I snap. I hurl my hand, at the speed of lightening into his face, and it really fucking hurts! *Ow!*

Marcus immediately cups the side of his face with his hands and laughs. "Shit, she's got a mean fist, my friend. You got a good one there, Danny boy. Call me when you fuck up, I'll gladly fill your shoes." He laughs as he walks off. I'm shaking, I want to chase him and sink my stiletto heel into his head, the cocky, fucking bastard.

Daniel loosens his grip on my waist and turns to look at me, wary, "You okay?"

"Yes, I'm fine, I didn't realise that'd hurt as much as it did, I've never done that before."

"You shouldn't have, he's a worthless piece of shit. Let me see your hand."

I show him the palm of my hand and he lifts it to his lips and kisses it. Oh heavens above, Daniel is here. Here! "How... when? How long have you been here?"

"I only just came in here and saw the two of you. You looked... cosy."

"Oh god, Daniel, no. It was *so* not like that, I was just about to push him away and tell him to knob off, he's such an idiot! How do you know him?"

"Oh, from a long time ago, it's a long story, we don't get along."

"No shit. You seem... off-ish, are you annoyed with me?"

"I... I just saw that prick with his arm around you and his face in your hair and thought you... you know."

"Please don't think that, Daniel, I have been trying to get away from him for ages. He had literally just pulled me against him when you arrived. Thank god you did, you saved me."

"Sorry, baby. I don't mean to be pissed at you, I know he's an asshole. You look... incredible, baby. Wow!" He stands back and looks me up and down.

"I am so happy to see you Daniel," I say as I look into his beautiful eyes, a warm feeling spreads over my skin.

"Hey! Bea, that was some slap! Way to go!" Luke high fives my good hand. "He's such an asshole, Danny, don't let him get to you."

"I won't, thanks bud. Hey, Tilly."

"Hi, Daniel! I'm very surprised to see you two here, you seem to be everywhere we go!"

"Actually, Bea was texting me and mentioned where she was, I live... well, I live here."

"Here?" I ask. *In a hotel?*

"Yes, in the residences, I own an apartment here."

"Oh! So that's how you got here so quickly! What a co-incidence, I was texting you from downstairs all the time!"

Daniel turns and notices Gemma and Jay on the sofa. "Gemma, I'm sorry, I didn't see you there, hi. You must be Jay? I'm Daniel."

Jay stands to shake Daniel's hand. "Hi, Daniel, good to meet you," Jay says before returning his attention to his wife.

"I think I could use a drink, champagne anyone?" Daniel says with a smile. He clutches my hand, taking me with him to the bar and leans against it, pulling me close to kiss my neck. "You look so beautiful, baby. I've missed you," he says, nuzzling his face into my hair. "And you smell so good."

Goosebumps spread like wildfire and my stomach flips. *Feels so good...*"So do you, Daniel, you always do. I slept on your side of the bed so that I could smell you last night. And the night before."

He pulls away suddenly and gapes at me. "Really?"

Oh god, I should stop drinking if I insist on talking. "Umm..." I frown and smile hesitantly, "yes?"

He smiles that stunning smile with the teeth and the lips and the eyes. Oh god, he's lush.

"I like that."

"Daniel, I am a bit drunk, as you already know, and am likely to get more drunk. I am saying things that I wouldn't

158

usually say, sober, so please ignore the embarrassing things, remember the good things and stop me if I go too far. Okay?"

"Absolutely, baby."

"I really wasn't interested in him you know, it's only you. I can't see how I'll ever be able to meet anyone else and not compare them to you."

"Whoa, you really do talk, don't you."

"Oh god." I smack my hand over my mouth in a bid to shut myself up.

"No, baby, no. It's good. I want to hear it, it has been awful these past couple days. I can't bear to hear you talk about meeting someone else." He shakes his head, looking down. "And I don't want anyone else, I only want you."

"But one day we will meet other people, Daniel, we can't be together. Yes, we could have text sex and talk on the phone at certain times of the day, but it won't last if we can't touch each other and kiss each other, see each other."

"Bea," he says, kissing my lips softly, "baby," and again. I wipe my lipstick off his lips with a smile, red lipstick was a bad idea! "Please, let's not talk about meeting other people. I didn't expect to see you again, and then you texted me, saying you were right downstairs. Wherever you were, I'd have come to you. You know that? While we're together, let's make the most of it. You are the only woman to make me feel... this. I'm besotted."

Tears pool in my eyes. This beautiful man, who I have been pining after and crying over for the past two days, has just said *that*. Oh shit, I'm... falling.

I take a couple of deep breaths to compose myself. I look him in the eye and kiss him tenderly, meaningfully. I want to say how I feel, like this. No matter how drunk I get, I'll never admit this feeling. That would make everything so much harder and he'd probably freak out and run a mile.

"Hey, Daniel, it's a week."

"Since we met? I know, who'd have thought I could feel the way I do, in just a week. With anyone else, I'd have had one date, possibly two by now. But You? You're something else."

"Daniel, I'm so, so happy to see you, but I'm still going home, please don't make it harder."

"I know, baby. So anyway, in your texts, you said you wanted my arms around you." He wraps his arms around me. "And you said you wanted to kiss me." He pulls me close and kisses me. A soft, slow, gorgeous kiss. I close my eyes and the hairs prick up on my arms.

He nuzzles my hair and whispers in my ear, "And you also said that if I was here, you'd rip my clothes off and straddle me on the sofa... how are my chances, baby?"

I open my eyes and grin at him. God he's breathtaking. "Well, I'm sure the women and gay men in here would love me to strip you naked, however, I think I'd cross a line by straddling and fucking you senseless. Maybe we can do that later?"

"Mmm, I want it now."

"Oh, me too, but we have people waiting for champagne, so we better deliver."

"Quite right, baby."

He flags down the barman who comes running.

"Mr. Berkeley, yes sir?"

"Two bottles of Dom Pérignon and six glasses, to that table, please," he says, pointing at our table and the barman nods and gets straight to it. *Hmm, sexy*.

Daniel continues to hold me around my waist as we re-join Tilly and Luke by the sofa. One of my favourite songs is playing in the background, 'Underwater Love' by Smoke City. It's sexy and smooth, another piece of music to 'make love to', as Daniel likes to put it.

"Daniel, can you speak Portuguese?"

He frowns and grins at me, "No, just French, why?"

"I just wondered, I love this song and I think some of the lyrics are Portuguese, I don't know what they mean."

"Oh, sorry, I have no idea. It's very sexy though, I like it."

"And do you like my dress, Daniel?" I do a turn to show him the whole thing.

"Bea, You are the most beautiful woman in here, that dress is stunning, you look incredible in it, but you could wear a sack and look like a princess. I love the feathers at the bottom, I want to run my fingers beneath them." As he says it, he runs his hand up my thigh and under the back of my dress, skimming the bottom of my buttock.

"Daniel! Stop that!"

He grins, salaciously, "Okay, baby, later. And you can keep those shoes on later too. I can't wait to get you to myself. I was planning a night in with Luke and now look at me, down here with my hot, British beauty. You'd better prepare yourself."

I lean in and whisper in his ear, "Why, what are you going to do to me? Because I know you don't like 'fucking' me anymore..."

He closes his eyes and presses my body against his, his cheek pressed against mine. I sway my hips against him in rhythm to the music. " I'm going to make such sweet love to you, all night, good, hard, deep love. I am going to touch you and make you come, I'm going to kiss you and make you come, I'm going to fill you and make you come. Baby, you're so hot, and tonight, you're all mine. I'm going to make sure you know it."

Oh, fuck me now you beast! Could I be any hornier? A lascivious smile spreads across my face; I grind into his body and stroke his neck with my hand.

"Daniel," I murmur in his ear, "I know it already; I'm wet and aching for you. I want you now, I want to touch you, I want to feel how hard you are inside me. Please, let's go, I need you to... make ... love to me."

"Oh god, baby, you've got me horny as fuck. We can't go, we're with people, and I can't move, I have a huge erection!"

"Mmm, can I feel?"

"Bea, please, I promise, it'll be worth the wait. It certainly will be for me."

"Good. Until then, hold me?"

"Of course." He tightens his arms around my waist, nuzzling his face into my neck. I slip my hands around his back and enjoy every second of this closeness, how I have longed for this. I don't want to let go, he's all I want. With a few drinks in me, I can quite happily stick two fingers up to the UK and the business, if it meant I could stay in this man's arms forever. God, I am in so much deeper than I ever thought

I would be, I knew I had strong feelings for him, but I never thought I'd be feeling *this*. I want him to want me, forever. I want him to love me. *Jesus*.

We manage to stop canoodling and converse with the others. Tilly and Luke are all over one another, we look like three, happy, long-term couples. No one would know that Daniel and I have known each other for just a week, and will never see each other again after Sunday, or that Tilly and Luke are merely, temporary fuck buddies.

"We're going to head up to the party in Drai's, do you guys fancy coming?" Jay asks.

I smirk at my dirty thoughts and whisper in Daniel's ear, "I know I fancy coming. All over you." *Good lord, is it the drink that's doing this to me? I need to shut my filthy mouth.*

"And you will, baby. All night." He winks at me.

"Drai's sounds good to me, Tilly?" Luke responds.

"Yep, I'm up for a party."

"Let's go on up, then," Daniel adds and we all make our way towards the club. He holds my hand and raises it to his lips as we walk. "So where did you go to get that outfit? You look beautiful."

"Thank you. I love it. We went to Beverly Hills, I found loads of stuff I liked on Rodeo Drive, but it was all too expensive, even this cost a fortune but it wasn't as much as the other things that I liked. And I've never spent so much on shoes before, but aren't they gorge?"

"*Gorge*, baby. I wish I'd have been there; I'd have bought you everything. Tell me if you want to go again before you leave?"

"Daniel, you're too sweet, but it's fine, thank you. I'm happy with what I got."

"I want to spoil you; I want to buy you gifts."

"Spoil me with you. That's all I need."

"I can't wait. In fact, can we join the others in a moment, I need to kiss you."

"Even with this bright red lipstick on?"

"Even with the lipstick," he says, his eyes glued to my lips. "We'll catch you up in a minute," he calls to Luke as he walks us over to the wall, turning my back to it and pressing me against it. He runs his fingers down my cheek and leans in so that his face is brushing against mine. He whispers in my ear and my eyes close in anticipation. "Kiss me, baby, please? You look so beautiful, you're mine tonight and I need you." His hand slides behind my neck and pulls my face towards him. My lips parted, ready for him. His bottom lip skims mine and I can feel his warm breath against my mouth, I sigh as tingles flow under my skin.

I reach my arms up and around his neck, tilting my head and pressing my lips against his. He reciprocates, pressing his body firmly against me, opening his mouth to introduce his skilful tongue. He moves slowly and sensually, it's romantic and so arousing. I moan as we pick up the pace a little, I can't get enough. His hand slides around to my backside and he grabs my buttock through my dress and squeezes it hard, pressing my groin against his thigh.

"Ah..." God, that feels good.

"Oh, baby," he mumbles against my lips and pulls away, gently.

"Please, Daniel, don't make me wait, let's go to yours. I want you to feel what you're doing to me," I whisper, breathlessly.

"Are you getting hot for me?"

"That's putting it mildly. I'm hot, wet and need you there, now."

"Need me where, baby?" he asks as he kisses my neck.

"Oh god, Daniel, I need to moan, I need to make noise, please let's go."

"Need me where, baby?" he repeats, sternly.

"I need you inside me. Please, I want to go, I want you to take my clothes off, I want to put my hands on your naked body, I want you to touch me," I whisper, breathlessly, lifting my head to give his soft lips easier access to my throat. His hand still against my buttock and his leg in between mine, pressing his thigh against me, there. I want to grind against it, although if I do, I'll come in a matter of seconds.

"Let's go." He looks me in the eye and smiles.

"To yours?"

"No, to the club." No, no, no! I need to get some Daniel sex!

"Daniel, no!"

"Come on, baby, we can continue this later."

"Can we at least go to yours so I can check my make-up? I must have lipstick all around my mouth, because you do..." I say as I run my thumb along his lips.

"You won't try to get me naked?"

"Cross my heart. I'll sort my lipstick and we'll go. I hope we don't see many people on the way, I must look awful!"

"You could never look awful, Bea, and you don't have lipstick everywhere."

"I'll just touch up."

As we wait for the lift, my drunken honesty makes a come-back. "Daniel?"

"Yes, sweetheart?"

"I love it when you call me that. My mum calls us sweetheart."

"So, you like it when I talk to you like your mom?" He frowns and I giggle.

"Well, no, but she loves me more than anything in the world, so when anyone calls me sweetheart, it makes me feel loved."

He looks at me for a moment, without saying anything. *Oh shit, what have I said...? Oh god.*

"Oh... um, I didn't mean... um..." *Oh, crap.* "Anyway, what I was going to say was, I'm looking forward to seeing where you live. I, um, I didn't want to see it before."

"Really? Why not?"

"It sounds silly, but I thought if I saw where you lived, saw your belongings and everything, that I'd feel closer to you and it'd make it even harder - you know - to say bye."

The lift arrives and we step in. Daniel leans his back against the wall and I rest against him.

"I don't want to make anything hard for you - well maybe one thing - "he winks, "if you don't want to see it, we won't. I can come back to the pool-house with you; that's if you want me to stay with you tonight, of course."

"Daniel, there is no way on gods earth that we're not spending the night together. I can't wait to get that hot, sexy, masculine body of yours out of those clothes."

164

He smiles at me, his eyes glistening. I must remember to take some pictures before I go; I need to be able to see this beautiful face again, even if it is just a picture. The lift opens on the eleventh floor and I step out, following Daniel's lead.

"And I want to see where you live now, I've already gone past the point of no return, I'm going to be broken hearted when I leave, whether I have seen where you live or not. So show me, baby!"

"I'm 'baby' now, huh? I like it. But I can't bear to hear you say you'll be broken hearted, I'll be the broken one, baby. Here, we need to cross the sky bridge here." He uses a key fob to open a door and leads me across a small bridge, up in the air, joining the two buildings.

After a short walk, we arrive at Daniel's door. I put my hand on his shoulder and he turns to face me. "Before we go in, Daniel, I just want to say..." I stroke his neck with my hand trying think of the words. I can't think of anything to express it, so I lean forward to kiss him, tenderly. He welcomes it, releasing a slight, deep groan as he grabs my face and deepens the kiss. Our tongues meet, and immediately we are taken to a wild place of passion, in the hallway.

"Oh god, Bea. You have no idea," he says against my lips as he somehow opens the door behind him, our eyes still fixed on each other. We stumble inside, resuming where we left off, slamming the door behind us. As we fall against the wall, Daniel slides his hand under my dress and grabs my bare buttock. I lift my leg at his side, trying to feel more of him against my skin, and I moan, loudly.

With his other hand, he slowly lowers the zip at the back of my dress. *Yes!*

I release my bag and take the dress off my shoulders so it drops to the floor, it's heavy, and the beads thud as they land on the wood. He gazes at my body, making me feel sexy in my Manolo's and nude, lace underwear. I slowly take a step forwards and tug on the bottom of his shirt before letting my fingers crawl up his chest and start unbuttoning his crisp, blue shirt.

As I see more and more flesh, liquids pools, and I need him to touch me. I peel the shirt down his shoulders and it falls to the floor with my dress. His arms are so muscular and beefy, his torso is phenomenal. *Grr.* He kicks off his shoes and pulls his socks off. "Come," he says as he grabs my hand and yanks me down a hallway, before taking a swift right turn through an open-plan kitchen and then bursts through the door of his bedroom. The lighting is dim, sexy... perfect, and the decor is minimal but extremely stylish. Dark brown furniture, cream and beige soft furnishings, clean lines, it's very masculine, yet warm and welcoming at the same time.

He holds both of my hands and turns to face me, walking backwards towards the bed. When he gets there, he pauses, gazing at me with those beautiful eyes full of desire. "I've got you in my bedroom, baby."

"Uh huh, and what are you going to do about it?"

His mouth curls and he cocks an eyebrow, his fingers slowly unbuttoning his jeans while his eyes remain, burning into mine. He slides his jeans and underwear down his toned thighs, letting them fall to the floor before stepping out of them and slipping his hands around my back to expertly unclip and remove my bra.

Our lips meet again, and with one hand on my back, he caresses a breast with the other. I moan loudly, his touch sending an electric current directly to my clitoris. He slides the other hand down my back and underneath the lace of my knickers, gliding them down until we are standing against each other, perfectly naked.

I gently place my hands on his chest and drag my fingertips down past his taut abs, slowly bending to my knees until I'm face to face with his impressive erection. It turns me on, seeing just how much he wants me. I hold one of my hands around him and squeeze him, indulgently. I look up at his face, his eyes fixed on me, his lips are pursed and I can see his heart beating hard through his chest. I twist my hand slightly and glide up and down, squeezing just enough that I can feel him harden even more under my touch. *This is so hot.*

I pick up the pace a little and Daniel groans as he tips his head backwards. I place my other hand on his backside and squeeze it as I lean forward and place his tip in my mouth.

Daniel gasps and immediately looks down at me again, his mouth open.

"Fuck," he moans as I take as much of him into my mouth as I can, sucking hard and swirling my tongue around him. My mouth continuously rises and falls around him, gradually increasing speed. I'm enjoying the feel of him against my tongue, seeing his sexy stomach move as his breathing quickens, hearing his groans. I want to make him come, I've never had someone come in my mouth before, I've always thought it was a bit gross, but I want it with Daniel. I want to feel him coming undone, I want to do this for him, pleasure him, give him something that I haven't given to anyone before.

I keep sucking, hard, following my mouth with my hand, squeezing harder. I can hear him getting closer, his panting and quiet moaning giving it away.

"Oh, baby, stop."

"Uh uh," I murmur around him, moaning as I speed up again, increasing the pressure, I'm enjoying it so much, I want to do this for him, I want to give him this."

"Baby, please, I'm going to..."

"Mmm..." I pull away briefly, still working my hand. "Go ahead, I'm not stopping." I continue my rhythm, sucking, swirling, pumping... I'm so turned on.

"Oh god, oh baby... oh!" he shouts loudly. I feel a warm spurt in the back of my throat and I swallow immediately, hoping I don't taste anything. I slow and loosen my grip on him, but keep him in my mouth. I swirl my tongue gently, and slowly slide him out of my mouth, swallowing again to make sure it's all gone. I'm pleasantly surprised, not gross at all.

I look up at Daniel's face and he's biting his lip, gazing down at me. I stand and wrap my arms around him, tilting my head to bury my face in his neck, kissing him. Daniel's hands slide around my naked back, pulling me closer.

"Bea, that was *incredible*. You are... incredible, at everything. Oh god, baby, I..."

"Mmm, Daniel," I mumble into his neck, laying tiny kisses all over him, "I really enjoyed it, I like the way you feel in my mouth, I like how you taste. I've never let anyone do that before but it's different with you, I want you to have something no one else has."

167

"Oh, Bea, don't say that, I can't bear that I can't have you. How am I going to carry on as normal when you leave? I could barely handle the last couple days," he says, squeezing me tightly.

"I don't know how I will."

"We're together now. Come to bed with me."

"Mmm, and you can make... um, love to me. Will you? Please?"

"Baby, I'll make love to you non-stop until you leave for the airport; if that's what you want."

"So we're not heading to the club?"

"Club? What club?" he says with a smile, before taking me into his arms again and kissing me.

I lay on the bed, hot and panting after a wickedly intense orgasm. Daniel's head still clamped between my thighs, my fists clutching his hair. My ankles are crossed above his body, the glittery Manolo's gloriously catching the light. I slowly open my eyes and relax my thighs and fingers, enabling him to come up for air.

"Oh, wow..." I whisper, huskily, "That was amazing."

"For me, too, baby," he says as he crawls up my body, resting on top of me and kissing me gently.

"Can you taste yourself on my lips?"

I can, and it's not as weird as I thought it might be. It's actually quite arousing. "Yes, I like it, strangely."

"I love the way you taste."

I smile at him, he's just so gorgeous. "Tonight is amazing, Daniel, and we haven't even had... made... you know, yet."

"You mean we haven't made love yet?"

"Yes." I blush and look down.

"You've said it a few times, Bea, why do you feel uncomfortable now?"

"You know what I think about that, I never say it until I'm, you know... in a relationship where the other person and I are in love with each other. It's very unusual for me to have been saying it, like I have, recently."

Daniel looks at me in that way again, the silent way. It's so awkward, like he doesn't know what to say because he thinks I'm asking him to tell me he loves me, or something. I'm not.

"But anyway," I break the weird silence, "I'm looking forward to... making... it. I love tonight, thank you for coming."

"Don't thank me, I'm just so glad to be spending another night with you, I didn't think I'd see you again."

"Me neither," I say as he kisses my nose.

"So, baby, I know how you feel, and I know that you wanted to distance yourself, but do you think we could spend your last day together, tomorrow? I want to be with you every second until you get on that plane, Sunday."

How can I say no to that? I should, but I don't even want that anymore. I want as much as I can get. "I'd love to Daniel."

"Really?" he asks, and his face lights up. He's adorable!

"Really. I kind of broke the whole 'no contact' thing when I started sex texting you earlier."

"I'm so happy to hear that, Bea; I'll make your last day, one to remember. I promise."

"I've no doubt that you will, Sexy."

His eyes sparkle. "So, instead of *'making love'* right now, why don't we get some clothes on, get a bite to eat and some drinks up here, and ask the others if they want to join us?"

As disappointed as I am that we have to get out of bed and stop this wonderful 'skin-on-skin' contact, I think that's sounds really fun. "Sounds great, where will we get food from?"

"That's not an issue when you live here, sweetheart, I can have 'Whatever, Whenever'. Literally, it's like a 'thing' they do here. We can call down and get some food sent up."

"Wow, sounds fabulous! I love where I live and everything, but you don't get that there, this sounds very indulgent!"

"It's great, although I'm not totally spoiled, I like to keep my feet on the ground, I don't ask for the tub to be filled with candy or anything."

"Shame, I love sweeties!" I giggle. "Do you have something I can put on? I adore my new dress, but it's not for chilling about indoors in, I don't want to ruin it."

"I don't know what I've got that will fit you, but you're welcome to wear whatever you like. Come," he says as he climbs off me and walks towards one of the two side doors. I follow him through one of them, and find myself in the most enormous walk-in wardrobe, full of Daniel's clothes and shoes and accessories. It smells divine! "Oh Daniel, it smells like you in here, I love it. Mmm."

He raises an eyebrow and smirks slightly. "So you *'love'* how I smell, huh? What else to you *'love'* about me?"

170

"You '*love*' that word, don't you? Are you just saying it to make me feel uncomfortable? Do you '*love*' doing that to me?"

"I know what I do '*love*' doing to you," he says with a grin, looking me up and down. "Holy crap! You're still wearing the stilettos! Oh my god, baby, you're standing in my closet, completely naked except for those sexy heels. I '*love*' that and I want to do what I '*love*' doing to you right now, in here," he says and wraps his arms around me, walking me towards the doorframe.

"We're supposed to be getting me some clothes, young man. I don't think we should be fucking in the walk-in wardrobe."

"I don't plan on 'fucking' you, baby, and you know that. Turn around."

I do as I'm told, and Daniel scoops my hair up and pushes it over one shoulder, leaving my neck clear for him to kiss. He puts both of his hands on my waist and pulls me back against him; my heels make me the perfect height, his erection pushing through the gap at the top of my thighs. I grab hold of the door frame with one hand, and reach down, in between my legs, with the other, to press him against me. He's so warm and hard, I need to push him inside me and let him fuck... make love to me.

"I can feel how wet you are."

I moan, loudly, and he cups one of my breasts, smoothing his fingers over my hard nipple.

"Your body is beautiful, Bea, every tiny bit is perfect, your skin is so soft, I crave every inch of you."

"Daniel, please... do it..."

"Do what, baby?" he asks, kissing my jaw.

"Just fuck me, Daniel."

"That's not happening, Bea."

"Please!" I shout, urgently, I need this so badly.

"No, baby. Say it."

"Please, Daniel."

"I want you to say it and I want you to mean it."

I pull my head away from his shoulder and look down. I close my eyes, psyching myself up. I really, really do want to say it, I want him to do it and I want to do it with him, but it is actually starting to mean something to me, and it's just a 'turn of phrase' for Daniel. I believe he prefers to say 'make love', because he thinks 'fucking me' is derogatory, but he doesn't realise how much 'making love' means to me. He says he wants me to mean it but I don't think he realises that by meaning it, for me, it would mean I'm in love with him.

Somehow, after only a week or so... I think I might be.

"Please, please, Daniel."

He pulls back and presses the end of his erection into me.

"Oh god!" I yell, "Yes."

He slowly eases into me and I bend forward slightly to push myself onto him. I moan, loudly. "Yes, baby, make noise for me, I love your pleasure, I love your body, I love..."

"Oh, yes, it's so good, you're so good."

He slides out slowly and pushes into me again, deep. "Bea, you're amazing," he whispers, moving a little faster, harder, deeper.

"You too, Daniel, so amazing, keep going, keep doing it, keep..."

"Yes baby?" he asks breathlessly.

"I want to, I want to say it."

"Then say it, Bea, please? It means something."

His pounding hits the spot, head on (so to speak), over and over and it's agonisingly pleasurable. The huge waves are building inside as heat rushes to my groin. "I can't see you, I can't say it to the wall, but don't stop, oh god don't stop! Later..."

His fingers grab my chin and he turns my face to the side, leaning forward so his face is immediately in front of mine and he kisses me. "Look at me, don't stop."

I look into his eyes and I know I can say it, say it and mean it, I want to. "Make love to me, please make love to me, oh... yes, oh god... make love to me, make love...yes... yes...ah!" I explode around him, hard and passionately. "Oh, Daniel!" I shout, louder than loud.

"Oh god, baby, yes!" Daniel groans as he thrusts into me, hard, before stilling and resting his hand on the door frame in front of us. He splays his other hand on my stomach and drops his face to my shoulder.

I raise my hand and stroke the back of his neck, resting the other with his, on my belly. We stand in silence for a moment, calming our breathing, Daniel gently kissing my shoulder.

"Stay?" he whispers and I smile.

"If I could, believe me, I would."

"Can't you?"

"Sadly, no. Come with me?" I ask, knowing the answer.

"This is when I wish I had a boring, normal job that I could just quit. Then I'd come and be with you."

"What if you hated living in England?"

"I wouldn't care if I could be with you."

"You're sweet, Daniel,"

"More like smitten."

I grin and turn to face him, wrapping my hands around his neck. "I don't think you're real; there is nothing wrong with you, literally, nothing! Apart from living thousands of miles away, of course. You will make a California girl very happy, one day, as much as it pains me to say it."

"Don't say it." He kisses my nose again. "I don't want to make anyone else happy."

"One day you will."

"I won't. I don't want you making anyone happy either." He pouts like a child.

"You're so cute Daniel," I say, turning his pout into a shy smile.

"I need to use your bathroom, please. Where is it?"

He tightens his arms around me and nuzzles his head into my hair. "Don't go..."

"I have to, but I'll be back in a minute and you can get me something to wear and then show me around."

"Okay, baby. It's the next door on your right."

"Thank you."

~~~~~~~

I check my face before I leave the bathroom, it's still fine, the lipstick has gone and there are no ugly red smears, so all is good. I wash my hands and collect my underwear from the bedroom floor before making my way back to the walk-in wardrobe. Daniel has put another of his super-sexy polo shirts

173

on, this one is a pale blue Ralph Lauren one, and it skims his muscles perfectly. He has teamed it with a pair of navy cargo shorts and he looks *hot*. I kick off my shoes and wander over to him, still completely naked. How do I not feel uncomfortable? Must be the booze.

He offers me a beautiful, huge smile. God, I do love him. "Hello, baby."

"Hello, again, you look gorgeous."

"So do you, as always."

I smile. "So, what have you got for me to wear, Sexy?"

"I really don't know, my pants will be way too big, you're tiny."

"Okay, I'll have a look."

"Help yourself to anything, I'll go and put some music on and fix us a drink." He puts his arm around me and kisses me before leaving.

I put my underwear on, looking around at all of his clothes, wondering what on earth to wear. After a good rummage around in this 'Daniel-scented haven', I find a v-neck, lamb's wool, navy jumper which looks very comfy, and a pair of pale blue and white striped cotton boxers. I dress and roll the waist band of the boxers over so they fit me better. I am the most comfortable I think I've ever been. I head back out to the bedroom and make the bed before joining Daniel in the kitchen.

"Fuck," he says, looking me up and down, "how do you make a pair of boxers and a sweater look so hot?"

I giggle and roll my eyes. "I'm sure I don't, you'd probably say I make granny pants and flip flops look hot."

"I think you probably would!"

"No one can make granny pants look hot, Daniel."

"Well, you've already told me you don't 'do' granny panties so it doesn't matter does it? I love your panties."

"And I love your pants Daniel, these are super comfy!"

"Keep them, something to remember me by."

"Okay, I will, thank you. Shall I text Tilly and see if they want to come here?"

"Yes, great." I walk back out to the hall to retrieve my clutch bag and dress from the floor, pulling my mobile out.

There is a text from Tilly which I open as I walk back to the kitchen.

~

> **Tilly 22 Sep 00:20**
> **Hey! Are you two still snogging in the**
> **hallway?! Are you coming here? It's gorge!**
> **Let me know what you are doing. Luke is**
> **THE BEST DANCER on the planet. He is**
> **going to get some tonight! Xxxxxxxxxxxx**

~

I laugh as I lean against the kitchen work top and hit reply.

~

> **22 Sep 00:50**
> **Sorry, doll! We got a bit**
> **sidetracked ;-) We're at Daniel's**
> **apartment and about to get**
> **something to eat. We wondered**
> **if you all wanted to come and**
> **join us for food and drinkies? I**
> **need to talk to you, too. Please**
> **come? It'll be fun, promise. Xx**

~

"Here, baby." Daniel hands me yet another glass of champagne.

"Thank you, darling, I will not feel good in the morning!"

"I'll take care of you. Cheers." We clink glasses and I take a sip, it's freezing cold and delicious.

"Mmm, Daniel, it's lovely. Is it Veuve?"

"Veuve Clicquot? Yes, how did you know that?"

"It's my favourite."

Daniel smiles and takes another sip. "You called me darling; you haven't called me that before."

"Did I? When?"

"Just now."

"Oh, do you like it?"

"Yes, I love it; it makes me feel like your boyfriend."

"Well, you are, kind of, for a bit anyway. My holiday boyfriend," I say with a grin.

175

"I like that. I'd rather be your real boyfriend, but holiday boyfriend will do."

"So, can I have a look about?"

"Sure! This is the kitchen as you can see..." It's a lovely modern kitchen with dark wood cupboards and cream, marble work tops. It is open plan so behind the long kitchen island is a dining area with a large dark wood table. Beyond that is the living area, it's all very co-ordinated. A huge, cream, deep, shag-pile rug sits in the living area under one large, taupe fabric sofa and two black, leather Barcelona chairs opposite. At both ends, are large, square, cream furry poufs. In the centre of the seating area is a huge, square, striped fabric coffee table in taupe and black with a glass top. It's so stylish, I want to live here.

The balcony is beyond the living area and it's large but I can't see too much in the dark. To the left of the living area is the spare bedroom and it's decorated in bright red and white. That has an en-suite too. There is a utility room and toilet further up the main room, opposite the kitchen entrance and then around the corner is the corridor to the front door.

"It's not big, but I like it. I initially bought it as an investment to lease out, I was going to get something else for myself, a little larger, but decided I liked it here so I moved in. Do you like it?"

"I love it Daniel, I think it's huge. I thought my apartment was quite big but it's not at all, not compared to this."

"I'm glad you like it," he says as he approaches me from behind, snaking one arm around my waist and kissing my cheek.

My iPhone chimes on the kitchen work top and he walks over to get it for me. "Sit, make yourself comfortable," he says, handing me my phone. I stroll over to the taupe sofa and curl myself up in the corner, putting my champagne down on the coffee table in front of me.

~

Tilly 22 Sep 00:59
You don't need to ask twice, sounds great. I would like a bit more quiet time with Luke too ;-) Gemma and Jay aren't coming; they're

176

**going home to do it. Lol. Be there in a bit. I'm
STARVING! Xx**

~

"They're coming," I call to Daniel who is fiddling with
his iPod. "Just Til and Luke, though, Gemma and Jay got
horny and are going home apparently," I say with a smile.

"We're not the only ones then." He wanders over to join
me on the sofa as the music starts to play in the background.
He sits next to me and puts an arm around my shoulders,
pulling me close to him. "You look so damned hot baby, you
have incredible legs," he says, gliding a hand along my thigh.
"I'd never have thought my clothes could look as sexy, as they
do on you right now." His eyes lingering around the v-neck of
the jumper.

I smile and snuggle further into him, tucked under his
arm, listening to the music like we've been together, forever.

"How's your hand, baby?" he asks, holding his hand out
for mine.

"Oh, it's fine, I can't feel it anymore," I say as I show
him and he raises it to his lips. They're so soft.

"Thank you, it's fine. Really." I caress his cheek. "I
smell of you, in these clothes. Mmm."

"You make me smile all the time, you're so sweet."

"Well, I won't complain about that because I love your
smile," I say with a huge grin.

"Another thing you 'love', Bea," Oh, I love you,
Daniel...

"Yet another, Sexy Berkeley. This is really relaxing;
you, me and Veuve, a bit of music, your fabulous apartment. I
wish I could stay forever."

"Why don't you stay on a couple extra days?" he asks,
hopefully.

"Don't say that, I can't. I need to get back for work, and
staying on a little longer won't make it any easier to leave. I'll
still have to."

"I know, I just thought we could get a little more time."

"I know and it would be wonderful, Daniel. But I have
a flight booked and don't fancy flying back alone, and before
you offer to do the journey with me, I really don't think
delaying things will help."

"Okay, baby, I'll stop now."

"Thank you. I really don't want to go, if it makes you feel any better."

"It does... and it doesn't. I want you to want me, but I don't want you to be sad when you go."

"I do want you, so much, and I will be *really* sad. So I'm afraid you'll just have to know it and get used to it."

"Yes ma'am!" He laughs.

"Til and Luke will be here soon, can we have a pash before they get here?"

"A pash?" he repeats, amused.

"Yeah, you know, 'make out'."

He chuckles, "Sure, baby. There's nothing I'd like more than a 'pash' with you right now." He clutches my chin with his fingers and draws my face up to his and our lips touch, caressing gently, unhurriedly. I could kiss this mouth for eternity, I love everything about it. I glide my hand slowly across his lap to rest on his cock, slowly stroking it through his shorts. Holy fuck, he's hard as rock.

He pulls away, gently. "Bea, you're making me want you again, but Tilly and Luke will be here soon... God, you're incredible, I want you, all the time."

"I want you, too," I say in a deep, wanton tone, keeping my hand firmly pressed against him. "I always do," I add as I lay a soft, slow kiss on his lips. "If Tilly and Luke weren't coming back, I'd ask you to take me to your office."

"What?"

"Uh huh." I kiss him again. "I want you to fuck me in your office."

"Oh, baby. I want that so bad! Can we ditch those two?"

I laugh. "No. We'll just have to imagine what it would be like."

"We'll see." At that moment, we hear Tilly and Luke laughing as they open the front door, Tilly's dirty cackle making me giggle. "We'll continue the pashing, later, baby," he says as he kisses my nose and stands to get some more champagne flutes from the kitchen.

"Hey love monkeys, what've you been up to, huh? You pair of dirty bastards," Luke asks with an amused grin as he rests against the kitchen cupboards next to Daniel. I bite my lip and look down with a shy smile. *Funny, but embarrassing!*

"You two 'got it awn' again," Tilly sings in her best American accent. She saunters over to the sofa to join me. "Whoa, look at you in your boy clothes," she teases.

"I happen to think Bea looks hot in my clothes, Tilly, don't you?" Daniel calls from the kitchen.

"Well, I can't say it 'tickles my pickle', I'm not that way inclined, but I will agree that Bea looks hot in just about anything, Daniel."

"I'd like you to tickle my pickle, sugar lips," Luke says with a wink and I gasp, amused by his outrageous innuendo.

"Okay, if you two want to do any 'pickle tickling', you can take it into the guest room, thanks." Daniel says, laughing.

Luke sits on one of the Barcelona chairs and pats his lap, gesturing for Tilly to sit, which she does. Daniel joins me, as we were, on the sofa. "So, are you guys hungry? What shall I get to eat?" he asks, absently stroking my neck.

"I'm starving," Tilly responds, "and I have a real craving for pizza, anyone else fancy pizza?"

"Mmm, sounds good!" I enthuse.

Daniel calls to get some pizzas sent up and we all chat about the 'W' and what's it's like to live here. I'm having a great evening, but all that's important, is being curled up next to my man, knowing I'm staying the night, in his bed, with him.

~~~~~~~

We eat a load of pizza, and talk for hours about everything and anything. We've gotten through two bottles of ice cold champagne and I've definitely had enough now. I am not totally drunk anymore, but I am squiffy and really tired, I could do with a nice cuppa. I'm still sitting, tucked under Daniel's arm with my hand resting on his toned stomach, trying to get used to the fact that I think I love him. No, I know I love him. Fuck, I'm in love with someone I met last week.

I look up at his lovely face while he's deep in conversation with Tilly and Luke about skiing in Aspen, and I want to run my fingers down his cheek and kiss that beautiful

179

mouth. The fine stubble covering his jaw is sexy as hell, god, I could look at him for hours on end.

He looks down and sees me gazing at him with a silly, contented smile on my face and he grins. "Hello, baby," he murmurs, quietly.

"Hello, baby," I repeat. Tilly and Luke still talking Aspen in the background.

"Are you looking at something?"

"Only my holiday boyfriend. You are so handsome."

Daniel grins, shyly and I want to gobble him up. "You are so much more beautiful, than I am handsome, Bea. And I don't think I'll ever get enough of you calling me your boyfriend, give or take the 'holiday' bit."

"I wish I didn't have to say the 'holiday' bit."

"Me too, baby. Would you like another drink?"

"Actually, I was going to ask if I could make a cuppa?"

"Cuppa? Tea?"

"Yes, sorry. Tea."

"Of course, I'll make it," he says as he takes his arm from around me and stands up.

"I can do it, Daniel, just show me where everything is."

"Okay, baby, I want you to feel at home. I'll show you," he says, holding out his hand and I take it, following him to the kitchen.

"Tilly, Luke, do you want tea?"

"Ooh, I'd love a cuppa," Tilly says with a thumbs up.

"Not for me, thanks. Dan, can I have a beer, dude?"

"Sure, help yourself, and grab me one too."

Luke stands, effortlessly lifting Tilly and placing her back down on the chair with an affectionate kiss to her forehead. He heads to a fridge specifically for beer... well; I assume it must be considering there's nothing inside but shelves full of perfectly aligned beer bottles.

"Baby, the tea bags are here..." Daniel opens a cupboard door, "sugar is in this cupboard next to it and the milk and lemon are in the refrigerator. The kettle is right here," he points to the stainless steel, state of the art kettle. "Are you sure I can't make it for you?"

"No thank you, darling, I'll do it."

"Okay, I'll watch," he says as he perches himself on the kitchen island and crosses his arms in front of him. I'm not sure what it is, but he looks incredibly sexy like this, sitting on the counter top, watching me with that gorgeous smile.

Throwing the second tea bag into the bin, I place the spoon in the sink and turn to Daniel, pressing up against him. "You're so sexy," I say, running my hands up and down his huge biceps. That Enigma song is on, and all I can think about, is making love to Daniel to it.

"Mmm, so are you. You know, your nose is such a delicate little thing, it compliments your beautifully curved mouth perfectly, that's one of the first things I noticed about you, on the airplane," he says as he slides his hands around to the bottom of my back and pulls me closer, in between his legs.

I smile an awkward, shy smile. "Um, thank you."

"Don't be shy. You're beautiful. I can't wait to get you to myself again," he whispers into my ear.

"Me neither, let's go to bed after my tea. I think Til and Luke are half way there too." I nod over in their direction, Tilly straddling Luke on the Barcelona chair; they are whispering and gazing at each other, admiringly.

"I think Til likes him more than she lets on you know."

"That's funny because I was thinking that about Luke earlier. In all the years we've known each other, I've never seen him with the same girl more than twice and I've never known any girl to make him laugh so much. She's good for him."

"Really? Hasn't he had a girlfriend?"

"Not really, he's been happy, single. He's never had to try with girls before; they have always fallen at his feet. He does with Tilly, though."

"Um, Daniel?"

"Uh huh?"

"Can we take your iPod to bed?"

"This is the 'sex song' isn't it?"

"Uh, actually, Daniel, 'music to make love to'."

He grins and raises his eyebrows. "Why, yes, sweetheart, that's what I meant. And yes, let's do that."

181

I hand Tilly her tea and head back to the large sofa to sit down.

"Wait, baby," Daniel says as he strolls past me and sits first, patting his lap like Luke did, earlier. I hand him my tea and curl up on his lap, enjoying the feel of his body under mine. He hands me back my tea and I take a sip.

"Hey, you two... " Tilly calls and we both look over as she snaps a photo of us on her iPhone. Daniel kisses my cheek and makes me smile, as Tilly carries on taking pictures. A final one of us kissing is taken before she takes a few of her and Luke.

"Memories of our fun holiday in Hollywood," she says with a smile as she puts her phone down on the table.

I close my eyes and rest my head against Daniel's shoulder. "Mmm. This is lovely."

"Mmm..." Tilly says, "really nice, thanks for the tea, Bea, thanks for the hospitality Daniel and thanks for being a comfy chair, Luke," she says with a grin as she closes her eyes and mirrors my position. Luke wraps his arms around her, and rests his head on hers, eyes closed. It makes me smile, his affection towards her - given my earlier opinion of him as a serial philanderer - is really quite surprising. He clearly likes her, and she him. I wish they'd admit it.

I have another sip of tea and close my eyes again. I'm so comfortable, I could nod off. Daniel's beer arm is wrapped around my chest, moving occasionally as he sips, and his other hand is stroking my legs, slowly. It's so relaxing.

"Bea, baby." He disturbs my near snooze.

"Mmm hmm?"

"Shall we go to bed? I don't want you to fall asleep here, you look tired."

"I am, really tired, and I'm not ready to fall asleep yet," I grin, eyes still closed, I can't see Daniel's face but I am pretty sure he's grinning too.

"Let's go. Hold your tea tight..." He sits forward with me and places his bottle on the table before standing with me in his arms, like a baby. *Whoa! He's so god damned strong!*

"We're going to bed guys, see you in the morning."

"See you later," I add.

182

They both bid us a sleepy goodnight and Daniel makes his way to the way to his bedroom, grabbing the iPod on the way. He lowers me onto the bed, careful not to spill my tea, and dims the light so we're almost in darkness. I sit on one side, drinking my tea and watching Daniel as he strolls around the bedroom, sorting out the iPod and beginning to undress.

He lifts his shirt over his head, my attention is focused on his taut body again. In all of my ten, sexually-active years, I have never been with a man with a body like this. Dylan had an 'okay' body, but nothing like this. He walks, gorgeously naked, into the bathroom to clean his teeth. I can't wait to wrap myself around that naked body.

As he comes out, he stops and smiles at me. Oh, I love you, I love you, I love you, I LOVE YOU, you gorgeous man. I wish I could tell you.

"Nearly finished your tea?"

"Uh, huh," I murmur, taking a last sip before putting it down on the bedside table. I sit up and slowly pull Daniel's jumper over my head before unclipping my bra and throwing it to the floor.

Daniel watches, intently, as I lie down, raise my hips and lower his boxers and my knickers together to my thighs. He pulls them down my legs before crawling up my body and kissing me. He tastes of toothpaste; delicious. He points a remote to his iPod and the song starts to play. He drops the control on the bedside table and brings his hand to my face, looking me in the eye. He whispers the French words that he translated for me, the other day. "Dit Moi."

What does that mean again? Tell me? *Tell him what?* I place both of my hands on the sides of his face and say what I think he wants. "Make love to me, Daniel. Please, I need you."

He closes his eyes and lowers his lips to mine again. I bend my legs either side of him automatically, hooking my feet around his legs, my body rippling underneath him in time to the music.

I'm still gripping his face, kissing him fervently, moaning and sighing in undiluted pleasure. I slide one hand around to the back of his neck, one of my favourite 'Daniel places' and I move the other to his side, pressing him against me. I can feel myself getting warmer and wetter, the buzzing feeling in my stomach getting stronger, moving down to my pubic bone as I moan loudly again.

"Bea, you're so beautiful," he murmurs before moving his head down to take my nipple into his mouth. I arch my back and groan as his tongue ripples against me, his other hand gently massaging my other breast.

"Oh, Daniel..." I moan as I bring my knees up to either side of his body again, and push my pelvis up against him.

"Baby," he whispers as he moves to caress the other nipple with his mouth, "your body, your skin..." he says against my breast, running his hand down to caress my thigh, firmly. He rises up my body again to kiss my lips, the pressure increasing with our need. Daniel's tongue elegantly entwines with mine and the deep, velvety groan that escapes his throat into my mouth, only increases my desire for this lovely man, whom I now know, I love. The thought makes me yearn for him even more, to feel him as close as he can be, deep inside me.

His fingers move slowly towards my inner thigh and rise until he's gently circling my clitoris, so gently he's barely touching me but it's agonisingly good. "Oh!" I cry, passionately, closing my eyes, pushing my head back into the pillow. "Daniel, I crave you, I am hungry for you all the time, I feel deprived when I don't have you."

"Oh, Bea, you don't know... you don't know," he whispers between soft, delectable kisses on my neck.

"What don't I know?" I ask, my hands in his hair. *Tell me you love me...*

He squeezes my buttocks before positioning himself at my entrance. He gazes deep into my eyes. "You just don't know." His voice mellifluous, he closes his eyes and shakes his head as he slowly fills me.

"Oh!" I cry, it's divine, so slow. "Oh, yes, deeper, oh god, it's..."

He kisses me and thrusts deep and hard. This feels so incredible, not just because he's seriously good at this, but also because he's Daniel, the man that I want nothing more than to spend all day, every day with... because I love him.

~~~~~~

We lay, totally entangled, kissing gently as our breathing settles. Daniel smiles at me. "How can we make this work, Bea? I can't lose you."

"If I knew, Daniel, I would have suggested it already," I say, running my fingers down his darling face. "I want something with you, so much. Come and live with me?"

"Baby, I've thought about it, believe me. But I couldn't leave the business, I can't leave my family. My dad made this business for my sister and I, and it's my life. I can't turn my back on it, although I feel like I can't let you go either. Come and live with me?"

"I adore Los Angeles, I adore the people here, I adore where you live, I adore you. As much as I think that living here is a much more attractive option, you know why I just can't. I have fallen in love with Los Angeles." *And you.* "I want to come back here on holiday, but I can't up and leave everything I've worked so hard for. I wish I could, I wish I had a boring job that meant nothing to me."

"I know. Me too. We should stop having this conversation, it's depressing, huh?"

"Yeah, it really is. Will you send me the odd text?"

"Try and stop me. You'll be all I think about for a long time."

I smile and snuggle into him. "I draw the line at video-calling though, talking to you face to face will be far too painful. Okay?"

"Sure, baby. But don't you forget to send me a picture of you... in that nightgown."

I giggle. "Okay, *baby*, I'll remember."

"Do you need anything, sweetheart? A drink or anything?"

"No, thank you, Daniel. I'm fine and I don't want you to move, I'd like to stay like this until Sunday."

Daniel grins. "Okay, but I'd like to get out of bed tomorrow, if you'll let me, to take you out somewhere."

"Go on then, hopefully I won't be too hung-over." *Doubtful.* "Daniel...?"

"Beatrice...?"

"What did you mean when you said 'you don't know'?"

Daniel closes his eyes again, his mouth curling into a sad sort of a smile. "Don't worry about it, it's just what you mean to me, that's all."

CHAPTER FOURTEEN
SATURDAY 22ND SEPTEMBER

"Ugh," I groan as I roll onto my belly. I grab my pillow and bend it over my head. Hmm, smells nice...

I feel something touching me. No, I need sleep... oh... but that feels good, mmm... "Mmm," I murmur in appreciation, as the hand massages my neck, gently. "So good. Helping."

"You don't feel good, baby?" A surge of excitement runs through me when I realise where I am and who I'm with, but it quickly evaporates as the feeling of nausea returns.

"Daniel, I feel... ugh," I say with a whimper, my face still buried in my pillow.

"I'll keep rubbing your neck. I made you tea, too," *Oh, he's amazing.*

"Oh wow, I love you..." I mumble into my pillow before I realise what I'm saying. *Fuck! What am I saying?* "Oh, god, I mean... for making me tea.. um, thank you..."

Daniel chuckles, "Don't worry, I knew what you meant. Can I get you anything else?"

"A new head?"

"Hmm, not sure I can do that, and besides, I like the one you've got. Shall I run you a bath?"

"Oh, Daniel." My voice still muffled in the pillow. "You are amazing, how do you know what I need?"

"I'm just guessing, baby. I'll go turn on the faucet and come back and hold you for a while."

"You need to come back to England and live with me. That's an order."

I hear the lovely sound of Daniel's faint chuckle as he makes his way to the bathroom.

~~~~~~~~

I am woken again, this time by strong, warm arms, wrapping around me, the feeling of comfort helps alleviate my nausea. I just want to tell him, all the fucking time.

"I could hold you all day," he whispers.

"Yes, please," I murmur.

"But if you start to feel better, I really would like to take you out."

"I will, Daniel. Once I drink my tea and have a hot bath, I'll feel much better. Oh shag..."

"Shag?" Daniel laughs. "What's up?"

"I don't have any clothes or make-up..."

"That's already being sorted, just tell me specifics and I'll arrange for it to get here."

I slowly sit up and reach for my tea. "What do you mean?" I ask, taking a sip. He remembered how I like it from last night, I'm impressed.

"I have an assistant, she'll get what you need." He props himself on his elbow, iPhone in hand. "So, what do you need? Jeans? Top?"

"I need everything, Daniel, it's too much, we'll just have to go back to the pool-house."

"Bea, baby, she's getting stuff for Tilly too, Luke's taking her out straight from here. Tell me everything you need, she's there now."

I need a casual outfit and make-up. I reel a list of basics to Daniel, mascara, kohl liner and some concealer for under my eyes, if I look like I feel, I'm going to need a whole tube. A pair of jeans, a vest top and some flats. Christ, I hope she doesn't go over the top and buy a load of designer stuff, I can't afford to spend much more.

"Consider it done. Now, finish your tea, have a bath and I'll get some breakfast."

"Where did you come from? You're like some make-believe, ideal man, how are you real?"

Daniel laughs, "Baby, as long as I'm making you happy, then I'm happy. As for where I came from, that's a conversation you'll have to have with my parents, I'd like to stay out of the room for that one."

I smile, he's so gorgeous!

My nausea is already subsiding as I pull back the duvet and swing my legs out of the bed. How unusual, I'm normally hideously ill with a hangover, until at least after breakfast. Maybe Daniel put some magic in my tea. Maybe it's just Daniel. I slowly make the bed before strolling into the steamy bathroom. Daniel has run me the most fabulous looking bubble-bath, it's so inviting, and I step right in. I sigh as I sink into the hot, soothing water. I close my eyes, rest my head on the back of the bath and take a long, deep breath. Bliss.

"Hey, baby. Is the bath okay?" I open my eyes and Daniel is standing next to the bath in nothing but boxers. He looks delicious.

"Yes, Daniel, it's perfect, thank you. Want to join me?"

He grins, "I really do. Can I?"

"Of course, please do."

"I'll sit behind you," he says as he takes off his boxers, so I sit forwards.

He sinks into the water and I slide backwards in between his legs. It's a deceptively big bath. I lean back against his chest and he wraps his arms around me. Oh, wow. This is even more amazing, a hot bubble-bath with my favourite Californian hunk.

"Relax," he says as he kisses my hair.

"Mmm, this is wonderful. You know exactly what to do, Daniel."

"Just lucky guessing."

"You were made for me," I say as I run my hands along his thighs either side of me.

"And you for me, baby. I refuse to believe that you can't be mine."

I smile. "Well, if you figure it out, I'll be waiting."

"I will figure it out, somehow."

We lay together in the bath until our fingers are pruney and the bubbles have dissolved. I turn to face Daniel to wash my hair so I don't cover his face with shampoo. I didn't realise it was quite so interesting, he watches me intently. I position my feet in the spaces at either side of his waist, and arch back, lowering my hair under the water to rinse off the foam. I feel Daniel's hand slowly glide between my breasts, into the water and over my stomach. He rests on my pubic bone, gently circling my clitoris with his thumb. *Whoa!*

I raise my head from the water and smile, salaciously at my man. "Daniel..." My voice low, sultry.

"Mmm?" he responds with a raised eyebrow and slight grin.

"You're being naughty and I'm...trying to... ooh...mmm." I can't continue, it feels so good.

"You like it though."

"Uh huh, Mmm, yes. I. Do."

He turns his hand and gently circles my entrance with two fingers. "You can't sit in front of me and arch back like that without expecting me to touch you. You're so beautiful, every inch of you."

"Oh that feels so good. I really do... need to... oh."

Daniel slowly eases his fingers inside me, still circling my clitoris.

"Oh god... oh yes."

"I want to make you come, baby."

"Oh, I want to. Mmm. I... do... hair..." I moan as my head rocks back again, my hair under the water, my eyes closed. He pushes his fingers deeper and picks up speed with his thumb.

"Oh god! Yes, that's so good..." His fingers circle inside me, deeply, he pushes them again and it's incredible. His other hand reaches forward to massage one of my breasts and he squeezes my nipple gently, rolling it between two fingers.

"Oh fuck, Daniel, I'm going to..." *Talk about quick! Jesus.*

"I want to feel it, baby." I grab hold of his thighs and pull myself towards him, his fingers caressing me masterfully. *Jesus Christ*, I'm supposed to be washing my hair, not indulging in wild, orgasmic bath pleasure.

"Oh, yes, Daniel, yes... like that..." His hand moves to my other breast and as he pinches my nipple, the waves begin to erupt deep inside me.

"Fuck! Yes! Oh!" I cry as the waves build quickly together to form a magnificent, mind blowing orgasm. Water sloshing everywhere from my writhing, I arch backwards again, moaning.

"I love watching you come. I love feeling it, your hot, sweet body exploding around me. You squeezed my fingers so tightly," he whispers.

"Daniel, how do you do that?" I ask, breathlessly. "You can give me the most amazing orgasms in a matter of seconds."

He smiles, victoriously. "Some people aren't compatible, baby and some are. We just, are. You do the same to me," he says as he pulls my hands from his thighs and kisses them both.

"Now, shall we finish your hair? You want conditioner?"

"Hmm," I groan, my head heavy, my eyes closed. What a hangover cure.

I turn back around and Daniel conditions my hair.

We wrap big white towels around our bodies as we step out of the bath, and walk back into the bedroom together. I'm shocked to see everything I need, laid out for me on the bed. "Where did all of this come from?"

"I told you, my assistant got it."

"Is she superwoman? How did she manage that? How did it get in here?"

"She arrived just before I joined you in the bathroom, I left her to lay it out."

"Wow, thank you, and please thank your assistant."

"Of course, but it is her job to do stuff like this."

"She works for you, not me, so please thank her."

"I will, baby. Is it all okay?"

I stroll over to the bed and look through everything, there's so much more than I asked for, she's even bought me a handbag! It's a gorgeous pale peach, leather bag. Looks expensive. *Shit*. There's also a small, clear make-up bag containing the few bits I'd asked for, only, it's all designer. Don't get me wrong, I love these brands of make-up, but today, I think Daniel's darling assistant has cost me a flipping fortune.

The jeans look great, hopefully they'll fit, and the white floaty camisole vest is fabulous, provided it doesn't come with a hefty price tag. I open a small paper gift bag containing a pair of white Hanky Pankys and a white lace bra, in my size. My mouth falls open when I see an open shoe box with a beautiful pair of beige, snakeskin flats inside.

"Oh my god, I love these," I say as I pull one out of the box, gasping as I see the name on the shoe. "Holy moly, these are Stella McCartney! Daniel!"

"Is there a problem?" He frowns. I start rummaging around all of the bits on the bed looking for labels. *Jesus Christ!* The jeans are designer too, love them to death but not exactly twenty quid. I check the handbag. It's Chloe. This bag cost £1000 at the very least.

"Jesus Christ, Daniel, I can't afford all of this! Does she think I'm made of money or something?"

"Don't be silly, Bea. You know I've paid for all of this."

"What? No, Daniel, you're not buying me all of this stuff. I only needed a few cheap bits for today, we could have just gone back to the pool-house to get me a change of clothes for free!"

Daniel looks worried. "Baby, I didn't want to go back to the pool-house. If we decided to go out today, I didn't want to waste any time. I want to treat you, too. You like it, don't you?"

"I do like it, I love it all, Daniel, but it's unnecessary. I don't need you to buy me clothes, I can pay for my own things. Well, unless your assistant decides to spend my money for me."

"I know, Bea, but you needed some things, and I have very little time left to spoil you. I thought I could get you a few bits that you need, plus a few little surprises. I'm sorry if it's upset you, that wasn't my intention."

Okay. Now I feel horrible. His face looks uncertain, and I've just ruined his gift to me.

He strolls over and takes my hands. "Please let me buy these things for you, I really want to." *Just be grateful and accept it. Bitch.*

"I'm sorry. Thank you, Daniel. I love it all and can't wait to wear it. Thank you, thank you." I kiss his cheek, I still haven't cleaned my teeth. *Bleugh.*

Daniel smiles at me. "I'd like to spend money on you today, and it's not up for further discussion," he says with a wink.

"Yes, sir! How did she know my size?"

"I told her."

"How do you know?"

"Bea, I touch you, I explore your body. I know what size you are. Plus, I checked your shoes."

"You're the best. Let's hope it all fits and that you don't have some 'Shallow Hal' syndrome."

Daniel laughs and holds me in a warm, lustful embrace. He leans down and kisses my cheek. "Can I kiss you yet, baby? I've cleaned my teeth..."

"I'd love to, but I still need to clean mine, so no. Where's my toothbrush?"

Daniel looks around the bed and finds it amongst some super-dooper expensive looking toiletries. I look at him, questioningly. "Face cream, face wash... girls stuff, I don't know," he says by way of explanation and shrugs. "By the way, Bea, what fragrance do you wear? I love your smell."

"It's Chloe, funnily enough. Now I am going to smell Chloe and have Chloe hanging from my arm." I grin, excitedly, I'm looking forward to strutting about with my new, mega-money handbag.

"Lucky Chloe! I'm glad you like it," he says. "Now, clean your teeth."

Daniel isn't in the bedroom when I leave the bathroom ten minutes later. My face done, teeth clean and feeling like I didn't even have one drink last night. Remarkable. I remove my towel and put on my new, white underwear and jeans. There's a knock at the door and I automatically cross my hands over my chest to hide my body. I'm not sure why, it's not like Luke would be about to walk in here.

"Bea, it's me," Tilly calls through the door.

"Oh, come in, Til." She walks in looking beautiful in a short, summery floral silk dress. "Wow, you look gorgeous,"

"Thanks! Whoever Daniel's assistant is, I love her!" Tilly replies.

"I can't believe how much Daniel has spent on me, he bought me this bag!" I pick up the Chloe bag and show Tilly.

"Wow, that's gorgeous! It's Chloe! I told him I'd pay for my stuff, it wasn't a lot anyway. He said 'no' and then Luke piped up, wanting to pay for it, but I shoved the cash in his hand anyway. I'm not having either of them buying my shit. I need to borrow this bag at some point, Bea, you know that, don't you?"

I giggle. "Maybe."

"Goody! So, you said in your text last night that you wanted to talk to me?" We both sit on the side of the bed next to my beautiful new shoes, Tilly holding my bag on her lap, stroking it like a kitten.

"Yeah."

"What's up? Everything okay?"

"I'm just having such an amazing time with Daniel. I want to bring him home." I pout and frown.

"I know that feeling, babe. I actually really like Luke."

"You don't say?" I roll my eyes and grin, widely.

"Alright, alright. I'm not in love with him or anything." My face falls and I look down at my hands in my lap. "Oh, doll," Tilly says, putting a gentle hand on my back. "You've fallen, haven't you?"

I nod and turn to look at her, my eyes begging her to tell me what to do.

"That's not such a big surprise, Bea. He's amazing, and you two are so hot together, you can practically see the sparks."

"I don't know what to do, Til. How will I live? I'll be so far away from him, knowing I may never see him again. The thought actually hurts... like physically, hurts, Tilly." I clench my fist and press it into my sternum, as if holding it there will somehow relieve the pain.

"Darling, would you move here?"

I shake my head.

"Bear's?" she asks.

"Yes, and my family, and you and Clare."

"And I assume he can't move to the UK? How about long distance?" She shakes her head and scrunches her nose as soon as she says it, knowing that wouldn't be a viable option.

"Oh, dear. You're in a right old pickle aren't you?"

I sigh, loudly, "Oh, yes I am. But I don't want that to ruin my day today, I have the rest of my life to be miserable. Today, I'm with him."

"Have you told him?"

"Oh god, no! So don't you go blabbing!"

194

"Of course I won't," Tilly says, rolling her eyes. "Does he love you? Silly question, I think that's obvious."

"Really?" I ask, butterflies flitting in my belly. "He hasn't said anything. I don't think he does. It has only been a week!"

"I think you'd be surprised, Bea. But of course I won't mention it. Luke's taking me somewhere this morning and then I'm taking him back to Gem's for the day, she's making us dinner tonight, but call me if you need me, okay?"

"Ooh! He's socialising with the fam!"

"Yeah, yeah, it's just because I won't see him for another six months or something, don't read into it."

I grin, knowing it's more than that. "Yes, I'll call if I need you. You too, Til, call if you want to chat."

"Oh, I'm fine, babe, you're the one in love."

"Hmm, well have a lovely day, I don't know what's happening later but I imagine I'll stay here, I'd like to."

"Yep, no stress, as long as you're back in time to pack tomorrow. We don't have to be at LAX until about half six, so we have all day."

"Yes, that's great. I'll be back to pack at some stage. I'll see you tomorrow."

We both stand and share a long, welcome hug. "Love you," I say, because I do, I love her so much.

"You too, Bea. I'll look after you."

"Thank you. Now go and have a day of hot sex or whatever it is that you two do." She winks and turns to leave the room with a grin.

I feel better for talking to Tilly, although she hasn't come up with any alternative solutions as to how Daniel and I can be together, she is a huge comfort, and I know she will look after me when I get upset. I have the best friends in the world.

Daniel enters the room as I bend over the bed to pick up the white camisole. "Hey, baby."

I smile at him, he looks gorgeous yet again, in fitted navy shorts and a tan belt. He's teamed it with a white fitted shirt, tucked in with the collar open and sleeves rolled up at the elbows. He's such a well dressed man, I wonder if he wears much other than Ralph Lauren. "You look hot," he says as he approaches me, slipping his hands around my bare waist. I smile and he closes the distance between us to kiss me. It's not just any old peck, he is getting right in there, snogging me passionately and it's delicious. *God, I love you.*

"Baby, you need to get that top on before I get carried away. Do you need the hair dryer?" he asks, breathlessly, still holding me, running his fingers through my wet hair.

"Yes, please. One more kiss though?" I ask sweetly and he smiles a huge, beautiful smile before kissing me oh-so-tenderly, again.

"Come on baby, less kissing, more hair drying, breakfast is in the kitchen," he says, swatting my behind.

I pout and move away to put my new top on.

"Here's the hair dryer, I'll see you out there, will you be long?" Daniel asks as he puts it down on the bed.

"No, just a few minutes."

Once I've done my hair, I quickly pack all of the essentials into my lovely new handbag, before heading out to the kitchen. A selection of delicious looking food is spread out on the breakfast bar. "Ooh, yum!" I say to Daniel who is sitting, waiting for me.

"I made you tea, come sit and choose what you'd like."

"Thanks, Daniel. Did you get this all sent up?"

"Yes, I thought it'd be quicker and easier." I sit down and put a couple of pancakes on my plate with maple syrup and some strawberries. It's more like a dessert but I love pancakes, and they're so much more delicious in America. I take a sip of my tea, which Daniel has made perfectly again, and start to eat my breakfast. He watches me with a smile on his face.

"Is something funny, Daniel?" I ask when I have finished my mouthful.

"No, baby, not at all. I'm just enjoying how happy you look this morning. You like pancakes, huh?"

"I *love* pancakes. Thank you for breakfast."

"You're welcome, enjoy," he says as he continues to eat his scrambled eggs and streaky bacon. His looks delicious as well, I fancy eating that, too, I'm ravenous!

"When you're ready, we'll have a few hours out. I wanted to take you to a couple of places, that okay?"

"Sounds good, Daniel. I'm ready to go after this," I say, having another sip of my tea.

Fifteen minutes later, we're making our way down to Daniel's car.

"Thank you again, for my clothes and everything. I really love it all, Daniel." I clutch my bag and grin from ear to ear as we get into the car.

"You're welcome, again. Stop thanking me and enjoy it. Here..." He hands me a sunglasses case and I open it to find a pair of Ray-Ban aviators.

"I know you like aviators because you have some already so I thought they'd be the safest bet. Are they okay?"

"You bought these for me?"

"We can't go out for a day in LA without sunglasses, baby. Do they fit?"

I put them on and look in the wing mirror, "They're perfect, Daniel. Thank you, you didn't need to."

"I wanted to. Stop thanking me," he says, nonchalantly, whilst lowering the roof. I lean over and kiss him on the cheek. "Shall we go or do you want to do some more kissing?" he asks.

"Don't ask me that question, my answer will always be kissing."

"Oh, really? I'll ask you that tomorrow then, when your plane is about to depart," he grins a conspiratory smile.

"I wish I could canoodle with you on the flight home." I pout, and he leans towards me, cradling my face in his hands and kisses me, softly.

"Me too, baby," he says against my lips, kissing me once more. We pull out onto the road, and Daniel puts on his Ray-Ban wayfarers, they really suit him. "So where are we going?"

"Well, first, I want to show you something."

"Okay," I'm intrigued. I wonder what it is.

As we stop at some lights after a few minutes, Daniel says, "Look up there." He points to the top of a large office building, and I see the words 'Henry Berkeley Inc." in large letters at the top. *Wow*, I realise now just how huge the company is.

197

"Your work!"

"Uh huh," he says, pulling into an underground car park, removing his sunglasses and nodding at a security guard, "I thought I'd show you my *office*," he adds with a huge, cheeky grin and a sly wink.

"Oh! I see!"

He smiles, "Actually, I thought I'd show you where I sit and think of you all day. Is that okay? Or would you rather go somewhere else?"

"No, Daniel! I am really excited to see where you work."

"Really?" He looks surprised.

"Yes! You always seem surprised when I ask about your work, I want to know! It's a huge part of your life. I would also like to have a mental picture of you at work, so when I look at the clock and it's a time you'd be there, I can imagine you, sitting at your desk." I grin.

Daniel is silent for a moment as he parks. When he turns the engine off, he remains still and then turns to me. "Will you really think of me, like that, when you're home?"

"Of course I will, what do you mean?"

"Like, you'll look at the clock and wonder what I'm doing?"

I nod, shyly, "Is that weird? Have I freaked you out?" I ask quietly, wondering if I've just completely put him off. Not that it matters really, considering I'm leaving tomorrow.

He stares at me and it feels like minutes pass. Oh shit. It is weird. How do I come back from this? "Daniel, I..."

He grabs my hand. "Baby, it's not weird at all, sorry. You take me by surprise sometimes, you're so interested in parts of my life that most girls don't want to know about. When you say things like that, I like it because I know I'll be the same, only I can't picture you at home or work. There's so much about you that I don't know and I want to know it all, I want to be part of it, I want to see you at work, I want to meet your folks and Oliver and Clare, be in your car with you, see your apartment, sleep in your bed with you," he stops and shakes his head.

I offer him a small smile. "Daniel, I wish it wasn't like this, I wish you could see all of those things and be a part of them. And I'd like you to understand that I am so interested in your work, I think it's fascinating, what your dad created, and what you and your sister are now part of. What an incredible achievement for the family, and huge opportunity for so many employees."

Daniel smiles. "Come on then, it makes me feel happier bringing you here, knowing you really want to see it. I like to show off what I'm proud of. I'd show you off, given the chance."

I smile as Daniel steps out of the car and comes around to open my door for me. He takes my hand and walks with me to an awaiting lift.

We step out into a huge, marble floored reception hall with a large desk between two pillars, opposite the main doors to the street. There is a great, sweeping marble staircase behind the reception desk, and three more lifts to the right of that. I can imagine it bustling in here during the week. Daniel takes my hand and walks me towards the other lifts.

"Good Morning, Mr. Berkeley," the girl at reception says, blushing a little.

"Good morning, Sarah," Daniel responds with a warm smile, walking purposefully, towards the lifts.

We enter another lift and he presses a button for one of the top floors. As the doors close, he pulls me into his arms and beams, beautifully. "I like having you here. I'd rather it was a week day so I could show you off, but never mind," he says as he kisses my nose and loosens his grip on me as the lift comes to a halt. He takes my hand again and leads me out onto the office floor.

It's a very large, open space with many, modern office cubicles to the left, a large reception desk to the right with a seating area beyond it. Around the back of the huge room, are doors to what I presume are, private offices.

An older lady sits behind the reception desk, typing at the speed of lightening. She looks up as we walk towards her and immediately stands. "Good morning, Mr. Berkeley, I wasn't aware that you were coming in today."

"Good morning, Iris," Daniel says, confidently. "Don't worry, as you can tell from my attire, I'm not here to work, just showing my girlfriend my office. This is Beatrice Hart."

His girlfriend! I wonder how many of his 'girlfriends' she's met...

"Good morning, Miss Hart," she greets and nods with a smile. I can see a hint of surprise in her expression but she's hiding it well.

"Good Morning," I respond, not wanting to use her first name for fear of sounding patronising. Daniel tugs my hand and leads me towards the far end of the room.

"It's huge Daniel," I remark, looking around me as we walk.

He smirks. "I'm aware of that, baby, but what do you think of the office?"

I giggle. "The office is pretty big, too."

He opens a door, and inside, working behind a large desk, sits a very attractive girl, maybe twenty-five or so, with honey blonde hair and a very fitted, suit dress on. She stands immediately.

"Good Morning, Mr. Berkeley, I didn't know you were in today."

"Morning, Heidi, don't worry, I'm just picking something up and showing Miss Hart around." He turns to me, "Bea, baby, this is Heidi, my assistant."

My heart sinks a little, she's too damned attractive to be his assistant.

"It's great to meet you, thank you so much for running around for me this morning, everything is perfect."

She holds out her hand for me to shake. "Miss Hart, it's great to meet you, too. It wasn't a problem at all, I just followed Mr. Berkeley's instructions. I'm glad you like everything, you certainly look lovely."

"Thank you. I do like it, very much."

"Mr. Berkeley, Miss Hart, can I get you anything?"

"No, Heidi, thank you. You can go now, finish whatever you're working on on Monday. Have a great weekend."

"If you're sure, Mr. Berkeley, thank you."

"See you Monday," Daniel says as he walks towards a connecting door.

"Mr. Berkeley, Miss Hart," she says with a nod.

"Nice to meet you," I call behind me, as Daniel tugs me through the door of a huge, beautiful office.

"Is this your office, Daniel?" I ask, wide eyed.

He chuckles and frowns, "Yes, why? Something wrong with it?"

"Daniel, it's amazing! It's huge and so... nice!" There is a large, old-looking, wooden desk in the centre of the room with a big leather chair behind it. In front are two smaller leather chairs. There is a seating area to the right of the door with four Barcelona chairs, like the ones in his living room, and a small, wooden coffee table, matching his desk.

The meeting table and eight chairs is to my left in front of floor to ceiling windows, the view of LA is breathtaking. Against the far wall, is an extra wide, built in cabinet.

A framed photo sitting on the top catches my eye, a man that looks a lot like Daniel with a young girl and boy, outside a building with 'Henry Berkeley' above the door. I am drawn to it and automatically stroll over to take a closer look. "Is this you?" I ask, knowing the answer, the little boy in cute denim dungarees could not look any more like Daniel if he tried.

"Yes, with my dad and sister, I must have been about five or six."

"Oh, Daniel, you were *so* cute!"

His eyes crease as his mouth curls into a slight, embarrassed smile.

"You still are," I say, placing the picture back down and walking towards him. He's perched upon his gigantic, solid desk. I put my bag down on his chair and lean against him, between his legs.

"Is being cute a good thing?" he asks me, stroking my arms with his finger tips.

"Very," I reply, as I gently clutch his shirt at either side of his waist, and rise on tiptoes to nuzzle into his neck, trailing soft, open-mouthed kisses down his throat. His hands slide to my waist and around to the small of my back, where he holds me against him, tighter.

"Mmm, Daniel, you smell gorgeous."

Daniel stands and turns with me, lifting me so that I sit on his desk. He steps back and I sit, gently swinging my legs over the edge. He stares at me, arms crossed, grinning. "I knew I'd get you in my office, baby."

A rush of excitement warms my blood, when he gazes at me like that, it gets me so hot.

"Well, here I am, *baby*. Do you wanna...?"

"Wanna...?" he repeats, slowly stepping back towards me.

"Wanna... christen the desk?" And then a thought comes to me, "Hang on, has it already been christened?"

Daniel smiles as he presses against me, in-between my legs. "No. The only girl who has ever been in my office, not on business, is Holly, and we certainly *never* did anything remotely interesting in here. In fact she couldn't wait to get out."

"Really?" I ask. How odd, how could you be in here, alone with Daniel, and *not* want to rip his clothes off and be dirty on the desk?

"She wasn't really interested in work. Unlike you," he says with a grin. He slips his hands underneath my top and runs them up my bare back, undoing the clasp of my bra in the process.

"Naughty boy." My voice deep and libidinous. Daniel's turquoise eyes blaze with sensual anticipation, as he pulls one bra strap from the armhole of my top. I frown in question. *Why?*

When the strap is off, he takes the other with ease and pulls the whole bra through the other armhole. He looks down at my chest and I hear his sharp intake of breath. "Baby, you should *never* wear this top without a bra, unless you're with me. You can see everything, it's fantastic," he smirks, as he holds the back of my neck with one hand and caresses one of my breasts, through my top, with the other. His lips are on mine, immediately, and I melt as the goose bumps spread all over my body. I moan, running my hands through his hair.

He lowers his head to take one of my nipples in his mouth through the delicate fabric of my top. The warmth from his breath and gentle flick of his tongue makes my body quiver in anticipation. He pulls away suddenly to lift my top up and over my head. "My god, you're so beautiful," he says before pressing his lips to mine again and squeezing my torso against his body.

I un-tuck his shirt from his shorts and run my fingers up his abs. I could never get enough of feeling his immaculate body, his beautiful skin. I hold onto his arms, lying backwards onto the desk, taking him with me. There's paperwork beneath me, and I worry slightly that I'm going to mess it up, but as Daniel's kiss becomes increasingly carnal, I quickly forget.

He groans deep in his throat and reaches down to unbutton my jeans. The buzz behind my pubic bone is electric, unbearable. His tongue forceful in my mouth, not asking, taking. This is a Daniel I *really* like, if it's possible to like him anymore than I already do. I love this forceful, raw, animalistic Daniel, it reminds me of the first time, in Luke's apartment, when he fucked me against the wall.

He pulls my jeans and knickers past my hips, without breaking away from the kiss, and I push them a little further, but they get stuck on my knees. Damn skinny jeans! I attempt to unbuckle his belt, but it's one I can't figure out and I fumble, clumsily, flustered. *For fucks sake!*

"Grr!" I groan, impatiently.

Daniel rises and smirks. "Impatient, Beatrice?"

"Yes! I just want you to fuck me!" I snap, irritably.

He smiles, stepping back and raising his eyebrows, slowly unbuckling his belt. I sit up and quickly shove my jeans off my legs, leaving me bare naked on the desk, waiting. Daniel takes his sweet time with his fly.

"Daniel..." I tap my finger nails on his desk beside me.

"Yes, baby?" His voice is so fucking sexy.

"Hurry up, please?"

"A little horny?" he grins.

I roll my eyes, *seriously*? "Yes! Get a move on! I need you, like, five minutes ago."

"...and you want me to '*fuck*' you, right?" he asks, gazing at me, his eyes slowly licking my naked body from head to toe.

"Yes, I do. Hard," I whisper.

"You don't want me to make sweet love to you?"

"Not this time. I want you to really fuck me, hard, on your desk."

"Hmm, I see. Are you wet for me?" he asks, his voice quiet and gravelly.

Oh, okay, two can play that game. I slink back onto my elbows and smile, slowly. "Really, really wet, *baby*." I respond slowly, my tone low and sultry. I move my hand down my belly languidly, skimming over my landing strip to touch myself with my fingertips. He gasps, audibly. "Are you hard for me, Daniel?"

"Very," he says, staring at me, touching myself.

"Mmm," I moan, licking my lips.

He drops his shorts to the ground. *Finally!*

"You look incredible, lying there like that."

"I want you."

"I want you too, baby, but I like watching you."

"Watching me... touch myself?"

"Yeah, it's so fucking hot," he says, his eyes hooded, burning into me.

I bend my knees and raise my feet slowly, to rest on the drawer handles, either side of the desk. I'm fully exposed to him, but bizarrely, I don't feel shy in the slightest. I throw my head back and circle my clitoris with my middle finger. "I want you here," I whisper.

"Jesus Christ..." Daniel groans and leans forward, grabbing the back of my neck, covering my lips with his passionately, carnally. I feel his hard cock, eagerly pressing against me where I'm touching myself. I move my hand and grab the back of his neck, pulling him closer, deepening the kiss. My other hand pressing into the flesh of his buttock.

Daniel groans desperately, slowly sinking into me.

"Uh!" I throw my head back and tighten my legs around him. "Yes!" He starts to move, hard and fast. He thrusts into me again and again, harder, with each thrust, deeper.

"Fuck, Daniel, yes... yes!" He pounds stronger, faster. *Christ!* This is so good, the true definition of 'fucking'.

"Fuck me, Daniel, fuck me!" I cry, nearing the imminent explosion.

"Oh, baby, you're so wet, so good!" he groans, his eyes burning into mine as he continues to pump hard.

"I'm going to... uh huh... yes..."

204

"Yes Bea, come all over me, come on, baby."

My feet start to tingle and curl, and the waves inside me burst into an almighty, crashing orgasm that has me shrieking out loud, crying his name.

"Fuck! Bea! Yes!" Daniel cries, as he comes hard inside me, with me. He slumps on top of me, panting. "Fuck..." he murmurs, between breaths.

"Quite," I respond, trying to catch my breath.

He lifts his head and kisses me. "Baby, you're something else. This time, you got truly, fucked," he says, amused. "But, as outstanding as this was, next time, I'm making sweet love to you, okay?"

"Mmm. Anything you say, sexy. I love it all," I respond with a huge smile on my face, closing my eyes, dropping my head back on his desk.

Standing slowly, he slips out of me and gazes at me for a moment before finding his clothes and putting them back on. I remain sprawled on the desk, trying to find an ounce of energy, with which to move. Daniel steps towards me and holds my hands. "Come, up you get. Let's get you dressed."

"Oh..." I grumble, I can't be bothered to move.

He sits me up and stands between my legs, brushing my hair off my shoulders. "You're so beautiful," he whispers, before softly caressing my cheek with his fingers.

I smile, shyly. *If only I could tell you, Daniel. I love you so much.* "Thank you, you do mention that, a lot."

Daniel steps back and picks up my jeans from the floor, he takes my knickers from inside and hands them to me. "I want to take you someplace else, and after that, you can decide how we spend the rest of the day. Does that sound okay?"

"It sounds lovely, Daniel." I get down from the desk and put my underwear back on, already planning what I want to do.

Suddenly, we hear voices in Heidi's room and I pause, looking to Daniel for reassurance that no one is about to walk into his office. I don't get it, he is looking almost as wary as I am so I yank my jeans on as fast as I can.

"It's my dad," Daniel says, grinning like a naughty school kid.

"Oh my god!" I whisper, panicked, "Where's my top?"
I'm running around in circles wearing jeans and a bra, trying to
locate it. I slip my shoes on and crouch down under the desk,
just in case he comes in. *Bingo*! It's under the desk. I quickly
throw it on and Daniel pulls me up just as his office door
opens. I spin around to see a very well dressed, attractive
couple, smiling.

"Darling! We didn't know you were here, Iris just told
us you came in," the lady says warmly, before looking
between Daniel and I, waiting for an introduction.

"Hi Mom, Dad. She didn't mention that you were here,
I only came in briefly to show Bea the office. This is Bea,
Beatrice Hart."

"Of course, Beatrice, I've heard a lot about you,"
Daniel's dad says, smiling, as he strolls purposefully towards
me with his hand held out. I shake it and smile back at him.
Heard a lot about me? Intriguing.

"It's lovely to meet you Mr. Berkeley, Mrs. Berkeley." I
extend my hand to Daniel's mum who shakes it gently.

"You too, Beatrice, please do call me Rose, and my
husband is Henry." Rose walks around the desk to kiss her
son, and I become suddenly self conscious, recalling the
deliciously dirty deed performed on this desk just a few
minutes ago. I hope I don't have sex hair or anything. *Oh god,
does it smell of sex?* I look down at my body, double checking
that I have all of my clothes on. Luckily the wet patch where
Daniel was so skilfully sucking my nipple through my top, has
dried off.

Everything is in place, and I'm pretty sure there are no
icky odours, so I can stop panicking and thinking about hot
desk sex, to focus on Daniel's parents.

"Darling, how are you?"

"Good, thanks, Mom."

"Will you both be around tomorrow? Maybe you could
bring Beatrice for Dinner?"

"Thanks, Mom, but, unfortunately, Bea is going home
tomorrow."

"Oh what a shame. Hopefully you'll be back again soon
so that we can get to know you a little better." *If only.*

"Bea lives in London, she's on vacation so she doesn't know when she'll be back. I hope soon," he says as he reaches for my hand and smiles at me. I am shocked by his display of affection in front of his parents. I look at them to gauge their reaction but they don't seem too phased by it. Henry is smiling at me with an almost sad look on his face. He's extremely good looking, Daniel looks exactly like him, only younger, obviously.

"Well, if you can't come tomorrow, are you busy now? Maybe we could have coffee?"

Daniel looks at me, questioningly. I smile and nod. "I'm taking Bea out shortly, but we have time for coffee, shall we take it in here?" he asks, gesturing towards the Barcelona chairs.

"I'll ask Iris to arrange it. What would you like Beatrice?" Henry asks.

"Could I have tea, please?"

"She likes English breakfast tea, Dad," Daniel adds.

"Of course, I won't be a moment."

Daniel continues to hold my hand as he strolls over to the seating area, sitting opposite Rose and gesturing for me to sit next to him. It's a little nerve wracking, meeting the folks.

"So, Beatrice, have you had a good vacation?" Rose asks.

"It has been wonderful, actually." I smile at Daniel, "Los Angeles is fabulous."

"We like it, don't we darling?" she says to Daniel, who smiles warmly at her. "I'm so glad you've had a good time, hopefully Daniel has shown you around a little."

"Mom, Bea has her own business, just outside of London, she owns a cakery."

Daniel's dad returns and sits opposite me. "Iris will bring the drinks shortly."

"Thank you, darling. Bea, what exactly do you do?"

"I have a cake shop, we make wedding cakes mainly, but also sell the usual cupcakes, occasion cakes et cetera. I love it."

"How fabulous," she says, enthusiastically, "you must be very creative." I like Rose instantly, she's sweet and warm. I bet she's a wonderful mum.

"It's a great business, hard work, but I wouldn't have it any other way."

Iris interrupts us with a huge tray of refreshments. She puts the tray on the meeting table and serves us all our drinks, individually, before placing a tiered stand in the centre of the coffee table. It's piled high with delicious looking biscuits and gorgeous miniature cakes. She promptly leaves the office, closing the door behind her.

"Wow! This looks lovely," I say with an exuberant smile.

"Coming from the cake maker, that must be good! When Iris started... how many years ago, Dad?"

"Eight, son."

"...Eight years ago, she suggested we serve platters like this for clients and during staff meetings. It went down very well, so we've done it ever since, in all of our offices, even the London office has the same arrangement."

"That's great, cake is the way forward in business, I always say."

Daniel and his parents laugh and Daniel smiles, affectionately at his mum. At this moment, I think I want to stay here and never go home. I could cuddle him every night, make love every day, see his beautiful face and mouth-watering body whenever I like. How am I going to live without him? He looks at me and smiles, and I melt. I want to blurt it out right here with his parents as witnesses. I LOVE YOU, DANIEL! More than I've ever loved anyone. I am so in love with you.

Meeting Henry and Rose was lovely. They seem wonderful parents, I can easily see how Daniel has grown up to be the amazing man he is today.

Daniel and Henry talked work which turned me on, no end. Daniel in work mode is one of the sexiest things I've ever seen. The girls in this office must walk around with their tongues out all day long, not only because he's a super-hot slice, but also because, when he talks business, he has a powerful, masculine, super-intelligent air about him, and it makes me want to strip him naked and ravish him like a wild animal.

They discussed global integration, foreign market entry, consumer behaviour and in all honesty, I had no idea what the hell they were talking about, but I nodded and smiled, all the while thinking how I'd like to be a fly on the wall in this office, perving at 'work-mode-Daniel' all day long.

When they left, they each kissed me on the cheek, and Rose wished me the best of luck with the business, saying she hoped I could make is back to LA very soon so that she can take me out for lunch. She kissed Daniel and told him that I was obviously very good for him because he had colour in his cheeks. I tried to conceal the grin spreading across my face at that point, but it didn't work and Daniel glanced at me, winking in response.

~~~~~~~

As they close the door behind them, I turn to Daniel with a grin, "Your parents are so lovely, Daniel."

He holds my hands and pulls me into his chest. "So are you, baby. They like you."

"Do you think so?" I ask, my smile growing. Not that it matters.

"I know so. Who wouldn't?"

"You're sweet," I say as I kiss his lips and wrap my arms around his neck.

"So, Bea, would you like to make a move now or..."

I raise my eyebrow, amused, "...Or?" I ask, as if I don't already know.

"...Or christen another part of my office?"

"You're insatiable."

"I could say the same about you, Beatrice," he murmurs, sexily.

"Let's go wherever you're taking me, because I know what I want to do with the rest of the day, and the sooner the better."

Daniel pouts like a child. He looks gorgeous. I kiss his pout and pinch his cheek, "Come on, grumpy, let's go. Plenty of time for more fun later." I scoop up my new bag from his chair and pause, deciding to sit down and check out Daniel's view, day to day. I wheel the chair up to the desk and look around. I pick his phone up, put it to my ear and put it down again.

He's staring at me, baffled, but amused. "Baby, what are you doing?"

"I'm just playing."

"Playing?"

"Yes, you know, 'Daniel at work'."

He looks at me like I'm crazy. "Uh huh, that well known game we all played as children." He shakes his head and I laugh.

"I just want to see how the world looks for Daniel all week. It's completely different to how I work. This is much more... civilised, I make animals out of sugar paste and get covered in cake batter all day. If I lived here as your full time girlfriend, I don't think I'd be able to stop myself coming to visit you and watching you all day. You're so hot when you talk work."

Daniel approaches his desk and leans towards me. "I'd love that. I could have you in here to '*pash*' between meetings." That amazing thought unfortunately reminds me of his hot assistant who works right next door. I wonder if he ever thinks of taking her into his office for a bit of afternoon delight.

"Um, don't you find Heidi..."

He frowns. "Find Heidi, what?"

"Attractive?" I ask, looking down at the desk, nervously.

"She's not ugly, but no, she's not my type at all. Why do you ask that?"

"Just because I think she's pretty damned hot, and she's lucky enough to work in close proximity to you all day. I can't imagine how she manages to keep her hands off."

He chuckles. "Well, you've nothing to worry about there, I'm not her type either. My dad is probably more her '*thing*'," he says with a compassionate smile.

"Really? Wow, that's surprising, she's so young."

"I know, her boyfriend is in his fifties. Are you jealous, baby?" he asks, a cheeky grin spreads across his face.

"Well, yes, actually. I don't want to think about your next... female companion."

"Neither do I."

I sigh, fighting back the sadness that's threatening my day. "Shall we go?"

"Yes, baby." He takes my hand and we make our way down to the car.

~~~~~~~

About twenty minutes later, we're in a car park somewhere in Beverly Hills. He still hasn't told me where we're going and I have no idea. We walk for a short while before he stops outside a shop.

"This is it," he says, pointing to the large shop.

"What's this, Daniel?" I ask, already spotting something inside that's luring me in.

"This store sells really cool cake stuff, my mom used to bring us here when we were kids if she wanted to make cookies at Halloween or something. According to Mom, it sells all sorts of cake paraphernalia."

"Oh, Daniel, this is *so* my 'thing'! Can we go in?" I'm itching to get in there and have a good look around, I had *not* expected this!

"Of course, please," he says with a smile, "I'm sure you have everything you need, already, but I hoped you might find something different."

"Thank you so much, I'm really excited! I love places like this!"

The shop was made for me, I'm sure of it. I fill my basket with Halloween decorations for the shop, Spider cake-pop stands, loads of little nick-nacks and a couple of beautiful bundt cake tins. Hopefully I can fit it all in my luggage!

"Thank you for bringing me here, Daniel. It really is the best place to bring a cake maker!" I say, walking out of the shop, Daniel carrying my purchases.

"You're welcome, baby, I'm glad you found some new things for the cakery."

"Me too!" I say, excitedly. "Clare will be so excited to see it all."

"So, would you like to do some more shopping in Beverly Hills, sweetheart?" *'Sweetheart'.* It makes me turn to Jelly.

"Do you need to do any?" I ask, more interested in getting him home.

"No, but I'd like to get the things that you wanted the other day. Please let me?"

"Daniel, no. Thank you so, so much, but no. I don't need those things, and I would really like to pash for the rest of the day," I say enthusiastically with a beaming grin.

"When you put it like that, going home sounds much more interesting. But when can I spoil you? I really want to get you something special."

"You already have, you've got me loads of stuff, Daniel, and this bag is the most gorgeous bag I have ever owned. Every time I wear these shoes, I'll think of today and you. Every time I wear any of this again, I'll think of you. Thank you. So can we please go home?"

"Home?" Daniel grins, "I like you calling my place 'home'."

"Your home," I add and he pouts again.

Soon after, we're pulling back into the car park at the 'W' Residences, and making our way up to Daniel's apartment. He opens the door for us and I stroll though to the main room, depositing my handbag on one of the kitchen stools.

"What shall we do for lunch?" Daniel asks as he plops down onto the sofa and pats the cushion next to him. I smile, walking towards him and sit down, tucking one foot underneath me, facing Daniel. I stroke his face and he gazes at me, affectionately.

"I'm so lucky to have met you, Daniel."

His eyebrows shoot up and a shy smile grows on his beautiful face. "I wasn't expecting that. I think I'm the lucky one, baby."

"Thank you. I mean for everything, I've had a wonderful holiday and the time I have spent with you has been amazing. I've loved every minute. I'm going to miss you so much."

Daniel closes his eyes and drops his head, shaking it. "Me too, baby, it's going to be so hard to say goodbye tomorrow, you know that?"

"Of course I do. I'm dreading it."

He looks up at me and smiles, sweetly. "But you're here now, and we have all afternoon, all night and all morning, together." He kisses me gently, an appeasing warmth spreads through my body.

"Quite right, darling. So, what shall we have for lunch?"

"We can go out or down to the restaurant if you like, or we can order something up."

"Can we order something up? Then we can chill out in our comfies and snuggle under the duvet all afternoon? I don't want to go anywhere, I want you all to myself."

"Whatever you say. Comfies?"

"You know, track suit bottoms, pjs, that sort of thing."

"Okay, so are you going to wear my sweater and boxers again?"

"I can if you'd like me to, Daniel," I say, grinning from ear to ear, "I'd definitely class those as comfies."

"Good, then I'm all for comfies, you look hot in them. Let's get some food ordered and get changed."

I'm excited at the prospect of spending the rest of the day, tucked up with Daniel. I plan cuddles, kissing, talking and lots of Daniel sex. *Mmm, Daniel sex.* I need to stock up on it while I can.

Twenty minutes later, I've changed into my new favourite comfies, and Daniel's got some low slung track suit bottoms on and a grey, fitted t-shirt that shows off his out-of-this-world body.

I emerge from the bedroom with Daniel's heavy, fluffy duvet wrapped around me as the food is being laid out on the breakfast bar. He stands with his arms crossed, looking questioningly at me, amused. I grin in response. The staff leave and Daniel thanks them, politely.

"Okay, so what's with the comforter? Are you cold?" he asks.

"No. I know it's hot outside and everything, but this is what I do at home when I want to get cosy on a rainy day." I slump on the sofa, still wrapped in Daniel's duvet. "I want to do it with you." I add with a raised eyebrow as Daniel grins cheekily at the double entendre.

"You got it. Do you want to eat lunch over there or at the breakfast bar?"

"Um, I don't mind, but I don't want to get food on your duvet... comforter... whatever you call it."

"Who cares, let's eat on the couch, I'm sure the *comforter* will be fine." he says with a big smile on his face. He passes me my Caesar salad and puts his steak sandwich down on the coffee table, before returning to the kitchen to collect two champagne flutes and a bottle of Veuve Clicquot which he serves up swiftly. "Cheers." Daniel raises his glass to mine and we clink before taking a long, refreshing sip.

"Mmm, lovely. Thank you Daniel."

"Are you feeling okay now?" he asks.

"Yes, thank you, I don't have a hangover at all, surprisingly."

"Good, I'm glad. Let's eat."

"Yes, let's, my salad looks yummy but your steak sarnie looks even better."

Daniel takes a bite out of it and nods. "Mmm, it is," he adds, holding his hand in front of his mouth. When he's finished his mouthful, he continues, "Do you want a bite, baby? I'll swap if you want."

"You're so sweet. No, you eat it, but I will have a little bite, please?"

"Of course," he says, holding it in front of my mouth.

My eyes widen in appreciation. "Wow," I say as I finish chewing, "that really is good. So is my salad," I add, taking another sip of my freezing cold champagne.

"This is really nice, baby, sitting here like this, with you."

"It is, isn't it? I'm glad we came back."

"Me too."

We finish our lunch, chatting and enjoying every minute of 'togetherness'. This is what Daniel and I should do every weekend, but of course, we can't. I take the plates over to the kitchen and stroll back to cosy up, next to him, under the duvet.

He pulls me onto his lap and wraps his arms around me, kissing my head. "Hmm, this is good," he murmurs.

"Yes, it is. How will I survive without this?"

He sighs, "I don't know, baby, probably better than I will. There must be *something* we can do."

"I don't know what. Even if I was able to keep coming back for holidays - which I can't - the time between each one, without you, would be horrible. It has to be all or nothing."

"I agree, sweetheart. I'll keep thinking. In the meantime, please, please can we stay in contact? I know you didn't want to, initially, but I can't just stop how I feel for you, I need to speak to you when I can." *How do you feel for me, Daniel?*

"I can't either. We can stay in touch, but maybe we should limit it a little, we do need to get over each other at some point, we will have to meet other people, as much as it pains me to say it."

"The thought of anyone else having you..." He shakes his head. "I want you to be mine, every day, I don't want it to stop tomorrow, when you leave."

Tears threaten and I manage, somehow, to keep them at bay. "Please, Daniel, I can't talk about it anymore. I just want to stay here with you, I don't want to get out from under this duvet and if I have to, I want it to be because you're taking *us* to the airport so that *we* can get on a plane and go to England, *together.*"

Daniel holds me tight, saying nothing. I want to burst into tears but if I start, I won't stop, and that'll ruin what precious time I have left. I wrap my arms around his waist and squeeze him as tight as I can, resting my face against his chest. It almost slips out; '*I love you so much'*, but I manage to control myself. Just.

I sigh and loosen my grip on Daniel to lean forward and take my drink from the table in an attempt to lighten the mood. I sink my champagne and hold the flute in front of him. "More, please," I say with a wide, cheeky grin.

Daniel rolls his eyes, jovially. "Off you get then, sugar lips."

When he returns, he brings a tray with two clean champagne flutes, a fresh bottle of champagne and a cardboard box on a plate.

"Ooh, what ya got?" I ask, my eyebrows dancing.

"Patience, Beatrice," he scolds as he places the tray down on his fabulous fabric coffee table.

He pops the champagne and pours us another glass each. "Here, baby," he says, handing me mine and sitting down next to me, "here's to you and me and the universe making it happen, somehow."

"To us and the universe," I repeat, praying to god that the universe has some sort of trick up its sleeve.

"Anyway, I got you something delicious," Daniel says, reaching for the plate with the box on.

"Oh, I'm intrigued, what is it?"

"Close your eyes and keep them closed." I do as he asks. I hear the cardboard box opening, and another container. "Open your mouth, baby," he says, and as I do, he pops his finger in. "Suck."

I suck and taste delicious, warm, chocolate sauce. Just like we had after our dinner at The Palm. I feel a buzz in my belly, recalling the sexy things we did with it. "Mmm, chocolate sauce," I say as he removes his finger. I open my eyes and he's grinning at me.

"Uh huh, and warm doughnuts, I enjoyed it so much last time..."

"Me too," I respond, my eyebrows raised, "are you going to lick it off me again?" I ask, excitedly.

"If you want me to, I'd be more than happy to oblige." He takes my champagne and places it on the table before holding my face in his hands and kissing me, deliciously.

We spend the next couple of hours, covered in chocolate, laughing and making lots of lovely, dirty, chocolaty love. I fall asleep in Daniel's arms and wake after about an hour, when the deep, evening sun is shining through the huge windows of the room.

It must be about six and Daniel is still fast asleep beneath me. I nuzzle into his chest, inhaling his scent and savouring the feel of his silky skin against my body. He tightens his arms around me and groans appreciatively. "Mmm, hello, baby," he says, his voice course and gravelly.

"Good evening, Daniel," I reply gazing up at his face and smiling at him. It's so nice waking up, wrapped in his arms.

"How long have we been asleep?" He asks, reaching for his phone on the coffee table.

"I'm not sure, about an hour?"

"Mmm, it's just after six. That was good."

"Yes, it was, do we have to move?"

"Nope," he says quickly with a beautiful smile on his face. He tightens his arms around me again and kisses my hair.

"I need to clean my teeth though, if I am going to kiss you, that is..."

"Well, we gotta move, then, because I need kissing."

"You need something else too, judging by the bulge digging into my belly..." I say with a salacious grin on my face.

"That's always the case, when it comes to you, Beatrice."

"I'll take whatever you're offering. I can't get enough of you."

"Did you enjoy earlier? With the sauce?" he asks, and I think back to all of the licking and sucking from a couple of hours ago. *Mmm, it was incredible.*

"Oh, I more than enjoyed it."

"You're so shy when I do that," he says and I squirm.

"Well, you know..."

"No, I don't. Why are you shy?"

217

"Oh, Daniel, do we have to talk about this?" I grumble.

Daniel props himself up on his elbows and looks down at me, frowning. "Yes, we do, Bea. What's up?"

"Nothing's up, Daniel. I'm just shy when it comes to you looking down there. It's not the nicest part of a ladies body, is it?"

"Are you kidding me?" Daniel cries, "You're beautiful, I love it. It's one of my favourite parts of you, I could spend a week with my head between your legs." I flush scarlet. *This is too embarrassing, my god.* "People have told you that before, surely?"

"Look, to be honest, Daniel, Dylan was never really into it, he didn't like venturing 'down under' and we probably only did it a couple of times while we were together. After that, I always avoided it really. Whenever someone has done... *that*, I've just closed my eyes and waited for it to be over. It makes me really uncomfortable, vaginas are so ugly, Daniel, I don't know how you do it."

Daniel has a look of disbelief on his face as he strokes his chin with his fingers. "So, when I've been down there, loving every minute, you've been clenching your eyes shut, waiting for it to be over? It seemed, to me, like you were enjoying yourself."

"It's different with you, Daniel, you seem to be some sort of expert and it's amazing. I really do enjoy it, although I still wonder what you're thinking when you gaze at it the way you do. You can't call a vagina, pretty."

"Is a penis pretty? Hell, no! Yet you happily gaze at that, I can assure you, your bits are a hell of a lot prettier than mine. Bea, I love it, I really do. I could gaze at it all day. I wish I could!"

Oh god, I cover my face with my hands, *this is so embarrassing.*

"I mean it, please don't hide," he pleads, pulling my hands from my face, "you're beautiful, baby, everywhere. Whatever your ex said, forget it, he's an ass who obviously can't appreciate something special. I'm telling you, you're beautiful, believe me, please? You must understand that he is not normal, just because he didn't like it, it doesn't mean there's anything ugly about you. I mean seriously, a couple of times in five years? The guy was loco! But we know that already," he adds, under his breath.

My word, he really does like it. He *'loves'* my va-j-j and wants to spend all day gazing at it. He desperately wants me to feel less self conscious, and is doing a pretty damn good job of it. "Thank you, Daniel. You're the only person I'd let spend a day in my lady garden. You're welcome back, anytime."

He laughs and tightens his arms around me. "God, you're incredible." He gazes at me, saying nothing. A few moments pass and I wonder what the hell he's thinking because he's just staring at me in total silence.

"So... shall I clean my teeth then?" I ask, breaking the silence as Daniel looks away and then back at me with a totally different expression. Now he's smiling, sweetly.

"Yes, baby. Then I'd like to kiss you non-stop until it's time to get some dinner."

"I'm up for that!" I reply as I slowly pull myself away from his warm, delectable body. I stretch and yawn before making my way to his en-suite, completely naked. Daniel joins me at the vanity, beautifully naked, and starts to brush his gorgeous, sparkly, white teeth. He smiles at me, mouth full of foam, and stands behind me with one hand resting on my belly. He pulls me close and closes his eyes, briefly. Butterflies flutter in my tummy. *I love you.*

We spit and rinse and make our way back into the living area. Daniel grabs me by the hand as we pass the kitchen and pulls me into a warm, muscular embrace, holding me firmly. He gazes into my eyes and kisses me, tenderly, his tongue slowly caressing mine. I rise onto tip toes and wrap my arms around his neck, returning every ounce of his affection. A small moan involuntarily escapes me, as Daniel presses his hand firmly at the small of my back, holding me against his muscular body.

He slows the kiss and gradually breaks away. His eyes closed, he runs his nose up and down mine. "Mmm," he murmurs.

"Mmm," I echo, grinning.

"Stay? Please, please stay? I need you here, I want you so much."

I look down, frowning, it would be so easy to say yes. But I just can't. "I want to say yes, so much. I need you too, Daniel, I want to stay with you, I want to stay here. I love it here."

Daniel's eyes remain passive. He lets out a long sigh and rests his forehead against mine. "I'm going to find a way, baby."

"I hope so, darling. I really do. I'd say I'd wait for you, but I don't think it's wise for us to make a commitment like that when we can't see any future."

"I wouldn't ask you to, baby. Although I can't bear to think of you out on a date with some schmuck. Promise me you won't let any assholes near you?"

I smile at him, he's just adorable. "Cross my heart. And the same goes for you, no gold-digging whores."

He grins at me. "Done. No one will be good enough after you, anyway."

I am starting to wonder if - maybe - he does love me. Many of the things he says point to it, but I'm probably looking into it too much, being over-optimistic. I mean, no one falls in love after a week. Except me. It'd be too much to hope that Daniel had done the same. I know he feels strongly for me, I believe everything he says and I don't think he acts like this with any old passing tourist, but I don't think he could have fallen in love, as much as I want him to. It's kind of irrelevant anyway, it's not like we can be together.

"What do you want to do, Bea?" He asks, still holding me, leaning against the breakfast bar.

I don't hesitate with my answer. "I want to make love, *baby.*" I kiss him softly on his neck, over and over.

I can hear the smile in his response, "You do? You don't want to 'fuck' now?"

I continue kissing his neck. "As much as I enjoyed 'fucking' earlier, because - let's face it - it was damned hot, now I want you to make love to me. Sweet, slow, Daniel love."

"Baby, I want nothing more," he says as he grasps my behind.

"Take me back to bed?" I ask and Daniel immediately sweeps me off my feet, carries me to his bed where he crawls on top of the mattress and gently lowers me. He leans over me and strokes my face with the backs of his fingers.

"You know, your asshole-ex had everything I could ever want. He had you, he had five whole years of you loving him, being faithful to him, making love to him. And he threw it all away. I bet he regrets what a dick he was every day of his life. I've only had you for a week or so and I can't bear to think what I'll do without you. He wants you back, doesn't he?"

"Well, we had the conversation a few times a while back, he still asks after me when he sees the girls out and stuff like that. They think he does but he has a girlfriend, who hates me - incidentally - so I don't think he still does."

"He does," Daniel says, sharply, his face serious, almost angry.

"Hey, what's the matter?" I stroke his face and he closes his eyes.

"I can't do it, Bea, thinking of you at home, of that mother fucker coming on to you, wanting you and begging you to go back to him. The thought makes me feel sick," he says, disgust is his expression. *Oh my, where has this come from?*

"Daniel, he's done all that already, I said no and I always will say no. I'll never get back with him. It wasn't right, and anyway, he has his girlfriend now, he won't ask again."

"And she hates you, baby, because she knows he wants you. More than her."

"I don't necessarily think that's true, darling, but either way, it's irrelevant. I have no feelings for him. I feel for you, a gazillion times what I feel for him. I'm more likely to be with you, living over five thousand miles apart, than I ever am, to get back with Dylan. Okay?" I ask, running my fingertips down his cheek.

"I need you. I want you with me, every day."

"Look, Daniel, please don't do this. I want that so much, more than you know. You don't understand just how painful tomorrow is going to be for me, in fact, just talking about it now is making me want to cry," my voice wobbles as I speak, my eyes prickly as the tears begin to well above my lashes.

221

As one escapes, trickling down my cheek, Daniel closes his eyes briefly and frowns. "Oh, baby, please don't cry, I'm sorry. I... I just... I can't..."

"I know Daniel," I say through a sob, "it's okay, it's just hard to leave, you know? Leave you, leave all this..." I wave my hand around at his beautiful apartment, "leave Hollywood, I love it here. I love it all." *And you, my darling Daniel, especially you, more than any of it.*

"I know, baby. I'm sorry for bringing it all up. I just..." he shakes his head and gazes at my face, his beautiful eyes look pained and exhausted.

"I know," I respond, caressing his stubble with my fingertips. I move my fingers slowly around the back of his neck, pulling his face down to meet mine. Instead of kissing my mouth, he gently presses his lips against my wet cheek, slowly caressing away my tears with his beautiful mouth. It's so intimate, so close, so loving.

He moves slowly, gradually moving down to my throat - soft, gentle open-mouth kisses. I moan quietly, running my fingers through his hair, his touch so soothing, kissing away my sadness, making me want him, love him even more.

"Daniel," I whisper, "I..." *Tell him... tell him!*

"Mmm, baby?"

"I will miss you so much." *I can't.*

"Me too," his voice warm and calming, "you mean so much to me."

"I'll never forget you."

"I won't let you. I told you, I'm going to find a way."

I close my eyes and smile, letting myself believe, for a moment, that he will come up with a plan. "Yes. We'll be together, like this. We'll kiss every day, I'll see your smile every day, you can make love to me..."

"Every day, baby." He moves one of his hands slowly down my body, over my breast, making me gasp, and down over my hip to my thigh. He skims over to my inner thigh before slowly gliding his fingers back up to hover over me, I can feel the heat from his hand before his fingers gently stroke me, there. I arch my back and groan.

"Mmm, Daniel..." I murmur as I hold his face with my hands.

He lowers to lay a soft kiss on my lips, still lightly circling my clitoris. He kisses me so gently, so slowly, matching the movement of his fingers. I raise my knees either side of his body and wrap my legs around him, inviting him, I want him. "Bea, baby," he murmurs as he pushes his fingers inside me.

"Oh god!" I cry, throwing my head back into the pillow, "Please, make love to me."

He moves his fingers away and I feel the tip of his erection. I grab his neck and press my mouth against his, forcefully, my tongue fervently searching his. He groans loudly and slowly eases himself into me, deeper and deeper.

He moves gently, kissing me intensely, passionately. I close my eyes, savouring the feel of him deep inside me, the feel of his tongue on mine, his body moving against my skin. My hands explore his sculptured back, my fingertips rippling over his taut muscles.

"All I want to do is make love to you," he says, his voice strained, full of emotion.

"We are, we're making love, Daniel." My eyes search for his. "Look at me," I whisper, and his stunning turquoise eyes gaze into mine, I can see the longing, he needs me too.

I hold his darling face. "Daniel, we're making love. I am making love... with you." I'm telling him. Maybe not outright 'I love you', but I'm telling him in my own way. Yet another tear escapes over my lashes, telling him I love him, in not so many words. I can't help the tidal wave of emotion crashing through me.

He gazes at me and smiles a beautiful, sad, Daniel smile. "Me too, baby. With you."

Daniel makes slow, meaningful, incredible love to me and it's beautiful. I've never experienced feelings like this before, I think this is my first time, truly making love. And quite possibly, my last. We lay in each other's arms, gazing at each other, I don't want to let go of him, I don't want to stop touching. I make the decision to try not to cry anymore, I'll do enough of that when I'm gone.

I stroke my fingers up and down his impressive bicep as he lays on his side, facing me, his hand over my waist,

223

gently circling my lower vertebrae. "Are you cold, baby? Shall I get the comforter from the sofa?" He asks.

"I'm fine, thank you, sexy. You can cuddle me if I get cold."

"We should grab some dinner soon, if you're hungry, it's almost eight thirty."

"I'm not hungry, lunch filled me up. I could forego dinner."

"Okay, we can always get a snack later. What would you like to do?"

"Lay here. Cuddle you. Make the most of you."

Daniel smiles at me and pulls me against his body, and I wrap my leg over his. "That's fine by me."

I wrap my arm around his torso tightly and squeeze him. "Mmm, Daniel, Daniel, Daniel." I breath against his chest. He smells wonderful. "Daniel...?" I look up to his face.

"Yes, baby?"

"Can you spray some of your aftershave on something of mine so that I can smell it when I miss you?"

He grins and kisses my nose. "Of course, sweetheart. But what am I going to smell when I miss you?"

"You'll have to hop on a plane and come and smell me."

"Is that allowed?"

"Hmm, I suppose not. But if you happen to be in the UK on business, I think it'd be okay for you to come and smell me."

"And if you've moved on by then?"

"I can't see that happening for quite some time, darling, but I think I'd still want you to come and see me. I'd have to be unfaithful to whoever the new bloke is."

"You couldn't resist me, huh?"

"Definitely not," I say as I run my fingers up and down his gorgeous back, "you're always going to be the one that I compare new men to. If I date someone and you turn up... poor them."

He grins. "Just don't date anyone. Then I'll be happy."

"I didn't date you and look what happened."

"Hmm. Okay, just don't flirt with, hold hands with, press up against, kiss, *pash*, fuck, make love to... anyone other than me."

I giggle. "Okay, if the same goes for you and any other girls, then we have a deal."

"Done."

We both laugh and he kisses me, softly. "If I could really make you agree to that, I'd be happier."

We continue to hold each other and talk 'what ifs' for much of the night. Daniel fetches the duvet from the lounge and we fall asleep underneath it, wrapped in each other.

CHAPTER SIXTEEN
SUNDAY 23RD SEPTEMBER

Daniel kisses my face as I stir. I'm sad, my chest convulses with a small sob. "It's okay, baby. Shh."

I open my eyes and look straight at his concerned face.

"Are you okay, sweetheart? What were you dreaming about?"

I pause for a moment, frowning. I'm not sure. "I don't know... but I can probably guess." I take a deep breath in and exhale slowly. "Good morning," I smile and squeeze him, pulling closer.

"Good morning, baby," he smiles, "you were really whimpering, it took a while to wake you."

"I'm okay." I reach my hand to his face and stroke his cheek. "I love waking up next to you."

"Me too," he says, kissing my nose.

"I'm so glad my flight isn't until tonight. I'll need to go back to pack at some point."

"Okay, should we do that first? Then we can have the day together, knowing it's done."

"Good idea but I don't want to get out of bed just yet, I want to make the most of it."

"Okay, baby," he says softly, holding me close, "let's lie here for a while, then have a bath and get ready." He looks over to the alarm clock on the bedside table. "It's early, only seven thirty. We have plenty of time."

"Mmm, good. Let's do that, and then you can take me out for brunch."

"Sounds good, I know just the place."

I nuzzle into his chest, remembering that I, sort of, told him last night, and if I recall correctly, he said the same back. I wonder if he was talking in code too, he probably didn't even realise what I meant.

"Baby..." Daniel murmurs in his terribly sexy, deep morning voice.

"Sexy?"

"I miss you already."

I look up into his face and smile. "I'm still here, darling. Enjoy it, I am."

"I'm trying, baby," he says as he runs his fingers down my cheek and kisses my forehead, "you're so special to me."

"So are you, to me, Daniel."

I realise that this is the calm before the storm, I'm in heaven now, wrapped in his arms, listening to his lovely voice, but tonight, I will be in hell, desperately needing him but knowing I can't have him. *God, I really love him so much.* How is this even possible? It's fucking sods law. I meet the man of my dreams, who happens to think I'm amazing, I manage to fall in love with him in a week and now I have to leave him, forever.

"I'm going to clean my teeth so we can have a little pash fest. Sound good?"

Daniel chuckles and squeezes me tightly. "Sounds perfect. Would you like tea?"

"I'd love tea, thank you." We tear ourselves away from each other and Daniel strolls out of the bedroom, totally naked, to put the kettle on. I admire the view of his gorgeous behind before I head to the bathroom.

He joins me in there shortly after, wrapping an arm around my waist to pull me against his chest. I look in the mirror at our naked bodies touching, Daniel's hand holding onto me, my spare hand wrapped around his bicep near my face, and think just how well we mesh together. We're really made for each other.

I wonder what he's thinking as he gazes at me in the mirror, his eyes warm and affectionate, full of... lust? Longing? Love? I don't know, but whatever it is, he could look at me like that for the rest of my life and I'd be the happiest woman in the world. He makes me so happy, but at the same time, so very sad, because I love him so much. I love him and I can't have him. Who'd have thought that falling in love could be such a sad thing.

When we finish staring at each other, Daniel heads to the kitchen to make the tea and I crawl back under the duvet and wait for my man to come back and join me. I pick up the remote for Daniel's iPod and press play; a bit of music to preoccupy my thoughts.

A beautiful song plays softly in the room, one of my favourites, 'Last Request' by Paulo Nutini. As it plays, the lyrics - which I have always known but never really thought about - now mean something new, something heart wrenching. Although I'm pretty sure the song is about another situation entirely, many of the words relate to the situation Daniel and I are in, right now.

My heart aches listening to the sad, sad words, and the tears stream from my eyes instantly. I raise my fingertips to my mouth and try my hardest to keep the sobs from erupting. At that moment, Daniel walks in with my tea, completely naked with a gorgeous smile on his face. He takes one look at me and his expression falls, concern etched on his face. He puts the tea on the bedside table before sitting next to me and pulling me into his body. The song continues and I pull back to look at him, the lyrics poignant. I sob and he knows exactly why.

"We're going somewhere, baby, just hang in there, I'll work it out," he says, softly as he holds my face and gazes sadly into my eyes, "please don't cry." He crawls into bed next to me and holds me, gently rocking while I sob, uncontrollably into his chest. *So much for no more fucking crying.* "This isn't a last request, baby. We'll do this again, we'll be together, maybe not tomorrow or next week, but one day, soon. I promise."

"Daniel," I manage between sobs, "don't make promises you can't keep, we both know we're not going anywhere. We've only known each other for nine days, we can't move heaven and earth to make something happen that might not even last more than a couple of months."

"I don't care how long I've known you, I know how I feel and I know that we've got something worth fighting for. I..." he drops his head to the top of mine and shakes it, kissing my hair, "...I just need you so much."

We sit, gently swaying, listening and holding each other until the song comes to an end. Another Paulo Nutini song follows; 'Loving You', which is equally as beautiful. He repositions himself, facing me, and holds my face in his hands, kissing me tenderly. We kiss slowly, listening to Nutini sing about making love, being in love, before Daniel pulls away.

228

He tilts his head to one side and looks down before locking his beautiful eyes with mine.

"What these words mean, is what I feel, for you," he whispers.

I stare at him, trying to decipher exactly what he's telling me. A tear spills over my lashes as I gaze into the beautiful turquoise. Searching. He simply nods with a terribly sad, but gorgeous smile, and instantly, I know.

He wipes the tears from my face with his thumbs and I just stare at him, fresh streams sliding over my cheek bones. "I love you, baby," he whispers, and I whimper as I wrap my arms around his neck and squeeze him.

"I love you, too. I love you so much," I cry, "I thought I'd never get to tell you." His arms wrap around my body and we hold each other, tightly. We love each other. He loves me. *He loves me!*

Looking into his eyes, I lean forward to rest my lips against his. He opens his mouth slightly, inviting me to deepen the kiss, and I readily accept. I close my eyes and lose myself in this incredible moment of togetherness. I'm with the man I love, who loves me back. I may not be with him again, but I'm here now.

I open my eyes, still immersed in a perfect kiss, to look at his face. His eyes are firmly closed and he's frowning, as if in pain. "Daniel..." I whisper against his lips, pulling away, "Daniel, are you okay?"

He keeps his eyes closed for a moment and drops his head. When he lifts it, he looks straight at me, his eyes glisten with moisture. "Baby, I'm fine. I've wanted to tell you so many times. Now I have and you feel the same, but you're leaving. I love you, you can't leave." *Oh dear god, if I wanted to stop crying, I did NOT need to hear that.*

"Oh god, please don't say that. I don't want to leave... I have to. I want to stay and love you," I say as my voice wobbles and trails into a whisper.

"Make love to me," he asks, "real love."

"Oh, Daniel."

"Bea..." he whispers as he grabs my face and kisses me, urgently. He manoeuvres, pulling me down the bed slightly so that my head rests on his pillow. He lies on top of me, kissing me fervently as I thread my fingers through his hair, pulling him closer. His hands running all over my body, feeling every inch of me, trailing love all over my body.

"I love you, baby," he says, as I feel him hovering between my legs, "say it... please?"

"I love you, so much. Make love to me, Daniel." He moves in between my legs, parting my folds with his tip. He runs it gently up and down, over my clitoris and back down to my entrance where he gently eases into me, agonisingly slowly but incredibly deliciously. He stretches me as he gradually pushes deeper and deeper. I let out a long, loud groan and rock my head back into the pillow. I'm still sore from yesterday, but feeling him inside me almost soothes it away, he's my medicine, my cure.

"Oh yes, Daniel, you're amazing, I love you."

"I love you, baby, I love you so much," he says as he presses his lips against mine and kisses me, passionately, amazingly. He slowly eases nearly all the way out of me and back in again, pushing hard as he sinks deeper. My moans are so loud, I can't help it, I'm making incredible, sweet love with my Daniel and nothing in the world is better than this. And I can tell him I love him!

As I run my hands over his impeccable torso, I feel like the luckiest girl in the world, this body is mine, because the man who it belongs to, loves *me*. Not one of the super-amazing Hollywood girls, not Heidi the hot assistant, not Holly the ex... me. Beatrice Hart from Rickmansworth.

I wrap my legs around him and he slowly grinds into me, over and over.

"Oh yes, baby. My beautiful girl, you're all mine," he whispers, between kisses.

"Uh huh, oh yes, Daniel, yes. I'm yours, only yours. Oh, oh!" I cry, everything building up, slowly; the intense waves, the tingles, the toe curling, the imminent explosion brewing deep inside. My muscles tense in anticipation.

"Fuck, you're unbelievable. I've never known anyone like you." The volume of his voice increasing with each word, "Oh, baby... I'm... I'm... I..."

And as my orgasm bursts and crashes around him, I scream out loud. "Fuck! I love you, I love you, Daniel, oh fuck!" And he immediately comes inside me, calling out my name.

Daniel rests on my chest, panting. "Me too, baby. I love you, so much."

I stroke his hair and smile. "How will I live without you telling me that every day?"

"I will tell you every day. I promise." I decide not to disagree with him. I can't see how he will ever be able to find a solution to our problem, but I'll let him believe, or try to make me feel better, if that's what he's doing.

"Shall we have a bath now?" I ask.

"Sure, baby, I'll go fill it," he says as he kisses my lips and slowly rolls off me to sit at the side of the bed. He pauses for a moment and turns back to look at me, smiling. "I wanted to tell you so much, baby, but I didn't want to make things worse for you leaving. I'm glad you know, though, because now I do too, and I feel so lucky to have someone as incredible as you, love me."

I reach up to run my fingers down his stubble and smile at him. His handsome face looking at me, lovingly.

"*I'm* lucky, Daniel. I never knew a man as perfect as you could exist, and not only have I found him, but he feels this way about me... after only ten days."

"I felt it before ten days, I can assure you. I've never felt this way before."

"Me neither. What I felt with my ex was nothing, in comparison."

He leans down and kisses me gently. "Good. Don't get back with him."

"Of course I won't! I don't feel anything for him, Daniel, it's only you. Now go and run the bath, I need to pack and then we can spend the day telling each other that we love each other. Make the most of being able to say it, face to face."

"Sounds like a plan," he says as he stands to walk to the bathroom. I close my eyes and take a deep breath in, and exhale slowly. *I will not cry.* I don't want to ruin the day. Be strong, Beatrice, be strong.

After our wonderful, relaxing, hot bubble-bath together, we dress and I disappear off to the bathroom to wash my face and reapply my make-up. As I emerge, Daniel is sitting on the end of the bed, looking gorgeous in his Ralph Lauren casual attire, holding an envelope and a small box, wrapped with a ribbon. I stroll over to him to kiss him on the lips. "Hello."

"Hey, baby," he replies, "this is for you." He hands me the envelope and box and I look at him, questioningly.

"Don't open it now, save it until you're gone."

"Oh," I pout, "what is it?"

"Just a little gift, not much. I can't let you go without giving you a little something. But I did arrange this all by myself, Heidi didn't help with this. Just so you know."

"You've given me so much, Daniel, thank you. I'm very intrigued and I'd like to open it now!"

"Patience is a virtue... apparently," he says with a grin.

"Thank you, darling," I whisper as I bend to kiss him again before placing the card and box in my handbag, smiling, wondering what it is.

"Why won't you ever wash your make-up off in front of me, sweetheart?" Daniel asks as I start to make the bed.

"No one sees me without make-up on, Daniel. Well, except for the girls and my mum, and even then I can't stand feeling so exposed."

"But you're beautiful, what do you have to be self conscious about?"

"I just hate it, I don't look like this in real life, I need, at the very least, a bit of mascara to be able to show my face."

"Okay. I just wondered. I wish you'd feel comfortable enough to let me see you without, though. I love you, all of you."

I smile, he's so cute! "Thank you, Daniel, but it's very unlikely that you'd ever see me without make-up on. It's how I've always been."

"I'll consider that a challenge then, Bea. One day, you'll let me see you. The beautiful, make-up-free you."

"I'm not beautiful without make-up on."

"Don't say that, baby. You might not think so, but I do. I may not have seen you without, but you're the most beautiful woman in the world to me, either way."

"Thank you, Daniel. I'm going to say it for the millionth time this morning... I love you."

"I love you, too. I think you know that now," he beams.

"I do. But I'll never tire of hearing it, so you can say it all day long."

Daniel stands and holds his hand out to me. "Shall we go to the pool-house and pack? I'm starting to get hungry."

"Yes, let's. Oh and one more thing..."

"Yes, baby?"

"I love you."

He chuckles, "I love you, too."

I climb into Daniel's car and as he sinks into his seat, next to me, he hands me a Nordstrom bag. "Here."

"What's this?" I ask, he hasn't gone and bought me more has he?

"It's my boxers and sweater, your new comfies. I put my cologne on them, as you asked, so you can smell me."

Tears threaten as my eyes heat and prickle. I gaze at him, smiling. "Thank you, Daniel. I would have been really upset if I had forgotten something to sniff you by."

"Well, I sniffed my pillow this morning and it smells so much of you, so at least I can bury my face in that when I need you. I will never let the maid wash my bed linen again!"

~~~~~~~~

We arrive at the pool-house while Tilly is packing in the bedroom with Luke.

"Hi kids!" she shouts as we walk through the french doors.

"Hi Til, hi Luke."

Luke strolls out and high-fives Daniel. "Hey, bud. Hey Bea, how's it hanging?"

"Hey," Daniel responds.

"Hi, Luke, have a good day yesterday?"

"It was great, thanks Bea." He doesn't seem as jovial as usual this morning, although I expect maybe he's tired, I know they'll have been up all night having wild, good-bye sex.

"Bea, your case is in here, doll," Til calls from the bedroom and I walk in to meet her. She hugs me, long and hard, saying nothing, rocking slightly.

"Are you okay, Tilly?" I ask, this isn't like her.

"Yes, of course, I'm fine, Bea. How are you?" Her voice lowers to a whisper as she pulls away, "How was yesterday, did you tell him?"

I look down. "He told me this morning... and I told him back."

"Oh, darling, how are you?" She wraps one arm around my shoulders.

"I'm okay, constantly trying not to cry but I'm coping. For now. Listen, Til?"

"Uh huh?"

"I'm going to be a right old mess, later. You know that, don't you?"

"Yes, babe, I'll be right next to you. I'll look after you."

"I apologise in advance."

"Don't be daft, Bea," she raises her voice back to a normal volume to continue, "now, get on with your packing, you've got..." she looks at her watch, "eight hours until we need to be at the airport."

Daniel appears in the doorway. "Actually, ladies, you've got ten hours."

"No," Tilly responds, "our flight leaves at nine-twenty, and we need to be there for check-in, three hours before."

"It's only three-hour check-in for economy, in upper it's one hour before departure."

"We are in economy," I add, "remember? I told you my uncle got us upgraded but only one-way?"

"Baby, trust me, you're travelling in upper."

Tilly and I look at each other confused. "Hang on, what?"

"You're in upper class, baby. Okay?" Daniel says, exasperated.

"Daniel! What have you done?" Tilly gawks at him.

"It's nothing," he says with a shrug and a smile. He walks over to swiftly kiss me and swat my bum before leaving to join Luke in the lounge.

"Oh my god, Bea, I think I love your boyfriend."

I smile, astonished. He just keeps doing these lovely things. I walk, purposefully, into the lounge and throw myself at him, wrapping my arms around him, kissing him,

234

passionately. I couldn't give a fuck if Til and Luke are watching, I love my man and I'm going to let him know it. He stumbles back a little, clearly not expecting my forceful display of affection, but he quickly steadies, snaking his arms around my waist.

"Thank you, darling, thank you," I mumble against his mouth.

"You're so welcome, baby, it's nothing."

"Yes it is, Daniel. Thank you. How did you manage that?"

"Oh, Heidi knows."

"She's good, she might be super hot and gets to see my man every day, but I like her, you should keep hold of her," I say with a grin.

"Yeah, yeah. If she liked guys her own age, you probably wouldn't like her so much."

"Probably not, but she is good."

"That she is, now come on. Pack." *He's amazing.*

It doesn't take long for me to pack all of my stuff up and change into a short summer dress, and before I know it, we're all sitting on the decking, finishing a cup of tea, about to leave for brunch. Tilly and Luke are joining us.

I'm tucked under Daniel's arm on the step, holding my tea. As Luke and Tilly chat to Gemma, Daniel looks down at me and I up at him, he smiles beautifully and kisses my nose, making me grin from ear to ear. "Love you," he mouths, his eyes twinkling.

"Me too," I whisper, gazing at him. I stroke his cleanly shaven cheek. "You're so handsome."

He smiles and rolls his eyes, he's so damned cute! "Will we have time to make love again, before you go?" he whispers.

"I'm sure we can arrange it, darling," I reply, my voice a whisper, "Daniel...?"

"Bea?"

"When are you next coming to the London office?"

"I don't know, as soon as I can. I'll make sure it's soon, I promise."

"We aren't doing long distance though, you know that, don't you? If we can't figure out a way to be together, we just can't be. Okay?"

"I know. Let's not talk about it now, sweetheart."

"Okay, but I still want you to visit me when you go to the London office. Every time."

"Oh don't worry, baby, you couldn't stop me."

"Good. Shall we go? I'm starving."

"Me too, come on," Daniel stands and holds out his hand to pull me up.

"Ready to go?" Tilly asks before we take our cups indoors and head out to Luke's car.

~~~~~~~~

We arrive at a restaurant at The Grove, and pick a table outside in the lovely sunshine. I like the sound of the brioche french toast, which Tilly orders, but I decide on eggs Benedict, someone on a nearby table is having that and it looks amazing. I could eat a horse.

I've been working up quite an appetite, I don't think I've ever had so much sex in such a short space of time in my life! I can't even count how many times Daniel and I have had sex since we met. *Oh, so good.* How long will I have to wait until I get to make love to him again? Maybe forever, if he meets someone else before his next London visit. I shake my head, clearing the nasty thought from my mind and take a sip of refreshing, ice-cold pineapple juice that the waiter has just placed in front of me.

"You okay, baby?" Daniel asks, clutching hold of my hand on the table, lacing his fingers between mine.

"Yes, I'm fine thanks."

"Good." He gazes at me and smiles, lovingly and I can see Tilly, staring at me, out of the corner of my eye. I look over at her and she's got her head tilted to one side, she's frowning and gazing at both Daniel and I, with a sad smile on her face. She looks like she's going to weep.

"Alright there, Til?"

"Oh... yes. Sorry." She quickly looks away, shaking her head.

She's sad! Is she sad for me and Daniel? Or is it because she's leaving Luke? She'll never admit it if it is that, but these two are acting strangely today, I think they're realising just how much they like each other. But I could be totally wrong.

My food is delicious. There aren't enough places to go for a proper brunch where we live, obviously you've got the 'greasy spoons' for fry-ups - but that's not really my thing.

"What are you guys doing now? Need a ride back to your car or are you going out hang out around here or at mine for a while?" Luke asks.

Daniel looks at me, eyebrows raised in question. "What do you want to do, baby?"

"We could have a stroll, I'd like to get something for Clare and my parents. Maybe we can go back to Luke's after and...um... chill out for a couple of hours?" I say, trying to hide the salacious grin growing on my face. I may as well have said 'let's go back to Luke's for a shag.'

"Oh yeah...? I know your game," Tilly says with a wink, "good plan though."

I giggle and watch her as she eyes Luke with a grin. He gazes at her and leans in before gently kissing her. Their eyes close and I can feel the emotion between them. This is no fuck buddy relationship. I realise I'm staring so I look away and busy myself looking through my bag for my new aviators.

"I'll go and pay inside," Daniel says as Luke pulls away from Tilly and strokes her face, affectionately.

"No, Dan, I've got this," Luke says, standing and entering the restaurant. These boys don't let us pay for anything. I offer Tilly a supportive smile and she grins, shaking her head and rolling her eyes.

When we leave, Daniel and I walk hand in hand towards the shops, waving good bye to Tilly and Luke who are heading back to his apartment for a swim. Or so they say.

I get some bits for Clare and my parents and then we sit on a bench, in the sun, with our arms wrapped around each other, people watching. "Everyone seems happy, here."

"Do they? Is everyone miserable in Rickmansworth?"

I giggle. "Not exactly, but we don't walk around looking joyful all the time. It's nice to see happy people. I'm going to be the most miserable of the lot, when I get back."

Daniel pulls me closer and kisses my forehead. "Me, too. Hey! Do you want to go and look at underwear in Nordstrom again?" he asks excitedly.

I laugh and look up at his delightful face. "Do you?"

"Yes, I do. And I'd like to buy you a bunch of night gowns that you can't wear for anyone else."

"Come on then, let's go. But no buying me anything. You've spent enough on me over the last ten days."

"I haven't even come close, baby."

As we await the lift, Daniel looks down at me and puckers his lips, silently requesting a kiss. He's irresistible. I stretch up on tip toes and do just that, savouring the feel of his soft, gentle lips against mine. He smiles and winks at me as the doors to the lift open and we step in.

Stepping out again, a moment later, Daniel grasps my hand and walks, purposefully, towards the night gown section, collecting a basket on the way.

"You look like you're on a mission, Daniel."

"I am, baby. I'm going to buy you everything you want... and everything I want you to want, starting with the robe that matches your lace night gown. I'd like to know that when I come to see you, you'll have all of it, ready and waiting for me. No one else though, baby."

"You don't need to get me anything, Daniel."

"I want to. Just let me. Please?"

I smile, knowing this isn't just for me. It's for him too. Buying me these things helps him, somehow.

"Thank you, darling."

"You're welcome, baby. Now, let's shop."

Returning to the lift a while after, holding the bags of goodies that Daniel has just bought for me, I decide that I would really like to buy him something special. But what the hell do you get for Daniel? He can have anything he wants. Suddenly, an idea comes to me, and then another! *Yes!*

"Daniel," I say, as we stroll out of the lift, "I want to get some gift boxes in here for the my parents and Clare's goodies, but I'm so thirsty, would you mind getting me one of those freshly squeezed juices from that place we walked past, while I get some bits?"

"Sure, I'll meet you outside on the bench. Apple?" he asks.

"Oh, yes please. I'll see you in a minute."

He kisses me and lingers a little. "Mmm, I love you," he mumbles against my mouth, making me smile.

As he walks towards the door, I wait for a moment, making sure he's gone, and then dart over to the menswear department where I pick up a lovely soft, plaid winter scarf and then head straight to the gift wrap department where I get a few bits and bobs. I pay quickly before dashing back outside to meet Daniel. He's sitting back, waiting for me, looking edible.

"Hi, I'm back," I say as I approach him. He hands me the juice and I take a sip. "While you're sitting, there's just one more thing I want to get for my brother in Barney's. Can you stay with the bags and I'll just run down and get it quickly, that okay?"

"Sure, baby. Take your time. Do you want me to come with you?"

"No thank you, Daniel. I'll only be two ticks." I dash down to Barney's, managing to take the bag with the gift boxes and scarf in, without Daniel noticing. When Tilly and I were looking for bikinis last week, I saw something that caught my eye in Barney's. I now know, it's the perfect gift from me, to Daniel.

On my way back, I stop at another bench, out of view of Daniel, and make up one of the gift boxes. I fold the scarf and place it inside, followed by a layer of tissue paper and the gift I just purchased. I fish my pen from my handbag and write in the card I bought before I package it all up.

As I stroll back to Daniel, I see yet another gift in a shop window that I *have* to buy, so I run in and get it quickly. I prepare it before shoving it in the gift box with his other gifts and get back to him. I feel thoroughly pleased with myself. I have spent a small fortune, but right now, I don't care.

I plonk myself down on the bench next to him, panting. He hands me the juice again and I take a long, welcome, refreshing gulp through the straw. "Mmm, delicious. Thank you, Daniel."

He looks amused. "Why were you rushing, baby? I told you to take your time."

"I didn't want to waste a minute of my time with you..."

He grins and leans in to kiss me again, clutching my face with his hand. "You're beautiful and I love you. Shall we head back to Luke's? It's two, so we've got just over six hours until we've got to get you to LAX."

I frown and pout, looking down and then back up through my lashes, into his gorgeous eyes. "I don't want to go home."

"Don't go, baby. Stay with me."

My heart is breaking, so painfully slowly. I tilt my head and kiss him, my eyes prickling.

"I know. I'll find a way," he whispers.

I nod and take a deep breath to steady my emotions. "Let's go to Luke's. I can't concentrate on you and me with all of these people around us." He stands and takes my hand and we walk together, hand in hand, back to Luke's apartment.

When we arrive, Luke and Tilly are nowhere to be seen. They may be swimming, or they may be in the bedroom. Either way, we decide to go up to the guest/Daniel's room to have some alone time.

I place my bags down on the floor at the end of the bed and pull out Daniel's gift and card. He sits on the edge of the bed and I join him, handing him the box.

"Here, Daniel. I got you a little goody box."

He looks at me with an excited smile on his face, clearly surprised. "Baby, You didn't have to do that!"

"I know, darling, but I wanted to. Open it, I hope you like it."

"I know I will. Thank you, baby. What a wonderful surprise!"

"You're welcome. Open."

He opens the envelope first, pulling out the card with beautiful, hand painted butterflies all over the front, and the words 'Thank you'. As he opens it, jumbo butterfly confetti pieces fall out. He looks at me with a small smile and a questioning frown.

"Read it." I tell him.

'Darling Daniel,

Thank you for everything

*You have given me butterflies from the very first
moment I met you. I thought it only fair that I give you
butterflies in return. I have never met anyone as special as
you, I will miss you so, so much.*

I LOVE YOU,

Bea. Xxxxxxxxx'

"Baby..." he says as he wraps his arms around me,
tightly, "I love you so much." He kisses me on the lips,
tenderly and gazes into my eyes.

"Open the present." I point to the gift on his lap.

He looks down at the box and lifts the lid off. He pulls
out the last gift I bought. A small, knitted, stuffed cupcake
with a cherry on top. He grins.

"Smell it," I prompt and he lifts the cake to his nose.

"Mmm, it smells of you."

"Something to smell me by, just in case the maid
washes the bed linen."

He sniffs the cake again and sighs. "Mmm. You smell
so good."

"Open the next one."

"Okay, bossy," Daniel says with a smile.

He pulls out the small black box with 'Deakin &
Francis, England' written in silver on the top.

"England?" he asks.

"Well, it is an English company, so that's an extra thing
to remember me by, but I bought it here, in Barney's."

"Okay," he says as he opens it. Inside are bumble bee
cufflinks, painted beautifully in yellow and black with
detailed, veined silver wings and sapphire eyes.

"Oh, wow! They're... bees!"

"Yes, I thought that when you wear them, you'll always
have a 'Bee' near you, even if it's not this one."

Daniel laughs and shakes his head. "Baby, that's
brilliant. I love them, thank you so much. Wow, they're really
something aren't they?" he says, inspecting the fine detail,
closely.

"I liked them, I hoped you would too. You don't have
to wear them, I just wanted you to have something to remind
you of me."

"Of course I'll wear them, baby. I'll wear them tomorrow! I love them. These can't have been cheap, baby?"

"Daniel, don't think about that. Now, there's one more gift in there."

"Okay, sweetheart," he says as he places the cufflinks on the bedside table and removes the tissue from the box. He pulls out the scarf and smiles. "This is great, just my style..."

"I know it's a little warm to wear now, Daniel, but it's going to be cold when you come to London on business over winter, and I want you to have something to keep you warm. Now you have to make sure you come. Okay?"

He grins. "Try to keep me away, sweetheart. Thank you."

Putting the box to the side, he cradles my face with both hands, kissing me, lovingly. He pulls back and gazes into my eyes. "Thank you for the gifts, I love them all. I'm going to keep the cupcake on my desk, at work, it'll remind me that you've been there."

"And I enjoyed every minute of it." I climb onto his lap and push him down onto the bed. "And I'd like to enjoy every minute of being with you, now." I lean down and kiss his neck whilst undoing the button on his fly.

I sit up on him and push his polo shirt up his abdomen before lifting my dress over my head. I slowly sink back down to kiss his taut belly, all over. He crosses his arms over his chest, clutching the hem of his raised shirt and pulls it over his head so he is naked from the waist up.

My gorgeous, sexy, delicious man. I move up his chest with my lips, over his neck and up to kiss his mouth fervently. I can't wait, I need him. I moan, loudly as I kiss faster, impatiently.

"Mmm, baby..." he mumbles as he unclasps my bra and pulls it off before flipping us over so that I'm underneath him. He wriggles free of his shorts and boxers before slowly lifting off the bed to take my knickers off. He stands, staring at me, completely naked before him.

"Daniel, come and touch me, make love to me." I stretch my arms out towards him.

He remains standing, gazing at my body. "You're so beautiful, baby."

I grin and giggle a little. "You must have told me that a thousand times, Daniel."

"Because you are. No one else can have you, baby, I couldn't bear it. I'm going to make sure that you're mine, forever." *Forever?! Holy cow.*

"Daniel, you sound a bit crazy right now."

"I'm crazy for you. But don't worry, I'm not planning on kidnapping you and locking you up in my apartment. As much as I'd like to," he says with a grin as he crawls back over my body, kissing me, gradually making his way up to my face.

"Oh..." I pout and giggle.

"Would you like that?" he asks, between gentle kisses.

"Mmm, sounds heavenly."

"Don't tempt me."

I smile and narrow my eyes. "What would you do to me? Locked up in your apartment?"

"Baby, I'd make love to you twenty-four-seven."

"Ooh, yes, please."

He grins and we resume kissing, passionately, before we make delicious, emotionally charged love, for the last time.

Tears stream down my face and my sobs erupt uncontrollably from my chest as Daniel wraps his strong arms around me. I can feel his heart thumping through his chest onto mine after our love making.

"Shh. It's okay," he whispers, "we'll be okay, somehow."

"No... Daniel. We... won't," I splutter, sobs marring my ability to speak coherently.

"It seems that way, baby. Something will change. I promise."

I lay, quietly sobbing against his chest. I won't argue with him, if it helps him to think like this then so be it.

"Cry it out, if it helps," he whispers, gently rocking me. How can I continue with normal life? It seems so small and pointless without him in it. Could I give it all up? Right now, I want to, but something inside is forcing me to go back. I know it's the right thing to do, but I don't want to, god damn it! I want to pack it all in and come and live here in LA, in Daniel's apartment, with him.

We lay, quietly, wrapped in each other and drift off into a deep, afternoon sleep. When I wake, I am clinging onto him for dear life, one of my legs is wedged between his and my arms wrapped around him, my head buried in his chest. It feels wonderful and I forget, for just a second, that I'm going home today.

I gasp loudly, attempting to pull away from Daniel. He holds me tightly so I can't break free.

"Shit!" I murmur, finally escaping Daniel's arms and sitting bolt upright, feeling disoriented. "What's the time?" Waking up from that deep sleep with such a jolt makes me feel dizzy and queasy. I put my hand on my head and close my eyes.

Daniel checks his phone and pulls me back down into his arms.

"It's okay, baby, don't panic. We have plenty of time. It's five-thirty."

"I feel sick." I still feel disoriented and am trying to get my head around today's schedule. "So, how long have I got?"

"We need to get you there for eight, baby. Latest. We should aim to be there earlier so I can park up and come in with you. Then we have time to say good bye at LAX."

"You don't have to come in, darling."

"I want to. There's no way I'm dropping you at the door."

"Thank you, Daniel. You're the best."

"Are you still feeling sick? Would you like me to get you some water?"

"No thank you, don't let go. If I lay still for a bit, I'll feel fine."

"Okay, baby. Let me know if I can get you anything, I don't like you sick."

"Don't worry, I'm okay." I close my eyes and snuggle back into his warm body, holding one of his huge biceps. I kiss his chest, over and over as if it'll somehow help alleviate the pain of leaving.

"Daniel..."

"Mmm?" he responds, gently, stroking my back slowly with the tips of his fingers.

"I know you don't know yet, but I feel like I need to know when you'll be coming to England. Like it'll make it easier to leave... knowing how long I have to wait before I can touch you again."

"I know, I'm sorry, I want to know too, sweetheart. I can come on vacation? I'd come straight away."

"No, Daniel. We'll get stuck in a difficult long distance relationship situation if we keep having holidays to see each other. Whenever you come on business, we can meet, but that's it. Don't come just to see me."

"I don't know when that'll be, baby. But I'll let you know as soon as I do. It's going to be real hard, not being able to come and see you for the heck of it. I need you."

"Me too, I love you. So much." I squeeze him tightly and kiss his chest again, repeatedly.

He lets out a long, quiet groan. "I love the feel of your mouth on my skin."

"I love the feel of your skin on my mouth," I say with a grin, "in fact..." I add as I slowly move my fingers down to Daniel's growing erection and squeeze him gently, "I'd like to feel more with my mouth."

He gasps and smiles as I look up at his face. "Be my guest, baby."

I slowly run the tips of my fingers up and down the back of his thick shaft before I wrap my hand around him again. I reach up with my other hand and wrap my fingers around his neck, pulling his face towards mine and into a sensual, erotic kiss.

My tongue exploring his mouth slowly, I close my eyes and moan as Daniel's hands run firmly, up and down my bare back, clutching at the nape of my neck.

I push him so he's on his back and move to straddle him. I gently run kisses down his body and crawl backwards until I rest on his legs, taking him in my hand and hold a tight grip as I glide up and down.

I look up at him through my lashes and he's gazing down at me, his eyes hot and glazed, he looks sexy as hell. My eyes locked with his, I lick my lips slowly and lower my tongue to his tip to lick the bead of liquid from the top, all the while, maintaining this incredibly erotic eye contact.

Daniel's mouth opens, ever so slightly and I see him take a long, deep breath in. I move lower and gently kiss his balls, gradually moving up the length of his erection, laying wet kisses all the way up.

"Oh god, baby..." Daniel moans, he hasn't taken his eyes off me, "you are..."

I smile, enjoying the effect I'm having on him. "Uh huh?" I murmur, before licking his tip again. I'm so sad, but I feel a real need to be naughty, to preoccupy my feelings.

"You are..."

"Mmm. I am... good at this?"

Daniel smirks and I lick him again, applying more pressure with my tongue. "Oh yes, baby, you're *so* good at this."

I look up at him again and raise one eyebrow, smirking slightly as I take his tip in my mouth. "Uh huh," I mumble, my mouth full of him.

He rolls his head back into his pillow again and groans. "Fuck me. Bea, what are you doing to me?"

"Sucking you, Daniel," I purr, my voice as deep and sexy as I can get it. I take his whole tip into my mouth again and suck him, very gently dragging my teeth over him. His skin is so powdery smooth.

"Oh god, baby, shit," Daniel moans and I take him all in, as much of him as I can. I swirl my tongue around him and rise and fall, sucking all the while. I flick my hair over to one side so it doesn't get in my way and look up at Daniel's face. He's biting his lip, gazing at me, as if he's amazed by something.

I move faster, sucking harder, pumping down on him. It feels so good, I've never enjoyed giving blow jobs as much as I do with Daniel. Same as most things I suppose, everything is better with Daniel.

I want more, I want to be... naughtier. I rise onto my knees, taking him from my mouth, and move around until I am facing the foot of the bed, beside him, fully exposed. I glance around at him, slightly shy but trying my hardest not to be. As I place my mouth back around him, I move my spare hand slowly down my belly and over my landing strip to touch myself. Daniel's gasps. I try not to think about the view he's got, I know it's turning him on so it can't be that bad.

"Fuck, baby, you're so hot," I pick up the pace and pressure and start to really pump him, simultaneously with my hand and mouth.

"Let me touch you..." he whispers, as he replaces my fingers with his own. *Thank god, I'm no multi-tasker when it comes to bedroom activities.* Jesus, his fingers are magical. I'll be there in a matter of seconds. I moan loudly as I suck him, and he hardens even further in my mouth, signaling his imminent climax. It turns me on even more, sparking the flutters and waves, his fingers pushing and turning inside me. *Oh Christ it's coming and it's so strong, so good.*

I suck hard, pumping him, and as he yells my name loudly and the warm liquid shoots to the back of my throat, I immediately detonate around his fingers, swallowing his release between groans. My legs are like jelly and I quiver as the orgasm shudders through me, taking over. I take one gentle last suck before raising my mouth from him, and let out a loud, desperate moan as the spasms begin to ease.

He grabs me to pull me up on top of him and wraps his arms around me, burying his face in my neck. My heart thumping through my chest onto his, I lay there, consumed. My insides still pulsating from the sheer strength of my orgasm.

"My god, baby, that was unbelievable."

"Mmm," is all I can offer in return.

"You turn me on so much."

I grin slightly against his chest, I could fall asleep all over again. "I'm so tired, Daniel," I mumble, "I want to go back to sleep."

"Me too. We can't though, sweetheart."

"I know," I sigh, "that was really good for me, too. I love doing that to you. It has never been something I've enjoyed so much before. Must be because I love you so much, that turns me on." I smile.

"Everything about you turns me on, baby. You're damned good at it, too, Christ."

"Well, It's like you told me, Daniel, we're compatible. Our bodies work well together."

"Too damned well, if you ask me, considering we'll be miles away from each other from tonight. How will I cope without you?"

I kiss his neck and snuggle into him as he lifts the duvet over us again. I need to commit to memory, the feel of his body. "You coped without me last week and every week of your life before that, I'm sure you'll find a way."

"But I didn't know you then. I know you now, I know how amazing you are, baby, I know what 'love' really means. How will I deal with being so in love with someone I can't even see?"

"I can't bear the thought of only seeing you once in a blue moon while you're on a business trip."

"Me neither."

I lean up and kiss him. "You're an amazing man, Daniel. I am so lucky to have met you."

"I'm the lucky one. I'm not prepared to let you go without a big fight."

I gaze into his beautiful eyes. "Well, you're going to have to fight, baby, because I'm going tonight."

"You're going home, sweetheart, that's not the same as letting you go. You're my girl and I want it to stay that way." *His girl, how cute.* "I think we need to get going soon, baby. I'd like to leave yours by seven so we have plenty of time to reach LAX and park."

My heart sinks again. I don't want to. "Oh. I am enjoying naked Daniel. I wish you could come with me, cuddle me on the flight."

"I'd love to. If you want that, I will get a seat booked, baby, I would jump at the chance to spend an extra eleven hours holding you, but I don't want to make it harder to get back to normal when I have to come back tomorrow."

"No, Daniel, you can't do that, you have work and you're right, it would make it harder."

Daniel's arms tighten around me and he kisses my head. "Well, it's six now, I should probably go find Luke and see when he and Tilly are ready to go get the bags, I forgot I don't have my car here."

"Okay," I sigh, so sad to let him go, this is the last time our naked bodies will touch for... I don't know how long.

Daniel rolls us both over so that he is laying on top of me. He kisses my lips tenderly and brushes the wispy hairs away from my face. "You're the most beautiful woman, Bea. And just in case you aren't aware, I love you." He kisses my nose.

"I love you, too."

"Guess what, baby?"

"What?"

"I kissed you, after you had a nap, without us cleaning our teeth."

I gasp, putting my hand over my mouth. "So you did! Well, that's a first, I've never done that, ever!"

"Relax, baby, it was fine. Can't have been too bad if you didn't even notice. You must love me," he says with a smile.

"I must do, Daniel, I'm shocked that I forgot, I never forget that! But you're right, I didn't notice, you must have nice morning breath. Oh no, did you notice?"

Daniel laughs quietly, he looks gorgeous when he laughs. "Of course not, I only just realised. You shouldn't be so self conscious. Everything about you is perfect, even your morning breath."

"Oh Daniel. You are so sweet."

"So's your breath," he chuckles. "Okay, I'm getting out of bed now, sweetie. I'll go find Luke and I'll bring you up a drink."

"Thank you." He gets out of bed and puts his clothes back on before heading out of the door. I am so cosy and warm in this bed, I don't want to get up but somehow, I drag myself out and put my underwear on before making the bed. I look over at the bumble bee cuff links on the bedside table and stroll over to pick them up. They are sweet, I hope he really does like them.

Daniel walks back into the room with a chilled glass of sparkling water. I put the cuff links down and take the glass.

"Thank you." I take a long gulp and it's so refreshing.

"What were you doing with my bees, baby?"

"Just having a look at them, I think they're cute."

"They are, I really like them a lot. Thank you," he says as he kisses me again, "I'll think of you whenever one catches my eye. I'll think of you nonstop."

"Me too," I say with a shy smile, "so, what did Luke say?"

"He and Tilly are down in the living room, they're ready when we are."

I'm surprised to hear that they're not in the bedroom, to be honest, knowing what they're like. "I hope they haven't been waiting for us."

"No, they've been eating, something we forgot about. I'll get you something on the way."

"I'm fine thanks, Daniel, to be honest, I'm not that hungry. I can eat on the plane." I couldn't eat a thing, my stomach is in knots, counting down the minutes until I need to say goodbye to Daniel.

"Well, you let me know if you're hungry. You look so hot in your underwear," he says, distracted.

I smile. "Make the most of it, I'm getting dressed."

He wraps his arms around me and runs his large hands all over my naked flesh. He buries his face in my neck. "Mmm. You're skin is so soft and you smell so good, baby. Mmm. I. Love. You." he says, emphasising the last words with three sharp squeezes around my middle, making me giggle.

I wrap my arms around his neck and hug him close before we reluctantly break away and I start to get my clothes on. Daniel sits on the edge of the bed and packs his gifts back up into the gift box. I watch him as he smiles broadly, inspecting each item like a little boy at Christmas. He sniffs the cupcake plush and places it in the box before replacing the lid. He looks up at me and notices me watching him.

"Hello," he says with a smile.

"Hello, Daniel. I think you like your gifts."

"I love them. I like surprises, no one has ever really known what to get me before, for my birthday or Christmas, but you have given me the most perfect gifts, there's so much meaning in them. Thank you, baby."

"You are so welcome," I say as I stroll over to him and stroke his cheek before bending and kissing his lips tenderly. "Shall we go? I'm ready."

Daniel closes his eyes and grunts. "I wish I could keep you here. What would you say if I told you that I locked the door and lost the key?"

"I'd say that someone is telling porky pies because the door is still ajar."

"Huff. Okay then, let's head to the pool-house and get your bags." he says with a cute pout and stubborn tone, "And what are '*porky pies*'?

I giggle and explain the cockney rhyming slang, as we make our way down the stairs. Entering the living area, we find Tilly and Luke sitting aside each other on the sofa in silence. It seems so odd, they're usually joking about or practically ripping each other's clothes off, but here they are, deathly silent, gazing into thin air.

"Hello you two, are you ready to make a move?" I ask quietly, breaking the awkward silence. Tilly stands and straightens her clothes.

"Yes, let's go," she says, almost a whisper. I look at her with a frown, trying to assess the situation, have they had a fight? She doesn't look at me, just collects her hand bag and makes her way to the door. *Fuck, have I upset her?*

"Hey, Bea, you want to take a bottle of water or something?" Luke asks as he stands slowly and smiles a beautiful smile at me. I can't help but notice that the twinkle in his eye is missing, what the hell is going on?

"I'm fine thank you, Luke."

Daniel and I follow them to the car, they walk ahead, next to one another but there doesn't seem to be any interaction between them. I look up at Daniel and frown, gesturing towards Tilly and Luke and he shrugs, he doesn't seem to know what's going on either.

Soon after, we pull up outside Gemma and Jay's house and I take a deep breath in, knowing that the next port of call is the airport. I desperately don't want to go. All the way here, in the back of Luke's SUV, I have held onto Daniel, my head resting on his shoulder as he gently chatted away to me, his deep, masculine tone vibrating, welcome through my body.

Daniel gets out of the car and holds out his hand to help me out. He shuts the door and as I move towards the house, he gently tugs my hand and pulls me back into his arms. I look up into his beautiful eyes and he gazes down at me. "Let me hold you for a minute," he says, quietly, and I smile, resting my cheek against his chest, wrapping my arms around his muscular torso.

Tilly has already made her way around the side of the house with Luke following her. I look up at Daniel's face again.

"Shall we go to the airport with Luke and Til, or in your car?"

"Let's go in my car, I'm not sure what's going on with those two but I think they could use some space. And I want my last few moments with you, alone."

"Okay, I want to have one last journey in my new favourite car, too."

"Your new favourite car, huh?" Daniel says with an amused, smug look on his face and I giggle.

"Let's go and get the bags."

"Do I have to let go?

"Just for a minute." I smile.

We load the bags into the car and stroll back around to the garden. As we have a short while before we need to leave, Tilly, Daniel and Luke sit by the pool, talking with Gemma, while I take some photos of the pool-house to remember it by.

I take photos of everything, I want to remember every tiny detail of this lovely little holiday home, it's a shame I didn't think to take any of Daniel or Luke's apartments, considering we've spent a fair bit of time there too.

Just as I take a shot of the kitchen from the doorway, I feel strong arms wrap around my belly and soft kisses trail up the back of my neck. I close my eyes and sigh, it's heavenly. "I love you," Daniel whispers into my ear.

"I love you, too. I'm going to miss you so much."

He turns me in his arms and kisses me, tenderly. It unexpectedly escalates as our tongues desperately caress each other. I close my eyes and moan, lasciviously into the kiss, as Daniel's hands slide over my body. The river of emotions flowing through me, makes the urge to sob uncontrollably whilst, simultaneously, tearing his clothes off, almost impossible to contain.

Daniel moans deep in his throat as he grabs the back of my head through my hair, his other hand at the base of my back, holding me against him. My leg automatically drags up the outside of his thigh as his hand runs under my dress to my bottom. I groan loudly. Still completely caught up in the passionate moment consuming our senses, Daniel closes the door to the kitchen and gently, pushes me against it. *Oh, Déjà-vu.*

His hand caresses my behind while my leg wraps around him, we have no time to have 'kitchen-goodbye-sex' but, oh, how I want to. He lifts the skirt of my dress up around my waist and runs his hand down my belly and inside the lace of my knickers. As his fingers slowly circle my clitoris in time to the gentle caress of his tongue, I grab his face and moan loudly.

"Shh, baby..."

"Oh, Daniel..." I whisper, leaning my head backwards, against the door and he kisses my neck.

253

"Mmm," he murmurs against my skin, "you're my girl, baby. Don't let anyone else here until I come for you." And as he says it, he pushes two fingers inside me, exquisitely slowly.

"Oh, fuck..." I whimper, my voice a croaky whisper.

"Please, baby?"

"Daniel, we can't, long distance... oh, god... it feels so good."

"I love you," he whispers into my ear, his fingers slowly, but forcefully circling inside me, brushing against that all important spot, "I want this, I want you."

"I want you, too, you know that. I love you so much. Oh, yes, Daniel... keep going, don't stop..."

"I want you to come, baby, I want to feel it, see your body react to my touch, one last time."

"Yes, yes... I will... I am... Oh yes, Daniel!" And as the waves of sheer ecstasy roll through my body, I pull his face to mine and kiss him, forcibly. I hold his face, his lips against mine as the ripples inside, fade around his fingers. I frown and pant against his mouth.

"Fuck, Daniel. That was so good," I whisper, "and naughty, someone could have tried to walk in!"

"But they didn't and I got to pleasure you one more time." He grins, cheekily.

"And what a pleasure it was, my Daniel," I say as I stroke his cheek with my fingers, "you're an amazing man."

He smiles at me, affectionately and we stare into each other's eyes for a moment.

"Bea... Daniel..." Tilly's voice disturbs us and I immediately straighten myself out, Daniel turning to the sink to wash his hands as I respond.

"In the kitchen, Til," I open the door and she's in the living area, her eyes are red and she looks so... fragile.

"I've just said my byes to Gemma, Jay and Jack, so Luke and I are going to head to the airport now." Her voice is small and gentle, and I know immediately that she's really sad. I offer her a sympathetic smile.

"We're going to leave now, too, Tilly," Daniel says in a soothing voice as he walks over to her and puts his arm around her shoulders, "you'll be back here before you know it, Tilly. It must be difficult to live so far away from someone you're so close to." His voice is so caring and comforting, *oh*, he is adorable.

Tilly looks up at him with a smile and a frown. "You're amazing, you know that?"

Daniel chuckles, shyly, that's the second time that he has had that compliment, in about a minute.

"You really are, Daniel, and sadly, in a few short hours, you're going to find out just how difficult it is to live so far away. I really hope you two manage to figure something out. You're perfect for each other." *Oh, Tilly, so do I.*

"We will. I'll make sure of it. Now, let's make a move. Baby?" He holds out his hand to me.

"Oh! Let me just put this out for Gemma..." I pull a gift and thank you card that I bought at the shops today, from a bag, and place them on the coffee table. It's only a candle that matches the pool-house blue decor, but I thought it was pretty and hoped she would appreciate it. "Okay, I'm set."

Before we get to Daniel's car, I hug Gemma and Jay and give Jack a big squeeze. They've been so wonderful, especially considering I've spent so much time doing other things, they're the most perfect, accommodating hosts.

"You're welcome back, anytime, Bea. Although I'm sure you'll have another place to stay when you come back to LA...." Gemma says with a wink, and I thank her, again, for her fabulous hospitality.

Daniel starts the engine and pulls away from the house. "So, this is it. I'm officially on my way home," I say, solemnly.

Daniel looks at me briefly and smiles before putting his hand on my knee and squeezing it gently. I don't know what I'll do when you're gone, baby. I'm going to feel like crap. Maybe I should go home, try to sleep."

"So am I. Maybe you and Luke can go and chill out together, I think he's a bit sad that Tilly is leaving, do you?"

"I think so, and that's a real first, if someone had told me, last week, that I'd be thinking Luke had fallen for someone, I'd have laughed in their faces."

"Do you think he loves her?"

"I really don't know, I've never seen him in love, but I've never seen him like this before, either."

I like the idea of someone being in love with Tilly, she's so blasé about falling in love but secretly, I think she'd love it. She's been hurt before and I think that has discouraged her from showing her true feelings, claiming to want 'fun' and nothing more.

I gaze out of the window, taking in my last views of LA, and my thoughts turn back to our lovely day, and Daniel's face as I gave him his gifts. It gets me thinking.

"Daniel, what do you do at Christmas?"

"That's very out of the blue, baby?"

"I know, I was just thinking about the presents I got you and it made me think of you at Christmas. I'm trying to picture you, all festive."

"Oh, okay, well we usually go to Aspen for the holidays, my mom likes the snow and festivities. I'd love you to come there with me, you'd love it."

"Oh wow, how festive! I love snow, especially at Christmas, I'd love to do that."

"Well, maybe, one day, you will."

I reach over and rest my hand on the back of Daniel's gorgeous neck, stroking his short hair. "I hope I will."

Daniel takes a turning off the highway towards the airport and my stomach flips. I feel sick. I can't bear leaving him. As he finds a spot to park in, I tell myself that it's okay, we might be at LAX, but I still have a little while until I need to leave. He turns the engine off and looks at me with a gorgeous, sad smile on his face. "Well, we're here." He shrugs.

I simply nod and look down into my lap, if I continue to look into his beautiful turquoise eyes, the floodgates will open and that'll be all I do for the next... well, I don't know how long.

Daniel reaches for my hand and brings it to his lips. "Look at me," he says against my knuckles.

"I don't want to cry, Daniel," I whisper, but the tears are already flooding my eyes and as one drops down into my other hand, he lifts my chin and leans in to press his soft, soothing lips against mine. I instantly wrap my arms around his neck and kiss him back.

"We'll be okay, baby. I'll make sure to find an urgent reason to come straight to the London office for a meeting," he says with a small smile.

"Really? I hope so."

"I'll do my best." He nods as he runs his thumb along my bottom lip. "Let's go get you checked in so we can have a moment to say goodbye, before you go through to the lounge."

"Okay," I respond, reluctantly.

I notice Tilly and Luke as soon as we near check-in. They're standing facing one another, talking quietly. It's so odd that they're not horsing around. Tilly doesn't have her suitcase so she's obviously checked in already, so I head straight to the desk, clutching Daniel's hand as he wheels my case behind him.

After check-in, we stroll over to a wall and Daniel leans his back against it, holding me in his arms. I wrap mine around his warm torso and rest my head against his chest. The sound of his breathing, the rhythm of his heart thumping under my ear, the soft thread of his polo shirt beneath my cheek, I notice every tiny detail and try to lock it all in so I'll remember it when he's not there.

His arms are wrapped so tightly around me, his cheek resting on the top of my head and we stand in silence, enjoying each other's warm embrace. My eyes close and I try to forget where we are for just a tiny, split second, so I can enjoy my boyfriend without the heart ache of knowing I'm leaving for good.

"I love you so much, baby," he whispers and I pull my head back to look up at his darling face.

"I love you, too."

He smiles and leans down to kiss my lips. "Now, you promise me? No assholes."

"I promise. And no gold digging whores?"

"Cross my heart, baby. Please, please look after yourself, I want you in one piece when I come for you."

"Of course. But Daniel, please don't wait for me. It's not going to happen and we both know that."

"Shh. Don't," he says as he pulls me in close again.

"Tilly is waiting for you sweetheart."

"No!" I cry, "No, Daniel... we haven't had enough time!" The panic in my voice evident as I plead with him. Tears cascade once again, only this time, I start to sob. My body convulses against his as I break down, knowing that I need to leave. It's so, so unbearably painful, I feel like my heart is ripping through my chest, all I want is him. "I don't want to go, please, Daniel."

"Bea, I don't know what to say sweetheart, I don't want you to go either." He holds me tightly, soothing me, like a child, with a gentle rocking motion.

"Bea, darling, it's time to go," Tilly says in a gentle, caring tone as she rubs my back.

"Uh huh. Just two minutes, Til, okay?" I manage to mutter from the fabric of Daniel's shirt, my face buried in his neck.

"Okay doll, I'll be right here," she replies and I hear her step away.

"Baby, I want to know the minute you get home, okay?"

I nod.

"And make sure you eat; eat and sleep all the way home. You don't want jet lag."

"I'll try. I'm opening my gift first though," I say with a sniff as I look up into his perfect face. His eyes are awash with emotion.

"Good. I hope you like it."

"I'll love it, Daniel. Like you." I stand on tiptoes and gently touch my lips to his for our last kiss. His arms tighten around me and he lifts me from the ground as we lose ourselves, momentarily, in the connection. I keep my lips against his for as long as I can, tears trickling down my cheeks. Eventually, we unwillingly end the kiss, and Daniel returns me to my feet.

"Off you go, baby. Remember to text me when you're home. I love you so much, sweetheart, so, so much." He clutches my hands as we begin to separate our bodies, our lives.

"I love you too, I'm going to miss you so much, I can't bear this, I don't want to leave you."

"I know you don't, baby, I don't want you to go either."

"Good luck Daniel, with everything."

"I'm going to see you soon, okay? Please don't be sad."

I step away from him and pull his hands to my lips to kiss. "I'll try, I can't promise though. I love you."

"I love you too. Have a safe flight."

"Bye Daniel..."

"Bye bye, baby." I reluctantly, painfully let go of Daniel's hands and step back, turning towards Tilly as I start to break down again, the tears pouring down my cheeks. Tilly wraps her arm around me, her eyes welling up too, as we walk away from our men.

I turn one last time as we walk, he seems so far away. He still looks beautiful, waving gently with a small smile. Luke stands with him and watches us as we go. Daniel blows me a kiss and I send one straight back, as I take in his beautiful features for the last time, before turning and heading deeper into the airport.

~~~~~~~~

Take-off was horrific. I felt as sick as a dog and it was unbelievably bumpy - I'm sure it's not normal for it to be like that. We seemed to be dragging along the runway on the back wheels for about half an hour, I'm surprised that we got off the ground at all. All I wanted, the whole time, was that hand, that caring, masculine, soothing hand, to comfort me. Thank god we're airborne now, just turbulence to deal with.

Tilly is sitting right behind me, thankfully, and we have been trying to console each other. I don't think I'm doing a particularly good job of it, honestly, but I can't really tell how Tilly is feeling, she's not as open a book as I am. I can tell she's not herself but she's not admitting to anything, apart from being sad to leave Gemma and Jack.

My eyelids are swollen and my head aches from the non-stop crying; I don't seem to be able to switch it off once it starts these days. I probably look like a deformed panda but I couldn't give a shit right now, I feel crap and the general public will just have to deal with my ugly mug.

As soon as the aircraft is on an even gradient, I ask the cabin crew to turn my seat into a bed and I change into my airline pjs before curling up under the covers, clutching Daniel's delicious smelling jumper. I think back to our

259

wonderful time together and how amazing Daniel made me feel, all of his compliments, his undivided attention, constant kisses, his wonderful gifts... and I suddenly remember the gift in my handbag.

I practically jump off the flatbed to grab my handbag and pull out the little ribbon-wrapped box and card. I sit, cross legged in my aeroplane pyjamas and place the gift box in front of me, wiping a tear from my face.

I slowly open the envelope and pull out the card. On the front is a picture of a jumbo jet, flying through a beautiful blue sky with fluffy white clouds dotted here and there. At the bottom, Daniel has hand-written: *Where it all began...*

I smile and open the card, bracing myself for the deep ache that will torture my body the moment I have read it. I am immediately excited to see just how much he has written, and his handwriting is beautifully neat. Of course it is, Daniel is perfect, through and through.

> *'My beautiful Bea,*
>
> *At the moment, I'm sitting at my breakfast bar and you're in my bathroom doing your make-up. I miss you already. I can't wait for you to finish so I can see you, even though you've only been in there for a few minutes. How will I cope without you?*
>
> *If you managed to wait until you left before you opened this, then I know you'll be feeling sad right now and you can be sure, wherever I am, I'm so miserable, missing you. You're the best thing to have come into my life in... forever, and I don't know how I'll manage to carry on, every day, without you here.*
>
> *A moment ago, you told me that you love me. I have never felt a feeling like it in my life, I've never wanted anything as much as your love, and you gave it to me, just like that. I think the one thing that I want now, even more than that, is for you to be by my side. I love you so, so much. I don't think it's possible to express how much I love you. And all this happened in ten short days. It was so easy, baby, and I fell hook, line and sinker.*
>
> *I won't give up trying to find a way for us to be together and trust me, baby, we will be together.*

I know that you'll enjoy getting back to Bear's and also seeing your friends and family. Tell them all about me and that I'll be sure to meet them, real soon.

Have a good flight, sweetheart, let me know when you're home safe. Now get those sexy airline pajamas on and cosy up in your bed, make the most of the night flight. I wish I was there to wrap you in my arms. Don't forget to dream about me, I'll be dreaming of you, every night.

Thank you so much for a truly wonderful few days, I have never been so happy, as when you were curled up in my arms (apart from when you told me you loved me, of course).

I love you so much, my beautiful, BEAUTIFUL Beatrice.

Always,

Daniel xxxxxxxx'

I press the card against my chest as if it somehow makes him closer to me. How can I possibly have anymore tears left in me? There's an endless supply and they are freely pouring down my cheeks.

Tilly pokes her head into my space. "What's up cherub? You okay?"

I nod and sniff, and hand her the card.

"Oh darling, he wrote you a note! That's so sweet. Can I read it?" she asks and I nod.

I watch as her eyes move from word to word, frowning a little more with each line. She puts her fingertips to her mouth as the tears well in her eyes. I'm glad I'm not the only one who becomes emotionally unstable at the drop of a hat. I know she's about to sob when her nostrils twitch and she takes a sharp, deep breath in.

As she finishes reading Daniel's last few words, she shuffles out of her bed and comes around to crawl onto mine. "Oh Bea, I can't bear how hard this is for you. What an incredible letter, he loves you so much."

She wraps her arms around me and kisses my cheek, before wiping the tears from my cheeks and then her own. We both sniff together and let out a giggle.

"What do we look like, eh?" she asks with humour.

"He got me a gift too." I pick up the box and show her.

"Oh! Open it, open it!" I tug at the pretty red ribbon and it slips off the box. I remove the lid and a small bundle of tissue before I see his gorgeous gift for the first time.

"Oh..." I whisper, holding my hand over my mouth.

It's a thin, delicate gold chain with three different gold pendants: The first is a small, yellow-gold doughnut and I let out a little giggle, knowing exactly what that represents; the second is a white-gold aeroplane, how perfect; the third, a rose-gold cupcake.

Each pendant is very small, about the size of a pea, but they are so intricately designed, the aeroplane even has little windows and doors. The cupcake has a corrugated edge, just like a cupcake case, and has swirly icing with a cherry on top. He knows me so well. It's absolutely stunning and I love it to bits.

I silently turn the box to face Tilly and she tilts her head, frowning with a smile. "Bea, it's gorgeous. It's so you, he knows you so well!" She knows what each pendant represents, I told her about the super-hot doughnut and chocolate sauce sesh and the other two speak for themselves.

"I know, that's exactly what I was thinking. I love it. Will you put it on me please?"

She fastens the clasp at the back and I immediately close my fingers around the precious pendants. The chain is just long enough for me to hold them up and see them.

"Do you want to try to get some sleep darling or shall I stay and chat?"

"To be honest, Til, I'm not very good company. I can't think about anything but him, so I might try to catch a few winks, give the swollen eyelids a chance to relax."

"Okay, doll, I'm going to do the same then, but if you need me, I mean it, wake me up. Okay?"

"Thank you, I will. Please let me know when you need *me* though Til, okay? You don't have to be strong just because I'm weak as shit, I will do my best to be there for you too. I love you."

"I know, thank you. I love you, too, but I'm fine."

~~~~~~~

Mmm... I'm so cosy, curled up in Daniel's nice warm bed, against his chest and wrapped in his arms. He smells so good. I snuggle into him but I can't feel his soft skin, so I reach out. My hand hits the seat back and immediately, I am brought back to the present, to the monotone hum of the aircraft engines. My stomach churns and I draw my knees to my chest with a quiet whimper. *Oh god, how will this ever go away, it hurts so much.*

"Ma'am, can I get you anything?" asks a stewardess, making me jump.

"Oh, um, could I have a cup of tea, please?"

"Of course, can I get you something to eat?"

Oh good god, no. "No thank you, just tea."

I sit up and cross my legs underneath me as the pretty stewardess returns with a steaming hot cup of tea. I put it down and pull a pack of face wipes and a mirror out of my bag to clean up the panda eyes that I'm no doubt sporting right now. I'm shocked at the face that looks back at me, I look like absolute and utter shit, nearly as bad as I feel.

The cool, refreshing wipe obviously does nothing to help my agonisingly knotted stomach, but at least I look a little better. I'll try to get back to sleep after my tea but I must remember to put some mascara on before we land; the rule still applies, no matter how crap I feel.

My tea pre-occupied me for all of four minutes, but as nothing other than sleep can stop me crying, I think I'll try and get a little more. The last thing I need, on top of this miserable, dull ache, is hideous jet lag.

I curl back up in the surprisingly comfortable bed, hug Daniel's jumper close to my chest and play with the pendants on my necklace. I let my mind wander to the first time Daniel and I met, on an aircraft the same as this. His beautifully handsome face took my breath away.

CHAPTER EIGHTEEN
MONDAY 24TH SEPTEMBER

"Oh Daniel, mmm..." I moan as Daniel tenderly kisses my neck, his hands caressing my breasts, his fingertips lightly squeezing my hardened nipples. Papers underneath me rustle as we move together, writhing in anticipation.

"Oh, baby, I love you so much," he says, as he eases himself into me, exquisitely slowly. He sweeps a pencil pot and some papers off the desk as he leans down to press his lips against mine.

"We need to pick up the pencils," I mumble, breathlessly against his lips as he thrusts into me, forcefully. It feels so good... but the pencils...

"It's okay, baby, let me make love to you."

"No, pencils first..."

"Shh, baby," he says as he rolls onto his back, taking me with him. The soft, white bed sheets below my knees are satin. I could have sworn we were on his desk, must be one of those desks that doubles as a bed. I ride him slowly, it's incredible, he's so deep and hard and with every rock I can feel myself getting closer and closer. I look down to find Daniel's beautiful eyes, but I can't see them, his face, a blur. I blink a few times to clear my vision but I still can't see him.

"Daniel, I can't see you, I need to see you."

"I'm right here baby," he says as he clamps his big, warm hands on my waist and rocks me faster, back and forth against him.

I can feel him, I can smell him, but I can't see his darling face. I know, somehow, that if I pick up the pencils, I will be able to see him again.

"Daniel, I need to... oh yes..." I'm getting closer, the waves inside building stronger and stronger. "Oh, god, it's so good! I need to see your face!" I cry, desperately.

"Baby, look at me," he shouts, letting go of my waist to clutch my face and, suddenly, he comes into view. His delicious mouth, his unbelievable turquoise eyes, his chiseled jaw... god, he's so handsome.

"Oh, Daniel! Oh I love you so much, oh yes... oh..."

"Ride me, love me, baby, oh god, yes... yes!" Daniel shouts loudly as he comes hard and fast inside me and I immediately detonate around him silently, it's so strong and goes on and on and on. I look into his piercing eyes and he smiles at me, gorgeously. "I've got my beautiful girl. I love you."

~~~~~~~

"The pencils!" I shout loudly, waking myself with a jolt, the pulsating orgasm ripping through my body. *Oh, wow....holy fuck. Hang on... am I... did I just...?* I frown and rub my eyes, remembering clearly, the very odd but very pleasant dream I was having. I have definitely just come, I still feel the aftershocks. Christ, I hope I didn't make any noises.

Daniel's beautiful smile is the clearest part of the dream. I smile, thinking how he'd love to know, that not only did I dream about him, as he asked, but I had an orgasm doing so. What was with the weird desk-bed? And the pencils? Bizarre.

"Hey, sweetie, did you sleep well?" Tilly's head appears over my seat back.

"Hi, Til. Um... yes I did actually." I smile and frown, such an odd dream. "I had a sex dream and... you know..." I raise my eyebrows and rock my head from side to side by way of explanation.

"Oh my god, did you... you know?"

I nod and giggle and Tilly follows in surprise.

"That's hilarious! On an aeroplane!"

"I know! Shh!"

"I'm going to ask for something to eat, we need to pack up the beds for landing soon, the stewardess just told me."

"Okay, I had no idea I'd been asleep that long."

"Yep, we'll be home very soon." A heavy ache lingers deep in my gut at the reminder of being so far away from Daniel, but the tears don't appear of their own free will this time. I'm making a little progress. I hope.

About an hour and a half later, Tilly and I have disembarked the aircraft, collected our bags and are on our way to the collection point to meet my dad. Neither one of us is particularly loquacious; we're cold, tired and miserable. As we reach the doors, the smell hits me first, a wet, smoggy,

265

mossy smell, surprisingly homely but very depressing at the same time. We're definitely home.

"Bloody hell, it's colder than when we left, isn't it," Tilly says, wrapping her cardigan around her as we look for my Dad's car.

"I was thinking that, but it always seems cold at the airport."

"Yeah, suppose so. Come on Eddy-boy, we're freezing our tits off here," Tilly calls to the row of cars, making me laugh.

"I'd appreciate you not discussing your tits with my dad, Til." She grins at me as a huge 4x4, almost identical to Luke's, pulls up in front of us and beeps, making us jump.

Oliver jumps out and jogs over to us with a huge smile on his face. "Hey BB! Hi Tils!" he calls out, giving us both a giant hug together.

I can't express how good it is to see my brother, it's such a comfort to have him here. "Oliver, it's so nice to see you, I thought Dad was collecting us?"

"Yeah, something to do with Mum's car having problems so he had to take her somewhere... or something, I don't listen. So, good holiday?"

Tilly and I both smile at him. "It was lovely thanks, Olly, we're sad to be back," Tilly replies.

"You look hot Tils, what's his name?" Oliver jokes and Tilly rolls her eyes at him. He loads our bags into the boot and we all climb in to make our way home. Tilly and I quiet and somber. "Oh come on girls, why are you both so glum? You've just been to sunny California!"

"Sorry, Oliver, we're just knackered and a little down in the dumps. Thanks for coming to get us. I like the new ride." I offer, realising we must be terrible company.

"Oh no, I know that tone, did you have a holiday romance? Actually, I don't think I want to know."

I giggle. "I'll spare you the gory details, but yes, we both met someone and we didn't want to come home."

"Some *one?* I really hope there were two of them..." he says as his mouth twists with mock disgust, making me laugh again.

"Thankfully, yes. They were best friends. We had such a fantastic time, Oliver, you'd absolutely love LA."

"I bet I would, we should all go sometime, get a few of us together."

"That would be so much fun," I say and look around to Tilly in the back who seems to be on another planet, gazing out of the window into the rain. "Til? You okay?"

"Hmm? Yes, sorry, were you talking to me?"

"Oliver was just saying it'd be great to get a few of us together and go back to LA."

"Oh, yeah, that would be fun," she says with a half smile, lacking all of her usual enthusiasm. I offer her a sympathetic smile and decide to leave her be. She obviously has other things on her mind. I, however, am glad for the distraction, Oliver isn't taking my mind off Daniel, but he is keeping the agony at bay for a short while. It's great to catch up with him.

"So, been up to anything while I've been gone?" I ask, genuinely interested.

"Not a lot, work as always, got a couple of new big contracts which is good news. We all went out on Saturday night, that was a laugh. I talked to Clare quite a bit, she's missed you guys loads."

"Ah, we've missed her too, I wish she could have come with us."

"Dylan turned up with that girl, what's her name? Lee... Lena?"

"Leah."

"Yeah, Leah; face like a slapped arse. He asked after you, again. You wouldn't get back with that dick-head would you?"

"Oh for god's sake, Oliver, how many times? No, I am never getting back with him." This is something I seem to be discussing a lot lately. "Especially not now."

"Not now? Why's that?"

I sigh loudly and shake my head. "Oh never mind, it's a long story." I rub my hand over my forehead, the sadness creeping back.

"Bea? What's going on? Is this about the bloke in LA?"

"Daniel." I nod, "Yeah, he's... oh, never mind, I'll cry and I really don't want to. Can we talk about it another time?"

Oliver frowns at me, knowing something's up. "Okay, but if you want to talk, just call or come over, okay?"

"Yes, thanks Oliver."

"Mum asked me to ask you if you want to go for dinner tonight, I'm going over, she's making that lamb thing."

"Can you tell her thanks but I'm knackered and just need to get some sleep? I'm not really in the mood for talking about the holiday and stuff, I just want to be on my own and go to bed."

"Yeah, no worries, she thought you might say that anyway, after such a long flight."

As we arrive in Watford, I turn to look at Tilly and she's fast asleep in the back. I hope she's okay, I've been so wrapped up in my own sadness that I haven't given Tilly enough thought.

"If Tilly is asleep, I'll drop you back first. Unless you want me to come in for a cuppa?"

"No, it's okay, I've got to sort out my suitcase and washing and all that. Can you make sure she gets in okay?"

"Of course I will."

At home, Oliver puts my suitcase in the lounge for me and gives me a big hug before leaving to take Tilly home. I put the kettle on and lean back against the counter, closing my eyes and taking a long, deep breath, to steady my emotions. When my tea is brewed, I take the toothbrush pot-come-mug to the lounge and sink into my plush sofa with my handbag, and pull out Daniel's jumper. Bringing it to my nose, I inhale long and deep, closing my eyes, imagining he is with me. I pull my iPhone out of my bag and switch it on, curling up, cuddling my Daniel-jumper.

The ache is back with a vengeance and I feel helpless. I'm so lonely but I only want him, I could go to Clare and Tilly's place or my parents house if I wanted company, but it's Daniel that I need.

As a tear runs down my face, my phone chimes. I look at the screen and the butterflies immediately flit with excitement in my belly when I see his name.

~

Daniel 24 Sep 18:03
Hey baby, are you home yet? I checked online
so I know you landed safe and sound. Let me
know when you're home. I miss you so much.
I Love you. Xxxxx

~

I weep and reply immediately.

~

24 Sep 18:05
Hello darling. I'm home now
with a nice cup of tea. Thank
you so much for my beautiful
gift, I love it almost as much as I
love you. It's so perfect. The
card made me cry. I can't tell
you how much I miss you,
already. Are you at work? Did
you sleep well? I slept most of
the flight home and you will be
pleased to know that I most
certainly dreamt of you! I will
tell you about it another time,
you'll enjoy it! The best bit was
the VERY happy ending. It was
good ;-). I love you so, so, so
much. I can't stop crying. I wish
you were here. :-(Xxxxxxxxxxx

~

I send the message and re-read his as I walk to my
bedroom to get a box of tissues. My bed looks so inviting, I
can't wait to crawl into it, but I need to stay awake until after
ten so the jet lag doesn't set in.

The strangest thing that I'm noticing, is how horny I
am. I have had so much sex over the last week, you think I'd
be sated, but I'm feeling depraved already. Looking at my bed,
I can picture Daniel laying in it with me, making love to me,
relieving this need to have him inside me every five minutes.

The chime of a text message disturbs me from my
reverie and I head back to the lounge so I can curl up with my
tea and enjoy his reply.

269

~

Daniel 24 Sep 18:12
Hi baby! I wasn't sure if you were going to reply. You're so welcome for your gift, I'm glad you like it. I didn't sleep too well, I wanted to have you curled up in bed with me. Yes, I am at work, I'm not doing much because my mind is on you 24/7, but I'm here, at my desk, smelling my cupcake :-) I LOVE the sound of your dream, was it a sweet sort of happy ending or a moaning in ecstasy one??? ;-) I wish I was there too or at least that you were here. Please don't cry baby. How's home? I love you. Xxxx xxxxxxx

~

~

24 Sep 18:14
Of course I would reply! Home is very wet, cold and lonely. My place is lovely though, my mum has left flowers and food so I don't even need to go to the shop. I'm trying not to cry but it's not really working! It's so nice to text you though. Well, the happy ending was definitely a moaning in ecstasy one, in real life! I'm really horny for some reason, I can't stop thinking about you and me in the throes of passion. What I'd give for a bit of that right now... Mmm ;-) You should get back to work, you don't want the bosses on your back ;-) I LOVE YOU TOO. XXX

~

I smile and blow my nose, determined to stop crying for a while. It's so lovely just to be able to communicate with him. I open my suitcase to start sorting out the washing, considering I have some time to kill before bed. I've been dreading going through my clothes because I know when I see the things that Daniel bought me, I'll hurt more. But as I'm feeling a bit jolly for hearing from him, I'll make the most of it and get as much out of the way, as possible.

I put all of my toiletries away in my en-suite and sort all of the dirty washing into the laundry basket, putting one load in the washing machine at the same time. I hang up my beautiful, expensive dress that I wore to the 'W' and place my sparkly Manolo's in centre place amongst my other shoes in the wardrobe.

When I have finished unpacking everything else, I put my suitcase away, feeling extremely proud of myself for doing such a good job, very quickly, without crying once. It's taking Daniel a very long time to reply, but it's okay, he's at work and that comes first. I realise, as my stomach churns painfully, that I haven't eaten since brunch yesterday. I always lose my appetite when I'm upset but I have got to eat before I start feeling lightheaded.

I look through the fridge and there is just nothing I fancy, whatsoever. I pick at a few grapes and have a slice of goat's cheese but it doesn't taste of anything but cardboard. It's not like I have any plates to eat from anyway, so I give up and go back to the lounge to flick the TV on. I wonder what's taking Daniel so long to reply, it has been over an hour now and I'm starting to feel crappy again. I fiddle with my necklace and pull his card out of my handbag to read again.

Oh dear god, this is just so hard, the lump in my throat aches, my eyes hot, ready to flood. This is so much more painful than I had anticipated, even when I was trying to prepare myself, back in LA, I had no clue that it would be quite *this* bad. My body aches, my heart physically hurts, I don't know quite what to do with myself.

Maybe I should have a bath. The TV is an irritating noise, I'm not looking at it, it's not distracting me, so I turn it off and head to the bathroom. I pray that a hot bubble-bath will do me some good as I return to the lounge and wait.

My phone eventually chimes and I grab it excitedly, but feel a stab of disappointment and immediate guilt - for feeling that way - when I see Clare's name on the screen.

~

> **Clare 24 Sep 19:47**
> Hey doll-face, welcome home! Hope you're okay, Til won't tell me why she is so upset, just says she is sad to have left Gemma but she's never normally like this when she gets back. Do you know? I hope it was okay leaving your man. Let me know if you need me, I'm here. Work is fine, nothing major to report, had a business call to discuss a regular contract which will be excellent, I'll tell you about it when you come in. When are you planning on coming back? Don't rush, we're fine but we miss you like mad. Love you xxxx

~

Poor old Tilly, it must be about Luke, and poor old Clare having two miserable best friends.

~

> **24 Sep 19:50**
> Hi sweet cheeks, sorry I haven't been in contact for a little while... Okay, I think it must be to do with Luke. I'm not sure, she wouldn't admit it, but she has been acting very uncharacteristically over the last few days. They defo had a special spark. I hope she's okay. Contract at work sounds good, I might come in for a bit tomorrow, just to say hi and see what's new. I will be back in on Wednesday, hopefully that'll give me a chance to cheer the hell up. I love you too, missed you xxxxxx

~

~

Clare 24 Sep 19:51
Great, can't wait to see you and get the goss.
Coming back from hols is always a crapper,
you will feel better in no time, I know you
miss him, must be hard. :-(. Xxxxxxxx

~

I smile, I don't feel any better, but I appreciate her sympathy. I'm really looking forward to getting back to the cakery and seeing everyone, I've missed it. I check the time; nearly eight o'clock, my eyelids are so heavy already but I have at least two hours until I can let go and sleep. I also note that it has been nearly two hours since my last text from Daniel.

Stop it Beatrice! He's busy and you told him to get back to work! I can't help but wonder, though, if I said anything in my text to upset him, or if, maybe, he isn't interested in staying in contact. Funny, considering I was the one saying we couldn't keep in contact. What if he's hurt? What if he had a car accident or something? *Oh my god, please let him be okay.* Oh, this is getting ridiculous, I need to stop this. He's at work!

I turn my bath off and undress, lighting a few candles and turning the light off before sinking into the hot steamy bubbles. *Oh.* It's wonderful. The moment I close my eyes and start to drift, my phone starts ringing from the top of the sink, making me jump out of my skin. *For fucks sake, I really DO NOT want to talk right now.*

I dry my hands and reach over to grab it and check the caller I.D.: 'Unavailable'. Someone trying to sell me something, as always. I'll answer and tell them to fuck off, then at least they won't keep calling.

"Hello?" I say in my most monotone, uninterested voice, preparing the salesperson for the tough job they've allocated themselves by choosing to call this number.

There's a long pause and then... *"Baby?"*

I recognise the voice instantly, it's deep and rich and mellifluous. I can hear his smile. It's my man! *"Daniel?"* I ask excitedly, knowing it's him.

"Hey, sweetheart, are you okay? It's so good to hear your voice."

273

"Oh Daniel, I miss you so much, I was worrying because you didn't reply..."

"I know, I'm sorry about that, I had to go out of the office for a meeting and my battery drained while I was gone, so I decided to come home afterwards and give you a call, is that allowed?"

"Not really but who cares. So you're home now?"

"Yes, baby, where are you? It sounds echo-y"

"I'm in the bath."

"What?! Oh my god, I wish I could see you."

I giggle. "I wish you were with me."

"Me too. Especially after you told me about your dream! I'm glad that I could still make you come when I wasn't even with you," he says, his voice amused and sexy.

"I know, it was wild, you did a great job." I giggle.

"After your last text, I had to talk to you, you can't tell me you're horny baby, it drives me crazy! On top of scaring the shit out of me."

"Why does that scare you?"

"Baby, my girlfriend is over five thousand miles away, telling me she's horny. I'm going to worry about how that tension gets released, I sure know I can't do it..."

"Oh god, Daniel, just because I'm horny, it doesn't mean I'm about to go and grab some stranger off the street for a shag. Besides, I'm not your girlfriend, darling."

"You are in my eyes. Anyway, I'm sure you know certain people who aren't strangers, that would be more than willing."

"Is this about Dylan? What is with you people? I AM NOT GETTING BACK WITH DYLAN. Nor am I calling him up for a quick shag. I never will, I don't even like him very much. God!"

"Hey, hey! Okay! Calm down! Anyway, what do you mean, 'you people'?"

"You and my brother, I had him double checking I wasn't going to get back with him earlier, too. Jesus."

"Okay, sorry, sweetheart. But I'm glad I have an ally in your brother."

"Yes you do, not that you need one because it's never going to happen. But this is sounding a bit too much like a *long distance relationship to me, and Daniel, I miss you horribly and I love you more than I think is physically possible, but we can't have a long distance relationship."*

"I know. I'll drop it, and we can set some rules about how and when we contact each other, if that makes you happy, okay?"

"Thank you Daniel, it hurts to even think like that, but it has to be that way."

"I know. So. About this 'horny' problem of yours, just how bad is it?"

I grin, appreciating the change in conversation. I lift one leg out of the water and point my toe in the air, running my hand from my ankle to my thigh, as if he can see me.

"Really bad, I don't know why, I just need you all the time."

"Baby, I'm always horny when I think about you. You give me a permanent erection, I had to calm myself after your text, I thought I was going to have to take a cold shower before the meeting. Even now, hearing the water sloshing about, thinking of you laying there, naked..." he makes a growling noise and I laugh, loving that I can turn him on, even when he can't see me.

"Oh you've really cheered me up, Daniel."

"Good, I don't want you sad. Tell me what you're doing."

"Oh... like that is it?"

"Uh huh..." God, his voice is so damned sexy.

"I am mostly submerged in the water, candlelight flickering against the walls, soft bubbles floating on the surface, my body hidden underneath them, apart from my..."

"What? Apart from your what?" He's so funny, I grin broadly.

"Apart from my two, hard, pink... toe nails."

"Hey, baby! That's not fair! I was going for some phone sex there!" he grumbles.

"Sorry, Daniel," I giggle. *"I couldn't help myself. I do need to have a wash though, maybe you can talk me through it."*

"That's more like it... are you dirty?"
"Yes."

"Good. Keep the phone in one hand, and put a little soap on the other, can you do that?"

"Uh huh."

"Good, now, slide your hand from your neck, down in between your beautiful breasts, to your stomach..."

"Okay..."

"Slowly glide from hip to hip, washing your sexy belly..."

I do exactly as he says. *"Okay, it's clean. What now?"*

"Wash your chest, gently caress each breast in turn..." His deep voice, talking so seductively down the line, turning me on, big time.

"Mmm..."

"That good? Run your fingertips over your left nipple, gently rub it between your forefinger and thumb."

"Yes, that's nice."

"Close your eyes, baby, imagine my mouth is doing that to you, my lips around your nipple, my tongue flicking and stroking..."

"Mmm, yes, I'm running my fingers through your hair... oh Daniel, this is getting me wet."

"That's the plan, baby."

I smile, this is fun, this is hot! *"Mmm, what now?"*

"Now the other one. I'm circling it with my tongue, nipping it between my lips..."

"Oh, Daniel... I want you here."

"I am, I'm moving my hand down your body, move yours baby, imagine it's me."

"I am..."

"Down to stroke your inner thigh, in circles, with the very tips of your fingers."

"Yes."

"Imagine I'm kissing your neck, my hand between your legs, stroking your thigh, closer and closer..."

"Oh, yes, touch me."

"Put your fingers against yourself, feel your warmth, gently circle your clit."

"Oh god, that's so good, Daniel, keep going," I urge him.

"Nice and slowly, feel how turned on you are, forget it's you, it's me. What would I do now, baby?"

"Mmm, you'd go a bit faster, you'd lick my neck a little between kisses, mmm, yeah..."

"You sound so hot, baby, are you feeling it? Are you close?"

"Oh uh huh... keep going."

"Pick up the pace again, feel my fingers playing with your hot spot, I want to be inside you."

"Oh, yes, me too, yes Daniel..."

"Think of me, hot and hard, pushing inside you, stretching you..."

"Oh god, oh yes, yes..."

"Now slip two fingers inside, circle and push and come hard on your fingers, baby, imagine it's my cock pushing deep and hard..."

"Yes, yes, oh god, oh... oh..."

"Now baby!"

"Fuuuuuck!" I shout as I come hard, water sloshing everywhere from my writhing. I can feel myself clench against my fingers, over and over. It's a strange sensation, but so hot because Daniel was guiding me all the way. I moan quietly into the phone. My eyes still closed and my heart racing.

"That sounded so good," Daniel growls, his voice is so sexy.

"It was..." I whisper, dazed.

"Don't go to sleep baby, you're in the tub."

He makes me giggle. *"I won't, darling, but you're lucky I didn't drop my iPhone in the bath... that was delicious."*

"Well, those noises you were making definitely turned me on."

"Were you... you know - at the same time?"

Daniel chuckles and it makes me smile broadly, his voice is the caress to my ache. *"No. That was just for you. But hearing you and imagining you doing those things has definitely left me with an erection that will stay with me for at least a week."*

I laugh. *"Oh, Daniel, you do know how to cheer me up, I love you."*

277

"I love you, too, sweetheart. What time is it over there?"

I check the time on my phone and put it back to my ear. *"It's nearly eight thirty p.m. So it's about lunchtime there, right?"*

"Right. I don't think I'm going to go back to work today, I think I'll mope around here and picture you asleep in your bed."

"I wish you could be in it with me. Do you want me to talk dirty to you so you can have a turn?"

Daniel laughs. *"No, it's okay, baby. You just relax. I suppose I'd better let you go and get some sleep soon."*

I immediately feel bereft at the thought of hanging up. *"Oh... do you have to?"*

"No, of course not, I don't want to keep you though, if you need to get to bed. I'm happy to talk as long as you want, I've got all day!"

That thought is wonderful, being able to talk to him all night if I want to, is exactly what I need to hear. We continue to talk and when I'm pruney, I get out of the bath and wrap myself in my big fluffy dressing gown.

I warm myself a bowl of chicken noodle soup that Mum has left in the fridge, and chat to Daniel throughout my dinner, while he eats his lunch. Shortly after, I lock everything up before crawling into bed with him... with my phone.

"You sound cosy, baby."

"Yes, I am, not as cosy as I am in your bed, but I'm cosy enough. I'm so tired."

"I'll go then, sweetheart."

"No! Don't go! Stay until I go to sleep, please?"

"Sure, if that's what you want, baby. So what do you want to do about contacting each other? I want to be able to text or call whenever I like, but is that what you want?"

"I wish we could, but we should limit it so that we can gradually get used to not having each other. This isn't a long distance..."

Daniel cut's me off. *"Relationship, yes I know Bea, you keep telling me. Would it really be that bad?"*

"Yes, it would. We can't be together so how do you move that relationship forward? You can't live here, I can't

live there... we can't see each other apart from the odd two days every few months, if that. One day, one of us will meet someone else and it will be a much more attractive relationship because we'll be able to see, touch, feel, make love to that person. I can't live with that. One of us will end up being deceitful and I'm not prepared to put myself in that situation. As it is, yes, I'll admit that you feel like my boyfriend and you've already said that you see me as your girlfriend, but the only way for us to go forward, is to try to distance ourselves, because what we want is never going to happen. I can't pine for you forever."

A long silence follows. *"Daniel?"*

"I'm still here, Bea, taking all that in. But what if? What if we did manage to find a way?"

"It's highly unlikely, unless you're prepared to give up everything, but if we did, amazing. Until such time, though, we need to go forward as if it's never going to happen."

"Wow. Brutal."

"But you knew the score, Daniel."

"I know I did, I just didn't think I would need you this much. I didn't think it would be this hard."

I sigh, I don't want to argue, he's sad and I'm panicking that I'll spend the rest of my life crying for him. I don't know how you get over something like this. *"Neither did I. Sorry, Daniel, I don't mean to sound so... harsh."*

"It's okay, baby. Like you say, I knew the deal all along."

"I really do love you and wish, more than anything, that there was a way."

"Me too."

"So, in the interest of our future sanity, why don't we limit ourselves to only texting a couple of times in the evening... my evening, your lunch time, and maybe speak on the phone twice a week, going down to once a week... how does that sound?"

"And email?"

"I think no email..."

"That's not a lot of contact, baby."

"I know, it'll be really hard for me but we need to keep it to a minimum."

"Okay, if that's what you want." He sounds forlorn.

"What I want is for you to be here with me, snuggling me into your big, strong arms, kissing me."

"Big, strong arms, huh?" I hear his smile.

"Oh yes, your gorgeous, toned body... mmm. I love how small I feel when you're wrapped around me."

"You're tiny anyway, I love that. I miss touching you. Will this get easier? It's only been a day."

"I don't know, I hope so because I feel bereft when I'm not communicating with you. I don't know how long I'll manage if it doesn't ease."

"Me neither."

I yawn, my eyes closed as I snuggle into my pillow. *"I love that I'm all snuggled in my bed falling asleep, talking to you. I can try to imagine you're next to me."*

"I will be soon."

"This call must be costing you a fortune."

"Don't worry about it, baby, I'm not. Sweetheart, if we carry on as you say, not in a relationship, would you come to LA on vacation?"

"If I got invited back with Tilly, I might."

"What if you got invited to come stay in a nice apartment in the 'W' for a couple weeks? Would you come?"

"Hmm, that's a tough one, I'd be sorely tempted."

"Okay, good to know it's not completely ruled out."

"Two weeks of Daniel would be heavenly, but the hell of going home would make me rethink," I respond, sleepily.

"Okay, we'll discuss another time then."

"Mmm..." I'm almost drifting off but I don't want to stop talking.

"Baby," he says softly, *"you're falling asleep, I should go and leave you to rest."*

"Oh..." I moan.

"Yes, Bea, I'm going to go, you need to sleep now. I want you to drift off into a lovely, deep sleep and dream about me kissing you, all over your beautiful body."

"Mmm..."

"I'll wait for you to text me tomorrow night, your time and I'll speak to you same time on what, Wednesday?"

"Mmm, can't wait. I love you, Daniel."

"I love you, too, baby. So much. Night night, sweetheart, sweet dreams."

"You too. Love you."

"Goodnight."

And with his beautiful, sexy deep tone held in my mind, I do exactly that and drift off into a deep, lovely sleep where Daniel is laying next to me in my bed, talking to me about work, playing with my hair and trailing gentle kisses all over my face.

Waking up the next morning was odd. I'd had a wonderful sleep, I'd had my Daniel with me (albeit in my dreams) and I felt happy for speaking to him for hours last night, but I still felt miserable. I was still over five thousand miles from my boyfriend, I knew I had to stop calling him 'my boyfriend', I had no plans to see him, and I wasn't going to speak to him until tomorrow night. And to top it all off, I got my period. Joy. At least it waited until I got home so I could have all the sex in LA.

I managed to pull myself out of bed and get dressed, ready for a long day of mixed emotions. After breakfast, I toyed with the idea of shoving Daniel's jumper in my handbag so I'd have it on hand whenever I needed a sniff, but decided that was taking it too far, and tucked it neatly under my pillow.

I left my apartment and drove around to the girls' place to see how Til is. I've missed driving and I've missed my lovely little car, but it does seem particularly basic next to Daniel's gorgeous Bentley. *Oh, Daniel.*

As I pull up outside their maisonette, I notice that the curtains to the front room are still closed, which is unusual. Maybe Tilly is still asleep. I should get her up, it's almost ten. I open the front door using my key and close it gently so I don't give her a fright. As I walk around the corner to the lounge to open the curtains, I am surprised to see Tilly walking out towards me looking horrendous. I know immediately that she is *not* okay.

"Tilly..." she looks up slowly, hunched over and pale and her mouth twitches downwards at the sides. I drop my bag and head straight over to wrap my arms around her, she doesn't even hug me back, just breaks down, collapsing against my body.

"Oh, darling, it's okay." I try to console her. Apart from the terrible time she had when her dad died, I've never seen her in a bad place. It's quite disturbing to see her like this. "What's happened Til?"

"N-noth-ing," she mumbles, hardly able to get any noise out between the violent sobs shuddering her chest.

"Come on Tils, this is me. I know something is up, Clare and I both do, you had been perfectly fine on holiday and then you suddenly changed - I'm not stupid, so you're going to sit down and talk to me about it. Right?"

She smiles slightly at my bossiness and nods before padding over to the sofa and curling up in a ball.

"I'll be right back." I go to the kitchen and flick the kettle on, they have cups here! I get a glass of water for Tilly and grab a box of tissues before returning to the sofa. "Here." I hand her the tissues and water, and sit on the sofa, facing Tilly with my legs tucked under my body. "Now, tell me what's going on, and don't even think of trying to tell me this is about leaving Gemma."

"I... I just... I don't know, Bea."

"It's Luke, isn't it? What happened? Something did."

"Nothing happened. We had a great time. I just... I kind of realised that I'm not happy with how I am. I want... I want more now."

"Tilly, I know you say that you only want a bit of fun, but I know you. You don't want to get your heart broken again, so you don't open up to anyone, but you can, Tilly." I think back to the time, years ago, when she had a hideous break-up with her boyfriend Scott. He was a total bastard, but even then, I never saw her like this. At the time, she shed a tear and quickly bounced back. She hasn't had another 'proper' relationship since, but she always swore that she was happier that way.

"I know, and I do want all that happy ending shit - don't tell anyone I said that or I'll kill you - but I don't see how I can have it, without the fucking heart break. I mean - no offence - but look at you, you're right in the shitter, and he hasn't even put a foot wrong! I felt myself, you know... with Luke, and now I'm in all sorts of shit because he's possibly the last person on the whole planet I should have let that happen with."

"Do you love him?"

"Don't be stupid."

"Tilly, I'm not being stupid."

283

"No. I just... I opened up to him. I don't do that. I shouldn't have either because he doesn't want all that crap."

"Did he say that?"

"Oh come on, Bea, he didn't have to. He's a ladies' man, he'll have forgotten about me already. I knew that all along. I just, I hate that I like him so much, I know he's my type, but my type has always been happy-go-lucky, hot ladies boys who I can have a brief fling with, with no strings. I don't want to want more with one of those kinds of guys."

"You want more with Luke though?"

"If I lived in LA - yes, I'd want more with him. That's what scares the shit out of me. He'd never want more with a girl like me... he'd never want more with anyone. I'm angry that I let myself feel that way for him. I really thought the fuck buddy thing was great, a super-hot piece of eye-candy for me to visit every time I go to my sister's, but now, I don't think I could do that. It won't happen though because I told him we won't see each other again."

"Why?"

"Because I freaked out. I didn't like how much I liked him and decided that if we see each other again, I might feel more."

"What did he say to that?"

"It all got a bit weird, we kind of stopped talking after that. Carried on fucking obviously." She shrugs and smiles.

I grin. "Obviously..."

"But we stopped talking about anything when we weren't in bed, and it just got weird."

"That makes sense to me now. The thing is Tilly, how do you know he doesn't like you more than just a fuck buddy? Daniel said he'd never seen Luke like this before."

"He would! That's what blokes do for their mates, play games, he knew you'd tell me."

"Daniel's not like that, Tilly." I bite back, sternly, defending my man. *I really need to stop thinking of him as mine.* "He told me that Luke hadn't been with any other women while you were there and that he's never seen him act the way he does around you. And that's not bullshit, Tilly."

"Well, it's good to know he wasn't shagging anyone else, but he didn't really have a lot of free time," she says with a grin.

"You two definitely had a spark."

"I felt a spark. I never get that anymore. Ever."

"Why don't you contact him?"

"Absolutely not. No way. We're not seeing each other again, Bea. I'm not going to put myself in the position you're in. Sorry."

"No apology necessary, it is really awful and I wouldn't wish this feeling on anyone, but doll, you look like you *are* in my position. You look like you feel as shit as I do. No offence."

She shrugs and smiles. "None taken, I look like shit, I know. I'm not in love with him, Bea, I'm just having a little early-to-mid-life moment. I'm realising that what I've been wanting, isn't really what I want. I'm sad to be back, I miss my sister, I do really miss Luke, I miss LA and I've got jet lag. I'm just emotional and am about to get my period so everything has come together and is making me miserable."

"Oh, tell me about it, I got mine today. At least we didn't get it on holiday though, to ruin all the sex."

"Yeah, there is that I suppose." Tilly giggles.

"Come on, I'll run you a bath and you can get ready and come out with me. I've got to go and get some plates and cups and all that crap, and then I'm going to go to Bear's and see what's new. You up for that?"

"Not really, but I need to stop moping. I'm sure it'll make me feel better."

"It will. I'm sorry I was so wrapped up in myself all the way home. I knew you weren't yourself."

"Oh shut up, don't be stupid. Bea, you are going through something horrible and I wish I could make it better for you. I wish I could magic Daniel here so you could live happily ever after, I love him you know, he's my favourite of any guy you've ever been out with."

"Oh, I love him too. But let's not start, I don't want to get crying again, I am trying to be strong."

"Thank you, babe. Thanks for looking after me and making me tell you, I really did need to talk about it, but it's hard for me, you know? Clare, as gorgeous as she is and I love her, just wasn't there in LA, so she doesn't really know, I didn't feel like I could tell the whole story without breaking down."

"I know, and so does she, she'll understand. Do you want me to tell her?"

"Yes please, I want her to know why I'm sad, and I'd hate for her to feel excluded, but I don't want to have to go over it all."

"Okay. Consider it sorted. Now, I'm running the bath and making a cuppa. I'll give you an hour!"

"Yes, Miss!"

~~~~~~~

It was really good to get out with Tilly. We both needed something to preoccupy ourselves with. Tilly helped me pick out some crockery, it's nothing like the lovely set that my parents bought me, but I will have to wait a while if I want to think about buying that set. I spent far too much in LA to be splurging now.

We chatted about the fun times we had in Los Angeles, it made me feel closer to Daniel, somehow, talking about it. It was painful, but a pain I felt I needed to endure because it made me happy, remembering things like our indulgent shopping trip in Beverly Hills, our night at the 'W' and afterwards at Daniel's, our chilling out time around the pool... it was all so wonderful.

We pull into a rare, available parking space on the High Street and walk towards Bear's. I'm really excited, I've never been away from it for this long and I have missed it. I smile as the familiar chocolaty aroma that always lingers outside the shop, wafts over to me, welcoming me back.

Everyone is happy to see me, as I am, them. There are no appointments for the next hour or so, so Tilly, Clare and I sit around one of our tables with a pot of tea and a cake, chatting. Clare tells me about the new contract that we're about to finalise with a company in London, supplying a selection of cakes daily. It reminds me of the cake selections that 'Henry Berkeley' do, it's along the same lines. We have a similar contract with another local firm although the new contract seems a lot bigger and will be an excellent opportunity.

Tilly nips out to the pharmacy, and I take the opportunity to fill Clare in. She's relieved to know, because she had been worrying about her, but she understands why Tilly didn't want to bring it up.

By the time we leave and make our way back to Watford, it's already nearly four, and we're both a little on the tired side, no doubt our long journey and all the crying is catching up on us. Tilly decides to come back to mine for a bit, we both admitted we'd rather be alone but knew it wasn't the best idea because we'd just end up wallowing and crying all evening.

We chill out on the sofa with a glass of wine and some music in the background. Today has been a fantastic distraction and I have loved having my best friends with me, but it hasn't taken the sting away. As the talking winds down, exhaustion takes over. My thoughts are, as always, with Daniel.

The slow music in the background plays along with my solemn mood and I can't help but reach for Daniel's card to read. It's my undoing, I knew it would be. Tears trickle down my cheeks, an endless stream of warm saline. I hold it to my chest, weeping silently, I miss him so much, I don't see how this feeling of utter loss will ever go away. It's ridiculous, he's alive and well, all I need to do is pick up the phone and I can talk to him, but it's a short term gain for long term suffering. I'll never get over him if I just pick up the phone every time I get sad.

I sniff and Tilly turns to look at me and I at her, noticing that she is in exactly the same state. What a pair. "Do you want to stay tonight?" I ask.

"I'd like to, but I'm back at work tomorrow and I'm not sure that I fancy getting up early and walking back to our place. I know it doesn't usually bother me but I need to get my head organised before I go back to work."

"Okay, well the offer is there, and my super comfy spare bed."

"Thanks, it's tempting. I'll see how I feel later. I'll hang about for the evening though if you don't mind?"

"Course not. The last thing I want to do is eat, but we need to, so what do you fancy for dinner? I have a fridge full of food or we could get a take-away?"

"Let's get a take-away, we're sad, we shouldn't have to cook."

"Too right, okay what do you want, pizza, Thai, Chinese?"

"Not pizza, after that amazing one at Daniel's that night, no take away pizza will ever be good enough. Let's get Thai. Shall we ask Clare over?"

"No, she's out tonight. Oliver mentioned yesterday that a few of them are going to the pub."

"Oh, okay. I obviously wasn't listening. Is there something going on with Oliver and Clare?"

"No! What makes you say that?"

"They just seem a bit... friendly."

"You've just got it on the brain."

"Yeah, you're right. Okay, I'll order the food and get it delivered so we don't have to go out looking like shit." I giggle, she makes me laugh even when she's not trying.

When the dinner arrives, it's eight o'clock and I get butterflies knowing that I can text Daniel now.

I put the plates and cutlery on the coffee table and Tilly serves up while I rummage through my bag for my iPhone.

~

25 Sep 20:07
Hello sexy :-) I've been waiting all day to text you. How's your morning? I slept so well after talking with you all night. I still miss you like mad. I have been thinking about you all day, I want to kiss you so much. Reply when you can, I know you're at work.
XxxxxxxxxxxxxX

~

"There you go, doll." Tilly hands me my plate and I top up our wine.

"Thanks, shall we watch something?"

"Ooh, yeah, can we watch Mad Men or do we need to wait and watch it with Clare?"

"No, she watched it while we were away." I respond excitedly, hoping that getting back into routine might help our depressive moods. Within about three minutes of watching, my iPhone chimes next to me and my belly lurches.

~

Daniel 25 Sep 20:13
Hey baby! I have been waiting for you. I miss you so much. My morning is good, thank you, although I'm finding it hard to stop thinking about you, the scent from the cupcake keeps wafting over to me, I love it. I'm so glad you had a good sleep last night, baby, are you sure you don't want to do that every night? ;-). I want to kiss you so much too. I want to do so much more than just kiss. And, hey, where's my 'I love you'? :-(What are you up to? (I love you.) xxxxxxxx

~

"Who's that?" Tilly asks with a mouthful of phad thai.
"It's Daniel."
"Ooh, what does he say?"
"We're just chatting, he misses me and loves me."
"Ah that's so sweet. Say hi from me," she says, somewhat melancholy, before focusing her attention back on the TV screen."

~

25 sep 20:18
Sorry, I LOVE YOU. I wish we could talk every night. Don't tempt me, it's not allowed! I want to do so much more than just kiss you too. I want you to do all sorts of naughty things to me ;-). Right now, Tilly is over and we're having a take-away, watching Mad Men. She says 'hi'. Went to Bear's today which was fun, we have an exciting new

contract which is great news for the business.
How's Luke doing? (I love you 100 times
over) Xxxxxxxxxxxxxxx

~

I tuck into some more dinner, smiling, and I try to figure out what I have missed on the TV. I don't really care, texting Daniel is so much more interesting than anything on TV.

"Do you know what, Bea? I think I might stay, I'm cosy, is that okay?"

"Of course it is! There are some pjs for you and Clare in the drawers in the spare room."

"You are the best, Bea," she says as she kisses my forehead and heads to the bedroom to change. I notice that she has hardly touched her dinner. Neither have I. My phone chimes again.

~

Daniel 25 Sep 20:26
Don't tempt you? Does that
mean there's a chance I could? I
want to talk to you every day
baby, so badly. That's great
news about the contract, well
done to Bear's :-). Tell me about
it tomorrow night when I call?
BEATRICE, haven't I told you
enough times that you can't say
things like that to me? I WANT
TO DO NAUGHTY THINGS
TO YOU TOO!!! I am
visualising it now. Your hot
naked body buckling under the
work of my fingers... Mmm.
Damn it, I have a hard-on.
When I finally get to see you,
you'll be in big trouble! 'Hi'
right back to Tilly, is she okay?
Sounds like you're having a fun
evening. Luke is okay I think,
he's not really himself. He

290

wouldn't tell me but I think he
misses Tilly. They had quite a
connection don't you think?
Xxxxxxx

~

"See Til..." I say as she sits back down, dressed in pyjamas, "Daniel says that Luke isn't himself and although he hasn't told Daniel anything, Daniel thinks it's because he misses you."

"Oh my god, did you tell Daniel?" Tilly shrieks.

"No! Calm down! I asked after Luke, I'm allowed to do that aren't I?"

"Sorry, doll."

"I should think so too."

"I doubt it's about me though, he's not the type."

"Neither were you."

"It's different."

"Okay." I resume play on Mad Men and reply to Daniel. Nothing I say is going to convince her that I think Luke wants her.

~

25 Sep 20:32
You know the rules, we can't talk every night
and although part of me wants you to tempt
me, because I want to go to sleep with your
sexy voice in my ear tonight so badly, we just
can't do it. I'm miserable though, just so you
know. I'm not enjoying being such a square
about rules. I'm sorry for getting you hot
under the collar, now you're making me hot
for you. Your hands touching me, making me
moan, I need you, I'm so horny. Just thinking
about your hard on is making me lick my lips.
I like that I'll be in trouble, what will you do
to me? Yes, I do think T&L had a connection,
a big one. I want them to get together :-(I
want us to be together :-(We should stop
these mega-texts soon... Xxxxxxxxx

~

291

We continued texting for a short while longer, discussing all of the naughty things that we would do if we were together. It was great at the time but now I'm desperately horny, wet and in serious need of release. I'm sorely tempted to just call him up and ask him to make me come like he did in the bath last night, but I need to be strong, I can't.

I've done so well thus far, even though I can't see the good it's doing me, I still don't feel any better about living so far apart. The hurt is still as powerful, I'm trying to manage it better but I don't see, a year down the line, that I will feel any differently. But this is all I can do, without cutting ties with him altogether. I think that would kill me.

I kiss Tilly good night and go to my room to start to undress, opening my nightie drawer. I have folded all of my lovely new purchases from Daniel and put them to one side, waiting for him. I hope I get a chance to wear them for him one day. I decide to give him a little treat, as promised a little while ago, so I slip into my favourite polka dot nightie, his first gift to me.

Knocking on Tilly's door, I ask tentatively if she wouldn't mind taking a photo of me on my iPhone, and she's surprisingly into it! She tells me how to pose and takes a few shots, helping me pick the sexiest one; hand on hip, come-to-bed eyes, blowing a kiss.

After thanking her profusely, I return to my bedroom. I feel awful having asked her and in hindsight, it was probably really insensitive of me. She was very enthusiastic about it, though, so hopefully she was okay. I lay in my bed and forward the picture to Daniel. I smile as I roll onto my side and close my eyes, wondering if he'll reply when he gets it.

CHAPTER TWENTY
WEDNESDAY 26TH SEPTEMBER

I wake suddenly in a cold sweat, sitting bolt upright. My heart pounding, my face damp from tears. *It was only a dream, just a dream.*

I desperately need to know that Daniel is okay, my dream was so real, so vivid, I sob violently, fearing for him. I reach for my iPhone and there's a message from him from ten thirty. I check the time now; three in the morning, so that makes it about seven thirty in the evening in Los Angeles. I don't even bother to read the text, I call him immediately and he answers after the first ring.

"Baby?"

I sob, loudly into the phone, thanking god that he's okay.

"Oh god! You're okay."

"Of course I'm okay, baby, what's happened? What's the matter? Are you okay?" I can hear the panic in his voice, bless him.

"Yes, I had the most horrible nightmare, Daniel, it was so real, I needed to hear your voice." I break into sobs again. *"Oh god, Daniel, I don't think I can do this, I'm so miserable, I can't live like this."*

"Calm down, sweetheart. Everything is okay, I'm okay, you're okay, you've had a nasty dream but it's over now. It's okay..."

"I love you, I love you, Daniel," I wail.

"I love you too, Bea. Shh, it's over now."

"Uh huh..." I manage, between sniffs and chest convulsions. Just hearing his soothing voice is helping.

"Do you want to talk about it?"

"I... I just... it was so awful." My voice a quivering whisper.

"It's over now, baby. Just lay down, breathe. I'm only on the other end of a phone, sweetheart. I'm glad you called."

"I had to, I needed to know you were okay. I can't tell you how much I need you to hold me right now."

"I'm so sorry, baby, I wish I was there for you."

"I wish you were here, too. I love you so much."

"I love you too. Everything is okay."

"You're right." I lay back down, close my eyes and take some deep breaths. Daniel is safe. *"I'm sorry, Daniel. Are you busy?"*

"Not at all, I just got home and Luke is here, just having a beer and getting some food."

"Oh I'm sorry to interrupt, you get back."

"No, baby! You haven't interrupted anything, we're just chilling. I'm in my bedroom now anyway, Luke's watching a game in the living room. It's so late for you... or early, depending on how you look at it."

"I know. I had to call, though. I won't be long, I'm breaking all the rules."

"You and your rules," he chuckles, *"you're cute, Bea."*

"Cute? Because I'm a stick-in-the-mud about rules?"

"Because you can't help but break them," he says and I can almost see his cheeky grin.

"Trust me, if you'd had a dream like the one I just had, you'd break the rules too."

"I'm always up for breaking the rules, baby!"

"That's because you're a naughty boy." Oh wow, we've taken a turn for the raunchy...

"You make me naughty, I want to do all sorts of things to you right now, to make you feel better."

"Oh lordy, I'd welcome it. You need to hurry up with this business trip because I need it and I need it hard."

"Oh my god. Now I need it. I'm trying all I can, baby. Listen, sweetheart, let me come on vacation - and before you interrupt - I'll only stay a week, tops. You can go to work while I do some work from my laptop at yours, then we can spend every evening together."

I whimper, dramatically. *"Oh, Daniel! You're making this impossible! You can't, I'd only feel like this again when you left. It's too painful."*

Daniel growls. *"It's so fucking frustrating! I could be there in like, two days!"*

"I know, and god, I wish you could. Business trips are okay, they're short and you are here for another reason. Not solely for me."

"It's for me, too, you know."

"I know. Look, I'd better go, I've been very naughty, calling you."

"You had good reason, don't beat yourself up. Call me anytime, day or night, you hear?"

I smile. *"Yes, loud and clear. Thank you, Daniel. I do feel much, much better for speaking to you."*

"Are you going to tell me what it was about? The dream?"

"You're just trying to keep me on the phone..."

"You got me!"

"It was about you and I... and Marcus. He was forcing himself on me and wouldn't get off. Then you two fought and you got really, really hurt. I couldn't get to you because he was holding me back and no one would help. You were bleeding and unconscious, I was losing you, right in front of my eyes and I couldn't even hold you. You, you know..."

"Died?"

"Oh Daniel, let's not talk about this."

"Okay, sweetheart. Well, you'll be pleased to know that Marcus is about as capable of hurting me as I am of growing wings and learning to fly. The man's a weasel."

"He looks like one. I love you."

"I love you, too. Now, you get back to sleep, and have another 'happy ending' dream this time. I'm thinking of you in that nightie... it's making me hot."

"Mmm, I hope I dream about you and me being dirty."

"I hope you do too, baby. I hope I do!"

"Okay, well, enjoy your evening with Luke, say 'hi' from me and apologise for taking you away for a bit."

"Don't be silly, he doesn't care. Sleep well, still call me tomorrow, okay?"

"Okay, can't wait. Night night, Daniel."

"Night, baby."

I hang up and take a deep breath, I'm still not quite over that dream, but at least I have spoken to Daniel and know that he is safe and sound. Nothing to worry about. I check the text message that he sent earlier, after I sent him the photo.

~

Daniel 25 Sep 22:31

**Good god. Baby, you're so freaking hot!
Damn. I'm going to have to do something
about the state you've got me in. I'm taking
this picture to bed and it's not going to take
long to do what I gotta do! I hope it was Tilly
that took this picture?! You better not be
wearing this for anyone else! You're
something else, sexy girl, ILY. Xxxxxxx**

~

Oh, Daniel. ILY too. I smile and consider sending him a
reply, but decide that I need to be stronger. I'm going to talk to
him again tonight, I can wait until then. I roll over, grab the
Daniel-jumper and hug it to my chest before I slip into another
sleep.

CHAPTER TWENTY ONE
MONDAY 1ST OCTOBER

The next five days or so went by painfully slowly. Nothing has changed, I'm still just as agonisingly miserable as I was the minute I left him. Work is nice, but not enough. When I'm sitting at my counter, piping swirls onto a wedding cake or making sugar flowers, my mind is on him, the whole time.

I spoke to him the evening after my nightmare, which was lovely, I took him in the bath with me again. It was hot, but it didn't take away my constant sexual frustration. I still need him, rock hard, twenty-four-seven.

We spoke a couple of nights later, again for hours, and I fell asleep with him to my ear. Last night we were supposed to talk, but Daniel had a meeting all day and the same again today. Who has meetings on a Sunday? Not having spoken to him has gotten me in even more of a foul mood.

As it was Sunday yesterday, I went around to my parents with Oliver for Sunday lunch. They invited Tilly and Clare along too so it was a nice day, but as soon as I got the text from Daniel to say that he couldn't talk that evening, my 'okay' mood disintegrated entirely, so I went home and cried all night. The fading of Daniel's scent on his jumper is somewhat depressing, too. I know I have to wash it soon, I just can't bring myself to wash the 'Daniel' off it.

I could be paranoid, but I feel like he's distancing himself a little. I love him and miss him so much, if I don't speak to him when I'm supposed to, it feels like I've been kicked in the belly again. I wait all day long for the time I can pick up my phone and speak to him or send him a message.

I've woken in a foul mood today, my head hurts from crying all night, I don't want to eat but I feel sick because my stomach is craving food. Just knowing that I can't talk to him again makes me feel like complete shit.

When I get into work, Clare gives me her sympathetic smile, and throws her arms around me. "It's a bad day today, hey?"

Oh no, the flood gates open and I can't stop it. *God damn it!* I cling onto her and bury my head in her shoulder, nodding. "Uh, huh."

"Come around the back, doll. Talk to me."

I follow her around to the baking area which is somewhat out of view of the customers and grab a tissue to wipe my eyes. "I just can't handle it, Clare, it's supposed to get easier but every day is harder. I know we were finished the moment I left LA but we still talk, and although I shouldn't, I still consider him my boyfriend. This wasn't supposed to happen, I'm supposed to be getting over him, preparing myself to move forwards but I can't see how I ever will. He's been distant, too."

"He's had meetings, Bea, he can't help that."

"I know, but he could have called or texted at another time of day..."

"He's probably just trying to follow your rules, babe. I'm sure there's a reason."

"I'm right, aren't I? It's over-over."

"Come on, Bea, you don't know, you'll talk to him later."

"Nope, another meeting."

"Ah. Well, send him a little text now, see what he says to that. Who cares if you break the rules?"

"I do! I shouldn't still be so hooked on him, long distance doesn't work, why am I wanting it so much when I really don't want it at all? I've turned into a crying, needy, crazy person!"

"Because you love him. Just send a text, darling, it'll make you feel better."

"It will." I agree with a reluctant nod.

"Do it then," she says with a small smile and rubs my arm gently. "I'm going to go though the diary and get the samples ready for the tasters today. I'll do the appointments, you do the 'behind the scenes' stuff, okay?"

"Thanks, Clare, I don't know what I would have done without you the last few weeks. I'd never have even been able to go away if you hadn't been so 'okay' about it. Since we returned, me and Tilly have been such miserable cows, and you still manage to be the best friend in the world, to us."

"Be quiet. You'd do it for me, and anyway, you don't mind whenever I go on holiday, and I go away more than you so stop being grateful that you got to go once. Now, shh. Text him."

I smile at her, appreciatively and take my phone from my bag. I check the time... it's only eight thirty so it has just gone midnight in LA. Will he still be up?

~

1 Oct 08:33
Hi sexy, I know I am breaking the rules but I feel like I haven't spoken to you in forever. I miss you :-(. Do you still have meetings later? I wish we could talk. I love you xxxx

~

I smile and start to busy myself with the early morning prep, ready for the other girls to start baking when they get here. I hope he replies.

About fifteen minutes later, my phone chimes.

~

Daniel 1st Oct 08:50
Sorry, baby. I do still have meetings. We'll talk real soon, promise. Love you too. Night night xxxxxx

~

Is that it? I can't help but feel a little disappointed. He said he loves me and all that, but it was so short. We normally send great long messages to each other. It has done nothing to make me feel better. Looks like today is going to be a long day.

And it was. Damned long. I didn't eat and had a nasty headache. Now I'm curled up in bed, super early, hoping to drop off to sleep and forget for a while. Unfortunately, all I do is lay there, fantasising about him laying next to me, running his soft fingers up and down my spine in that glorious way, kissing my neck and telling me how beautiful I am. His fingers run over my bottom and back up to my waist before slipping down my belly to my... *This is torture!* I roll over and punch the pillow in frustration.

I don't understand why I'm still so fucking horny, I had put it down to my period but that's finished now and I'm still swooning at the thought of Daniel's delicious body. I'm constantly wet, my mind going back to our amazing sex sessions in the kitchen... the walk-in wardrobe... on his desk... *Oh yes, his desk.*

I finally drift off into a somewhat, frustrated sleep, waking every few hours sorely disappointed that he wasn't laying on top of me, going for it, hard.

By the time morning comes, I'm knackered from the broken sleep and seriously in need. I contemplate dusting off the vibrator in the box at the top of my wardrobe (the one that someone bought as a joke for my birthday years ago, which I was secretly really grateful for because I was too embarrassed to buy one, myself). I have only ever used it a handful of times because it's so damned noisy that I can hardly concentrate on the task at hand. But I decide to forget it, maybe if I manage to speak to Daniel tonight, he'll talk me through another unbelievable orgasm. Doing it alone just doesn't cut it anymore.

I have one of those mornings where I break things, drop things, get hot and flustered and make myself stupidly late. By the time I get to work, the other girls are already working on their allocated projects. I hang up my coat, wash my hands and put my apron on before sitting down and taking a long, deep breath.

"Like that is it?" Clare asks, paint brush in hand, looking up from the wedding cake she is buried in.

"Uh," I respond with an exaggerated, dramatic wave of the hand.

"Nice quiet day today, no appointments, so you'll be able to just get on with it."

"I know, I need it too. Sorry, I'm such a pain in the arse right now."

"Yes, you are, but it's about bloody time, I'm always the one in a flap while you're calm and collected. Now it's your turn. Besides, you've got good reason," she says with a sympathetic smile. "Anyway, on another subject, can you do me a really big favour?"

"What's that?"

"I know you were going to start the superhero wedding cake, but Marie has prepared the sponges for the 'boob-job' cake, and as your lace is so much better than mine, I was hoping you might decorate that one instead?"

"Yes, no problem."

"Can we have a quick meeting?" Clare asks.

We make our way to one of the appointment tables at the front of the shop, out of earshot of Marie and Jessica.

"Right, shall we get Jessica to do the superhero cake? Get her started on the more intricate work? She's good enough, if all goes well, she can take on much more wedding work and free up time for us. We will need to give her quite a pay rise though, when she proves herself."

"I was going to say exactly the same, but we need to figure out the money."

"Well, this new contract is really quite big, Bea, I'll go through it all with you later but it means we can give Jess a rise and get someone else in to do her old job."

"Really? Will there be anything left?"

"Yep."

"Wow! We'll need someone else anyway then, just to help with all of the new work."

"That's what I thought."

"Sounds really good, Clare. How exciting! Why don't you come over tonight to go through the contract?"

"Definitely. Okay, meeting over?"

"Over, I've got to put a bra on some boobs!"

The excitement of the new contract and Bear's growing is all well and good, but I feel terribly guilty that I'm not thinking about it much. An hour later, all I can think about whilst decorating this huge pair of boobs with a sexy lace bra, is texting Daniel. I haven't heard from him and I'm not likely to either, considering it's three in the morning in LA.

What if he's with someone? What if that's the reason he's being distant? Maybe he's just doing what I want and sticking to the rules. *Oh god, I can't concentrate.*

"I'm going to grab myself a cuppa from down the road, anyone want anything?"

"We do have facilities here you know." Clare looks at me in amusement, obviously it's daft to go out and buy it when we make tea and coffee for our appointments all the time, but right now, I just need to take a break.

"I know, but I need some air and I can't be bothered to make my own."

"Yeah, go on then, I'll have a latte, please," Clare says and the other decline.

I head a few shops down to get the drinks and wander back, trying to look at our lovely High Street through Daniel's eyes, wondering if he'd like it here. I want him to see it, I want him to see Bear's and my apartment, I want him in my bed with his hands on me, I want his lips, his tongue, his.... *Oh for god's sake.*

I get back to my work station and look down at the giant titties gazing up at me, pointy nipples under the intricate, sheer lace piping that I'm mid-way through. It's looking good, I'm pleased with it, although it's reminding me too much of Daniel ripping my bra off, god damn it.

I sip my scalding hot tea and wince as my tongue burns. Slamming it down in the counter, almost causing another injury, I rest my face in my hands and sigh loudly. I just want to cry. Cry and cry and cry. I want to talk to him and see him and make crazy, animalistic love to him. This is so fucking hideous!

The shop door opens and I quickly shuffle around to the baking area so the customers don't have to see my miserable, about-to-cry mug. Seconds later, Clare pops her head around the corner. "Bea, you've got a customer."

"Oh, what?" I whisper, seriously put out.

"Must be a groom, a hot groom though..."

"Ooh yay, someone's hot fiancé, how exciting," I say with an overly sarcastic edge to my voice. Clare raises her eyebrow in distaste at my tone.

"Okay, okay, I'm coming," I say, rolling my eyes. I stand straight and take a deep breath, putting on my fake happy face. I turn the corner, head towards the counter and lock eyes with my customer. I come to an immediate, abrupt halt. *What. The fuck.*

I stare. And I stare. I look at Clare and then back at him. She's looking at me like I've gone stir crazy, he's looking at me like... like he's in love with me. Like he's flown across the globe to see me. Tears sting the backs of my eyes and I blink, trying to believe what I'm seeing.

"Hey, baby," he says softly, excitedly.

The streams cascade down my face, a huge smile grows from ear to ear as I run to him, wrapping my arms around his beautiful neck. I press my lips against his and he lifts me, my legs wrapping tightly around his waist. We're immediately consumed, kissing passionately in the middle of the shop. With one hand holding me under my bum, he drags his other up my body to my neck and holds me against him.

"I take it he's not someone's groom then..." I hear Clare say from behind me, making me giggle against Daniel's lips. I pull away and gaze at him, stroking the hair on the back of his neck, taking him in. This has to be real, this can't be a dream, please don't let it be a dream, that would be too depressing to even contemplate.

"God, I love you, baby. I've missed you so much," he whispers. His gorgeous, sexy voice sends shivers through me.

"Daniel, I can't believe you're here. You didn't tell me!"

"I wanted to surprise you, sweetheart."

"You definitely did." I lay another kiss on his wonderful mouth and turn my head to see all three girls watching us; Marie, open-mouthed holding a dripping spatula, Jessica, clutching her chest, looking like she might cry, and Clare, resting on her elbows, sipping her coffee, enjoying the show.

I slide down to my feet, to stand at Daniel's side, holding him around his middle.

"Sorry about that, this is Daniel... Daniel, this is Clare, Marie and Jessica."

"Hi, ladies, great to meet you all. Clare, I've heard so much about you," he says as he walks forward to the counter and leans over to kiss her cheek.

"You too, Daniel. Wow, you're just as she described."

I can't stop staring at him and touching his body. "When did you arrive? How long are you here for?" I ask, already dreading him going home.

"I came straight from the airport, I told the driver the town and name of the store, and he drove me straight here. I'll be here for a few days, I'm not sure yet."

"Oh god, I'm so happy to see you! Do you have to go to work now?"

'No, not today."

"Oh good! So you can spend it with me?"

"Of course, baby."

I kiss him excitedly, over and over again, clutching his neck. He snakes his arms around my waist and pulls me into his amazing body, firmly. "Mmm..." he groans, deep in his throat, "I don't want to let you go," he whispers.

"Me neither. Where are you staying? Mine?"

"That's what I was hoping for."

"Bea, love..." Clare says, tentatively from behind the counter.

"Oh god, sorry, this is so unprofessional."

"Oh no, you carry on, I just wanted to ask, do you think you'll get the boobs finished or are you going to go home?" She looks worried, worried that she'll have to pick up where I left off and finish the bra.

"Of course I will, I wouldn't leave it half done, doll."

"I know, but.. you know, it's not every day..." She trails off, waving her hand towards Daniel and I. "It'll just look crap if I try to finish it."

"Daniel, do you want to go back to mine and have a sleep? I need to finish a cake I'm doing. You're welcome to stay here, might be boring though."

"Are you kidding me? I can't wait to see you work. Can I stay?"

"Of course you can. I was hoping you'd say that, to think of you alone in my bed would be too much for me to handle," I whisper so only he can hear.

I turn to the girls and clap my hands as I lead Daniel towards the baking area where I am working. "Spit spot, back to work, show's over!" They snap out of it and get straight back to work. "I'm over here, Daniel." I point to my work station. "Grab a stool and watch away."

"Whoa!" he says when he sees the boobies. "They look so... real! That's awesome! Great jugs!"

"Thank you. It's for a lady who has just had a boob job and she's having a party to celebrate!"

"What? That's crazy!"

"I know, each to their own." I wash my hands and get back to work, chatting to Daniel the whole time, he takes in

305

my every move, seeming to enjoy it. "I can't believe you're here, Daniel. I was having a really bad morning, missing you."

"I am so happy to be here, I missed you so much. I love watching you doing this, too, baby. You're so talented."

"Thank you." I smile shyly. Leaning in to give him a slow, soft kiss, I whisper in his ear so no one can hear. "When we get home, I need you to fuck me so hard and fast, we'll both come in seconds. And after that, I want you to make long, amazing, sweet love to me all day and night. Okay?" I look into his eyes and he's grinning from ear to ear.

"I've got a hard on now, baby. Don't make me stand up."

I giggle. "I'll take that as a yes."

"Good. You're so beautiful," he whispers as he kisses my neck, below my ear.

My eyes close and I exhale, loudly. "Mmm, Daniel... let me finish this so we can get home."

"Sure thing," he says with a wink as he leans away and looks around the shop. "It's really cool in here, Bea. I love the decor."

"Thanks, we like it, don't we Clare?"

"Yep. It's just what we wanted," she calls from the counter.

"So, tell me about this new contract," Daniel enquires.

I continue to tell him that the contract is to supply a large office building with cakes, similar to the arrangement he has at his company.

"That sounds cool, so what company is it?"

"I don't know yet, Clare has taken over the dealings with them, as she started it all while I was away. We were going to go through it all tonight. Clare?"

"The company is called... um..." She fishes through some paperwork in front of her. "Uh... Henry Berkeley UK', they sound like a huge corporation."

"What?!" I yell, turning from Daniel to Clare and back again. "Henry Berkeley?"

"Yeah... why?" Clare asks, looking confused.

Daniel smiles a guilty, cheeky smile and looks at me tentatively.

"Clare, meet Daniel. Daniel *Berkeley*. Daniel *Berkeley* of Henry *Berkeley* Inc."

"What?!" She cries. "Tell me it's all still happening and it wasn't some kind of weird lover's joke?"

Daniel chuckles. "Yes, Clare, don't panic, it's all still happening. I spoke to them and told them to change their supplier to you. Not a problem is it?"

"No!" Clare shrieks. "Not at all! Thank you, Daniel, that's amazing."

I turn to stare at him in disbelief. "Daniel! I can't believe you did that, how did you know we'd be good enough?"

"I know you, baby. I knew your business would be more than good enough, and no doubt better than our current supplier here."

"Wow. I don't know what to say, Daniel."

"Nothing, it's no big deal."

"It is for us, this means a lot for us," Clare says.

"Well, I'm glad. Now, let's get back to work," Daniel says, addressing all of us with a cheery smile.

I gaze at him, shaking my head and smiling.

"Come on, work, baby. I want to get home."

"I'm nearly done here. I'll just do the red trim and then..." I turn around in my chair to continue. "Marie? Can you add the message to the drum when I'm done? Not on the cake itself."

She agrees and soon after, I'm done. "Right, Clare, I'm done with that, do you mind if I head home? Anything happening this afternoon?"

"Nothing I can't handle! See you tomorrow. Daniel, will you be here for Bea's birthday?"

"Yes, I hope to be here, Friday."

"Great, you'll come out with us then?"

"I'd love to, thank you for the invite." *How did he know it was my birthday?*

We head to my car and both get in. As soon as his door is closed, I jump over to straddle him and kiss him like crazy. He laughs into the kiss and wraps his arms around me. He kisses my neck and I moan loudly. "God, Daniel, I'm so fucking horny, I can't explain. There's something wrong with me."

"Nothing wrong with you, baby," he says between kisses, "now, get back in your seat and drive me to your place before I strip you naked and fuck you right here."

"I'm not sure I can wait that long," I say in all seriousness as I clamber back into my seat.

"Drive! Fast!" he cries making me laugh.

"I've missed you so much, Daniel."

"Me too, baby. Me too."

I've never driven from Rickmansworth to Watford so quickly in all my driving life. I practically screech into my parking space and jump out of the car.

"It's nice here, baby, I like it," he says, turning and looking over the green in the centre of the development.

"Thanks, me too, I'll give you a tour... maybe tomorrow," I add, realising there's no way I'll let him out of my bed today.

Upstairs, I nearly break my key in the lock, trying to open my front door. When it finally opens, I slam it behind us and start to undress.

"Baby, baby, baby... slow down," he says pulling me close to him and gazing into my eyes.

"No, Daniel," I plead, "you don't understand, I need you so badly."

He pauses for a moment, his eyes burning before he presses me against the wall in the hallway, kissing me fervently. I moan and wriggle and grab, I might even come, just like this. He starts to undress me and I tackle the fly of his jeans. "Bedroom, baby. Now," he orders and I drag him straight there, ripping the rest of my clothes off as we go.

Stripped of my underwear, the backs of my legs pressed against the foot of my bed, Daniel is topless, crushed against me, kissing me like there's no tomorrow. Our mouths moving fast, desperately, tongues entwined. He tastes so good, his lips so forceful, yet soft as satin. Oh how I've missed this.

He pushes me down onto the bed and pulls his jeans and boxers off in record time. I gaze at his tanned, muscular frame and swoon. *Even better than I remember...* "Oh god, baby, I've missed you so much, this incredible body, your beautiful face..." He crawls, slowly up the bed, straddling me. He kisses me all the way up, making my skin tingle.

"Daniel, please fuck me... please?"

"I'll agree to that, baby, because I need you just as badly. But after, I'm savouring every last bit of you. Mmm," he says, closing his mouth around one of my hardened nipples.

"Holy shit, I'm not going to last two seconds, Daniel." I moan, feeling that buzz already.

"Let's go for it," he whispers with a huge grin, moving up to kiss my lips. I feel him in between my legs, just the feel of his tip close to me makes me gasp. He pushes gently, opening me, forcing his way in, slowly, deeper and deeper, and *oh my god.* It's spectacular. "God, baby, you're so wet," he croaks.

"I have needed you so much, Daniel, so much."

He pulls back, the feel of his cock moving inside me, hard as rock, is what I have craved since I left him.

"Hard, Daniel, really hard, please?"

He slams back into me and I cry out in ecstasy.

"Yes, yes!" I cry, begging for more and he repeats the motion, completely filling me.

"You like that?"

"Oh yes, faster, harder!"

"God, baby, you're so damn hot," he groans, each word louder than the last as he picks up his pace and slams into me, over and over and over. I bend my legs either side of him, pushing my pelvis towards him with each thrust, forcing him harder into me and that's it, it's here, the huge tidal wave crashing down inside me and I cry out, grabbing the back of his neck, my toes curling, legs cramping.

"Yes! Oh god! Daniel! Uh!"

"Fuck, baby!" Daniel shouts out loud as he explodes inside me, it's so hot, the combined moaning, grunting, panting. We rock together, waiting for the final waves to die down, kissing each other.

Daniel rests his forehead against mine and closes his eyes, breathing heavily. "Oh, baby. You're so freakin' hot."

I grin. "So you said."

"Fuck. I've never experienced the feelings I get with you. You've taken over my world, completely, you're all I

309

think about, morning, noon and night." He takes a few more heavy breaths. "I need you, baby, permanently."

"Let's not get into that now, I'm still reeling from getting fucked by you. Jesus, it was so good."

"I don't intend on leaving it there." He kisses me gently on the lips and opens his mouth ever so slightly. We enjoy the slowest, most delicious kiss - the perfect finish to the first of many 'sessions' today. We lay, wrapped in each other, smiling.

"I can't get over the fact that I have Sexy Berkeley in my bed."

"I don't know about him, sweetheart, but Daniel Berkeley is right here and loving every minute of it."

"You are so sexy, Daniel. My Sexy Berkeley. I was really worried, you know, I thought you were being distant over the last couple of days."

"I'm sorry, baby, I was so, so busy trying to sort things for this trip and I had to cram a load of meetings into the last couple days. I also wanted it to be a surprise and knew if I spoke to you, I'd tell you."

"I'm so relieved. I thought that was the end."

"No, baby, the end is nowhere in sight." He runs his fingers up and down my spine, just as I had envisaged during one of my many sad/horny/lonely moments. He spots my necklace and clasps it in his fingers, smiling.

"You're wearing it."

"I haven't taken it off. I love it so much."

He smiles and I'm reminded, yet again, how much this man means to me. I can't let him go.

"So, when do you have to work?"

"I'll go in tomorrow, I'll probably get the car to take me and then figure the trains out for Thursday. I thought maybe you'd like to do something Friday, if you don't already have plans? Before your night out."

"That would be lovely, we never work on our birthdays so I was just going to potter about. By the way, how did you know it was my birthday?"

"Tilly mentioned something while you guys were in LA, so I asked her, you weren't there, you must have been in the bathroom or something."

"I didn't think you knew."

"I couldn't miss your birthday, baby."

"But you are on a business trip, yes?"

"Of course, this is strictly, not a vacation," he says with a salute.

"Good. But you're allowed to have fun."

"Why, thank you, kind lady. What sort of fun?"

"Mmm, well..." I reach down and grip his already hard cock and smooth my hand up and down. "I think this might be allowed."

"Well, I am very pleased about that, sweetheart. What about..." his hand slips down my belly and cups me, his fingers gently circling my clitoris sending a buzz right through my centre.

"Ooh, yes, that's... mmm... fun," I reply, somewhat giddy. I close my eyes and drop my head back on the pillow as he leans over me, continuing with his talented fingers, and lowers his soft gentle lips to mine. I moan and curl both hands around his neck, selfishly abandoning his erection.

Daniel talks against my lips, between kisses. "I've missed you so much, baby. I love you, I love every single thing about you. Your body, your smile, I love your laugh, your rules, your sex... the face you pull when you're excited, and the one that tells me you're in love with me. I love how you love me."

His fingers still working up a storm, I smile, gripping onto his neck. "Oh I do, Daniel, I love you and I love that you know and love all of those things about me. I don't want to let you go back, I want you with me all the time, forever."

"Me too, baby. I also love how you feel right now, you're so ready for me, I'm going to make you come so hard." He slips two fingers inside me.

"Oh, yes," I moan, "it's so... oh, don't stop."

"Is that good? It feels so good, this is mine... okay?"

"If we can be together, it's all yours Daniel."

"I want it to be mine, whatever."

"Mmm, oh Daniel, I'm close, talk to me..."

"You want me to make you come, baby?"

"God, yes, and then I want you to make love to me, straight away."

"I'll do whatever you want. I can't wait to slip inside you, wet from what I'm about to do to you. Ready for it?"

"Yes! Yes," I plead.

Daniel's fingers begin to twist as he draws them out and sinks them back in deep, making sure they glide right against that hidden spot, sending my body into sexual overdrive. He lays his thumb gently over my clitoris, and works it, continuing his rhythm inside me. "I'm going to slide myself right inside you, I'm so hard and ready for you, baby, but I want you to come on my fingers first, now."

"Oh god, oh god, I need you, yes, yes, yes..." And suddenly he presses down with his thumb and pushes his fingers as deep at they'll go inside me, brushing that oh-so-important spot, triggering the almighty explosion that ripples through me, instantly. "Oh GOD! Yes!" I cry, digging my nails into Daniel's neck, biting my lip and screwing my face up in sheer delirium.

"Say you're mine, baby," he whispers.

"I'm yours! I'm yours! Fuck, every day, I'm yours... oh god!" We make sweet, tender love straight away and come together once again.

We both flop back on the bed, bodies glistening with sweat, panting like crazy. I reach out and drop my forearm onto Daniel's chest, and he squeezes my hand with his, raising it to his lips.

"You're so... damned good... at this," he pants.

"Mmm..." I respond, on another planet.

I hear him chuckle, mid-pant. "Come here." He stretches his arm out and pulls me into his side. I tuck my head against his shoulder and drape my arm over his belly, my leg over his.

"Mmm," I moan, appreciatively. I can't do much else.

"Baby, I can't go to sleep, I need to stay up as late as I can, if you go to sleep, I will too."

"Oh," I grumble, "tired..."

"Me too. I'm hungry, want to get some late lunch?"

"Mmm hmm."

"Want to use coherent speech?"

"Uh huh." I grin. "Okay, if you must pull me out of my sexual delirium." I raise myself up against him and look at his delicious face, his beautiful turquoise eyes that have so thoroughly enraptured me.

"I must," he responds, kissing my nose.

"Right, I'll make some food, we don't have 'whatever, whenever' here you know."

Daniel laughs and sits up, taking me with him. "Let's go raid the refrigerator."

"Okedokey, *baby*!"

I make a delicious goat's cheese and black olive salad with pitta which we eat, sitting on the sofa in our underwear.

"I love your apartment, sweetheart."

"Thank you, me too, I'm so glad you got to see it. Um, Daniel? Don't you have a suitcase?"

"Oh, that, I forgot. Yes, the driver is going to drop it off for me, I didn't want to bring it into the cakery. I better give him a call and tell him the address."

"Okay. You know, it's a shame you didn't bring Luke with you, I think he and Til could do with a little chat."

"Funny you should say that, baby, I was trying to get him to come, but he kept saying Tilly wouldn't appreciate him following her."

"Tilly is... I'm worried about her. She's not herself."

"They'll sort it out, even if they have to wait it out and forget each other. Anyway, at least we're together right now, and guess what?"

"What?"

"I can call you my girlfriend; we're together." Daniel grins, excitedly.

"I suppose you're right, boyfriend."

"If I come out with you and your friends on Friday... hold up, I know Clare invited me, but do you want me to come?"

"Of course! More than anything! I can't wait to show you off."

Daniel smiles. "Good. So, will you introduce me as your boyfriend?"

"Um... I don't know. It'd be a bit awkward having to explain that you're only my boyfriend when we're in the same country. Do you want me to?"

"Yes, I do." Daniel nods. To the point.

"Okay, let's see how it goes. I would love to tell people you're my boyfriend, but don't want all of that awkward explaining when you've gone back home, when we're single again."

"Okay, baby. Let's see how it goes. I love you, by the way."

"I love you too, my gorgeous, gorgeous boyfriend."

Daniel smiles a broad, shy smile. "I love that. I want to tell the world you're my beautiful girlfriend."

"For the next few days."

"Bea!"

"Sorry." I lean across the sofa and kiss his sexy, tanned shoulder.

The rest of the day is amazing. We shower together, make love some more and talk like we've been apart forever. After Daniel's case arrives and we've had dinner, we lay in bed, gazing at each other, deliriously happy.

"When you called me that night, sweetheart, after your nightmare, I knew I had to come to you. I wanted to hold you so badly. I couldn't bear that I was so far away, you sounded so scared."

"I was. Scared for you, though. Speaking to you made me feel a lot better."

He pulls me closer to him and squeezes me. "I love you so much, baby."

"I know you do. When we are together, we've got such a good thing."

"We'll be together properly, baby."

"One day." I swiftly change the depressing subject. "Anyway, what are you working on at HBUK? Is it something you fabricated so that you could come here, or is there really work for you there?" I smile, cheekily.

"Well, you think so little of me," he says in mock disgrace before continuing, "actually, baby, there is real work for me, the UK division are having a sudden restructure and one of us needed to come to London to oversee and give the 'go ahead'. It's quite a big job, and was fairly last minute, which is why I don't know when I'll go home. We decided I'd be the best man for the job, but honestly, I think Dad would have sent me anyway, he's been watching me pine after you since you left."

I can't help the grin that spreads across my face, *he's been pining after me!* "Okay, Daniel, well answered. I'm convinced, genuine, work related business. With a bit of play on the side with your UK girlfriend."

"Correction - my only girlfriend."

I grin. "So you haven't met anyone to take my place yet?"

"Of course not, and I don't intend to, sweetheart. I hope you haven't set your sights on anyone else."

"I've been crying for ten days straight, darling. I think that's unlikely."

"Oh, don't say that," he says as he squeezes me again, "well, the crying bit, the other bit I'm more than happy about."

"I'm so excited that you'll be here on my birthday," I say, laying a gentle kiss on Daniel's chest. "Daniel, aren't you tired?"

"I am really tired and if I wasn't with you, I'd have fallen asleep a long time ago and gotten jet lag."

"It's nine thirty, so you could go to sleep now and you should be fine tomorrow?"

"I could..." he says with a sexy smile and he leans over me, running his warm hand down my body, to my far knee which he hooks and pulls up, turning me towards him and placing it over his hip. He presses his lips against mine and kisses me with such want, such need. "But I'd like to make the most of you, one more time before you fall asleep in my arms." His beautiful lips already tracing my neck while his hand glides up and down my thigh.

"Oh, I do *not* have a problem with that. Mmm."

CHAPTER TWENTY THREE
WEDNESDAY 3RD OCTOBER

Soft, tender kisses, from my neck to my shoulder and back again, the most delicious way to wake up on a very rainy autumnal morning. I smile, revelling, knowing that my man is here, showering me with affection.

"Mmm, good morning sexy," I whisper, rolling over to meet Daniel's gaze with a huge smile on my face.

"It's a very good morning, baby." He kisses my nose and brushes the hair from my face with his fingertips.

"What time is it?" I stretch bent arms above my head and cover my mouth with my hand as I yawn.

"It's real early, baby, I'm sorry to wake you, I wanted a little time with you before we head off to work."

I grin broadly. "I'm happy with that, Daniel. You make it sound like we live together."

"I'd like that," he says, his mouth curling slowly into a shy smile.

"So would I, I'm going to clean my teeth, right now, I need to kiss you."

"Let's do it!" he shouts, animatedly, jumping out of bed. I giggle at his boyish excitement.

I stroke his gorgeous, brawny back as we brush, making the most of him, and press the side of my face against him. *Mmm, feels so good.* As soon as we have rinsed, Daniel has me tightly wrapped in his arms. His lips gently meet with mine, and he kisses me in the most sensual, tender way. I practically collapse against him in sheer pleasure.

"Let's get back into bed, baby. It's cold and rainy and I want to feel your warm body wrapped up in mine."

"Amazing. I'll sort breakfast in a bit." I say, crawling onto my bed and snuggling under the duvet. Daniel follows, wrapping me up in his hot, naked body.

We spend the next forty five minutes kissing and chatting and loving. It's definitely the best workday morning I've ever had. I finally get out of bed and slip on my dressing gown to go and make us breakfast, while Daniel showers. When I'm finished, I set the kitchen table and go to find him.

He is *still* in the shower! I enter the en-suite to tell him that breakfast is ready, and get completely side-tracked by his hot, wet, naked body. The hot, steaming water runs over his tanned, well defined muscles which flex as he smoothes the lathering soap over his torso.

He doesn't notice me standing here, gazing at him through the shower doors as he faces the wall, so I slip my dressing gown off and silently step in behind him. I slide my hands around his middle and press against his back. I feel him jump slightly and then he chuckles.

"Hey baby," he murmurs as he places his hands over mine on his taut belly.

"Hello, darling, you've been in here for ages. I came to tell you that breakfast is ready, but I couldn't resist you."

He turns around and leans down to kiss me, his lips wet and delicious. God, he is so fucking hot! Will I ever get used to that? Suppose I don't need to.

"Daniel, you are very handsome at the best of times, but in the shower, crikey..."

He smiles slowly, shyly, and runs his nose up and down mine. He turns me so that my back is facing the wall and he pushes me to it, pressing his body against mine. He starts to kiss me gently, and presses his rock-hard erection against me. I lift my leg instinctively and he holds it up, wrapping it around him, hoisting the rest of me up, holding me tight. With both of my legs wrapped around him, he swiftly, unexpectedly thrusts inside me.

"Fuck!" I groan, loudly, not expecting his sudden invasion, but it's oh so good. "Oh god, Daniel..."

"You like it?"

"I love it."

He thrusts over and over, the water thundering down on us, making our bodies hot and slippery. I wrap my arms tightly around his neck, playing with his hair as he presses his mouth on mine again. "Uh!" I cry into our kiss, his hard, wet cock sliding into me over and over again, his beautiful chest pressing against my hard nipples... *Oh yes.*

"Fuck, baby, you feel so good. ..." he groans.

Hearing him, feeling him, knowing he's about to...*oh, oh yes....* the waves of ecstasy flood through my body and I grind my pelvis against him, bringing it on. "Oh yes... oh Daniel! Fuck!" I yell loudly, whimpering as I come hard, pulsating, convulsing, squeezing around him.

"Oh yes, Bea! I love you...so...much!" he shouts as he thrusts hard inside me one last time.

He kisses me again and slumps against me, against the wall. He slowly opens his eyes and rests his forehead against mine, panting. "Wow, that was unexpected."

"Uh huh," I reply with a broad grin, "it was delicious."

"You are incredible. I love you so much."

I giggle. "You tell me that a lot, I love you too."

He smiles and kisses my lips tenderly. "Let's get out, breakfast will be cold."

"Okay, I'm going to quickly finish showering, as I'm here. You have breakfast, it should still be warm if you're quick. There is a pot of tea on the table."

"You're amazing," he says with a quick kiss before he puts me down and gets out.

Soon after, showered and face applied, I stroll into the kitchen in my work uniform to find Daniel drinking his tea and reading yesterday's newspaper. I bend down and kiss him, subconsciously stroking his gorgeous broad shoulders over his crisp white shirt.

"Mmm, thank you for breakfast, baby. It was perfect. Yours will be cold now, though," he says as he pours me a fresh cup of tea from the pot. As he moves his arm, something shiny catches my eye, and I notice his shirt cuffs.

"Your bumble bees! You're wearing them!"

Daniel grins. "Of course I am, baby. I have worn them a lot."

"Did they remind you of me?"

"All the time. My dad is particularly fond of them, I bought him a pair of their lobster ones, I thought they were amusing and he loves lobster. I did notice, online, that they make cupcake cuff links too, I might put them on by birthday list, baby, as I have a newfound love of all things 'cake'," he says with a raised eyebrow and cute grin.

A shy smile spreads across my face as I sit and eat a little of my cold scrambled eggs on toast - which isn't actually that bad - and gaze at the view in front of me. "I will remember to have a look on their website when your birthday comes around. Oh..." It dawns on me. "When is your birthday? I can't believe I don't know that."

"You've got a while to save up, August seventeenth."

"Okay. Maybe Christmas then," I say, wondering if we'll still be in contact at Christmas.

Daniel's iPhone chimes and he looks at it before standing and putting his plate in the dishwasher. "Okay, baby, that's my car," he says, slipping into his suit jacket before strolling over to me, clutching my chin and bending to kiss me, sweetly. I can't help but enjoy this feeling of normal domesticity. This is what married couples do, this is what normal boyfriends and girlfriends do. I wish he could stay forever.

He pauses, gazing into my eyes. "I love you, baby. I can't wait to get home later. Have a great day." He kisses my nose and stands straight before I follow him to the door.

"I love you, too. Have a fruitful day at the office, dear, but don't get too much done, I don't want you to go home yet."

He chuckles before strolling down the corridor and disappearing down the stairs.

I head to work with a huge grin on my face, although that niggling feeling, reminding me that this isn't permanent, isn't far away. Knowing that I have a few more days of him, however, makes it that little bit easier to bear. I'm going to try to make the most of every moment that I have. Clare greets me with a huge hug when she arrives at work, and tells me how thrilled she is that I get to spend a few days with Daniel, knowing how miserable I've been.

"Darling, you might want to give Tilly a text or call though," she says, cautiously,

"I was just going to, why do you say that?"

"Well, I told her that Daniel had arrived yesterday and she went a bit funny, locked herself away in her room and I didn't hear or speak to her again. I didn't even see her this morning, I don't know whether she had left already or was still in her room when I left."

I feel awful. I should have told her that he was here, I was just so wrapped up in the excitement that I didn't even think about it. I grab my mobile and call her straight away.

"Hello?" She sounds dreadful.

"Hi, Til, you okay?"

"Yeah, you? I heard Daniel's here, how amazing. I can't wait to see him." I'm hearing the words, but I don't quite feel the conviction behind them, she sounds odd.

"Tilly, where are you? You not at work?"

"No, I'm not feeling too great today, I'm in bed."

"Oh I'm sorry, I hope I didn't wake you? What's up?"

"Just a horrid head ache, that's all. Had it for a couple of days and I needed a day away from the office to try to get back to normal."

"Okay, are you sure that's all?"

"Yes, I'm sure. I still feel a bit crappy and I'll be honest, I am a little jealous that your Daniel is here, but I really do have a shitty headache."

"I'm so sorry I didn't tell you yesterday, I got so side tracked..."

"Yeah, I'll just bet you did! No, don't worry about it, doll, I know exactly how that panned out and I would have done exactly the same!"

"Tilly, Daniel tried to get Luke to come too..."

She cuts me off before I manage to say another word. *"Oh Christ, stop right there, Bea. You know I'm not in the same boat as you. I know he wouldn't have wanted to schlep all the way to the UK just to see some 'piece of ass' he shagged for a few days, and I don't want him here anyway, so don't do the whole 'pitying' thing, because I'm not having it."*

"Uh, hang on, let me finish would you, please?"

She says nothing.

"Right, as I was saying, he tried to get Luke to come too, but Luke said that you wouldn't like him following you home and didn't want to force the situation on you. Probably didn't want to feel unwelcome, either, I imagine." I add, under my breath.

She says nothing, again and after a long pause she finally speaks. *"Right... are you finished now?"*

"Yes."

"Good. I don't need to hear it Bea, we had a great time, we're not going to have a relationship, I don't need to see him again. That's it, end of. Okay?"

"Okay, okay. Sorry, I just wanted you to know what he'd said. Please stop thinking it's all macho bullshit, Til, some men really are nice, you know."

"I know that, darling, and you've got one of those. I know Luke is nice, he's gorgeous and caring and... fuck, he's amazing, but he's not a one woman man and he's not after a relationship with me. I know this and I don't hold it against him because I get it, I've been there. But I don't need to stay in touch with him and remind myself that I want something else now, and he isn't the one to give it to me. So let's drop it, okay?"

"Okay. Sorry. I won't bring it up again, I just wanted you to know. Anyway, do you need us to get anything for you? I can nip to boots for some ibuprofen or something?"

"No, I'm stocked up, thanks Bea."

"Get better for my birthday, won't you?"

"I wouldn't miss it for the world. I really am looking forward to seeing Daniel, you know."

"Good, because he can't wait to see you either. Come over whenever you're feeling better, okay?"

"Okay, I'm going to have a sleep now."

"Alright then doll, feel better. Love you."

"Love you too. So much, Bea, you know that."

"I do, darling, call me anytime."

"Night night."

At lunch time, Clare nips out to get us all a sandwich, while I continue with some Halloween cakes for the window display. It's going to be great this year with all of the new bits from LA, even though we're a bit late. I can't wait to see it when it's finished. My phone chimes and I wash my hands of all the black sugar paste before I reach into my beautiful Chloe bag to pull it out. My stomach flips... *why is it still doing that?*

~

Daniel 3 Oct 13:03
Hey, baby. You okay? I loved waking up with you this morning. Can't wait to see you later. It's weird texting you in the same time zone... The London office is great today, although I can't wait for the day to end so I can come home to you. How's work going? Xxxxx

~

My grin almost hurts my face, it's so wide. I'm going home to my Daniel tonight! I'm going to make him something super-delicious for dinner. That's if he wants to stay in...

~

3 Oct 13:09
Hi sexy ;-) my day is great thank you! I can't stop thinking about you, but that's okay because I get to come home to you tonight and make all my thoughts reality... I'm excited to see you. Do you want to go out for dinner? Or shall I put some sexy lingerie on and make us something special? ;-) (ILY, DYLM?) Xxx

~

I sigh loudly with a huge smile and pirouette over to Marie and kiss her on the cheek. "You're doing a great job, keep it up."

She laughs at me. "Can you make this hunk of yours stay forever? I like this Bea."

I frown. "Is there something wrong with the other Bea?"

"Nothing at all, she's a lovely boss, but the one that came back from LA last week has been a real misery."

"I'm sorry about her, but beware, she'll be back next week. Make the most of this one."

She laughs and my mobile chimes again.

~

Daniel 3 Oct 13:16
Of course ILY, do you really need to ask?! I LOVE BEATRICE HART. A LOT. Is that better, baby? I had thought about taking you out for dinner, but since you mentioned lingerie, I can't stop thinking about you cooking in one of those sexy purchases we made... I'll take option 2. I'm dribbling at my desk. I've got a meeting now, baby, I'll see you

322

tonight, the driver said I'll get home at about 6:30. Enjoy your afternoon. I LOVE YOU.Xxxxxxxx

~

~

3 Oct 13:22
I know YLM really :-) Okay, I'll make us a nice dinner. I'll dress 'appropriately'... Get a hanky and wipe up your dribble before your meeting. See you about 6:30 then, enjoy your day. Love you, sexy xxxxx

~

Later on, I arrive home with bags of food shopping and head to the shower to wash off today's layer of sugar. I have about an hour until Daniel comes home and I want to be clean and super-sexy, with dinner at the table. I re-apply my make-up and spritz myself with Chloe, before choosing a nightie from the pile in my drawer. I'm thrilled that I'm getting to wear one at last. Instead of a traditional nightie, I decide to wear the super-sexy, black corset style slip that has sheer panels running below the bra cups, between the satin. It has suspenders so I add some black stockings and my black satin stilettos.

I only have a short while to get dinner ready before Daniel gets home so I wrap my silky robe around me and head to the kitchen where I kick off my shoes to cook. I open the wine to let it breathe and set the table elegantly before efficiently making a start on the food.

Not long after, my potatoes are beautifully whipped, my green beans are artfully stacked on the plates and my steaks are about to come out of the pan when the buzzer for the front door goes. Perfect timing. I pour the melted garlic butter into a tiny jug and put it on the table before I answer.

"Hello?"

"Honey, I'm home..." Daniel sings, making me laugh. I buzz the main door open and swiftly serve up the steaks. I ram the pans into the dishwasher and wipe the surfaces at double speed. I put the plates on the table, dim the lights and light the

candles just as Daniel knocks on the door. I quickly slip my shoes on and throw my dressing gown behind the chair in the hall, before flicking my hair about and opening the door.

And there he is. Utterly gorgeous in his mega-expensive suit with a huge bunch of beautiful flowers in his arm. He stares at me, open mouthed as his eyes lick me from my head to my toes and back again. *Uh huh, baby, soak it in, you're gonna get some of this tonight!*

Daniel briefly snaps out of it to hurry into the apartment, slamming the door behind him. "Don't want any of your neighbours seeing you, baby, jeez," he says, "you're the hottest thing, and you're all mine. Come here." He drops his briefcase and reaches for me, wrapping his arm around my waist, pulling me against his chest with a thud. He leans down and takes my mouth with such animal force that my knees buckle and I want to totally forget dinner and make love right here, against the door. Finally, he releases me, taking another long look up and down my body. "I bought you these..." he hands me the beautiful flowers.

"Thank you Daniel, they're gorgeous."

"No, baby. You're gorgeous. Can we...?"

I giggle. "I'm afraid not, sir, dinner is served." I hold my hand out, gesturing towards the kitchen.

"Wow! That looks almost as good as you do, baby. You're spoiling me."

"You deserve to be spoiled," I say as I kiss him gently and return to the kitchen. Daniel removes his jacket and loosens his tie before we both sit.

"Wine, baby?" he asks as he picks up the bottle.

"Yes, please."

He pours the Temperanillo and raises his glass to toast. "To my *outstandingly* hot, sexy girlfriend, and the lingerie she's wearing. Thank you for dinner, baby."

"And to my gorgeous boyfriend, I love that you're here."

"Me too," he whispers before we both take a sip and tuck into our meal.

Daniel cleaned his plate, rejoicing how delicious everything was. We decided to have a break before dessert so retired to the lounge, where I lit a few more candles to continue the romantic ambience. Sitting together on the sofa, he kisses me gently on the lips. "Thank you, baby. Dinner was delicious and you look incredible, I can't wait to do things to you in that."

I smile and snuggle into him. "I look forward to it. Oh, before I forget..." I stand up again and walk into the hallway to my handbag, Daniel wolf whistling as I go.

"Christ, baby, your ass looks amazing in that thing, stockings are a hot look for you. Fuck, I'm a lucky guy."

"Lucky for a few days, anyway," I say, bringing us back to reality as I return to the sofa.

Daniel nods and then shakes his head, rolling his eyes, his demeanour changing to something less jovial. "Bea, you think you could stop doing that?" *Whoa... he looks serious. Cross even.*

"Doing what?"

"Stop *that*. Every time I say anything about us, you add some comment about how it's not forever and it's really getting to me."

"Sorry, Daniel, I just have to keep grounded about this, I can't get carried away. I know how hideous it was without you for the last couple of weeks and how hideous it's going to be, again, when you leave. It isn't forever, Daniel, you know it can't be that way so why pretend it is? I don't know how many times I have to say it, I do not want a long distance relationship."

"What do you think this is, if not a long distance relationship, for god's sake? Neither of us wants anyone else, heck, we love each other, Bea! This is what a long distance relationship is."

Oh fuck it. How did we suddenly go from a gorgeous, romantic evening, to a barney? I sit back down next to him, feeling quite awkward and rather uncomfortable wearing this revealing outfit during an argument.

I look up at his face, he's so serious. "I understand that, and yes, I suppose this is a 'type' of long distance relationship, but I refuse to be heartbroken every single day that I'm not with you, waiting for the 'once in a blue moon trip' when you come here on business. Neither of us has met anyone else yet because there hasn't been any time to, but when we've been apart for months, we are both going to feel the strain of having a partner we never see. Love or no love. What's to say you won't find a great girl who would be perfect for you? You'd throw that away because you have me, in England? Unable to touch me, see me? Or of course you wouldn't throw it away and would end up breaking up with me anyway."

"Baby, you're so negative. Firstly, *you're* that perfect girl for me, I've never met anyone more perfect and don't think I ever will again. Secondly, why can't you have a ray of hope for the future? Why don't you think that, maybe, we'll find a solution? And you're the one who says I can only come when I'm on business, I'd come more often if you let me."

"I'm not negative, I'm realistic, Daniel, and as for your trips over here, you still wouldn't be able to take that much time off work, to make it often enough for me to miss you less."

"Well, we'll see. We'll talk about this again, let's try to get back on track and enjoy this romantic night, huh?"

"Okay, but I really don't see what's going to change between now, and our next conversation."

"Bea!" he says with exasperation, "I'm just trying to come back from an argument, okay?"

"Okay," I respond, nodding and looking at my hands in my lap, still feeling stupid in this bloody corset thing and stockings.

"Oh, here." I hold out my hand to Daniel and deposit a set of keys into his. "They are spare keys to my apartment, to use while you're here. I asked my mum to drop them at the shop earlier. You might need them."

He looks at me and smiles. "Thank you for thinking of me. I'm sorry, baby, I just want to feel like a normal couple, I suppose."

"I know. I'm sorry I'm not more positive, I just need to protect myself. Leaving you and being apart hurt so much, I'm not sure how many times I can go through that."

"Okay. Let's forget it, for now... Baby?"

"Yes?"

He leans forward, to put the keys and his wine on the coffee table and the then turns back to me, holding my chin and gently kisses me. "I love you."

"I know you do, Daniel. Me too."

He continues to shower my face with soft kisses. "I love you... I love you..." he whispers between them and I close my eyes as the tingles run under my skin. The feel of his soft, warm lips on my body relieves all the tension from our 'discussion'. He slowly pushes me backwards until I am laying down, my head resting on the arm of the sofa. He crawls over me, lifting my legs onto the sofa under his arching body. I place my hands on his shoulders and enjoy his hands and lips seducing me.

I run my hands from his shoulders, up the sides of his face and into his hair as the pace picks up. I bend my leg, my inner thigh grazing his hard body through the thin, silky fabric of the stocking, it feels... sexy, different. Hot. I start to remove Daniel's tie, mid kiss, he's wearing far too much clothing, I want to feel his skin, I want him to feel my stocking clad legs, brushing against his flesh, I want his naked, ripped chest pressed against me. *Oh yes.* "Daniel," I murmur against his mouth, "I want to feel you."

He immediately kneels up and swiftly unbuttons his shirt and throws it off his shoulders before removing the cuff links. I hold out my hand, taking them from him. I look at them and smile, loving that he's actually been wearing them. By the time I have leant over to put them on the coffee table, Daniel has removed his shoes and socks and is pulling down his trousers and boxers. *Oh, heavens above. It gets me every time.*

He immediately rests back down on top of me with a sexy smile, brushing my hair behind my ear. "God, you're stunning, baby."

"I was just thinking something quite similar about you, actually, Daniel."

He leans down to kiss me again and as I bend my legs up his sides, he groans loudly and moves his hand down to my knickers, tugging them to the side and slowly slipping his fingers within my waiting folds.

"Oh, Daniel." I moan as he gently caresses my clitoris.

"Wrap your legs around me, baby."

As I do, he removes his fingers and sinks immediately deep inside me.

I lay, panting, crushed between Daniel's Herculean masculinity and my plush sofa, and he lifts his head from mine, looking down at our bodies, entwined. "This picture is so hot, baby; you, in this, with your stocking-covered legs wrapped around me like that... jeez, this is what wet dreams are made of. I want to take a photo." He chuckles.

"Ha! No chance!"

Daniel laughs. "I know, baby, but it's so..." He growls and buries his face in my neck, kissing me, making me laugh out loud.

I reach around Daniel to my feet, crossed behind his back, and slip my shoes off, tossing them on the floor behind the sofa. "Daniel?"

"Yes, baby?"

"Do you know when you have to leave yet?"

"Let's not talk about that now, Bea."

"I just want to relax, and if I know, I can mentally prepare myself. I'm scared you're just going to say 'I've got to go back tomorrow'."

"Don't worry, I'm not going tomorrow. Or Friday. In fact, I'm hoping I'll be here a few days beyond that. As I'm not going into the office on Friday, I may need to go in on Monday."

"Really? Oh goody! I don't mind you going in to work on Friday though, you know."

"No way, baby. Not a chance, it's your birthday."

I smile, knowing there is no argument here. He's so lovely, even when he was cross at me earlier, he was still lovely. How on earth did I find this man? I'm being punished for it, the universe has found me the most incredibly perfect man, but only giving me tiny tasters of him and then tearing him away from me.

"I was thinking, baby, why don't you ask Tilly and Clare over for dinner tomorrow night? I'd really like to catch up with Tilly and get to know Clare a little better, ideally before your birthday party."

"Sounds like a great idea, darling. I will, we can get a take away."

"I might be home a little later tomorrow, it's a big day for the restructure project, it's when the final decisions are due to be made as to its viability, so I could have a lot of meetings to get through if any problems are detected."

"Okay, well that's not a problem, you can let me know when you're on your way home and I'll arrange the food then."

"Perfect, I'll use the car again tomorrow, it might be easier."

"Okay. What shall we do now? Want to watch some telly? Or go to bed? Want dessert?"

"I'm still full from dinner, sweetheart, but you go ahead, and then let's go to bed."

"I'm not hungry either, I want you in my bed."

"Let's go then," Daniel says excitedly as he sits up, taking me with him, kissing me hard.

This morning was, of course, wonderful. We didn't have as much time as yesterday because Daniel had to leave early, but we still enjoyed each other, as much as we could. I left for work early too to receive a delivery which needed to be stocked before morning prep started, and it was my turn.

I feel sprightly and happy today, but lingering in the back of my mind as always, the niggling, the torment, the knowledge that he'll be gone soon and the pain will return. All I wanted was to see Daniel, I should savour every moment, but it's tainted with the unwelcome anticipation of his departure.

I have a great day at work, we're very busy with appointments and collections, and before I know it, it's time to go home. I've had two texts from Daniel today, he seems very busy, as he said he would be, and so am I, so we haven't communicated since lunchtime. I send him a quick text as I walk to my car to let him know I'm on my way home and that both Clare and Tilly are coming for dinner. I know he's probably still busy so I don't expect a reply. As I place my phone back in my bag, it chimes with a text from my brother.

~

Oliver 4 Oct 18:04
Hiya, you okay? Meant to pop in today for a quick chat and a cuppa but got too busy. So when are we going to meet this American that makes my little sister cry all the time? X

~

Cheeky git. I suppose he has a point, I have been mega unhappy since I met Daniel. But not because of him, my darling man, he makes me happier than ever. Just the bloody distance.

~

4 Oct 18:06
Yo yo yo! How are you? I'm only unhappy when
I'm away from him, and he's here now so I have a huge grin

on my face, see... :-D. Clare and
Tilly are coming over later, why
don't you come and meet him?
I'll take him to meet Mum and
Dad before he leaves, maybe at
the weekend. X

~

I get into my car and he replies immediately.

~

Oliver 4 Oct 18:07
Alright, alright, enough of that romantic crap.
Yuck. Yeah, sounds great, what time? X

~

~

4 Oct 18:09
I think they'll be over at about
7:30/8. Getting take away. See
you then :-) X

~

~

Oliver 4 Oct 18:10
Cool. Tell him to prepare for the Hart
interrogation.
X

~

He makes me laugh, he'd do anything to protect me, but
he'd never intimidate someone I was seeing, unless they were
a total idiot. He hates Dylan, and Dylan knows it, but that's
mainly because he was a dick all the time.

At about half six, I walk into my building and decide
I'll have a long, hot bath before everyone gets here, wash off
all the sugar and food colouring, and put some comfies on. I'm
really looking forward to tonight but I feel filthy and
exhausted and I need a relaxing soak first.

I open the door and jump out of my skin when I see
Daniel, looking unbelievably sexy in low slung track suit
bottoms and a not-too-tightly fitted, grey t-shirt, standing
barefoot in the hallway with a glass of wine. There's
something so sexy about his tanned, naked feet on my soft,
cream carpet. *Is that weird?*

"M'lady," he says in a very posh, exaggerated British accent. He takes my hand bag and keys and bows, as he holds out the glass to me.

I giggle. "Why, thank you kind, sir. What a lovely surprise!"

"I hoped it would be madam, you have a hot, candle lit, bubble bath awaiting your arrival in the main bathroom."

I giggle again. "Wow, thank you, I feel spoiled. To what do I owe this pleasure?" I ask as I lean against him, wrapping my free arm around his neck and gaze up into his delicious turquoise eyes. The feel of his hard body through that t-shirt, *mmm...*

"Well, I had a fantastic day at work, baby. It all went really, *really* well and I was done early, so I thought - what better way to finish off my day, than to surprise my beautiful lady as she gets in from a hard day at the office."

I grin from ear to ear. "Thank you. I love you being here, even if it's only..." I trail off, not needing to bring that up, and lean upwards to kiss him firmly on the lips.

"Bath time, sweetheart, no more kissing or we'll get pre-occupied."

"Oh." I pout. "Will you be joining me?"

"Why, of course, baby."

Stepping into the hot bubbles, I slowly sink down to rest against Daniel's chest. It's a bit of a squeeze but it's oh-so-blissful. "My bath's not quite as big as yours, is it. Are you too squashed?"

"Not at all, baby, are you comfortable?"

"Mmm. Very," I whisper as I close my eyes and fully relax against him. I tilt my head so I can look up at his face. "I love this."

"I love *you*. What time are your friends coming?"

"Between seven thirty and eight. Oh, and Oliver is coming too. He wants to meet you."

"Oh great! He's coming to check me out, make sure I'm good enough for his kid sister?" He grins.

"Something like that," I say with a broad smile, "don't worry though, he won't give you a hard time."

"I'm not worried, baby, I'm sure we'll get on... if he approves."

I want to comment that it really doesn't matter whether Oliver approves or not, considering Daniel is not my 'proper' boyfriend and we aren't going to be together for long, but I refrain from doing so because I know Daniel will get cross with me and I'm in far too good a mood to have that argument right now.

After a pause, I change the subject. "I'm not sure you really wanted to share a bath with me, Daniel, I'm really sugary and dirty."

"Dirty, huh? Just the way I like you," he says as he crooks his neck to kiss mine and I grin, raising my hand behind me to curl around the back of his neck.

"You've got a dirty mind."

"And your point is?"

I giggle and carefully turn onto my front against his body. He immediately places a hand on my buttock. "We don't have time for sexing, Daniel, but I do want a pash."

"Pashing in the bath sounds good to me. Then, I'll wash you."

I smile and lean in to gently bite his lip, before we start the most sensual, arousing, bath-time pash-fest one could possibly dream about. As I writhe against him and moan loudly, Daniel pulls away, breathlessly.

"Baby, god, if we can't have sex, then we've got to stop right now. I need you so badly."

"I can tell..." I grin, waggling my eyebrows and leaning in for another kiss. Naturally, we get carried away and end up have just enough time to throw some clothes over our wet bodies as everyone arrives.

~~~~~~~~

Dinner was great, one of the most fun nights in I have had in a long time. Tilly loosened up a little bit, compared to how she has been lately, although she still wasn't completely herself. She was genuinely excited to see Daniel and the three of us reminisced about some of our fun times in LA.

Oliver and Daniel seemed to get on like a house on fire, I think Oliver approves of my gorgeous man, there might even be a little bromance forming, although they probably shouldn't get too attached to each other.

All evening, as we chatted together, Daniel kept catching my eye and sending beautiful smiles my way. If he left the room for anything, he'd find a reason to walk past me and stroke my shoulders or place a gentle kiss on my cheek.

As we stand at the door saying our goodbyes in the wee hours of the morning, Daniel holds me tightly around my waist.

"Thank you for having us," Oliver says as Daniel releases me so I can hug my brother.

"You're welcome, are you coming out tomorrow night?"

"Have I ever missed your birthday?"

I smile and shake my head, no.

"Exactly. I'll be there with bells on."

As Daniel kisses the girls goodbye, Oliver whispers in my ear. "I approve, he seems a good bloke. I can't wait for Dylan to see you with him." He smirks and pulls back, chuckling to himself and I roll my eyes.

"See you tomorrow, Daniel. Good to meet you."

"You too, Oliver, I'm looking forward to it, should be a great night."

I say goodbye to the girls, and as we close the door, Daniel smiles and pulls me close to him, his arms snake tightly around my middle. "Mmm, I've got you all to myself again," he says before he leans down and places a soft kiss against my lips.

"Uh huh, and I can't wait to curl up in bed and fall asleep with you."

"Oh..." he says with a cute pout, "can't I ravish you?"

I giggle and wrap my arms tightly around his neck. "Go on then, just this once."

"Then we can sleep and your perfect birthday will begin."

"I'm excited."

"So you should be, baby. I'm going to spoil you."

"Not too much, I hope."

"Well, you'll find out tomorrow," he says as he releases me and swats my behind, "to the bedroom!"

"You're in a very good mood tonight, Daniel," I say suspiciously as I make my way to the bedroom.

"I am always in a good mood when I'm with you. Now get your clothes off," he orders jovially as he throws himself on my bed, rests his hands behind his head, crosses his ankles and watches me, intently with a huge smile on his face.

CHAPTER TWENTY FIVE
FRIDAY 5TH OCTOBER

I roll over to reach for Daniel as I stir, but my hand only finds bed sheets. I open my eyes to look at the clock, and I see that it's nine o'clock. It takes a few seconds to register that I'm not late for work because I'm off for my birthday. "Oh phew." I mumble as I stretch and smile in anticipation of the day ahead.

"Phew, what, baby?" Daniel asks as he strolls into the bedroom carrying a tray.

"Oh, nothing, I thought I was late for work. What's all this?" I ask with a smile as I sit up.

"Birthday breakfast in bed, happy birthday, baby." He rests the tray on his side of the bed and walks around to give me a kiss on the cheek. "And good morning, I want to kiss you properly, so you better eat up and go clean your teeth, unless you'll let me kiss you now?"

"Nope. I'll eat quickly." I grin as I look over to the tray. "Pancakes and strawberries! Yummy! Hey, I didn't have strawberries..."

"I know, I stopped at the grocery store on my way home yesterday. I know how much you loved pancakes and strawberries at my place, so I thought they'd be a good birthday breakfast," he says with a huge smile, clearly pleased by my reaction. "Now, eat up while I have a shower and then you can have a present." He wiggles his eyebrows, salaciously.

"Ooh, what sort of present?"

"Wait and see, eat up, sweetheart." He places the tray on my lap, plays a song on his iPod; 'I'm yours' by Jason Mraz, and heads to the en-suite. I look at what he has prepared on the tray; pancakes with maple syrup and strawberries, a cup of tea, a glass of orange juice, my iPhone, an envelope with my name on it, a pink rose and a small, navy, rectangular velvet box with a tag attached;

'Don't open me yet, put me in your purse for later...'

My stomach knots in excitement as I wonder what else is in store for today. I listen to the lovely lyrics, pretending they refer to Daniel and I.

The pancakes are delicious and I smile non-stop as I eat, listening to the music and Daniel whistling in the shower. I open my card while I sip my tea and a huge grin immediately spreads across my face when I see the front; *'For my girlfriend on her birthday'* and a picture of a beautiful pink rose, freakishly similar to the one on the tray. I open it, eagerly anticipating his message.

> *'Baby,*
>
> *Happy 28th Birthday!*
>
> *Prepare yourself for the best birthday you've ever had, I intend to make sure you enjoy every second of it. I am so happy to be able to celebrate with you, you mean everything to me. I'm a very lucky guy to have you in my life. I love you so much.*
>
> *Always,*
>
> *Your boyfriend, Daniel xxxxxxxxxx'*

An elated giggle escapes me - *'always'*. Oh, I wish. I place the card on my bedside table and smile at it, I absolutely *love* that I get Daniel here on my birthday. Placing the rose next to the card, I sit back against my headboard and check the messages on my phone whilst finishing my tea with a deliriously happy smile on my face.

I grin at the 'Happy Birthday' messages from Tilly, Clare, my brother and parents, and then I rest back, thinking about that card. I'm so far away in my happy daydream, that I don't even notice the shower turning off and I jump as he speaks. "Enjoy your breakfast, baby?"

"Oh! Yes, thank you it was so delicious. Thank you for my beautiful card too."

"You're welcome," he says as he wraps his towel around his waist and leans over to take the tray off my lap. He kisses my cheek and vanishes off to the kitchen. I take the opportunity to step into the en-suite to clean my teeth. When I return, I hear the bath running in the main bathroom and Daniel strolls back in. "Get back into bed, baby. Your bath will be ready in a little while."

"This is fun!" I giggle at the joyous feeling of being pampered.

Daniel crawls up the bed to plant a kiss on my lips, he lingers and curls one of his strong hands around the back of my neck. "Mmm," he says as he pulls back to rest his forehead on mine. "Are you ready for a gift?"

"Ooh yay!" My eyes widen with excitement, I feel like a child again.

Daniel hops off the bed again and goes into the spare room where his suitcase is. When he returns, he sits next to me and hands me a beautifully wrapped gift.

"Thank you!"

"Open it," he says with an excited smile. *Bless his cotton socks.*

I remove the ribbon and start to rip off the exquisite wrapping paper and a layer of tissue paper, before revealing the absolutely stunning strapless, red, Valentino jumpsuit that I fell in love with on Rodeo Drive. "Daniel!" I cry, bringing my hand to my mouth. "Daniel! How did you know? But this is so expensive!"

"You wanted it, didn't you?"

"Oh I love it! I wanted it so much but I obviously couldn't afford it, Daniel, this is too much!"

"Baby, you better get used to it, we haven't even gotten started yet."

"Oh, Daniel, thank you so much!" I grab him and hug him close, showering his face with kisses.

"How did you know?"

"I asked Tilly to send me an email of the things you wanted on Rodeo Drive so I could pick something I knew you wanted, remember you told me you loved a bunch of things on your shopping trip? Well, when I searched it all out, this really stood out. I like it a lot."

"Oh, you have gone to so much trouble for me, thank you so much."

"Nothing is too much for you, baby. Now, go try it on."

I hop out of bed excitedly, ready to try it on as Daniel slips out, I presume to get his tea or something.

As I do the zip up, I look in my full length mirror and squeal with excitement, it is gorgeous and fits perfectly.

"Got it on, baby?" Daniel calls.

"Yes! Come and see!" I sing back excitedly, and Daniel strolls back in with another beautifully wrapped gift in his hands.

"Wow, you look sexy as hell in that, I can see why you like it so much." He strolls over and wraps his arm around me from behind. Looking in the mirror, he kisses my neck and hands me the other gift.

"Another one? This really is so much, thank you, you didn't need to go to so much trouble."

"Shh, baby. Open it."

I turn and kiss him on the cheek before I place the gift on the bed and unwrap it. The tell-tale Valentino shoe box gives it away and I immediately gasp, knowing what's inside. "Daniel, Daniel, Daniel...oh my god." I open the box and swoon at the beautiful, matching, rock stud sling backs. I cradle one to my chest as I turn and gaze at him.

"You gotta have the matching shoes, huh, baby?"

"You are amazing, thank you so much darling. Thank you, thank you, thank you, I absolutely love them!"

He chuckles. "Try them on, I hope they fit." They are, of course, perfect.

"Wow, this is my favourite outfit of all time, thank you so much."

"You look stunning, sweetheart. And stop thanking me. I'm your boyfriend, this is what boyfriends do."

"Really? Well, my previous boyfriends have been seriously lacking then, because this is definitely a first for me. You really are incredible."

"Nonsense," he says, nonchalantly.

I turn and take another look in the mirror, another excited squeal escapes me and my face starts to ache from the constant smiling.

"Why don't you take it off and get ready, sweetheart, then we can start the next part of your day. Unless you'd like to go back to bed?" he says with no sexual connotation whatsoever, he's just being sweet and offering me more of a lie in.

I stroll over to him leisurely and wrap my arms around his neck, brushing my lips against his and pressing my body right up against him. "I think maybe *we* should go back to bed for a bit and then we can get ready in a little while, what do you say?"

His grin is hot, as is the feel of his warm tongue as it slowly runs across my bottom lip. "You might be onto something there."

An hour later, Daniel and I have bathed together and are getting ready for the rest of the day, when there is a knock at the door. I wonder who that is, I didn't buzz anyone in? As I open the door, the concierge greets me with a huge bunch of beautiful white roses.

"Oh wow! Thank you."

"Happy birthday, Miss Hart," he says and rushes off, leaving me in the doorway holding two dozen roses.

Daniel walks over and kisses me. "Happy birthday, again, baby."

"Are these from you? They are so beautiful!"

"I hope they're from me, who else would be sending you roses?" he asks jovially.

"Of course, nobody, thank you. I love white roses."

"Good. I chose white because I remembered the flowers at Gemma and Jay's pool-house were white roses, I thought I'd give you a little déjà-vu. Also..." he continues as he closes the front door and casually puts his hands on my hips, "white roses apparently symbolise sincerity and a love stronger than death. And as much as I hate to bring death into the equation today," he pulls a comical, awkward face, making me giggle, "I love you to death, baby."

I tilt my head and hold back the tears through a genuinely joyful smile. "I love you to death, too. I have honestly never been so spoilt. Thank you."

"Okay, sweetheart, the thank yous have to stop now, okay? It's getting old, I get it."

I laugh and kiss his gorgeous lips before placing the beautiful flowers in a vase, in centre place on the lounge coffee table.

"Now, this is what you need to do next, baby."

I look at Daniel, intrigued. "Okay?"

"You need to pack an overnight bag, you'll need an outfit for dinner and our night out tonight, clothes for

340

tomorrow, toiletries etc. I'm just going to make a call to work to check on the progress of their agenda today, I won't be long, I'll be done by the time you're finished. Can you be ready in, say, twenty minutes?"

"Yes, fine... where are we going?"

"Surprise, sweetheart. Okay, twenty minutes... ready, set, go!"

Fifteen minutes later, I'm standing by my overnight case, packing my make-up bag, when an overjoyed-looking Daniel appears at the doorframe. "Nearly ready, love-of-my-life?"

I laugh at his endearing, playful happiness. "Yes, just putting these last bits in. You're happy?"

"I am, life is good, work is good, I love you, you love me... what's not to be happy about?"

I smile and do a damn good job of hiding the one thing that sticks right out like a sore thumb, the one thing *not* to be happy about. It tarnishes everything and as much of an ungrateful bitch as I feel right now, considering all of the amazing, wonderful things Daniel has organised for me, I still can't forget it.

I wish I could, I wish I could spend this incredible day without a single negative thought... but I just can't. He's still going home next week and I will still feel like someone has ripped my heart out and ground it to a pulp. "Nothing, Daniel," I say with a convincing smile plastered across my face. I am happy, I am having a wonderful day. I will try my god damned hardest to ignore the elephant in the room, just like he is. It's the least I can do.

"Great, what can I take out to the car for you?"

"I hand him the dress bag containing my gorgeous new outfit that there's no doubt I'll be wearing tonight, and the Valentino shoe box. "I can take my case and handbag."

"Okay, let's go."

As we step outside, I see Daniel's driver waiting for us. He's exactly what you expect to see in a movie, an oldish, greying chap in a crisp uniform and chauffeur cap, standing next to the car, awaiting our arrival.

"I wasn't expecting this, Daniel."

"No? Well, it's a bit easier."

341

"I'm not complaining, it's wonderful!"

"Good. Enjoy it," he says with a loving smile as we walk towards the vehicle.

"Mr. Berkeley, Miss Hart. May I wish you a very happy birthday madam."

"Oh, thank you so much!" I gush, totally thrown by how important the driver is making me feel.

"Please, make yourselves comfortable," he says as he takes my bag and gestures towards the inside of the car.

I step inside, closely followed by Daniel who pops open a bottle of bubbly and pours a glass. "Here, baby," he hands me the glass and pours his own before returning the bottle to its allocated space. "Here's to you on your birthday."

"Thank you Daniel, here's to *us* on my birthday."

"To us, cheers, baby." We take a sip and the driver pulls away.

"I feel like a princess, you're really spoiling me."

"It's really nothing more than you deserve, sweetheart. I'm enjoying every second of it."

"Well, thank you. I'm having such a fabulous day already. So, where are we off to?"

"Okay, first stop; your parents place." *What?*

"My parents' house? What? Huh?"

Daniel laughs at my obvious confusion and clutches my hand. "You can't *not* see your mom on your birthday, baby, so I arranged to meet with your parents for lunch. I offered to take us all out but your mom said 'nonsense'," Daniel reverts to a British accent for the impression of my mother, "she said that she'd like to prepare something for us all to eat at the family home. I agreed with her that that would be a whole lot more personal and enjoyable. I can't wait to meet her, and your dad."

I'm thoroughly confused. "Okay, hang on, what? How have you been in contact with my mum?"

"I texted Tilly on Wednesday and asked for their number. She's helped me out so much. I hope that's okay? I thought it would be nice to surprise you?"

"Oh Daniel, of course it's okay, I'm just confused by how this has gone on without me knowing... so you've actually had a conversation with my mum?"

"Yes, and your dad, I introduced myself. Tilly said they knew about me so I guessed it was okay. They seem pretty cool!"

"Well, yes, they are cool... I'm still in a bit of shock about this."

"Did I do bad, baby?" he says with an adorable pout and I giggle, squeezing his hand.

"Not at all, darling, my parents are great, I'm happy that you've spoken to them. So... are we sleeping at their house?" I ask, wondering how on earth that would be better than staying at my own apartment where it's just the two of us, where we can actually have sex and make noise.

Daniel can clearly read my mind and laughs out loud. "No, no of course not, baby, I do want to have more birthday sex with you later, you know. No, we're going somewhere else later. You'll see."

"O-k?" I say with a confused smile on my face.

"You'll like it."

"I have no doubt that I will." I snuggle into his side and reach my head up to kiss him. His hand slowly tucks under my hair and cups the side of my face as our lips linger, his tongue slowly brushing at my lips until I stroke it with mine, and the kiss becomes more powerful.

I moan as the familiar buzz runs down between my legs and I suddenly need him, urgently, I need to feel him inside me, again. My moans become desperate, our tongues entwined, our lips caressing. Without breaking away, I slide my far leg over Daniel's lap and move over to straddle him. He smiles into the kiss and slides his free hand over my bottom, pulling me further towards him, against his erection. I break away to take a sip of my champagne and before I swallow, I clamp my lips against his again and release some of the champagne into his mouth. Daniel groans loudly and rocks my hips against him with his hand.

"Mmm, that's good, baby. I want to make love to you so badly."

"Uh huh..." I rock myself against him, feeling that tingle, the clenching inside.

"We're going to be at your folks soon, huh?" he asks against my lips.

"Yeah, fairly soon..." I cup his face in my hand and lock eyes with him. "Make me come, Daniel," I mumble, demandingly between soft kisses, still grinding in his lap.

"Oh god, baby, I love it when you're naughty," he whispers into my ear.

"Can he see us?" I ask breathlessly into his ear, referring to the driver.

"Nuh uh, he can't see a thing," he says as he unbuttons my jeans and slips his hand inside.

"Oh, god, yeah, there." I moan quietly as he hits the spot immediately and I continue to rock against his fingers. He moves down and pushes two inside me, pressing his palm against my clit.

"Oh fuck, uh huh."

"Come on, baby, come for me, let me feel it. You're so wet, baby, I wish it was my cock you were riding, I'm so fucking hard it hurts." And that just about sends me over the edge, I rock harder, throwing my head back, clutching onto his neck with one hand, my champagne glass in the other. I try to contain my moans but it becomes more and more difficult with each wave building higher and higher, rocking faster, harder against his hand, his fingers pushing deeper inside me. I bring my head back up to his and press my lips against his as the waves crash down and the sharp spasms shoot through me, pulsating around his fingers, the incredible pleasure coursing through my body.

"Jesus, baby, you're holding me so tight..."

"Oh..." I moan, high pitched, as the orgasm starts to fade and I become aware of my surroundings again. "Daniel," I breathe as I roll my head before bringing it back to his, "you're the only one who can make me come so hard. Every single time." I say with a lazy grin against his mouth and he chuckles, his chest rumbling against me.

"Are you ready to straighten out before we get there or you still coming down from the big 'O'?" he asks, kissing my face all over.

I giggle and open my eyes finally. "I'm ready, I'm surprised we're not here already," I say as Daniel slowly takes his hand back and I look out through the window. "We're just turning into their road now."

344

I straighten myself out and we soon pull up outside the house. Daniel knocks on the partition between us and the driver, and has a quick chat. The next thing I know, Daniel has wet wipes and hand sanitizer passed to him through the magic hatch. Thank god. The thought of Daniel shaking my dad's hand after... oh god I don't even want to think about it.

As our driver opens the door for us and we step out, my parents are both waiting at their front door with open arms. "Happy birthday my sweetheart," my mum says with a huge smile as she pulls me into her arms. "And Daniel, such a pleasure to finally meet you, we've heard so much about you from Beatrice and Tilly, and it was lovely to chat to you on the phone. We're thrilled we can finally meet you, aren't we Ed?"

"Absolutely, come in. Let me get you both a drink before we sit down to lunch," Dad says as he reaches out a hand to shake Daniel's.

~~~~~~~

Lunch with Daniel and my parents was great. My dad seems to think the sun shines out of Daniel's backside, and that he's the perfect man for me, even with the distance between us. Mum chatted away about me as a baby and little girl, and Daniel seemed to be really enjoying the conversation, squeezing my hand every time he thought one of the stories was cute.

I helped Mum take the dishes into the kitchen, leaving Dad with his new BFF, and we had a chat about everything. She thinks Daniel is wonderful, he clearly made a great impression on everybody, which is neither here nor there really, given our situation. I just know all future boyfriends will forever be compared to 'perfect Daniel'. Thinking of being with anyone other than him makes me feel empty and deprived.

"Sweetheart, we can see how happy he makes you, and I think it's clear that we all think he's lovely, but I know how down you have been since you got back from America, I know the heartache you will go through when he returns to the States. I'm worried about you, long distance relationships can be terribly draining sometimes, darling."

"I know, Mum, I don't know what to do. I told him I don't want a long distance thing, they rarely work, but I love him. He loves me, too. What can I possibly do, without getting my heart broken?"

"I don't know, Beatrice, I really don't know what to suggest. I'm worried about you, without him. Whatever you do, know that you have mine and Daddy's support. We're here for you, cry, laugh, whatever you want to do."

I tried to hold back the tears that were so determined to stream down my face, but couldn't. I whimpered and hugged my mum close to me. I'm not sure if I was happy or sad, I'm having a wonderful birthday, I love Daniel so much and am so grateful to have him here, but am also so sad to think of life without him again.

"I just don't want him to go. I love him more than I have ever loved anyone. I can't imagine meeting anyone else that would even come close."

Mum rubbed my back, soothingly." I know sweetheart, just do what feels right. Let him love you, enjoy him while you have him. It's early days, darling, but whatever you decide to do in the future, even if you want to move to America one day - we'd miss you horribly - but we'd always be there for you. Might even move over there with you, if it's half as fabulous as you say it is! "

I giggled. "Thank you, Mummy."

"Now, stop crying, it's your birthday and you're having a lovely day. You probably have lots more surprises waiting for you."

I smiled, wiped the tears from under my eyes and kissed my mum on the cheek before going back in the dining room to join Dad and Daniel for dessert.

An hour or so later, we are back in the car, on our way to... somewhere.

"Thank you, Daniel," I say with a huge smile, clasping hold of his hand. "Seeing my parents on my birthday was lovely. You're so thoughtful."

"You're welcome, baby. Were you okay, though? I thought you looked like you'd been crying at one point, everything okay?"

"Yes, don't worry. Just had a bit of a heart to heart with my mum."

"Okay, baby. Let me know if you want to talk, okay?"

346

"I will, but I'm fine now."

"Good. Now, time for another gift."

"What?" I cry. "Another one?"

"Of course, here you go." He passes me beautifully wrapped present number three. This one is in a box but it's quite light. I start to unwrap it and giggle in excitement. "Really, Daniel..." I say, peeling back the fabulous paper, "you didn't need to get me so much, I'm happy to just have you..."

I gasp when I see the Dolce and Gabbana cloquet lace mini dress hidden amongst a mass of tissue.

"You like it? Is it the right one?"

"Oh, my... Daniel, yes, I love it! I don't know how you managed to get the exact same things that I wanted back in LA. How did Tilly even remember all of this? Thank you so much." I reach over and kiss him, holding myself there for a prolonged time to ensure he knows just how grateful I really am.

"I can't wait to try it on, thank you so much." I run my fingers along the intricate lace of the dress, brushing the stylish collar that drew me to it in the first place.

"You're welcome, as you know. Stop thanking me."

"I can't, I will always say thank you. Thank you."

"Okay, baby. Well, it's almost three now, so I think we should head to where we're staying tonight and have a bit of chill out time before we get ready for dinner, what do you say?"

"Sounds wonderful, Daniel, where are we staying?"

"I checked it out online and booked us a suite at The Grove Hotel, I've heard you mention it before."

"Oh wow! I love it there! I go for dinner sometimes but have never stayed there, it's too expensive for me and I only live around the corner. Daniel, are you sure?"

"Of course, nothing is too expensive for you, sweetheart. It's the only local place I found that I thought looked right and I thought it was pretty apt since we met that second time at The Grove in LA. It looks a great hotel."

"Oh it is, I can't wait! Thank you, thank you!"

"Enough! So I wasn't sure if you'd like to have a massage or just chill out in the room for a bit so I booked a couple of treatments anyway, we can go have them if you like and go for a swim if you want, or we can just chill out in the room together. Maybe have the treatments tomorrow. Totally up to you, baby."

I raise my hands to my cheeks and gaze at him, I have honestly never before been made to feel so special. This is by far, one of the most amazing days of my life. "Daniel..." I say, shaking my head in amazement before he cuts me off and clutches my hand.

"Sweetheart, please, stop. Just enjoy it. Have a great day, okay? I love you."

"I love you, too. Let's decide what to do when we get to the room. A massage does sound amazing, but then again, so does spending the afternoon in bed, with you."

"Mmm, it does. You said we'll be meeting your friends in Rickmansworth at eight-thirty-ish, so I booked a table for us for dinner at six-thirty. So we have a couple of hours to kill before we need to start getting ready. That sound good to you?"

"Perfect," I say with a huge grin on my face as we pull up outside the main entrance to the hotel.

~~~~~~~~~

Sitting on the huge, curved sofa in the lounge of a vice-presidential suite in the mansion part of the hotel, I decide that, as long as Daniel doesn't mind, I'd like to stay in the room for a while and show him just how grateful I am for all he has done to make today so special.

This room is incredible, not to mention huge. The vase of two dozen white and red roses that awaited my arrival on the coffee table, are equally as stunning as the white ones that arrived at my door this morning. Daniel said that he chose these ones because white roses, mixed with red emphasise the meaning of love. Where on earth he gets this information, I've no idea, but I love the effort he has put into everything, to make it so perfect.

He is currently taking a call from work in the bedroom while I stretch out, enjoying a relaxing cup of tea. I close my eyes and rest my head back against the chair, thinking back to everything that has happened so far today. What a lucky girl I am, how differently this day would have been spent, had Daniel not been here. I realise that, yes, I am sad that he will be leaving, but I would never have had such a memory to look back on, had he not been here. I'm so lucky for this, whatever heartache awaits, later.

I am so relaxed and can feel myself dropping off just in the moment that soft lips press gently against mine. "Mmm, hello." I smile, eyes still closed.

"You look serene. Can I join you?"

"Of course," I say, opening my eyes. He is standing, hovering over me with another gift.

I grin a massive, stupid smile, knowing not to say a word about how he shouldn't have. This time, it's the matching peep-toe boot shoes to the lace dress he gave me in the car. They are stunning and totally extravagant.

"Thank you, Daniel, they are, as you already know, totally perfect. As with everything else today. And you. Thank you."

He sits next to me, leans forward to pick up his tea and rests back against the couch, one ankle resting up on the other knee. "So, sweetheart, what do you want to do?" he asks, taking a sip of his tea.

"If it's okay with you, I'd like to stay here. Chill out, get down and dirty a little bit, have a bath before getting ready."

The cheeky grin on Daniel's face tells me he approves of the idea. "Sounds like my kind of afternoon." He wiggles his eyebrows, making me laugh. "So how many of your friends will be out later, baby?"

"The usual crowd probably; Tilly, Clare and Oliver - obviously, Jamie and Laura who you haven't met, a few friends of my brothers who are now friends of everyones and a bunch of people from the college days. Probably about twenty people, or so. Oh yeah, I should forewarn you, Dylan and his girlfriend Leah will probably be there."

"Oh really? Okay..." he says with a scheming sort of smile on his face,

"Okay... what? What's that look for?" I ask with suspicion.

"Oh, nothing, baby, just looking forward to meeting the schmuck."

"Don't cause a scene or anything, will you?"

349

"Baby, of course I wouldn't do that. I just want him to know you're with me now, that's all," he says with a comical, wicked laugh as he inches closer to me, burying his head in the crook of my neck, licking and kissing his way up to my ear and back again.

~~~~~~~~

"Time to get up, baby," Daniel whispers in my ear, splaying a large hand on my naked belly, making me smile as I stretch and turn to face him.

"Mmm, morning... evening... whatever it is."

"Evening, baby, you looked beautiful laying there, so peaceful."

I blush a little and raise my hand to stroke his cheek. "I love you."

"Happy birthday..." he says, covering my body with his, kissing my neck and face. "I hate to have to stop here..." he mumbles between kisses, "but we have to get out of bed. Mmm, you taste good..."

"Don't stop, it's so relaxing. What's the time?"

"You've got an hour, sweetheart."

"Oh, we really do have to stop. But it's so good."

He pushes himself up onto his hands, looking down at me. "You want me to run you a bath, baby?"

"I can do it, you chill out in bed for a bit, watch some TV or something."

"Let me..." he starts before I cut him off.

"No, please, I'll do it, you haven't stopped doing things for me today. Just chill out here while I get my things ready and have a bath."

"Okay, but just so you know, I have really enjoyed spoiling you today. I look forward to doing it more often."

I grin and make my way to the bathroom. Why, I must always find the negative in everything, I have no idea, but when does he think he'll have the opportunity to spoil me more often? He's acting like we're never going back to reality. Oh well, that's a conversation for another day. I run the taps and start the 'getting ready' process in style in this fabulous hotel room.

Running my fingers through my bouncy hair, I check my face in the mirror and give a satisfied nod. Make-up complete, hair looking good, accessories in place. Now time to slip into my fabulous Valentino ensemble and head to dinner on my gorgeous man's muscular arm.

He's currently waiting for me in the lounge looking hot to trot in jeans and a tailored, crisp white shirt and sports jacket. My friends are going to think I paid for this man, he looks (and smells) far too good to be true. I'm not sure I'll be able to keep my hands off him.

"Daniel, can you please come and zip me up?" I call, holding my hair above my neck and slipping my feet into my beautiful studded heels, standing with my back to the door.

"Sure thing, baby," he says as he enters the bedroom and does as I ask. "Done. Let me see you, sweetheart."

I release my hair and turn to smile at him.

His eyes widen and a sexy little smile curls his lips. "God, baby, you look absolutely incredible. Wow."

I do a little twirl feeling somewhat shy, although thrilled by his reaction. "Thank you. I feel fabulous in this outfit."

"You look it, every guy in their right mind will be wanting to switch places with me tonight, how in the hell did I manage to get a girl like you? I am one lucky guy."

"No, I'm so lucky to have you here with me right now and for you to have made today so special. Thank you."

"You're welcome, baby. Ready to make a move?"

I grab my clutch from the dressing table and slip my arm into the crook of his. "Ready."

The waiter pours our wine and takes our orders as we sit opposite each other, smiling, enjoying. He takes our menus and makes a swift retreat as Daniel holds my hand across the table.

"So, Daniel. How was everything at work? Any problems?"

"None at all, baby, in fact, the task was set for HBUK to finalise the last few things today, contracts and the like, and it has all gone ahead smoothly, without a hitch. So things are looking really great."

"Oh that's fantastic, I thought you seemed very happy after speaking with work." I hope this doesn't mean he is going home right away. The thought lingers, unwelcome.

"Yes I was, and on this subject, I wanted to talk to you."

My heart sinks. "Oh?"

"Well, Bea, I wanted to talk about the future, our future." Here it comes. I brace myself for the bad news. "Firstly, what are you doing for Christmas?" *What?*

What the hell has this got to do with anything? I frown as I respond questioningly, "Um, I hadn't really thought to Christmas yet, probably spend it with the family as usual... why?"

"Well," he clutches both of my hands and leans forward on the table, "I was hoping that maybe you'd come spend it with me? In Aspen?"

I really don't understand how we got here from talking about work. "Oh, um... well, I think we ought to decide where we go from here first. I mean, it sounds amazing and I would love that, but you're leaving soon - judging from how things are going at work - very soon. We should really figure out how we're going to move forwards before we start planning Christmas. Maybe not tonight though, Daniel? I don't want to get upset, the thought of you leaving never really escapes me, but I would rather not discuss it on such a lovely day."

"I want to discuss it now, baby."

"Daniel, please? I *really* don't..."

"Baby, I'm part of the re-structure."

"Daniel, please, I'm serious, today has been..." *Wait... what?* "What?"

He smiles at me, tentatively, assessing my reactions. "I am part of the re-structure. It's based around me. The contracts drawn up today are mine."

I stare at him, frowning, not really sure if I'm grasping what he's getting at. "Which means... what exactly?"

He chuckles and reaches across to cup the side of my face with his big, warm hand. "I am going to be based here, in the London office, indefinitely."

My eyes widen as it dawns on me. I bring my hand to my mouth as the tears prick my eyes. "So... you're staying? Here?"

He nods slowly at me and shrugs questioningly, asking for my approval. His eyes searching mine for the 'okay'.

"Oh my god. Oh... oh my god!" Each word louder and higher in pitch than the last. My eyes flood with happy tears. "Daniel! So you're... we're... we can..."

"Be a normal a couple? Yes, please?"

I shriek out in excited laughter, attracting some enquiring looks from guests at other tables. They probably think he proposed, this is pretty much just as meaningful for me, so he may as well have. I jump out of my seat and move around to his side of the table. He stands with me and I throw myself at him, squeezing him as tightly as I can.

"Oh Daniel! I can't believe it! I just can't believe it!"

"Believe it, baby. It has been so hard not telling you that I've been working on this."

I kiss his neck and face over and over again. "Oh I love you, I love you!"

"I love you, baby. We should probably sit, people will think we're about to get dirty or something."

I giggle and wipe the tears from my cheeks, releasing Daniel to return to my seat. "So, will you get a place in the city? Or..."

"I can, sweetheart, and we can take things slowly, or..."

"...or you can move in with me?" I ask with an excited grin.

He smiles right back. "Are you asking me to?"

"Yes. Please? Please do. We can always get somewhere bigger later down the line, if you want."

"I was hoping you'd want me to move in, sweetheart, because I want that, more than anything."

The feeling of total and utter relief floods through me, I can finally let go, finally enjoy every minute with him. I just can't quite believe it.

"There is more that we need to talk about, and if you agree with what I propose here, you'll need to have a meeting with Clare."

"Right... so?" *Anything, I'll do anything!*

"So, my role here in London will be the same as my role back in LA and I'll still be working closely with my dad and Alexia. The difference being; I need to travel to LA for two weeks of eight, so basically, I will be working here for six weeks and then in LA for two. That's how my job will roll. What I want you to consider is that I want to share our lives, so I would like you to come back with me, for my two weeks in LA."

"Oh right, I see, every time?"

"Every time," he says cautiously, again, assessing my reaction.

"Well, I have to say that sounds like an amazing life, but Bear's? It's my business."

"I know, and I've thought about that, too. Maybe we can sit down and discuss that tomorrow. If you'd rather not go back so frequently, or think it won't work, then I understand, sweetheart, but if you think it might, we could be on to something just about perfect."

I press my palms to my cheeks and shake my head, I just can't believe what's happening right now. The waiter arrives with our meal, Daniel has the Rib-eye steak with fat chips and I have grilled sea bream with gnocchi. It all looks mouthwatering, but I can't seem to concentrate on what I'm supposed to be doing. I run my fingertips up and down the cutlery on the table, getting my head around this latest, amazing news.

"So, it's definite?"

Daniel smiles at me, he's just so handsome. "Yes. It's definitely definite."

"So that means, oh wow. This means you're actually my..." I wiggle excitedly in my seat with a smile that spreads so wide it almost hurts my cheeks. "My boyfriend? My real life, everyday, amazing boyfriend?"

His answering smile is just as gorgeous, his eyes light up. "That's right, baby. I'm lucky enough to be your boyfriend, and you're my girlfriend, my real life, everyday, totally incredible girlfriend, and I can't wait to tell the world about it."

"I can't wait either, sweetheart, but you're not skipping dinner, eat!"

"Oh yes, I am on another planet entirely. The food looks yummy."

"It does, I hope this restaurant is okay for you, I did try the others but couldn't get reservations."

"Oh, this is my favourite restaurant at this hotel, I love it in here."

"Great, so eat!"

"Okay, okay." I pick up my cutlery and make a start on the mouthwatering fish. There isn't a huge amount of gnocchi thankfully, it can be so filling and I can't get bloated in Valentino!

Still totally dazed by these new developments in our relationship, I realise I have so many questions to ask. "Daniel, what about your family? What about Luke?"

"Well, I had a talk with them all, I will get to see them every time I go back, six weeks isn't that long to be away, and besides, I would have been so miserable had I *not* done this, no one would have wanted to see me anyway!"

"But you spend so much time with them?"

"Yes, but I'll still be working alongside my dad and Alexia, like I said, so I'll be talking with them non-stop during the day anyway, I still have the same job, I'll just work, predominantly, from here. As HBUK is expanding so rapidly, it helps to have one of us here anyway, over-seeing everything. "I'll make sure I speak to Mom all the time so she doesn't miss her boy too much," he says with a smile. "Not seeing Luke will be quite difficult, we spend a lot of time together, but having spoken to him, he thinks I need to do this, we'll hang out during my two weeks at home and he said he'll try to come over here when he gets the chance. Having seen the golf course at this resort, I think he'll be more than willing to come try it out."

"Oh, Daniel that would be so much fun! It's such a shame he couldn't be here now."

"I know, but we'll see him soon enough."

It gets me thinking about spending two weeks in Los Angeles every six weeks. How absolutely amazing would that be? I'd get to see Luke and spend time with Daniel's family, go

355

back to all of the places that I loved so much when I was on holiday. Ooh and go for lunch with Rose like she said. It just seems a bit out of reach, what with Bear's and everything, I don't want to do anything to make the business suffer. I wonder what Daniel's idea about that is.

He disturbs my thoughts. "It would be great fun if he could come here once in a while, maybe he and Tilly can sort out whatever their problem is."

"I hadn't thought of that, oh Tilly will be really excited for us. Would you mind if we told her first?"

"You can tell whoever you like first, baby, as long as we can scream it from the rooftops by the end of the night."

"I just can't wait! So whether or not I manage to come back to LA with you, you're still going to be living here, with me, six weeks out of eight?"

"You really don't believe this is happening do you? Baby, I am going to be here with you, whatever the weather. I really hope we can sort something out so that we can live part-time at my place too, but if it doesn't work out as good business sense for Bear's, then that's fine. We'll have two weeks apart, but rest assured I'll be coming straight back home to you for another six."

"Maybe I could come on a few trips, just not everyone."

"We can figure it out, as I say, I had an idea that we can talk through tomorrow. If you and Clare think it will work - perfect - but if not, it's no biggie. I still get to spend seventy five percent of my time here, with you. But hopefully you can take time off at Christmas, so we can have a trip to Aspen."

"Oh, that's how this conversation got started, tell me your idea, as we're a normal couple now, discussing plans for Christmas is totally okay! Exciting actually, I can't wait to spend my first Christmas with you!"

"Me neither. Mmm, that was delicious!" Daniel says as he places his knife and fork in the centre of his plate and leans back, rubbing his beautifully toned belly as if he's about to burst. "The idea I had, tell me if I'm moving too fast, but I kind of hoped that, maybe, we could all go."

"All?"

"Yeah, my family usually stays together in one house, but my parents, my sister and I all have our own properties there so I thought that maybe your folks and Oliver might come, along with Tilly and Clare. Make a whole family 'do' of it. Luke often comes with us, so hopefully he'd come too."

"Wow! For how long?"

"Well, we could go for a couple weeks, everyone else could come for one if they want to? Unless they want to stay longer."

"That sounds perfect! Well, let's ask them and see what they say. Bear's will be closed for a few days over Christmas and I'm sure we could train the staff up to spend a couple of days without us. We can work on that. Oh it all sounds so exciting!"

"Great. I can't wait to show you 'our' place in Aspen, baby." His excited smile sends butterflies flapping around my belly.

"Our place, hey?"

"What's mine is yours, baby. Which reminds me, do you have that gift I left on your breakfast tray?"

"Yes, it's in my clutch."

"If you've finished eating, why don't you open it?"

I lean down to get the gift from my bag and push my plate away to set the little navy box down in front of me. I glance up at Daniel as I open it, he has one of his delicious smiles on his face. I focus my attention back on the now-open gift box, fully expecting some sort of necklace or something. "It's... a key?"

"Yes. It's *your* key to *our* home in LA, I want you to feel like that's your place, too. It never felt the same after you left, it felt empty without you, even though you were only there a couple nights. You know, I still have your pink toothbrush in the bathroom, as a little reminder of you being there. If you accept this, then anytime I'm there alone, I'll know a little bit of you is there, because you share it with me."

"That's so sweet, darling, I don't know what to say. Thank you."

He leans across the table and cradles my face in his hands, bringing his lips up close to mine. "You don't have to

357

say anything. Just know how much I love you." He kisses me gently and tears spring to my eyes.

"Thank you. I love you too. This has been, by far, the best birthday of my life. And you have given me the most wonderful present that I never, in a million years, imagined you'd be able to give me. You. You're really mine now, all mine!"

His delighted smile makes me giggle, his eyes sparkle and he looks almost childlike in his excitement. "Would you like dessert, baby?"

"No, thank you. As much as I love our alone time, I really can't wait to tell Tilly and Clare that you're staying!"

"Sure thing, let's go." Daniel takes his iPhone from his pocket as he stands, presumably to text the driver. We collect our coats from the restaurant reception and stroll, hand in hand through the bar to the main entrance, where the moonlit view of the golf course begins.

We stand to wait for the car and I turn to press my body against him, wrapping my arms tightly around his neck and raising up onto my tiptoes. His arms snake around my waist to hold me close. "I love you so much, Daniel."

"You don't know how much I love hearing you say that. I feel like I've loved you my whole life. I could never have gone back to my old life without you permanently in it. I feel so lucky, now I can have my cake, and eat it. Preferably a Bear's strawberry cupcake, of course."

I grin against his mouth and gently brush my nose along his. "I'll bring home a whole box of them, especially for my boyfriend, on Monday."

The driver drops us off in Rickmansworth, outside the pub where my friends are gathering for my birthday. My face is aching from the permanent smile plastered across it, but I don't care, I'm the happiest person in the world right now and I can't wait to introduce everyone to my 'real-life boyfriend, Daniel Berkeley.

He weaves his fingers between mine and clutches my hand tightly as we approach the door. Before we go in, he pauses, gazes into my eyes and tells me he loves me, one more time, before planting the most gentle, most gorgeously soft kiss on my lips. If I wasn't so excited to tell my friends our news, I'd be shoving him back in that chauffeur driven car and getting very naked.

A chorus of Happy Birthday's greets us as we step through the door together and approach the cosy corner of the pub that houses all of my friends. I greet everyone and introduce my gorgeous boyfriend, who gets more than a few appreciative looks from the girls in the crowd. *Yes, that's right bitches... this fine chunk of man candy belongs to me and I am loving every hot inch of him. Whoop!* I save Clare, Tils and Oliver until last so I can have a proper hug with them all.

"Fuck me, Bea, you look amaze-balls!" Clare cries looking me up and down. "I mean, you always do and everything, but there is something super-spectacular about you tonight... by the way, I'm borrowing those shoes."

"Thank you, but by the way, no you're not. Do you like the outfit? Daniel bought it for me."

"Ya, sweetie," Tilly butts in, "from Valentino on Rodeo Drive dahhhling."

Daniel rolls his eyes and chuckles as he shakes hands with Oliver and follows him to the bar.

"Wow, it's all gorge, Bea, I need me one of those," she says, nodding in Daniel's direction.

"He's pretty spesh, hey?" I'm momentarily dazed, eyeing up my sex-god at the bar. I must admit, he and my brother are a fine looking pair, they're certainly getting a hell of a lot of looks from the ladies, including Clare and I, as they stand, handsomely, head and shoulders above the other men in the establishment. I suppose I'll allow Clare to ogle my brother and my man, it's only natural, they're ridiculously good looking after all.

Laura taps Clare on the shoulder and asks her a question, giving me the perfect opportunity to chat to Tilly. "Got a minute?"

"Yeah, of course, what's up?"

"Come outside for a sec." We make our way out the back of the pub where canopies and a large gazebo are set up around picnic tables. Rolled up blankets are positioned sporadically to keep the smokers warm during the colder evenings. We head to the fire over at the far wall and sit in front of it to keep warm in our less than practical attire.

"What's going on Bea? Is everything okay?"

"Yes, don't worry, I just wanted to catch you on your own for a minute. I want to tell you first."

"Oh my god..." she grabs my left hand and after a quick glance at my ring finger, throws in back into my lap. "Okay, not that... what?"

I giggle, she just doesn't know how funny she is. "No, stupido, we're not engaged."

"I did think that would be a bit difficult, what with him living in Cali and all that. So what? Tell me for god's sake!"

"Well, he doesn't anymore. Live in Cali, I mean. He's moving here."

Her grin spreads fast and her eyes light up. I haven't seen a sparkle in her eyes since we were in LA so I know for certain that she is thrilled for us. She throws her arms around me and rocks from side to side. "Oh BB, I'm so, so happy! That's amazing. What a fantastic birthday present! You were destined to be together, I knew something would happen. How did it work out then?"

"Well, he's going to be working from the London office now. He'll be going home every six weeks for a fortnight, but his main home will be here. With me. He wants me to join him in LA every time he goes back, but I'm not sure that'll work with Bear's. He reckons he has a plan to discuss with me tomorrow but I'm just happy that for the majority of the time, he'll be here. I wanted to tell you first, you know..."

"Yeah, I know. I hope you weren't worried about telling me in case I had a crazy emotional breakdown?"

"No, I wasn't. I knew you'd be happy, but we started this journey together and I thought it only right that you know first. But now that you do, I can't wait to tell Clare and Oliver. Oh and the folks! They love Daniel."

"Bea, I am really, so happy. This is such lovely news. Congratulations darling, let's go and celebrate, you haven't even got a drink yet."

"I know, let's go in, but just quickly before we do, how are you doing? You still look a little under the weather, doll?"

"Yeah, I'm okay. Forget about that, let's just enjoy your night. This is the best news, ever."

"Love you, remember that, Tils, and thank you so much for helping Daniel with my birthday, you're the best."

"Of course, love you too, but stop worrying about me, let's go and party!"

After we returned to the rest of the party inside, Daniel handed me a drink and we made our way around the group, mingling. Introducing him to Dylan and Leah was amusing, Clare and Oliver were arm in arm watching from a far, laughing drunkenly as they observed Dylan's reaction to Daniel like it was some sort of wildlife programme. I didn't think there was all that much to it, but apparently, according to everyone else, Dylan looked like he had shit stuck to his top lip for the rest of the night.

Leah was as much of a bitch as she always is so I left them to it. Daniel enjoyed wrapping me in his arms to kiss me, in front of them, just a little too much, but the feeling of having someone so in love with me, so protective, a little possessive, was actually more endearing to me than anything else. So I let him enjoy it.

The evening's celebrations were twice as fun as usual birthdays, partly because we had more to celebrate, but mainly because I had the man of my dreams by my side. We were practically joined at the hip all night, apart from when he and Oliver were having one of their many bromantic moments.

Oliver was so excited to learn that Daniel would be staying. It's so cute to watch, I'm glad that they are forging a relationship already. I just know that when my brother meets Luke, they'll get on just as well as he and Daniel do.

~~~~~~~~

Drinks were drank, my beautiful cake, courtesy of Clare and the girls at work, was eaten, and laughs were had, all round. Truly the most amazing, fun-filled birthday I have ever had, thanks to my fantastic friends, my two beautiful besties, my gorgeous big bro and last but by no means least, my smoking hot, too-good-to-be-true boyfriend.

Back at the hotel, we laughed and kissed and had amazing drunk sex, long into the early hours, before passing out in each other's arms, sated and sickly happy. I never dreamed I would ever meet a man who made me feel so special, who I'd be absolutely certain I wanted to spend the rest of my life with. I so look forward to my future; enjoying him, one day marrying him, making and bringing up beautiful babies together, a lifetime full of happiness with my man, my soul mate, *my* Sexy Berkeley.

TILLY

Well, it has been two months since Bea's spectacular birthday bash, when we all found out that her California man would now be her permanent, hot lover. I am so happy for them both, Bea especially, after witnessing her torment when she got back from LA.

Even though I had my own issues, it was so fucking hard to watch her hurt so badly. She and Clare mean more to me than anything, and to watch one of them so broken, kills me. But, after all of her agony, her life has made a dramatic one-eighty, and now she is in her element, living here with Daniel and spending a couple of weeks in Hollywood now and again. To say I'm a little envious is putting it lightly. Lucky bitch.

They managed to get a plan in place at the cakery, so Bea will be able to accompany Daniel on most of his trips. Clare has one weekday and every weekend off, with Bea working all week and most Saturday mornings when she is here, and they also have some new staff.

The new contract with Daniel's company lead to another contract with a similar business, and tonnes of wedding cakes, so Bear's has profited massively, so I hear. I try not to get 'all up in their biz' about Bear's finances, I don't want to know; as long as they are happy, I'm happy.

Promoting a couple of their girls has meant that they can leave the shop, without having to worry. I'm so proud of them both, they have really made their business something to be super proud of and have even won some amazing awards in the process. My clever girls.

As things stand now, we're just under two weeks away from the big Christmas trip to Aspen. I know everyone is so excited, Daniel can't wait to show us around and introduce Bea to another new home. I'm sure it'll be fun, I just need to get my head around seeing Luke. Not that I've mentioned it to anyone, I'm sure they all think I'm just as excited as they are, and I am...no, really, I am. I'm not wishing I could stay at home all alone, curled up in a ball on my sofa for the entire festive period... no. Not at all. But anyway, this isn't about me, I'm supposed to be talking about Bea and Daniel and all their amazingness.

About six or seven weeks after the fab news - I think it was - the two of them flew to Los Angeles for their first trip back over thanksgiving. Bea said it was amazing, she was thrilled to be able to go back for a bit longer and actually enjoy her time, knowing she wasn't going to lose anything when she returned. I know - more than she realises - what she means. I miss Luke like crazy, which *is* crazy, considering I knew him all of a week or so. But anyway, back to the lovely couple.

We arranged a take-away night as soon as they got back, and heard all about the fab time they had.

She managed to spend a good amount of time with Daniel's parents who she has fallen in love with, and they with her, from what I gather. Bea and Alexia finally met, Bea says she's a lot like us, although she's a little more sophisticated, apparently. Bloody charming! Probably someone with a pole shoved up her arse. But we'll see when we meet her in Aspen, I'm sure we'll get on. Pole or not.

I was so jealous that Bea and Daniel got to meet up with Gemma and Jay for dinner a couple of times, I really felt like I was missing out. They were over there, enjoying all of the things that *we* were enjoying a couple of months earlier, with the people *I* want to see. But still, at least I can time my next visit for when Bea's going to be there. That'll be fun. *When* I'll be able to visit again though, is another story.

She has a constant sparkle in her eyes since her birthday, and it's been so lovely to watch her embrace her new life. I am still quite low, and at times, have found it hard to express my happiness for her, which makes me feel like the biggest fucking bitch in the world, because I truly am so happy for her. She and Daniel have something so special, so rare, and he adores her. She has what I want, without the issues I have, right now.

I have avoided them sometimes, trying to hide away so no one notices how badly I am coping. There's only so much of their oh-so-happy lifestyle I can deal with, without snapping and turning into a psychotic nightmare with a plethora of witnesses. Comes with the territory, I suppose.

Clare has noticed my depressive behaviour on a couple of occasions, although I must be a fantastic actress, because she hasn't realised - thank god - that I cry, without fail, every single day. Most of the time, I manage to contain it to when I'm in bed, or on my lunch break at work, or looking like a freak on the tube in the morning. She consoled me on those few occasions as best she could, she really is a beautiful friend. Shame she has no idea what's really going on.

Everyone is excitedly preparing for Christmas now, all of us are travelling together; Bea and Daniel obviously, me, Clare, Bea's parents and Oliver, though *some* of us won't be travelling in upper class this time. Also celebrating the festive period with us in Aspen, are Daniel's parents and sister, who Bea has been raving about, and of course, last but not least, the man who has turned my world upside down; Loverboy, Luke.

Nobody knows. Nobody knows the half of it. Sure, Bea and Clare know a tiny chunk, telling Bea I'm having a small life crisis seemed to keep her satisfied for a while, but that was only the very beginning, it's so much more than that now and it won't take long for it all to come out.

I lied. I *was* falling a little bit head over heels for Luke. I didn't want to believe it, I prayed I wasn't having those feelings for a well known playboy, but it was all happening too fast, and there was nothing I could do to stop it. That I could probably have gotten used to; toughened the fuck up and dealt with it, but now? Now it's not quite so simple.

I'm going to have to talk to him in Aspen, I have to tell him everything... and I'm not ready. Not yet. But, I have no choice, and the shit... well, it's going to well and truly hit the fucking fan. So, I've got two weeks to prepare myself before it's time to talk. He has no idea how much his life is about to change. Jesus fucking Christ, how the hell am I going to do this?

Hey, how did I get around to talking about me again?

###

Sexy Berkeley is Dani Lovell's first novel and introduces the Sexy series.

Although British, Lovell has quite an obsession with all things 'Stateside' and often dreams about the fabulous trips she'll one day take across the pond.

Lovell lives in Hertfordshire, UK, with Daniel, Luke, Oliver and the rest of the sexy gang (all in her head, of course), and her real-life family.

If she's not working on her latest Sexy story, you'll find her taking care of her children, planning her latest fantasy vaycay or eating her weight in goats cheese.

You can contact Dani here:
Facebook: **https://www.facebook.com/dani.lovell.3**
Twitter: @AuthorDaniL
Email: **authordanilovell@gmail.com**

Coming soon:
Book two of the Sexy Series; Sexy Summers - The story of Tilly and Luke.
Estimated:September 2013

4354486R00204

Printed in Great Britain
by Amazon.co.uk, Ltd.,
Marston Gate.